W9-AAC-657

A
FLICKER
of LIGHT

Books by Katie Powner

The Sowing Season
A Flicker of Light

A
FLICKER
of
LIGHT

KATIE POWNER

BETHANYHOUSE
a division of Baker Publishing Group
Minneapolis, Minnesota

© 2021 by Katie Powner

Published by Bethany House Publishers
11400 Hampshire Avenue South
Bloomington, Minnesota 55438
www.bethanyhouse.com

Bethany House Publishers is a division of
Baker Publishing Group, Grand Rapids, Michigan

Printed in the United States of America

All rights reserved. No part of this publication may be reproduced, stored in a retrieval system, or transmitted in any form or by any means—for example, electronic, photocopy, recording—without the prior written permission of the publisher. The only exception is brief quotations in printed reviews.

Library of Congress Cataloging-in-Publication Data
Names: Powner, Katie, author.
Title: A flicker of light / Katie Powner.
Description: Minneapolis, MN : Bethany House Publishers, a division of Baker
    Publishing Group, [2021]
Identifiers: LCCN 2021023575 | ISBN 9780764238314 (paperback) | ISBN
    9780764239427 (hardcover) | ISBN 9781493433766 (ebook)
Classification: LCC PS3616.O96 F55 2021 | DDC 813/.6—dc23
LC record available at https://lccn.loc.gov/2021023575

This is a work of fiction. Names, characters, incidents, and dialogues are products of the author's imagination and are not to be construed as real. Any resemblance to actual events or persons, living or dead, is entirely coincidental.

Cover design by Susan Zucker

Author is represented by WordServe Literary Group.

21 22 23 24 25 26 27   7 6 5 4 3 2 1

◆ *To Julia Marie (Leskiw) Reis* ◆

When I see a high-top shoe
A teddy bear or red canoe
I think of you

ONE

Secrets are like pennies. Everybody's got one, even the poorest among us. Some are new and shiny, and some are tarnished and worn smooth from age. I should've tossed mine in the Gallatin River years ago so I couldn't pull it out and turn it over in my hand, wondering why. Wondering if.

But I didn't.

"June? You out here?"

The screen door creaks as Rand steps onto the porch, and I tuck my secret away. He eases himself into the wooden rocker beside mine.

"It's nice yet."

I nod. Fall is in the air, but today the sun is shining over the valley, and the mountain standing tall and proud before us is still blue. Soon it will be sharp and white, but today it almost looks friendly. I've lived here long enough to know it isn't.

Rand reaches over and places a gnarled hand over mine. I like the weight of it, anchoring me.

"I'm waiting for the light."

This time he nods. "You talk to Mitch today?"

"No."

I've been meaning to call my son. Rand reminds me every

morning. But fear holds me back. I don't want to leave my home.

"There it is." I point at the mountain as if Rand can't see with his own eyes the light that appears there as the setting sun hits just the right position in the sky.

Rand's already-wrinkled face crinkles further as he smiles. "Wonder what the old codger's up to tonight?"

I squeeze his hand. "Searching for treasure, of course."

"Ah yes. Of course."

The old tale comforts me. When Mitch was little, I would say, "Look! Miner McGee turned his headlamp on," and Mitch would frown and ask, "Does Miner McGee really live up there?" Always skeptical, he was. But not Bea. No, when Mitch's daughter came along, my only grandchild, she would beg me to tell the story over and over, drinking it like water. She never questioned why an old man would live up there alone. Never questioned why the light only appeared on sunny days. Her only concern was, "What if he never finds the Big Sky Diamond?"

"He will," I would say. "He'll never give up."

The sun sinks lower, and the light disappears. The story fades away. First Mitch grew up and out of the story, then Bea.

I wonder what my son is doing.

Rand's boots scrape against the ancient porch as he struggles out of his seat. "You comin'?"

"In a minute."

He plods back into the house, his right leg dragging a little behind. His shoulders stooped under the burden of seventy-one years of hard living. Lord Almighty, I love that man. Forty-four years together and I've never wanted any other life. Never wondered if we could weather any storm Montana threw our way.

Until now.

TWO

Bea Michaels rubbed her eyes, blinked three times, and looked again. Yep. The two blue lines were still there.

"Hot coffee." Her version of a much stronger term fell a little flat. "Hot, hot, hot, hot coffee."

A rush of emotions crowded her heart. Her whole body. Joy, fear, confusion, anxiety, and amazement battled for control, flushing her cheeks and tingling her toes. This couldn't be real. Couldn't be true. But the little white stick said it was.

She was going to be a mom.

A strangled cry-laugh welled up from her throat, and she covered her mouth with one hand. Tears pricked her eyes. There was a baby inside her. Right at this very moment, her and Jeremy's child was growing. But she wasn't much more than a kid herself, was she? Even though she'd turned twenty-one a couple months ago, she'd never felt less like an adult.

She thought she'd have more time to prepare. More confidence about the future. More . . . something.

The sound of the apartment door slamming made her jump. Jeremy was home. But she wasn't ready to face him. She didn't know how to do this.

Why did you leave me, Mom? She gasped for breath and covered her face with her hands.

He found her standing in the bathroom, bawling.

"Whoa, Bea." He ran to her and gently put his hands on her shoulders. "Are you okay? What's the matter?"

"Y-yes." She worked to force words out between sobs. "I don't know. My m-mom will never . . . n-never . . ."

His face softened, and he pulled her close. "You're missing your mom today?"

"No!" she wailed and wriggled out of his arms. Why was she blubbering like this? She wasn't raised to blubber. "I mean, yes. But—but—look."

Since her words wouldn't cooperate, she held up the white stick.

Jeremy stared at it dumbly. "Um . . ."

"It's a pregnancy test."

His eyes widened.

She wiped at her tears. Swiped her nose with her sleeve. Enough with the crying already. "It's positive."

"You mean . . . ?" He searched her face for the truth.

"Yes." She started crying again. "You're going to be a daddy."

Wonder transformed his expression, giving her heart a little lift. She managed a shaky smile, and he shouted a questionable word.

She swatted his arm. "Don't swear."

"Sorry." He slid an arm around her waist and shook his head. "I couldn't help it."

Bea looked down at her stomach. "But she'll hear you."

He knelt so his face was level with her belly. "She, huh?"

Bea took a deep breath. She could do this. "Or he. Or one of each. Who knows?"

He stood and gave her a solemn look. "Hot coffee."

"Exactly." Her swollen eyes grew wide. "The hottest."

He reached for her. "With a double shot of espresso."

She leaned into him. "I just can't believe it."

He wrapped his arms tightly around her and laid his head on

top of hers. She breathed him in, thankful for his presence. His strength. For a few minutes, it was silent in their tiny bathroom except for the drip, drip, drip of the faucet their landlord had never fixed.

When Jeremy spoke, his voice was heavy. "You're sad because your mom's not here for this."

Bea nodded into his chest. Sometimes he understood her feelings better than she did, despite a childhood filled with dysfunction and neglect. Or perhaps because of it.

"She'll never get to meet her. Or him." Her husband's cotton shirt muffled Bea's voice. "She would've loved being a grandma."

In some ways, the last two years had flown by. Their whirlwind romance. Jeremy's college graduation. The wedding. But in other ways, it had been the longest two years of her life. Mom had been her best friend. Her confidant. The cancer took her so fast, it didn't even seem real sometimes. How would she get through this without her?

"I'm scared."

It wasn't something anyone in her family ever liked to admit, but it was a relief to say the words out loud. Jeremy released his hold on her and touched his forehead to hers. "Me too."

She avoided his eyes. "And you know what this means."

He took a step back and sighed. "Don't call him yet."

"But—"

"Let's just enjoy this for the weekend. I'll take you to dinner tomorrow to celebrate, anywhere you want. You can talk to him Monday."

Bea grabbed his hand and squeezed. The thought of food didn't hold much appeal. It had been her queasy stomach five days in a row that made her first suspect she might be pregnant. But talking to her dad didn't hold much appeal, either.

"Okay."

She let Jeremy lead her out of the bathroom into the small

living room that doubled as a dining room and connected to the kitchenette. He coaxed her onto the futon and insisted on making dinner. She smiled on the inside. He was going to be a good dad. But . . .

Would she be a good mother?

More tears began to fall. *Mother*. Such an innocent-sounding word, but it rang like a tornado siren in her mind. Her mother was gone. And the way her dad shut her out after? Well, it was almost like she'd lost them both.

She'd been getting used to how it was just her and Jeremy. Two hearts against the world. Free to do whatever they wanted. Free to chart their own course into the future. But now she watched Jeremy move around the kitchen and thought about the mold they'd found in the bedroom carpet. The electrical fire they'd recently experienced when the oven shorted out. The bad news they'd received from Jeremy's employer this week.

They couldn't stay here. Everything was about to change.

Again.

She rested her hands on her stomach. This was it. She was having a baby.

Hot coffee.

THREE

The sky stretched far and wide as the open arms of Jesus. That's what his mother used to say. Mitch Jensen hung one arm out his truck window and soaked up the sun. It wasn't going to last. Heck, it could snow tomorrow. But he couldn't remember a more beautiful start to fall.

He pulled onto a long gravel drive and slowed, the familiar sight of his childhood home doing something to his chest that he wasn't used to. Was that foreboding or exhaustion? It was only Monday. He shouldn't be worn out already.

When he turned off the truck's engine, the quiet was just the right kind. Not unnatural and forced, like when nature goes still in the face of potential danger, but alive. Moose Creek was a small town with little more than a four-way stop, two bars, a diner, and a post office, but it was downright chaotic compared to this. He was thankful his parents, the indomitable Randall and Juniper Jensen, had been able to sell most of the surrounding acreage so they could continue living here even after his dad retired from ranching a couple years ago.

Mitch braced himself as the front porch steps groaned under his weight. His dad had been calling him every few days, asking him to stop by. Dropping hints that something was wrong with his mom. Wondering if Mitch had talked to her lately. But Mitch wasn't exactly sure what to expect on this visit. He'd asked Dad if his mom was sick, and he'd said, "Mebbe." But that's what he always said. About everything. *Mebbe.*

His mom hadn't answered any of his calls, and he hadn't seen her or Dad in a few weeks. They hadn't left the house as far as he knew. Hadn't even been to church, from what he'd heard, which was a sure sign of debilitating illness. They never missed church.

The heavy oak door was propped open, but he banged a fist on the screen frame before letting himself in. "Mom? Dad?"

June poked her head around the corner from the kitchen. "Mitch? I didn't know you were coming by."

He wiped his boots on the rug and joined her in the kitchen, where he found her rolling out a piecrust. "I've left you a couple messages."

"Oh, that. Bah." She waved his words away like a pesky fly. "I've been busy."

"I can see that." Three pies already sat on the counter. He gave them a sniff. "You picked your apples already?"

"Stand back." She shooed him to the side so she could open the oven door and pull out a fourth pie.

He peered out the kitchen window. "Where's Dad?"

"Picking more apples. I reckon he saw your truck. Should be in any minute."

Mitch helped himself to a glass of water and covertly studied her as he waited for his father to appear. She looked healthy enough, scurrying around the kitchen same as always. Her cheeks had good color. Her movements appeared as smooth and confident at sixty-three as they'd been at forty. Unless there was something wrong on the inside . . .

Oh no. Cancer. Was that what this was about? No, he couldn't go through that again. Couldn't face it. His chest constricted.

The screen door creaked open and slapped shut.

"Mitch?"

"In here, Dad."

His heart beat faster as his father's footsteps approached. Maybe this was why he'd felt a foreboding when he pulled up here. His parents were hiding a horrible diagnosis from him. He should've made the drive out to see them sooner.

Rand carried a bucketful of apples to the table and set it down. "Howdy."

"Hey." Mitch shifted on his feet. "I got off work early and thought I'd stop in."

June snorted. "He's hovering is what he's doing."

His dad lifted his baseball cap to scratch his head. "Well, it's good to see ya."

"Don't just stand there staring at each other." June flicked at him and Rand with a towel. "Go pick some more apples."

Mitch followed his father as he went back out the door. It would be easier to have this conversation away from his mom, anyway.

He watched Dad take each porch step carefully, setting his left leg firmly on the next step before heaving his right leg down with a grunt. Mitch couldn't remember him ever moving so slowly. Had he been going downhill recently? Or had it been this bad for a while, and Mitch hadn't noticed?

He picked up an empty bucket at the bottom of the steps. "Why don't you tell me what's going on, Dad?"

Rand looked straight ahead and lumbered toward the three apple trees on the north side of the house. Mitch walked silently alongside, knowing his father would not be rushed. Rand wore his usual long-sleeved plaid pearl snap and faded jeans despite the sunshine, his wiry frame only managing to hold the pants up with the help of a worn leather belt embossed with his name.

When they reached the trees, Mitch plucked a low-hanging apple and bit into it. "Kind of tart."

"Yeah." Rand reached for an apple of his own and set it in

the bucket. "I would've waited another week or two, but your mother insisted."

Mitch frowned. She'd always had a knack for knowing exactly when the apples were ready. "What are all the pies for? Something happening at church?"

"Not that I know of."

"Then what are they for?"

Rand let out a long sigh and shrugged. "Your mother hasn't been herself lately, son."

Mitch's stomach dropped. Here it came. The bad news. "Has she been to the doctor? Is it bad?"

"No, no. No doctor. She won't go nowhere. Just fritters around the house."

Mitch's forehead crinkled. "Isn't that what she usually does?"

"Well." Rand paused with an apple in each hand. "I suppose so."

What was going on here? His mother was her usual busy self, and if they hadn't been to the doctor, there was no diagnosis. Mitch watched his father wince as he reached for an apple above his head and wondered which parent he was actually supposed to be worried about right now.

"Why don't you take a break, Dad." He gestured toward the house. "I'll finish this up."

◆ ◆ ◆

Mitch carried two pies into his house, one for him—like he could eat an entire pie—and one for "that sweet little neighbor of yours," as his mother put it. As if bringing five-foot-nothing Marge a pie wasn't the last thing in the world he needed. He set them on the table. What on earth was he going to do with two whole pies?

Even minus the two he took off their hands, his parents would be eating apple pie for breakfast, lunch, and dinner the rest of the week. But the excessive pie making wasn't anything to be worried about, as he'd tried to tell his dad before he left. The industrious Juniper Jensen just needed a new hobby or a new friend or something. That's all.

He threw some leftover meatloaf into the microwave and flipped through his mail. It was at dinnertime when he missed Caroline the most. For twenty years, she'd been there to sit next to. To talk to. To share food and life with. And now he had nothing but an empty table and a small plate of nuked meatloaf.

The words to "Sweet Caroline" played in his mind. Though he was a die-hard country fan, Neil Diamond's old song had a special place in his heart. He used to sing it at the top of his lungs when he'd burst through the door upon coming home from work, much to Caroline's chagrin. What he wouldn't give to see her roll her eyes at him just one more time. Have her swat his arm and say, "Good to see you, too, honey."

An elk bugle sounded. He shook away the memories and scanned the kitchen. Where had he put his phone? He checked the counter, his pants pockets, and under the pies. Who would be calling him at dinnertime?

The bull elk continued its high-pitched call, and he tracked the sound with his ears.

"Oh." Mitch hurried to the CINCH jacket he'd hung on the back of a chair and shoved his hand down the pocket. There it was.

"Hello?" He didn't even look at the screen in his rush to answer.

"Dad?"

This was a surprise. A smile grew on his face. "B.B. Hey. How are you?"

"You know no one calls me that anymore, right?"

"I know, I know. *Bea*. Sorry. What's up?"

"Just checking in."

Mitch pulled his meatloaf from the microwave and sat down

at the table. His daughter didn't call often. Not since getting married. He was still getting used to that. It had been hard enough when she left for college less than three months after Caroline passed away, but then to have Jeremy come along and—

"Did you have a good day at work?"

He set his fork down. Something about her voice sounded off. "It was fine. Is something wrong?"

Besides the fact she lived hundreds of miles away and he never got to see her, of course.

"We've just got a lot going on. Jeremy's company shut down unexpectedly last Monday, and we found out our landlord is selling our building. The new owners plan to kick everyone out and renovate since it's in such bad shape."

Mitch stiffened. "What? He lost his job?"

"You make it sound like he got fired, Dad. No. The company folded."

"So he has no job."

Silence.

Mitch pushed meatloaf around on his plate and tapped his foot. Jeremy was a good kid, especially considering the sorry excuse for a family he came from, but Mitch had long suspected he would have a hard time providing for his daughter. What exactly did one do with a degree in marketing, anyway? And now Mitch's only child was in distress, and there was nothing he could do about it from halfway across the country.

"They're just kicking everyone out?" He pushed back from the table and began to pace. "Is that legal?"

"It's a month-to-month lease."

"Huh."

"Anyway, I thought maybe—"

"You need somewhere to go." Mitch stopped midstride. Maybe there was something he could do, after all. "You'll come here, of course."

"Dad, I don't know."

He raised his eyebrows at the phone. What choice did she have? There would be no open arms waiting for them on Jeremy's side of the family, and they'd never find another apartment in Santa Clara without a job. How any young adult was supposed to afford housing these days was beyond him—even *with* a job.

Thank goodness they hadn't started a family yet.

"Temporarily." He gripped the phone. "You've got to live somewhere, B.B."

And if the temporary turned into something more permanent, all the better for him.

"Are you sure it's a good idea?" Bea asked.

It had been a tough pill to swallow when Bea told him she and Jeremy were going to live in California. Seriously, California? Montanans made jokes about people who lived there. But Jeremy had big ideas about working in Silicon Valley.

Just look how that turned out.

Mitch began making a mental checklist. Stock the fridge. Wash the sheets. Move the patio furniture out of the carport and into the backyard. He'd make everything perfect. Perfect enough that Bea would think twice before leaving again.

"Dad?"

"Yes." He looked around his lifeless, empty kitchen and smiled. His baby was coming home. "I'm sure."

FOUR

Bea shifted in the passenger seat, trying to get comfortable, but there was only so much she could do after two days in the car. She almost wished they'd powered through and driven the seventeen hours from Santa Clara to Montana all at once, just to get it over with. At the same time, she wished they'd taken a whole week to drive up here. The closer they got to Moose Creek, the less ready she was.

She turned to look at Jeremy's cat in his carrier in the back seat. Ha. At least Steve had finally fallen asleep after three hours of yowling.

"You doing okay?" Jeremy reached over and squeezed her knee. "Need a break?"

"I'm fine." She adjusted her ponytail and pushed her back against the seat. "Just tired."

Once the decision had been made to relocate—*temporarily*—to Moose Creek, she had taken her time packing up their small apartment. Their rent was paid through September, so there'd been no need to rush. Jeremy had helped her decide which few things to keep and which to give away, but he'd been strangely quiet about the whole moving thing, choosing instead to talk about the baby this and the baby that and the baby's name and the baby everything.

She loved how excited he was. Honest. But the queasiness in her stomach and uncertainty in her heart kept her from enjoying all the planning as much as Jeremy did. What was her dad going to say when he found out she was pregnant?

"Tomorrow's Monday, so you should be able to call and make an appointment, right?" Jeremy glanced her way with eager eyes as if he knew she'd been thinking about the baby.

Bea shrugged. "We'll see."

"You have to go to the doctor."

"I will." She messed with the buttons on the dash, searching for a new radio station. "But there's no hurry. Dad doesn't even know yet."

"You're not telling him tonight when we get in?"

"Uh . . ." She hesitated. The baby wasn't going anywhere, and she wouldn't be showing for weeks. Plus, they currently had no means to actually pay for a doctor visit. No sense in freaking her dad out right off the bat. "I want to keep it between us a little longer."

"Okay." Jeremy didn't sound convinced.

He turned left off the interstate, and Bea stiffened, her heart sagging at the sight of landmarks she'd known for years, tainted now by loss. The Prickly Pear trailhead where she and her mom used to go hiking. The wooden *Heifers 4 Sale* sign along the highway where she would take her mom for a picture every Mother's Day for laughs.

Bea's breathing became shallow, and she fought to keep control. Nothing was the same anymore. Not without Mom. It was a mistake to come back here.

Jeremy wrinkled his nose. "What's up with the country music?"

She blinked. Blew the air from her lungs. It didn't matter how she felt about it, there was no turning back. They had nowhere else to go. "We're almost there, that's what."

If the roadside signs didn't indicate Moose Creek was only

a few miles away, the radio would. Moose Creek picked up exactly three FM radio stations: two country and one classic rock.

Jeremy groaned at a song about a big green tractor. "I can't stand this stuff."

"You'll get used to it." She lifted one corner of her mouth. "And I should probably warn you my dad is a big fan."

Jeremy ran a hand through his thick sandy hair. "One more strike against me."

"There aren't any strikes."

He shot her an incredulous look. "You know that's not true. Your dad doesn't approve of me."

"How do you know that? You've only met him twice."

"I could tell. And now I'm unemployed with a baby on the way."

Bea looked out her window, not wanting to admit Jeremy might be right. Her dad had expressed concern about what their future was going to look like when she told him she was going to marry Jeremy. "You're so young," he'd said. "You're moving too fast." She'd scoffed at the time. What right did he have to an opinion about her future after emotionally abandoning her when she needed him the most? Yet now here they were, needing him to take them in.

No, she definitely wasn't ready to tell him about the baby.

"There's so much open space here." Jeremy scanned their surroundings. "Where are all the buildings?"

Bea studied the fields and hills and farmhouses, trying to see them through her husband's city-born eyes. "On the other side of the mountain."

Moose Creek, population 756, didn't boast many buildings of its own. The tallest structure for miles was the water tower, hovering over the town like a fat mother hen trying to tuck all her little chicks under her wings. Trying to keep them safe, keep them from wandering off into the big, bad world.

The small town had the essentials—a market, a gas station,

a school—but Ponderosa, just over the Bridger Mountains, was close enough that most people drove there if they needed a Walmart or a hospital. Moose Creek couldn't support such places. Didn't want to either—until someone was having a heart attack and the clinic was already closed for the night, that is. Or the pass was socked in with snow or fog or both, and you had to decide how badly you needed that forty-eight pack of toilet paper from Costco.

Jeremy applied the brakes as they approached town, and the speed limit dropped to twenty-five. The car slowed, but Bea's heart rate sped up. Moose Creek looked so . . . tired.

"It's nice," Jeremy said.

Bea gave him a tentative smile, aware of the descriptors he could've used. Like *rustic*. Or *Podunk*. "I love this time of year."

September in Montana was her second favorite month, right behind June. In September, everything was still alive and vibrant, before the leaves fell seemingly overnight, leaving behind skeletal trees and dirty snow piled up on both sides of the road. Nothing could beat June in Moose Creek, when the grass was green, the foothills blue, and the mountaintops white, but September came pretty close.

Jeremy glanced from left to right as he drove, taking in the town. The cross tattoo on his forearm rippled as he gripped the wheel. "Where is everybody?"

"It's Sunday," she said. "Turn right after that cinder-block house."

He turned onto an unpaved road. The low-profile tires on their Toyota Matrix hit a pothole, and their heads jerked forward.

Steve yowled.

Jeremy grunted. "Yikes. Should we notify the city about that?"

Bea laughed.

"What's so funny?"

She watched him from the corner of her eye. People didn't know the meaning of the word *pothole* until they'd lived in Moose Creek. "You know my dad works for the city, right?"

"Oh. Right."

She pointed. "That's it there on the left. The gray house."

When Jeremy steered the car over to park in front, she laughed again. "No, you have to flip around and park the right way."

"It's a one-lane dirt road, Bea. Who cares which way we park?"

"Officer Darryl."

"It's no big deal."

It was often the littlest things that were the biggest deal in a small town, but she let it go. Her eyes focused on the old gray house. Grandpa Rand's truck was parked in the alley. She hoped they hadn't been waiting long. When she'd told Dad they planned to arrive around five, he insisted he'd have dinner ready and that Grandma and Grandpa would be there, unable to wait even one more day before seeing their only grandchild again.

Bea's heart squeezed. She had missed them all. Her little family. But it had been easy to stay away and avoid all the memories. Easy to pretend the new life she'd found for herself had been her choice.

Not anymore.

Jeremy grabbed the cat carrier and a suitcase from the back seat while Bea carried her purse. The remainder of the few belongings they'd brought along could wait. How strange to be starting over already, after only a year of marriage.

She walked around the car and stood in front of the house, her mother's absence striking a near physical blow. She would never throw open the front door to greet Bea ever again. Never pull her in for a hug and say, "There's my girl." Never hold the child growing inside her.

Bea swallowed. "'The house that built me.'"

Jeremy stopped a few steps ahead and looked back. "What?"

"Nothing." She forced herself forward. "It's just an old Miranda Lambert song about going home."

He stood close and talked softly. "You okay?"

He was always asking her that. Always concerned about her welfare and happiness. She should be grateful, but sometimes . . .

She struggled to smile and nodded, wanting him to believe she was okay. But really, she had no idea.

FIVE

itch studied his mother as she sat in his favorite armchair, unusually still. Her arms were thin, belying their strength, and her short-cropped silver hair clung to her head like snow on the Crazy Mountains.

"When's Bea coming?" she asked.

His brow furrowed. She'd already asked three times. She must be more eager to see her granddaughter than he'd realized. Not that he could blame her.

"Any minute now."

A knock sounded on the front door as it swung open, proving Mitch's point. He sprang to his feet. "They're here."

He scuttled around the armchair and down the short hallway. He hadn't seen Bea since her wedding day, just over a year ago. He'd invited her several times to come up for a visit, but she'd always had an excuse. They were busy. They were settling in. They were trying to save money. She'd never reciprocated the invitation.

He rounded the corner and held open his arms. "B.B.!"

His daughter's brown hair had grown long. Her cheeks were rosy. She accepted his hug, and he held on tightly. She looked so different. So grown up. So much like Caroline. If only his wife could see her now.

"Mr. Jensen." Jeremy held out a hand as Mitch released Bea and turned to him. "Good to see you."

Mitch took the offered hand and pumped it hard. "Jeremy." His eyes dropped to Jeremy's other hand. "Is that . . . a cat?"

Jeremy lifted the carrier. "This is Steve."

Mitch blinked. How had he missed the fact they were bringing a pet with them? "You have a cat."

Jeremy glanced at Bea. "I thought you were going to talk to him about it."

The red in Bea's cheeks deepened. "I guess I forgot with everything going on. I'm sorry."

Aha. Mitch eyed the carrier. Folded his arms across his chest. Opened his mouth. Closed it.

They had a cat.

"Beatrice." His mother appeared and grabbed Bea's hands. "Look at you. Mylanta."

Bea hung her head a little, as if self-conscious. "Hi, Grandma."

"Well, don't just stand there," June said. "Come in, come in."

She pulled Bea through the entryway and down the hall to the kitchen.

Mitch turned back to Jeremy. It didn't appear there was much he could do about the cat situation at the moment. He narrowed his eyes at Jeremy's arm. "I don't recall your having a tattoo."

"Oh. We, uh . . ." Jeremy cleared his throat. "We got matching ones for our anniversary."

Mitch's Adam's apple bobbed up and down in his throat as he stared at his son-in-law. "Is that right."

He pictured some husky biker type in a leather jacket marring his daughter's fair skin with a dirty needle and shuddered. What had possessed Bea to get a tattoo? It must've been Jeremy's idea.

This was not how he'd pictured Bea's big homecoming.

A little sternness crept into his voice. "I hear you're out of a job."

"The company went under." Jeremy shifted on his feet. "But—"

"What do you plan to do now?"

"I have a few ideas."

Ideas. Boy, oh boy. "You can't eat ideas, Jeremy." That might've been *too* stern.

Jeremy's eyes flashed. "I'm aware of that, Mr. Jensen."

Mitch pressed his lips together. He didn't want to lay into the kid. He really didn't. Jeremy was respectful and kind, and Mitch actually liked him. He clearly loved Bea. But that didn't mean Mitch was okay with him marrying his daughter at such a young age and allowing her to drop out of college. She'd been on her way to earning the first college degree in his family until this guy came along.

He took a deep breath. There were a lot of things he hadn't gotten to say before the wedding. Bea hadn't given him the chance. But maybe it was time to have it out with his son-in-law. Lay it all on the table.

His mother called from the kitchen. "Time to eat."

Mitch glanced down the hall and saw Bea sitting at the table, watching him.

Then again, maybe not.

◆ ◆ ◆

Mitch chewed his bite of apple pie—and chewed and chewed. Much like the one he'd brought home Monday, this pie was chock-full of undercooked, tart apples. He glanced around the table as his mother handed plates to everyone else, wondering if they were going to notice. Maybe they wouldn't. With enough vanilla ice cream on top, it wasn't so bad. But what had gone wrong with the recipe? His mother's pies were usually cooked to perfection.

June finished passing out the dessert and put her hands on

her knees to look under the table. "And don't think I forgot about you, kitty." She plopped a small scoop of ice cream onto a spoon and set it on the floor. "There you go."

Mitch gaped. His parents had always been adamant about three things: you go to church every Sunday, you respect the mountain, and you don't let animals in the house. Animals were meant to serve a purpose. Dogs were for herding cattle and guarding the house. Cats were for keeping down the mice population in the barn. They were not pets, they were fellow workers, and no amount of begging as a child had persuaded his parents to change their minds about that.

Now here she was, feeding ice cream to Steve? And what kind of name was that, anyway? If he had a cat, he'd name it Buckshot.

Bea bent to watch the creature. "He's not supposed to eat people food, Grandma."

"Bah." June waved a hand in the air. "It's just a little ice cream."

His mother had always had a soft spot for Bea, letting her have her way more often than Mitch would've liked over the years, but this unexpected pet tolerance didn't seem to be for Bea's benefit. What had gotten into her?

A knock at the door tore Mitch's attention from the table. He wasn't expecting anyone else, but he hopped up and headed down the hall. His mind was still trying to process the sight of his mother feeding ice cream to a cat when he pulled open the door.

Oh no.

"Well, hello there." His neighbor's eyes were wide, as if he were the one who'd shown up unexpectedly at *her* door. "I saw the car out front and figured Bea must've made it in. I brought over a casserole."

Marge was forever bringing over a casserole. Ever since Caroline passed away, Marge had shown up at least once a week with a casserole. Then Mitch had to wait for Marge's car to be gone so he could return the dish when she wasn't home. He employed the same strategy when he rolled her trash can back in and mowed her lawn. Avoiding her took a lot of work.

"That's nice of you, but—"

"Marge! How good to see you." His mother came bustling up, wiping her hands on the apron she kept in Mitch's kitchen. "Come in, come in. How'd you like that pie I sent down?"

Marge beamed as she plunked a square glass pan into Mitch's hands and closed the door behind her. "Thank you, June. Now, what's this about a pie?"

Mitch gulped and glanced at the dish. "I'll go put this in the—"

"Do you mean to tell me you never gave Marge her pie?" His mother jammed her fists into her waist and glared at him.

"It was a busy week, Mom." He inched away. "By the time I had the chance . . ."

He gave Marge what he hoped was an apologetic look. She shrugged and pinched her buxom hips. "Don't you worry about it. I don't need my own pie, anyway."

His mom somehow wedged her way behind him and Marge and herded them down the hall like cattle in the chute. "I'll just have to make you another one." They entered the kitchen, where she pressed Marge into a chair. "In the meantime, I'll fix you a plate."

Instead of protesting, as Mitch would've preferred, Marge set a napkin on her lap and folded her hands on the table. "That would be lovely."

She settled in as if she came over every day. "Hi there, Bea. It's so good to see you."

Bea looked between him, Marge, and the dish in his hands with an inscrutable expression. "Good to see you, too, Marge. This is my husband, Jeremy. Jeremy, Marge."

Jeremy seemed unfazed as he stood to reach across the table and shake her hand. "Nice to meet you."

Bea raised an arm in the direction of Marge's house. "Marge lives next door."

Marge's long, dangly earrings jangled as she nodded. "I saw your car and wanted to say hello."

As they talked, Mitch opened the fridge and scrunched his nose. There was no room for a casserole. He set it on the counter with a thud and shut the door. "How did you know it was Bea's car?"

She'd left town in a black Chevy Blazer two years ago. Nothing like the yuppie-looking Toyota out front now.

"I heard it from Janice, who heard it from Ralph that she was coming in today."

Mitch frowned. Ralph. He loved the guy and had worked with him for years, but he sure liked to talk. Not that *anyone* could keep a secret in Moose Creek.

Marge caught him looking at her and blushed. "And I saw the California plates."

He looked away.

"How long have you been neighbors?" Jeremy asked.

"Since forever." Marge dug into the pie his mom had set in front of her, not appearing to mind the chewiness one bit. "Back in the day, our little block had all kinds of activity going on. Kids playing outside, and everyone coming and going. But now it's just me and Mitch. Two solitary souls."

Mitch pulled at the collar of his shirt. Why'd she have to say it like that? But he remembered those days. They were good times. Before Bill abandoned Marge, and her three kids grew up. Before Caroline died, and Bea got married. So much had changed.

He didn't like the way Marge was looking at him, but he resigned himself to the situation and sat back down at the table next to his father, who hadn't said a word since asking Mitch to pass the pepper at dinner.

"Now, Bea, listen." Marge pushed back the wild, curly frizz of hair encroaching on her face and leaned forward. "Janice said Ralph said you might be in town for several months. So I thought you might like to know that I heard Kathy's finally retiring from the Food Farm, bless her heart, and MacGregor's looking to hire someone part-time to replace her."

Mitch cringed on the inside. That was his daughter's best prospect? Replacing Kathy at the Food Farm? Then again, if a job would tie her down to Moose Creek . . .

"What a great idea." June clapped her hands together. "Caroline has always liked to keep herself busy, isn't that right?"

She turned to Bea with a smile, and Mitch frowned. Caroline? Where had that come from? Bea did resemble his wife enough to make his heart twinge every time he looked at her, but Caroline had been gone for two years. His mom had never made that mistake before.

Bea's brow furrowed, and she tilted her head. Before she could respond, another knock sounded at the door.

"What on earth?" Mitch muttered.

"Busy place," Jeremy said.

Mitch hurried back down the hall and yanked open the door for a third time. "Oh, hey, Darryl. What are you doing here?"

"Evening, Mitch." The officer jerked a thumb over his shoulder, then hooked it in his gun belt. "Somebody parked the wrong way in front of your house."

◆　◆　◆

"It's the easiest job in the history of jobs." Bea snuggled closer to Jeremy, thankful her dad had switched the twin bed that had been in her room for the queen bed in his. "It wasn't too bad when I worked there before. I kind of liked it. And it would only be part-time."

Jeremy spoke softly into her hair. "But what about the baby? Aren't you supposed to take it easy?"

She frowned. Only seven weeks pregnant and the baby was already dictating her life?

"I'm not exactly sure what I'm *supposed* to do," she said. "This is all uncharted territory."

But she knew one thing: they needed to make money. She'd googled "how much does it cost to have a baby" the other day and nearly hyperventilated. It seemed an impossible amount. And she knew another thing: she would go crazy hanging around the house all day. Grandma June had been right about that, even if she had called Bea by the wrong name.

"Maybe *I* should work there."

She stiffened. "Jeremy."

They'd talked about this already. Sixteen of the seventeen hours from Santa Clara to Moose Creek had been used up talking about what they were going to do now. What the plan was. How they were going to make it work. Jeremy had big dreams about starting his own company, being his own boss, and Bea was committed to helping him achieve his goals. That's what a good wife was expected to do. That's what Mom always did.

She and Jeremy had agreed they would stay with her dad for a maximum of three months so Jeremy could focus on researching ideas and methods and come up with a business plan. They had also agreed it would be ideal if she could earn some money in the meantime. A part-time job at the Food Farm wouldn't provide health insurance, but at least it would be something.

"I know we had a plan," Jeremy said. "But your dad—"

"Don't worry about my dad." Bea relaxed and nuzzled Jeremy's neck. "He's just a little overprotective."

"I don't think he's very happy with me."

"It's our life. Not his."

"I told him I had a few ideas about what to do now, and he said, 'You can't eat ideas.'"

"Well, he's not wrong." She shrugged. "You can't."

Jeremy tensed. "I need you on my side here, Bea."

"There are no sides." She kissed his ear, hoping she was right. Hoping he was just being paranoid. Dad might be thinking *I told you so* now, but he would be impressed when Jeremy launched his own company.

Right?

"It's been a long day." She knew how to take her husband's mind off his worries. She slid her hand across his chest. "Maybe we should talk about this tomorrow."

He exhaled. "You're probably right."

Though the room was dark, she found his chin with her fingers and turned his head toward her. She met his lips with hers, and he kissed her back, gently and deeply, but when she moved closer, he pulled away.

"Bea, I can't."

"What do you mean?"

"Your dad's downstairs."

"So?"

"So what if he hears us?"

She let go of his chin and laid her head on her pillow. "Jeremy."

"I told him about your tattoo."

She sat up with a gasp. "What'd you do that for?"

"He asked about mine, and it just kind of slipped out. I'm sorry."

Bea plopped back down in bed and stared at the ceiling, imagining what her dad's face must've looked like when he heard that little bit of news. She reached for Jeremy's hand under the covers and grabbed hold of it tightly.

It was going to be a long three months.

SIX

The darkness is one of the things I love most about this place. No city lights. No streetlights. Only stars and stars and stars, and a crescent moon.

Rand's boots rub against my bare calves as I stand in the yard looking up at the immense, all-encompassing sky. My boots were right there by the back door, too, but shoot, I like wearing his. The mountain stands before me like a sentinel keeping watch, but I wonder if it's doing its job. 'Cause I heard what she said. Beatrice. She thought no one could hear, but I heard.

Mitch and Rand were sitting in the living room, having one of their silent conversations, and Bea and her husband were in the kitchen doing dishes. Like I couldn't do them myself. Imagine, telling me to go sit down and take a break.

But I didn't do that. And I heard her say it.

Baby.

An owl hoots, and bats swoop and dive like acrobats in front of the moon. I put my hand in the pocket of the old dress I wear as a nightgown and wrap my fingers around a penny. Would there be any shine left in it if I held it up to the moonlight? I pull it out and lay it flat on my palm.

The screen door slaps shut and startles me. My heart shakes.

Oh, Lord, I dropped the penny.

"June, what're you doing? It's two in the morning."

I drop to my knees and skim my hands over the grass, searching.

"You got no coat." The porch steps groan as Rand limps down them one at a time. "You'll catch your death."

"Stay back." Nothing but damp earth meets my fingers as I press them into the ground. It has to be here somewhere. I was standing *right here.*

"June."

I lift my head and shout, "I said stay back."

My voice prowls through the night like a feral creature. I must stop him. I can't let him find it. I need to tuck it far away.

I pound on the ground. "No, no, no, no, no."

"Come back to the house, June."

He stands beside me now, and I slap at his legs. "Get away, get away."

"Juniper."

The fear in his voice reaches me, but I don't understand it. Does he know?

His hand is on my shoulder, soft and strong but unsure. I start to cry. Where is my penny? Why can't I find it? What if he sees?

"Come on." He gently grasps my arm and pulls me to my feet. Snot drips from my nose, and when I wipe at it, I feel the dirt smear across my face. It's better if I let him lead me inside. It's the only way to get him away from here. To keep him from walking all over the grass. When he isn't here, when he isn't looking, I will return.

We shuffle back to the house. Tears stream down my face and drip off my jawline. They fall like rain onto my nightdress.

It is dark, and I am cold.

SEVEN

Bea's foot struck a Cheerio as she placed her cereal bowl in the dishwasher, and it skittered across the floor. Steve chased it across the smooth laminate boards. She laughed as the cat batted the Cheerio under a chair and then pounced on it from behind the leg.

"At least Steve likes it here."

Jeremy slid the milk jug back into the fridge. "I never said I don't like it."

Her shoulders slumped. He hadn't said it out loud, yet she could tell being in her dad's house put him on edge. It wasn't where she wanted to be, either. But it was only temporary. They had no choice.

"I know."

"It's kind of nice being around family. Family that actually cares about you, anyway." Jeremy shook his head as if shaking off bad memories. "How does your stomach feel after eating? Is your morning sickness bad today?"

"Hot coffee, Jeremy." She glanced over her shoulder. "Keep your voice down."

His eyes twinkled. "Relax, he's not even home."

"I—I know," she sputtered. "I'm just, uh . . ."

Her voice trailed off as she let out a long breath. Was she

37

going crazy? Dad couldn't hear them. He'd risen with the dawn and headed off to work before Bea had even opened her eyes. No matter how many hours of sleep she got, her body wanted more.

Jeremy stretched his neck. "You can't keep it from him for long."

"I'm just not ready."

She scrunched her nose. *I'm just not ready* felt like such an understatement. She was more than *just not ready* to face her dad's reaction to the big news—she was terrified.

"Are you going to call the doctor at least?"

"Maybe later." She gave a half smile as she watched Steve's tail flick back and forth while staring down the wayward Cheerio. "I was thinking we could walk down to the Food Farm this morning."

"Walk?"

"I'll give you the grand tour of Moose Creek. Shouldn't take long."

"Okay." He followed her to the front door, where their shoes and coats waited. "But don't you want to drive?"

She opened the door and took a deep breath. "No way."

The air here was different from California. Thinner, for one thing, and drier. But also fresher. Santa Clara always smelled vaguely of an adolescent's bedroom that had been shut up for too long. Moose Creek smelled like ice water and Ponderosa pines. Unless the wind blew in just the right direction and carried the earthy scent of Dirk Reichman's cows into town.

They headed west on the dirt road, labeled Lewis and Clark Avenue but referred to by locals as Second Street. Bea breathed the familiar air, studied the familiar houses, and anchored herself on the familiar hard-packed dirt beneath her feet. Yet she couldn't deny an unfamiliar feeling. The feeling of being a stranger. She'd been gone only two years. How could Moose Creek no longer feel like home?

Jeremy scanned the street. "It's quiet."

She didn't answer. It had been hard to get used to the constant noise and bustle when she first moved away. Cities were so loud. But that's what Jeremy had grown up with.

An old four-wheeler manned by an even older driver puttered by at a slow and steady pace.

Bea raised one hand. "Good morning, Earl."

Earl nodded as he passed, his shaggy white hair streaming behind him.

"That guy looks like he's about a hundred years old," Jeremy said.

"Ninety-three."

Jeremy's eyes widened. "And he's still allowed to drive?"

"He's not really driving."

"Um, yes. He is. He's driving a four-wheeler."

Bea shrugged. "He likes to make the rounds. Just be glad we weren't here a couple months ago. In the summer, he rides around in cutoff jeans with no shirt on."

Jeremy narrowed his eyes. "And the police aren't concerned?"

It had never crossed Bea's mind that the police should worry about what Earl was up to. She'd seen Officer Darryl pull Earl's four-wheeler over many times but only for a chat. "After everything he's been through in his life, I think the police figure he can do just about whatever he wants."

She watched the four-wheeler disappear around a corner and chewed the inside of her lip. Part of her was annoyed Jeremy thought Earl was doing something wrong, but what if he was right? How long could Earl keep riding that old Yamaha around before someone got hurt? Something like that would never be allowed to happen in Santa Clara.

Sometimes the upsides of living in a small town were also the downsides. And vice versa.

As they continued walking, Jeremy checked his phone. "I'm not getting any reception."

"It's spotty all through the foothills."

"What's the elevation here?"

"About forty-eight hundred feet in town, but it gets up to six, seven thousand when you go through Bridger Canyon."

He pointed over his shoulder. "How high is that peak?"

"Around ninety-five hundred or so."

It was a long way up from Santa Clara, which sat pretty much at sea level. The air was heavier down there, similar to Atlanta, where they had met. Jeremy had been attending Georgia Tech, while she'd chosen Georgia State University in response to an overwhelming urge to escape Moose Creek after her mother died. So much for that.

They turned south on Town Road and exchanged the hard-packed dirt for a sidewalk. Town Road was the best-kept road in Moose Creek since it was part of Highway 288.

"Where does everyone work?" Jeremy asked.

"At the school mostly, but jobs are scarce. There are a few small businesses. Some people drive the canyon to Ponderosa every day."

"How far is that?"

"About forty-five minutes when the roads are good."

Bea glanced to her left at the mountain. It rose above the town with an air of authority, every peak and crevice distinct today.

Jeremy smiled. "And Ponderosa is where all the buildings are?"

She smiled back. "Yep."

"We'll have to drive over there and check it out sometime this week."

"Sure. It's easy to get there now."

"Not easy when it snows?"

"Well, there's an arm on I-90 that goes down and closes the road when the weather is really bad. The crosswind can blow strong enough to tip a semi. Then you have to go the long way through the canyon."

"And that's not as easy?"

"No." She shrugged. "But that's just how it is."

She thought back to the horror stories Dad used to tell her when she first got her license. He'd wanted to discourage her from ever attempting the long way to Ponderosa by herself and gave her the "people die ten feet from their front doors in a blizzard" lecture more times than she could count. Drivers needed to be careful in the snow, of course, but his stories had been exaggerated for her benefit, she was sure. Leftover tales from Montana's untamed pioneer days. He'd never been able to tell her exactly who these people were who couldn't find their own houses in a storm.

They reached Main Street, and she looked left, then right. Had the storefronts always been so grimy? When had the old video-rental store been boarded up? The store had been out of business for years, but now the windows were all broken. Nothing seemed as cheery as she remembered.

She linked arms with Jeremy, suddenly needing something solid to hold on to. "What do you want to see first?"

He gestured west, away from the mountain. They walked slowly.

"These buildings are old." Jeremy pointed with his chin. "When was this town founded?"

"I'm not sure . . . 1897, I think? But they look older than they are. Things wear down fast out here."

Including people. She thought of Grandpa Rand and the toll the ranch had taken on him. When she'd seen him last night, she was surprised at how old he looked for only seventy-one years. Old and tired. And his eyes had seemed sunken and troubled. She wished she could talk to her mom about how it bothered her.

She wished she could talk to her mom about a lot of things.

"Ms. Beatrice Jensen, is that you?"

Bea tightened her hold on Jeremy's arm. She knew that voice.

Spinning to face its source, she pasted on a smile. "Hey, Mr. Jamison. Why aren't you in class?"

He wore his signature gray newsboy cap and matching tweed jacket. The same cap and jacket he'd been wearing to teach history at Moose Creek High for decades.

"I figured I had made sufficient contributions to society, and I retired."

"Oh." Bea's eyebrows rose. It had seemed like he would be at the high school forever.

She glanced over at Jeremy and waved a hand in his direction. "Mr. Jamison, this is my husband, Jeremy."

The old man reluctantly grabbed Jeremy's hand but kept his eyes on Bea. "I heard a rumor you got married, but I didn't want to believe it. I thought surely you were too smart to drop out of school for some boy. No offense, Mr. . . . ?"

Jeremy gave him an enigmatic look. "Michaels. And none taken."

Bea felt her smile waver. Mr. Jamison had never been one to mince words. She stumbled over a response. "Well, I, uh, that's not . . ."

"And now you're back." Mr. Jamison crossed his arms. "Temporarily, I hope?"

She knew he wasn't saying that because he couldn't wait to be rid of her again. It was just that he always encouraged his students to dream big. Shoot for the stars. Go away to college and make a name for themselves. Plus, he'd taken a special interest in her back then. All the teachers had felt sorry for her when her mom got sick.

"Yes. Temporarily." The word sounded unconvincing in her own ears. She gave Jeremy a sidelong glance. "Mr. Jamison was one of my teachers."

Jeremy nodded. "And what are you up to now that you're retired?"

Mr. Jamison chuckled. "Causing trouble, mostly. My wife

keeps shooing me out of the house because I drive her crazy when I'm bored. I go for a nice long walk every day about this time."

Bea remembered all the long hours he'd put in at the high school, always going above and beyond the call of duty. Judging the Speech and Debate competitions, serving as senior-class adviser, administering PSAT practice tests. "I'm sure they miss you at the school."

He'd been a great teacher, despite his blunt way with words. One of her favorites. Which made the feeling she'd let him down all the more overwhelming.

He shrugged. "Every era must come to an end. You're headed to the Food Farm, I presume?"

Bea couldn't help but chuckle at the shocked look on Jeremy's face. He had a lot to learn about how fast news could travel in a small town.

"Yep." She tugged on Jeremy's arm. "My old stomping grounds. We better get going. It was nice to see you."

"You too, Ms. Jensen." Mr. Jamison gave Jeremy a pointed look. "I mean, Ms. Michaels. Don't stick around, you hear?"

She felt his words all the way through her heart and down her spine and to her toes. She wanted to say *I won't* or *Why not?* or *It's none of your business*, but instead only managed, "We'll see."

She stared at the brown leather elbow patches on Mr. Jamison's jacket as he turned away and wondered not for the first time how a man like him had ended up in Moose Creek. A man who'd never driven a truck or worn a pair of cowboy boots in his life.

"What was that all about?" Jeremy asked.

Mr. Jamison had gone left, so she turned right. "Don't take it personally."

Jeremy jogged to catch up. "I don't. I mean, I don't care what he says about me. But why would he talk to you like that?"

Bea slowed in front of an old brick building. "Every time a new freshman class arrived at his door, he would spend four years trying to convince them there was more to life than Moose Creek. I guess he thought . . ."

"What?"

"That I believed him."

Jeremy reached for her hand and squeezed. "Just because you're back for a little while doesn't mean you're settling."

What if it did? She squeezed back, still amazed at how well her hand fit in his. What if they got stuck here? She'd seen it happen to a lot of people over the years. They would come back because they couldn't find a job or needed to care for an ailing parent or wanted to save money for a new house and then never mustered the strength to free themselves a second time from the pull of small-town inertia.

Maybe that was what happened to Mr. Jamison.

"This is the fire station." She looked up. "It's the tallest building in town."

It was a little crumbly around the edges but stately. The redbrick walls and leaded arched windows gave the impression that the first fire engine Moose Creek ever parked inside might've been pulled by horses. Jeremy dutifully admired it, and then they walked on.

"The post office and pharmacy."

"Combined?"

"It's a long story." Bea chuckled to herself thinking about how she grew up believing it was normal for those two businesses to share a building. "And here's the newspaper office."

The *Moose Creek Messenger* went to print twice a week, every Tuesday and Friday.

"What do they—" Jeremy hesitated, like he wanted to choose his words carefully—"write about?"

Bea laughed. "High school sports mostly. And local news."

"Such as?"

"I don't know, police reports and community events and stuff. There was a whole exposé on Mr. Stuart's goat one time."

"Mr. Stuart has a goat?"

"Well, he *did*. It kept breaking out of his yard after dinner and coming back every night at nine, and no one could figure out why."

Jeremy raised his eyebrows. "Don't leave me hanging."

"Someone at Peggy's Place was taking the trash out to the alley every night at eight-thirty." She paused for dramatic effect. "The goat would hide out until they went back inside, raid the garbage, then trot on home."

She tried to interpret the look on Jeremy's face. He was amused by the story, but there was something else, too. What did he really think of Moose Creek? It didn't have all the bells and whistles of the city. It was a fishbowl she'd been eager to escape. But she'd learned quickly that a faster pace and greater population density didn't make life better. Didn't make you feel less alone.

Didn't change your memories.

Jeremy caught her expression and grinned. "It's charming, that's all. It all feels so Mayberry. I wish I'd grown up in a place like this. You were lucky."

Maybe that was true. Maybe she was fortunate to have belonged to a place like this. But things were different now. She wasn't sure where she belonged anymore.

"Here's the Food Farm."

The market had a dozen fliers taped to the large front window. A handwritten one said a kid named Wyatt wanted to earn money doing yard work. One from the school said they were selling butter braids to raise money for new basketball uniforms for the junior high team. A neon orange one said HELP WANTED. Nothing had changed.

A bell jingled as they entered. A giant of a man with a bristly salt-and-pepper beard looked up from the cash register and gave a triumphant shout. "Bea! It's about time."

❖ ❖ ❖

Mitch squinted at his phone in surprise. His dad never left a message. Ever. Something was wrong.

"I'm taking a break, Ralph." He checked the time as he loped to his truck. Dad had called a couple of hours ago, but it had been a busy morning, and Mitch hadn't noticed the voicemail notification until now.

He slid into his seat and slammed the door shut as he pressed the callback button, not wanting to waste time listening to the message.

"Pick up, Dad." He drummed the steering wheel with one hand. "Come on, pick up."

"Mitch?" Rand's voice was thin. Tired.

"Hey, what's going on? I saw you called."

A muffled thump, then the sound of a door shutting.

"Is it Mom?"

"She's poorly, son."

Mitch pressed the phone tightly to his ear. "She was fine last night. Did something happen?"

"I don't know. When it gets dark, she . . ."

Mitch eyeballed his keys as he waited, wondering if he should head out there. He could take an early lunch and be at his parents' house in twenty-five minutes.

"She what?"

"She isn't herself."

The raw way he said it gave Mitch pause. "Maybe I should—"

"Don't come by." His dad read his mind through the phone. "It'll upset her."

Mitch's brow furrowed. Was she mad at him? "Is this about the pies?"

Rand cleared his throat and lowered his voice. "If she hears us talking about going to the doctor, she'll pitch a fit."

Mitch rubbed his forehead. They were back to this. It had

been years since his mom had seen a doctor, but she appeared to be fit as a fiddle, as she would say. "What kind of doctor?"

Silence. Mitch fought to keep his frustration in check, the suspicion that his father was the one who needed a checkup growing more with every passing minute.

"Dad?"

"A head doctor."

Mitch sat back. "Like a shrink?"

"No."

A neurologist? But that would be for . . . Realization struck Mitch like a southwest wind ripping through the canyon. *"She isn't herself."* His father was worried about dementia or something. But his mom was way too young for that. She was only sixty-three.

"Dad."

"Please." Rand's tone leaned over the edge of desperation. "I don't know what to do."

Mitch couldn't ignore the tremble in his father's voice. Randall Jensen had never been the kind of man to exaggerate. Or see things that weren't there. Or be afraid. There must be something Mitch was missing. Even if his dad was way off, and Mitch was ninety-nine percent sure he was, it wouldn't hurt anything to make an appointment so he could put both their minds at ease. He'd need a referral, but Ruth Anne from the clinic would fax one to Ponderosa if he explained the situation.

"Okay." Mitch's shoulders slumped. He leaned his head back and stared at the mountain filling his windshield like impending doom. "I'll call tomorrow."

EIGHT

It was Thursday morning before Mitch had the chance to look up the nearest neurologist. He and Ralph had been scrambling to grade all the unpaved roads and clear all the drainage ditches before the freezing rain expected over the weekend. They'd worked long days, knowing the mess they'd be in for if they didn't. He loved working for the town, but he didn't relish being blamed when a road flooded or a car popped a tire in a pothole.

It took four minutes of scrolling through websites and three phone calls before confirming the hospital in Ponderosa did not have a neurologist on staff. Fortunately, two neurologists from Billings took turns driving the almost two hours to Ponderosa every Friday to meet with local patients. Unfortunately, this Friday was already booked up.

"Okay." He drummed his fingers on the counter. "How about next week?"

"Let me check."

The woman on the other end of the line was kind, if not apologetic. She put him on hold, and he watched for Bea and Jeremy out the window while he waited. Bea didn't start her new job until Monday. Where had they run off to?

The fridge made a suspicious sound, and he glared at it.

The on-hold music clicked off, and the friendly woman returned. "We have one opening next Friday at one-thirty. Would you like me to put you down?"

"Yes. Thank you." He kicked himself for not calling sooner. Hopefully, his dad wouldn't be too disappointed at having to wait another week. "We'll be there."

As he hung up the phone, he imagined Dad telling his mom about the appointment. *Consultation*, technically. She would be livid. Maybe they wouldn't tell her until they were already in the truck.

Then he imagined telling Bea. He had a feeling she wouldn't take it any better than his mother. Surely this was all for nothing.

The fridge made that sound again, catching his attention. What was the deal with that thing? When Mitch walked closer to listen, he nearly tripped over a cat.

"Watch it, Steve."

The cat scooted off to a safe distance and sat with his eyes fixed on Mitch. Mitch still couldn't believe there was a real live cat in his house. It was mind-boggling. But it hadn't been so bad. Steve mostly kept to himself, and Mitch had other things to worry about.

Like the fridge.

It didn't take long to diagnose the problem. Something was wrong with the ice machine. He'd never liked fridges with frills like ice and water in the door, but Caroline had talked him into it when they got married. *"Just think how convenient it would be,"* she had said. He smiled to himself, remembering the funny way she'd said the word *convenient*, holding out the middle *e* sound. She was always doing cute stuff like that.

As he pulled open the freezer-side door to inspect the ice machine, he sang softly to himself. "'Sweet Caroline . . .'"

"Dad?"

He jumped and spun toward the hall, where Bea and Jeremy were standing. "Oh, I didn't hear you come in."

"I heard you singing." The look on Bea's face was unreadable.

Mitch swallowed. Did it bother her to hear him singing her mother's song? "I was just trying to fix the ice machine."

Jeremy gave Bea a knowing look—what did he know that Mitch didn't?—and held up a large plastic bag. "I'll go put these clothes away."

Bea nodded but kept her eyes on Mitch as Jeremy walked away. "We went over to Ponderosa. Jeremy wanted to check it out."

He heard her words, but she seemed to be saying something else. He closed the freezer door slowly and took a couple of steps closer to his daughter. Her face seemed pale. "Orange Julius?"

She nodded. They always stopped at the mall for an Orange Julius when they went to Ponderosa. It was a Jensen family tradition.

Mitch leaned against the table and crossed his arms. "I haven't seen much of you this week. What have you guys been up to?"

Her expression softened slightly. "Not much. Jeremy's been spending a lot of time on his computer."

Mitch wrestled his face into a neutral expression. That kid was far too attached to his computer. It was like a third arm. And now he was going to sit around cruising the internet, or whatever they called it, while Bea worked her tail off at the Food Farm?

"Looking for work?"

"Sort of." Bea knelt to pet Steve on the head. "He wants to start his own company. Work for himself."

"What kind of company?"

She hesitated. "Consulting, I think."

"You think?"

"He doesn't know exactly yet. This is all new to us, Dad."

Mitch bit back a sarcastic reply. This was dangerous territory. Better to change the subject. "I've never heard of a cat named Steve before."

"He's named after Steve Jobs."

The name sounded familiar . . .

She stood. "The Apple computers guy?"

Ah yes. Of course. Mitch nodded. "I guess that makes sense with you living in Santa Clara. Was it nice there?"

Bea shrugged. "It was okay. Different."

Mitch had never been to California. Had Bea missed him as much as he'd missed her? "I guess we don't know much about each other's lives the past couple of years, do we?"

The look she gave him seemed filled with some kind of longing and also sadness. He was tempted to blame her for the fact they weren't as close as they used to be—she was the one who couldn't get out of Moose Creek fast enough—but his heart remembered the state he'd been in after Caroline died and wouldn't let him.

They stared at each other for a taut moment, then both spoke at once.

"I hear you got a tattoo."

"I miss Mom."

Her eyes widened. He cringed inwardly. They both spoke again.

"I miss her, too."

"I'm not sure it's any of your business."

She said it nicely, but it stung. He wanted to know why she would do something like that. He wanted to know what she was thinking. But she'd brought up Caroline. She'd tried to get him to talk about her, about what happened, lots of times after Caroline's funeral, but he never knew what to say. Looked like he hadn't come very far in that department.

A moment of significant expectation hung in the air between them. He should tell Bea how hard it had been for him since Caroline had passed. How alone he felt. How sorry he was for all the things he'd kept from her and how he wished . . .

"They're not just random tattoos, Dad. They're meaningful."

The moment passed. Regret stung his throat, and he gulped it down. Who was this woman who used to just be his daughter but now had an entirely separate life? It felt strange that she could go off and do something like get a tattoo without his knowing about it. Without his permission or approval. Without a second thought. Even though she'd turned eighteen three years ago, he was still struggling to accept that she was an adult. "What do they mean?"

"The two wedding bands circling the cross represent the way we want our marriage centered around our faith."

"Oh." Her words poked at something in his heart. They sounded like something Caroline would say. "I saw Jeremy's on his arm. Where's yours?"

Her face reddened. "Dad."

He pushed off the table and raised his hands. "Okay, sorry. None of my business."

Returning to the fridge, he pulled it back open to give his daughter some space. He tinkered with the mechanism inside the freezer door for a minute, then called over his shoulder, "Have you guys had dinner?"

Steve meowed.

He peered around the freezer door. "Bea?"

She was gone. He should've said something about Caroline. Should've asked Bea how she was doing instead of bringing up the tattoo. *Way to go, Mitch.*

A knock sounded at the front door, and his stomach sank into his shoes. Oh, great. He didn't have to answer it to know who it was. He closed the fridge and wiped his hands on his jeans. The knock came again.

"All right, I'm coming," he muttered as the words to Travis Tritt's "T-R-O-U-B-L-E" played in his head.

He forced a smile—a small one, nothing that might be mistaken for enthusiastic—and opened the door.

"Yoo-hoo!" Marge clutched a familiar glass pan between two potholders. "Janice told me how busy you and Ralph have been all week." She blew hair from her green eyes and grinned. "I brought burrito casserole straight from the oven."

He didn't want another Marge dinner. He hated pretending he didn't notice the hopeful look on her face every time she stopped by, or the disappointment when he didn't invite her to join him. But his stomach grumbled, betraying him.

"You must be starving. I bet you haven't eaten all day." She pushed her way into the house. "Let me just set this down on the counter for you. It's hot."

He stood in the doorway for a second, wondering how it had come to this, then resigned himself and closed the door. A man had to eat.

He followed Marge into the kitchen, racking his brain for something to say, but the only thing he could think to comment on was the weather, and he was sure she didn't want to talk about *that*.

She set the pan down and turned to him. "How about that winter storm warning, huh?"

He almost laughed. Maybe she did want to talk about that. "It's a storm *advisory*, technically. But yes, it could get messy."

"I'd rather have snow than that freezing rain." She began cutting the casserole into squares with a serving spatula she'd magically produced from nowhere. "It's miserable."

He opened his mouth but nothing came out. What should he say? Did he want to get into a conversation? He couldn't very well shove her back out the door.

"So, Marge . . ."

She looked up at him expectantly. He swallowed. Footsteps

sounded on the stairs, and he spun around as Bea and Jeremy came into the kitchen. Bea's face stiffened when she caught sight of Marge.

Bea gave him a weighty look. "Sorry, we didn't mean to interrupt."

Mitch's neck muscles tensed. She hadn't been interrupting anything. There was nothing to interrupt. He hadn't asked Marge come over here. Hadn't asked her to bring food yet again. But as he caught Bea's eye, he suddenly felt as though he'd done something wrong.

NINE

B ea had heard the expression "green around the gills" before and was pretty sure that would describe her current condition. She buckled herself into the Toyota with a groan.

Jeremy started the car and gave her a concerned look. "Are you okay?"

"It'll pass."

She pulled a Saltine from her pocket and nibbled on it. She'd learned to always keep some crackers in her coat in case the nausea got bad.

"I wish you'd go see the doctor." Jeremy navigated a pothole and turned down Town Road. "Maybe they could give you medicine or something."

"I don't think that's how morning sickness works. But I'll call next week."

She rolled down her window and leaned an arm out. There was a chill in the air this morning that hadn't been there yesterday, but it felt good on her flushed face. How long was this morning sickness stuff supposed to last? Mom would tell her everything she needed to know, if she were here.

Bea pictured Marge standing in the kitchen and frowned.

They reached Main Street, and Jeremy pulled up to the Bridger Brew Coffee Hut. "I miss Starbucks."

"It's only been one week."

"And fast food."

"There's a Subway inside the gas station."

"That doesn't count."

Jeremy ordered his drink, then pulled back onto the road and pointed. "What are those flags for?"

Blue-and-gold flags lined Main Street from one end to the other.

She spoke around another bite of cracker. "It's Friday."

"So?"

"Game day. The Moose Creek Spuds play the Whitehall Trojans tonight."

"Football?"

"Yep."

Jeremy squinted at the flags flapping in the brisk wind. "They're called the Spuds?"

Bea rolled her eyes. "I know. It's because of all the potato farms south of here. Other schools make fun of us."

"Why not the Moose Creek Mooses? Meese? Okay, I see why."

She smiled at him. "It's not so bad to be a Spud. Everyone loves potatoes."

"I thought potatoes came from Idaho."

"At least fifteen states mass-produce potatoes, Jeremy." She gave him a playful whack on the shoulder. "Don't you know anything about agriculture?"

He grinned. "Um, no. I don't."

"Idaho produces the potatoes people eat. Our valley grows seed potatoes. And sells them to Idaho."

"So this is where French fries begin?"

She leaned her head against the inside of the door. "Something like that."

"And what is that shop over there?" He pointed his latte in the direction of a tiny store with the word ANTLERS painted on the window in white block letters.

"Marty Van Dyken owns that place. He makes sculptures and furniture out of antlers."

"That sounds really cool."

Bea turned away as the shop disappeared from sight. It *was* cool. Mr. Van Dyken created amazing and unique art in that shop. But there wasn't a single customer in sight.

When they reached the edge of town and picked up speed, Bea closed her window but couldn't stop looking out. The leaves had turned to bits of sunshine trapped in the trees, and the beauty filled her heart with longing. She massaged her stomach and breathed slowly, willing the nausea away.

Jeremy focused on the road ahead. "I've never been to a high school football game."

She tore her eyes from the fall colors and sat up straighter. "How is that possible?"

"I never played sports."

"But didn't you go watch your friends play?"

"None of them played."

It boggled her mind a little. At Moose Creek High, everyone played sports or had friends who did. Sometimes the only way to field a team was if every eligible student turned out. And on Friday nights in the fall, there was only one place to be.

"We should go tonight."

"To the game?"

"It'll be fun. I can't believe you've never been."

Jeremy shrugged. "Sure, if you want to."

As they drove the rest of the way to Grandma and Grandpa's house in comfortable silence, Jeremy fiddled with the radio and grumbled about how all country songs sounded the same while Bea mentally sorted through her clothes. Nothing she brought from Santa Clara would be warm enough for a Montana night in October. Neither Georgia nor California had required heavy-weight wool socks or thermal long johns. But some of her old stuff was still tucked away in the closet. She'd have to dig out her Romeos. The rugged slip-on shoes would keep her feet from getting wet if it rained.

As the weathered ranch house came into view, her heart swelled. Grandma and Grandpa weren't the most affectionate people, but they'd always doted on her. She used to sleep over for weeks at a time in the summer and ride horses and help with the cows. Grandpa always had a piece of candy tucked in his pocket for her, and Grandma always told the best stories.

Bea scrunched her lips to one side. No one would ever be able to replace her mother as a confidant, but maybe Grandma would be willing to listen to some of Bea's troubles. It would be nice to have another woman to talk to.

Jeremy took the gravel drive nice and slow. "These tires aren't used to roads like this."

She pointed. "There's Rattler."

The old stock horse stood at the fence, black mane blowing and ears perked. Though they'd owned half a dozen horses in the past, Rattler was the only one her grandparents kept when Grandpa retired.

Jeremy parked the car. "That's quite a name."

"A lot of horses are afraid of rattlesnakes." Bea smiled to herself. "Rattler stomps on them."

Before they were out of the car, Grandma June was on the bottom porch step, waving and calling out, "Oh, Mylanta, look who it is. Randall, come see who it is."

Bea wasn't used to seeing Grandma June get so excited. She was always steady, like the mountain. And like the mountain, she was unmoving. A strong-willed rancher's wife. Bea's mother had been a strong woman, too, in her own way, but different from Grandma June. Affectionate and soft and always looking at things in new ways. It wasn't until Bea was a teenager that she realized how remarkable it was that Grandma June and her mother got along so well.

"Hi, Grandma."

Grandma June squeezed Bea in a side hug and eyeballed Jeremy. "You look hungry."

Jeremy smiled. "I could eat."

Well, that was about the same as telling her the only thing standing between him and utter starvation was a plate of her corn bread. She rose in height a good two inches and made her declaration. "We'll have pancakes."

Bea bit back a groan. Grandma's pancakes were even better than her corn bread, with homemade brown-sugar syrup to boot. Yet Bea's stomach protested the thought of eating anything heavier than a cracker. Grandma would be offended if she didn't fill her plate, though. Bea would need to keep Grandma talking about other things so she wouldn't notice.

Bea and Jeremy followed Grandma up the porch steps, reaching the front door as Grandpa Rand appeared.

"Hi, Grandpa."

His face looked weary, but his eyes sparked when they caught sight of Bea. He smiled and put a hand on her shoulder. "Good to see you."

He shook Jeremy's hand, and they all proceeded inside.

Jeremy eyed Grandpa's belt. "That's quite the buckle you got there."

Grandpa raised his eyebrows. "You like that?"

"I've never seen one so big."

"I've got twenty more bigger'n this." Grandpa stifled a grin and jerked his chin toward his office. "Come on."

Grandma and Bea shared an amused look as the men disappeared down the hall. Bea used to play with the buckles as a kid, organizing them by shape and size. With a glance back over her shoulder, she followed Grandma into the kitchen. Grandpa's buckle collection was extensive and each one had a story. If she was going to have a few minutes alone to talk with Grandma, now was her chance.

Grandma gave Bea a big smile as she tied on an apron. "It's so good to have you back, Beatrice."

She wasn't *back* exactly. Would Grandma understand if she said she didn't want to stay in Moose Creek? Better to start with an easier question. "Is Grandpa doing okay?"

Grandma opened a drawer and started digging around in it. "Of course, dear. He's fine. Are *you* okay? You look a little peaked."

She should've known Grandma would notice. "I'm . . . fine. I just . . ."

"What?"

Bea chewed on a fingernail. "I just was . . . uh, wondering. Did you ever have a secret you were scared to talk about?"

Grandma stopped measuring teaspoons of baking powder into a bowl but didn't respond.

"What I mean is," Bea tried again, "what if you knew the truth might change what someone thought of you?"

She imagined what her father's face would look like when he heard the news about the baby. If he thought her choice to get married at age twenty was irresponsible, what was he going to think of *that*?

A fiery feeling sparked in her chest. What right did he have to think anything of it? He'd told her he cared about her with his words, but his actions after Mom died had said otherwise.

Voices carried into the kitchen from the hallway. Had the belt buckle appreciation party ended already? Bea gave her grandmother a desperate look, hoping for something, *anything* that might give her some guidance about talking to her father. No one knew him better than Grandma.

Grandma's eyes seemed to stare at something far off behind Bea's head. "Secrets are like pennies . . ."

"What?"

Jeremy and Grandpa entered the kitchen. Grandma shook her head and focused her eyes on Bea's face. "You'll be fine, dear. Everything is fine."

Bea nodded dumbly, disappointment vibrating inside her. But what had she expected? She hadn't really talked to Grandma in two years, except on the phone at Christmas and her birthday. Maybe she could come visit another day and try again.

She turned her attention to her husband. "What did you think of Grandpa's collection?"

"Impressive." He grinned a big dopey grin. He was so cute when he did that. "The Montana state one with the blue stones was my favorite."

Bea returned his smile. "That was always my favorite, too."

Grandma pulled the griddle from a bottom cupboard. "So, Jeremy, tell me all about Colorado."

He gave Bea a quizzical look.

Bea chuckled. "California."

Grandma set a whisk and large spoon on the counter. "I've never been there, but I always thought Colorado would be a nice place to visit."

Bea frowned. "California, Grandma."

Grandma continued her preparations as if she hadn't heard, and Bea caught Jeremy's eye. He shrugged, unperturbed. Bea supposed it was normal for Grandma to start getting a little forgetful and confused as she aged. She was only human, after all. But she wasn't that old. Bea considered trying one more time to correct Grandma, but when she glanced at Grandpa Rand, the dejected look on his face changed her mind.

Pancakes soon appeared on the table as Grandma continued to chat away. She asked about Jeremy's family—a subject he delicately sidestepped—and mentioned his cat multiple times, though she kept calling him Stanley. Grandpa Rand rarely spoke, content to listen to the words flying around him. It had always been this way. Every so often he would open his mouth, and the whole world would stop to hear what he had to say. Most of the time, though, as their life puttered down the highway, Grandma was the driver, and he was in the passenger seat.

Until Jeremy asked how Grandma and Grandpa first met.

Grandma flicked her wrist. "Oh, we've always known each other from town."

"You both grew up here, right?" Bea asked.

Grandpa Rand's eyes lit up. "Sure, we'd always known each other, but the year your grandmother came back after spending the summer at her aunt's in Chicago—"

"Her aunt's?" Bea sat up straight. She'd never heard this story before.

"Miss Gladys Fennel. Like the seed." He offered a crooked grin, made all the more charming by a missing tooth on the left side. "Anyway, she was a sight for sore eyes when she returned, I tell you what. She wasn't just some kid from town to me no more."

Grandma went still, looking at him, and for a second, the years melted away from her face. She was a young girl again, falling in love with an older man. Bea could see it. The tenderness and longing. The hope. The fear. Bea understood.

"There was no going back after that, was there?" Jeremy asked, a twinkle in his eye.

"No, sir." Grandpa shook his head. "None at all."

Grandma passed a hand over her face as if wiping away the memories and jumped in with more questions for Jeremy. Whenever she wasn't looking, Bea slid some of her pancakes onto Jeremy's plate, and he happily ate them. Thank goodness he had a big appetite.

When Grandma June had used up all the batter, she sat down next to Jeremy. She ran her fingers through her hair, but it stuck out in the back, like she'd had a fitful night of sleep and forgot to comb it.

Jeremy patted his belly. "That was delicious. The best syrup I've ever had in my life."

"Oh, shoot." Grandma put a hand to her cheek. "It's just a little brown sugar."

"I didn't get much home cooking growing up."

Bea grunted, knowing he'd often been lucky to get any food at all.

Jeremy inclined his head in her direction. "My wife says you're quite the storyteller."

Grandma perked up. "We've had a lot of good story times around here, she and I. Haven't we, Bea?"

Bea nodded. "Tell him my favorite one."

Grandma waved a hand. "He doesn't want to hear that."

"Sure, I do." Jeremy pushed his plate away and leaned his arms on the table. "Tell me."

Grandma scooted her chair out. "I've got to clear the table."

"No, no." Bea jumped to her feet and gently pressed Grandma back into her seat. "I'll do that. You tell the story."

"All right, all right." She wiped her hands on her apron and folded them in her lap. "If you're sure."

"Of course, my lady." Jeremy gave a funny little bow and doffed an invisible hat. "Proceed."

Bea stifled a chuckle.

Grandma cleared her throat and put on the serious story-telling face Bea knew so well. "Once upon a time, many years ago, there was a man named Miner McGee. He had spent his life traveling all over the country, searching for treasure, and had found a little gold here, a few gemstones there, but never struck it rich. And, boy, did he want to strike it rich."

As Bea moved around the kitchen, she found herself keeping one eye on Jeremy as the story unfolded, wanting—needing—him to love it like she did.

"Eventually, his travels brought him to Moose Creek,"

Grandma continued, "on the first day of winter. The same day the whole town was abuzz with a fantastical rumor."

Bea smiled to herself. *Fantastical* was Grandma's favorite story word.

"The rumor told of an enormous diamond hidden away on the mountain—the Big Sky Diamond—and that only a man willing to give up everything else would ever be able to find it. Well, Miner McGee couldn't believe his ears. He knew he was that man. He'd been waiting his whole life for this. So he stocked up on supplies, strapped on his headlamp, and headed up the mountain."

Jeremy raised a finger in protest. "All by himself?"

Grandma nodded gravely. "All by himself. Everyone in Moose Creek begged him to wait until spring, but Miner McGee believed he had already waited long enough to fulfill his destiny. Up the mountain he went, just as the worst blizzard Moose Creek had ever seen fell upon the land. The wind began to blow, the snow began to fall, and the roads became impassable. It didn't let up for three whole days. When the sky finally cleared and the sun came out, the people of Moose Creek gathered to discuss whether to send a search party up the mountain for Miner McGee's body right then or wait until the thaw."

Jeremy gently pounded a fist on his knee. "He died?"

Grandma fixed her eyes on him, and Bea inched closer to the table, her task forgotten.

"Everyone believed so. No one could survive a storm like that out in the open. But as the townspeople talked, the sun sank low in the sky, and someone shouted, 'Look!' Everyone turned, and there on the mountain was Miner McGee's headlamp, shining bright for all to see as he worked away, searching for his treasure. And ever since that day, whenever the sun sinks low in the sky, if you look over at the mountain at just the right time, you will see his lamp click on."

"He's still looking?" Jeremy asked.

"He's still looking."

"What if he never finds it?"

"He will." Grandma June sat back in her chair with a satis-fied smile. "He'll never give up."

TEN

itch adjusted the pile of clothes in his arms as he stood outside Bea's bedroom, the words to Trisha Yearwood's "She's in Love with the Boy" taunting him in his head. *Argh.* The reason he loved country music was the same reason he hated it sometimes. It always hit him right where he lived. Why'd Bea have to fall for an unemployed computer geek who didn't know the difference between an elk and a moose?

He knocked on the door. "Bea?"

She opened it wide. "Just dump it here on the bed."

He didn't exactly *dump* it, but he let the clothes roll out of his arms onto the orange, green, and blue quilt he and Caroline used to sleep under. The quilt his mother's aunt Gladys had made for their wedding. "I hope something fits."

Jeremy stood off to the side as Bea dug through the items. He watched her with a bemused expression. "I still don't understand why I can't wear my own stuff to the game."

Bea scoffed. "Nothing you have is warm enough."

"It's not *that* cold."

Mitch snickered. This kid had no idea what he was in for. He grabbed two pairs of socks from the bed and held them out. "Here. These are the best ones."

"Two pairs?"

"One pair goes under your long johns, and the other goes over."

"I think one will be plenty. My feet will get sweaty."

"Is that right." Mitch held the socks out until Jeremy took them. It would not do to allow this greenhorn to neglect his feet. Speaking of which . . .

He nodded at the Romeos Bea was wearing. "Those look a little rough, B.B." He held out his hand. "Here, give them to me."

"Dad, they're fine."

"Just let me rub some Huberd's on them."

She huffed and kicked them off to hand over. "Leave in fifteen?"

Mitch nodded, and she turned back to the pile of clothes on the bed. He was glad to see her looking better than she had this morning. When he saw her at breakfast, he'd thought she might be coming down with something, but there was no sign of it now.

He left them to get dressed. Did it ever get below zero in Atlanta? It wouldn't be below zero tonight, but he did expect a very cold twenty-eight degrees or so. The air always felt colder when it was damp and when you were sitting outside on metal bleachers. With any luck, the freezing rain would hold off until the game was over, but in case it got wet out, he would give Bea's Romeos a good coating of Huberd's Shoe Grease for protection.

Once the shoes were rubbed down to his satisfaction, Mitch headed to the kitchen, stepping over Steve to reach his good thermos. As he filled it with coffee, he thought of his father and his stomach roiled with a touch of guilt. When he'd told his dad earlier that he couldn't get an appointment until next Friday, he'd neglected to mention his failure to call in a timely manner was to blame. His dad had sounded discouraged.

Then there was the football game. Bea hadn't exactly invited him along when she told him they were going tonight, but of course she must assume he would go, too, right? He went to all the home games. And it made sense to ride together in his truck. Why bother with two vehicles?

Not to mention he didn't want people seeing that Toyota thing with its hopeless tires anyway. They were never going to make it through a Montana winter. *And* not to mention Jeremy didn't know how to drive a stick shift. Mitch had made that disappointing discovery while they were discussing the ride arrangements.

At least he'd managed to dodge having Marge tag along. She'd been in her front yard pruning back her peonies when he'd come home from work, and she'd done her best to rope him into offering an invitation to the game. He'd wriggled out of it like a calf in the tie-down event at Ponderosa's annual rodeo.

He chuckled to himself, even as a heaviness landed on his shoulders. It was the kind of story Frank would get a kick out of. Mitch's fingers itched to dial up his old friend and tell him about it. Tell him about everything going on. Tell him his son-in-law couldn't even drive a stick shift. But he didn't know how to cross back over the bridge he'd burned two years ago.

A loud clatter made him jump, tossing thoughts of Frank from his mind. Ugh. That stupid ice machine. Now it was spitting out ice cubes whenever it felt like it. His tinkering had only made it worse. A chunk of ice slid across the floor and came to rest in front of Steve, who sniffed at it with contempt.

"Don't blame me." Mitch scowled at the cat. "It didn't start acting up until *you* got here."

Bea and Jeremy came bounding down the stairs, chattering happily together. Mitch's heart wrenched. He loved seeing Bea happy. Loved hearing her laugh and watching her smile, even if it was at Jeremy. But it made him miss Caroline. And he wanted to be the one to make Bea smile. To be what she needed. He'd spent her first eighteen years being everything for her. His only child. And now she looked at Jeremy like *that*.

He eyed the windbreaker in Jeremy's hand. "You got a coat?"

Jeremy looked down at the jacket. "Uh . . ."

Bea raised her eyebrows at him. "Dad."

"Okay." Let him freeze to death if that's what he wanted. "Let's go."

◆　◆　◆

Although there was some comfort in the sameness of everything—the home stands, the cheers, even the hot dogs—Bea fidgeted in her seat, wedged between Jeremy and her father. Everywhere she turned, there was someone in the sea of blue-and-gold team apparel wanting to ask invasive questions. When did you get back? What are you going to do now? And the worst one: Georgia State didn't work out, huh?

Georgia State. Sigh. It was tempting to believe going there had been a mistake. She'd spent the first six months in an aimless daze, changing her mind weekly about what degree to pursue and keeping the other girls in her dorm at arm's length. She couldn't remember a single thing she'd learned. But if it weren't for Georgia State, she'd never have met Jeremy.

She scooted a little closer to her husband and looked around, finding her eyes drawn to the land surrounding the football field. Cows grazed in the acreage to the west. The mountain loomed to the east, its face golden pink as it reflected the sunset. She caught her breath as she realized what time it must be. Miner McGee should be switching on his headlamp right about . . .

"There." She nudged Jeremy's shoulder and pointed. "Look."

His head swiveled. A flicker of light appeared, shining from one of the mountain's many folds.

"Miner McGee?" Jeremy asked.

She nodded. "There's an old forest service cabin up there. When the sun is low in the sky, it reflects off the window. Just for a minute."

They peered at it until the sun moved too far and it blinked out. Bea could remember being young enough to believe Miner McGee was really up there. She would shout with delight whenever the light appeared. Would her own child do the same one day?

The game started as the Moose Creek Spuds ran the kickoff back to the thirty-two-yard line. The thwacks and thuds of helmets and pads colliding echoed across the fields around the stadium. With nothing to absorb the sounds, people miles away could hear what was happening in the game. Many of them even stopped what they were doing to set their hands on their hearts when the national anthem played through the speakers.

"I've never seen so much camo in my life," Jeremy said.

She gave him a half smile. "Wait until opening weekend."

He leaned closer to her ear. "I didn't realize your dad was coming."

One eyebrow rose. She wasn't thrilled about it, either. But Dad attended all the home games, like most people in town. They couldn't just leave him home while they went out, could they?

A jolt of excitement rippled through the crowd as a man wearing a suit made from potato sacks appeared in the stands.

The crowd cried out, "Booger!"

He raised his fists and yelled. The crowd went wild, chanting, "Booger! Booger! Booger!"

Jeremy gave her a funny look, his lips looking a little blue. "Booger?"

She shrugged. "It's not his real name."

"What's his real name?"

"Beauregard."

"Oh." Jeremy stuck his hands under his armpits. "That wind is brisk."

The sky was clear as the harvest moon peered over the mountain to check the score of the game. But the damp chill portended the freezing rain to come. She looked at him sideways. "I thought your feet were going to be sweaty."

His face tightened. "I only wore one pair."

"Should've listened to my dad."

He frowned and looked away. She tensed. She shouldn't have said that.

"How are your shoes?" Jeremy asked, low enough only she could hear.

Was that what this was all about? She looked down at the Romeos and turned her face away from where Dad sat on her other side. "He was only trying to help."

"He wants me to know I'm out of my element here."

She spoke in an irritated whisper. "The leather needed some grease, that's all."

Jeremy didn't answer. She pressed her lips together. Was it going to be like this the whole time? What did he want from her?

The quarterback threw a short pass for eight yards, and the announcer's voice crackled over the loudspeaker. "First down . . ."

The crowd answered eagerly, "Spud Town!"

Never did Moose Creek embrace their potato heritage like during football season, which happened to coincide with harvest.

Dad elbowed her. "They're looking pretty good this season. You know they've won three games already?"

She raised her eyebrows. "Really?"

He pulled his beanie down tighter over his ears. "This could be the year."

Jeremy leaned forward to join the conversation. "The year for what?"

"The year we finally make the play-offs."

"That's never happened before?"

"Not yet."

The second quarter ended with Moose Creek up 14 to 7. People stood and stretched and shouted to each other from across the bleachers as "Callin' Baton Rouge" played through the speakers.

"Garth Brooks." Dad bobbed his head to the music. "The best."

"Garth Brooks?" Jeremy asked.

Bea turned to stare at him. Sure, he was raised in the city and everything, but how could he not know Garth Brooks? The bestselling country artist of all time?

"Garth is Dad's third favorite."

Jeremy winced a little. "Dare I ask who his first two favorites are?"

Dad's face took on a solemn look. This was a serious subject for him. "Randy Travis is number one, of course. Then Miranda Lambert."

Jeremy gulped. "Of course."

Bea laughed. "Dad loves him some Miranda."

"She's got spunk." Dad held up the fingers of one hand. "Then Alan Jackson and Taylor Swift round out the top five. If you must know."

Jeremy gaped. "Uh . . . Taylor Swift?"

"Oh, here we go." Bea rolled her eyes.

"Taylor Swift's not a country singer."

Dad glared. "You don't know what you're saying, son."

"Dad, please." Bea looked up at him, surprised at how easily she took on the role her mother used to play in this familiar discussion. "You've got to let her go. She moved on. It wasn't personal."

He crossed his arms over his chest. "She was born to be a country artist. She's going to come back."

"Taylor Swift is too gifted to be confined to any one genre, Dad. She has to be able to spread her wings."

"I didn't realize she was ever a country singer," Jeremy said.

Dad ignored him and gave Bea a meaningful look. "She'll be back. You wait and see."

"Okay, okay." Bea held up her hands. "If you say so."

Dad stamped his feet and rubbed his hands together. "I'm going to The Shack to warm up and get some popcorn. Want anything?"

"Ooh, popcorn." Bea smiled. "Get me one, too."

"You got it, B.B."

Jeremy watched him walk down the stairs with a guarded look on his face. "I thought you didn't like that name."

She chewed the inside of her lower lip. B.B. wasn't who she was anymore. B.B. was a kid with dreams and plans and a mother who was there for her no matter what. "I don't."

"Then why don't you say so?"

"He doesn't mean anything by it." She looked down to where he'd gone. "It's just a habit."

"Well, I don't—"

"Beatrice, I've been looking all over for you." A young woman holding a baby in one arm dropped into the seat Dad had left empty and threw her other arm around Bea's neck. "I heard you were back. I tried to text, but the number was out of service."

Bea stared at the child. His cheeks were rosy, and snot ran from his nose. She pulled away from the hug. "Oh, uh, hey, Amber."

Why had Amber Moss wanted to text her?

When she left Moose Creek, she'd ditched her old phone and old number as a way to leave it all behind. Start over new and all that. She hadn't been that close to anyone when she graduated anyway, having spent the last couple months of high school completely checked out as her mother's health faded.

She hadn't thought it would bother anyone that they couldn't keep in touch with her, least of all Amber Moss. Once you left town, people tended to forget about you.

Bea gave the baby a pointed look. "Who's this?"

Amber arranged the little one on her lap. "This is Hunter."

"Is he . . . ?"

"Mine?" Amber grinned. "Yes. Eight months old this week." It was her turn to give a pointed look in Jeremy's direction. "And who is *this*?"

"This is my husband, Jeremy." Bea leaned back a little to make the introductions. "Jeremy, this is Amber. We went to school together."

Amber greeted him effusively, acting as if she and Bea had been best friends. Strange. As she peppered Jeremy with questions, Bea stared at Hunter. He wore layer upon layer of warm clothes, giving him the shape of a lumpy snowman. A green knit hat with a triceratops horn covered his ears and tied under his double chin. He stared back, blue eyes wide and curious and carefree.

Amber turned her attention to Bea. "I heard you start work at the Food Farm on Monday. Won't that be something?"

Bea pulled herself from the staring contest. "What do you mean?"

"Nothing." Amber shrugged. "It's just kind of funny. I remember when you worked there in high school."

An uncomfortable pressure pushed on Bea's chest. "It's only temporary. To help Mr. MacGregor out."

"Of course." Amber smiled down at Hunter, and Bea couldn't look away. She was such a . . . mom.

"Your hair is so short," Bea said.

Amber touched her head, which used to sport long, wavy locks. "Hunter kept pulling on it and putting it in his mouth. I had to cut it all off."

"Oh." Bea fought the urge to touch her own shoulder-length

hair. Would she have to cut hers, too? It had taken her a year to get it this long. "It can always grow back, I guess."

Amber chuckled. "We'll see. It takes up a lot less time when it's short. I might keep it this way."

This time Bea couldn't resist fingering a chunk of her hair. Rubbing it between her fingers. "It looks cute."

"Thanks." Amber flashed a smile, then looked down at her boots. "By the way, I wanted to say I'm sorry about your mom."

Bea chewed her lip. "Oh."

"I never got to tell you. Before."

The funeral had been two weeks after graduation. While Bea clung to all her memories of what had been, everyone else in her class had been focused on what was to come. "Thanks."

Amber nodded. "Well, I wish I could stay, but I gotta get this guy home to bed. We should meet up for lunch sometime."

"O-oh," Bea stammered. "Uh, yeah. Sure."

Amber hoisted the baby onto her hip and carefully maneuvered down the steps. Bea watched them go, unable to tear her eyes from the tiny body in Amber's arms.

Jeremy scooted closer. His lips were definitely blue. And Bea was pretty sure she could hear his teeth chattering.

He caught her eye. "Cute kid."

She swallowed. Had Hunter's eight-month-old eyes seared her soul like floodlights shining on her every fear and insecurity, or had it been her imagination? "Yep."

"You know a lot of people."

"Everyone knows everyone around here."

"You must have a lot of friends then."

She hesitated. "Just because you know people doesn't mean they're your friends."

"So you *don't* have friends?"

Bea squirmed. Jeremy was always doing this kind of thing. Forcing her to talk about herself, explain herself. He always wanted to know everything. Understand everything. But how could she explain it when she didn't understand it herself?

"I had friends growing up, I guess, but never had a specific group. I kind of bounced around."

She'd always preferred working with Grandpa on the ranch or hanging out with her mom to school-spirit-type stuff. It was Mom she painted toenails with. Made ice cream sundaes with. Mom who helped her pick out a dress the one and only time she attended a school dance. Mom who had been her best friend.

"That doesn't surprise me." Jeremy nudged her with his shoulder. "You could get along with anyone."

"Maybe." Bea thought back to her mother's funeral. Though a dozen kids from school had been there, she'd felt lost and alone. "But sometimes getting along with anyone means not belonging anywhere."

None of her friends had been able to fill the void left by her mother. And Dad certainly hadn't. He hadn't even tried.

The crowd began returning to their seats as halftime wound down.

Jeremy scooted even closer and put his arm around Bea's waist. "Are you okay?"

"I guess." She watched him from the corner of her eye. "Are *you* okay?"

"Don't tell your dad"—he gave her a sheepish look and shivered—"but I've never been so cold in my life."

ELEVEN

It was a long-standing tradition, dating back to before Mitch was born, that any Moose Creek male who was so inclined met for breakfast at The Baked Potato on Wednesday mornings. They pulled chairs up to the big round table in the middle of the diner and chewed the fat over bacon and eggs. Mitch's dad used to be a regular—enjoyed listening to all the latest news, though he rarely participated in the chatter—but he hadn't made an appearance in over a month.

Mitch lifted his mug for the waitress to refill with coffee and grunted. Two more days until the neurologist appointment.

"I hear your son-in-law's riding the bench." Willy Batson peered at Mitch from across the table, his wiry gray eyebrows sticking out like antennae.

Mitch cringed inwardly. How did Jeremy know enough about anything for anyone to consult him about it? "He works from home right now, I guess. Technically. I don't really understand it."

Travis Kent peeled off his camo jacket and joined in. "He lookin' for something to do?"

Mitch straightened up. "You got something in mind?"

Maybe he could hook Jeremy up with a real job. Give him a chance to man up.

"You know the Duncans?" Travis looped his thumbs behind the fraying straps of his denim overalls. "Down past my place?"

Mitch nodded.

"One brother is down with a busted shoulder, and the other's got shingles."

"Is that right."

"All the way down to his hairy butt."

"So they're shorthanded?"

"As a three-legged dog." Travis bobbed his head, sweeping toast through the egg yolk on his plate. "They're pretty desperate for folks to put on the belt."

This was news to Mitch. He tapped a boot thoughtfully against a chair leg. The Duncan place was only thirty minutes away. And Jeremy hadn't done a thing all week, far as he could tell.

"I'll send him out." Mitch rubbed his chin. Bea wasn't going to work at the Food Farm while Jeremy sat around the house, not if Mitch could help it. "It'll be good for him."

Travis nodded, satisfied, and shoved the last bite of toast into his mouth.

Willy, who had been following their conversation, fixed an eye on Mitch. "Haven't seen your pop in a while." When Mitch hesitated, Willy added, "How are things up at the ranch?"

His dad wouldn't want anyone to know about Mom's troubles. A man kept his worries to himself. That was what Dad would say. "Fine." Mitch spun to look for the waitress so he could signal for his check. "Everything's just fine."

❖　❖　❖

Mitch watched with amusement as Jeremy's eyes widened. He'd been holding on to this information all day, eager to share it with Bea and Jeremy at dinner. What he wouldn't give to hear the thoughts swirling around in his son-in-law's head.

Bea seemed oblivious to Jeremy's discomfort as she ate the spaghetti she'd prepared. "That's awful about Mr. Duncan. I've heard shingles are terrible."

Mitch nodded. "That's why I figured Jeremy here could help out. Just through harvest."

"Of course he will." Bea smiled at her husband. "Right, Jeremy?"

Mitch knew that look. The look of a woman who knew she was going to get her way. It wasn't fair, but he could hardly say so. He wanted Bea on his side.

The deer-in-the-headlights expression hadn't left Jeremy's face. "How long does harvest last?"

Mitch shrugged. "However long it takes."

He discreetly assessed Jeremy's hand, which was holding a piece of garlic bread. Didn't appear suitable for much beyond typing on that computer of his, but surely he could pick rocks out of the potatoes as they rolled by on the belt. Anyone could do that.

"They're expecting you tomorrow morning. First thing."

In Jeremy's silence, Mitch chose to hear a favorable response. It was a win-win. Jeremy would get out of the house, the Duncans would get some much-needed help, and Bea wouldn't be carrying all the weight of earning an income on her shoulders alone.

"How's it going back at the Food Farm, B.B.? You getting the hang of it?"

She glanced at Jeremy. "It's fine. It's like riding a bike. Mac-Gregor hasn't changed a thing."

"It's handy you can bring groceries home."

Jeremy lifted his bread as if he were raising a glass to make a toast. "Yeah, thanks for making dinner."

Bea smiled. "I like cooking for you."

Pain pierced Mitch's heart like a fishhook through flesh, and he winced. She looked just like Caroline, smiling like that. He cleared his place and rolled his stiff shoulders. "I'm going up in the attic."

Bea tilted her head. "What for?"

"The carpet in my room was wet when I got home from work. I've got to check if there's a leak or something."

Jeremy stood with his plate and grabbed Bea's, too. "It didn't rain today."

The freezing rain predicted had come and gone, and the sky had been clear the past two days.

"I know, but there was a wet spot, right inside the door. Gotta find out where it came from."

It was the strangest thing. He always kept his bedroom door shut. Always. Where could the water have come from? His bedroom did share a wall with the bathroom, but if there was a pipe leaking somewhere, wouldn't the water be by the wall? And the attic was unlikely to yield the answer since his room was on the first floor, almost directly beneath Bea's.

Well, he'd figure it out.

"Need any help?"

Mitch paused. Jeremy didn't know the first thing about pipes, Mitch was sure of that. And this was *his* house.

"No, thanks." Mitch cracked his knuckles and headed for the hall. "I can do it myself."

TWELVE

Bea rotated the heads of broccoli and squirmed. She needed to pee. Again. But she couldn't keep taking breaks without raising suspicion, and the last thing she wanted was for rumors to start flying about her being pregnant before she'd even told her dad. If anyone so much as hinted at the truth, the news would make it back to her house before she did—thanks to the moosevine, as she liked to call it.

She'd mumble "hot coffee" through clenched teeth as if speaking about liquids wouldn't make matters worse. Was there no limit to how many times a woman could pee in one day?

"Ms. Michaels, good to see you again."

She turned to find her former teacher Mr. Jamison, the newsboy cap on his head and a large market tote hanging from one arm. "Good morning. Can I help you with anything?"

"No, no." He chuckled. "I know exactly where everything is. How are you enjoying your visit back home?"

He gave special emphasis to the word *visit*. Part of her appreciated his refusal to treat her reappearance in Moose Creek as a foregone conclusion. Another part did not appreciate the pressure. Whether she liked it or not, she wasn't going anywhere until some of Jeremy's "ideas" took on a more concrete form.

She lifted one shoulder. "It's a little strange to be back, living with my dad and working here. It's almost like the past five years never happened."

A piece of her heart broke off and fell to the floor. Why had she said that? If the past five years hadn't happened, if she could go back to the first time she worked at the Food Farm, Mom would still be here. None of the horror of the diagnosis, the heartache of her loss, would've happened. But neither would Jeremy have happened. And she definitely wouldn't be expecting a baby.

She involuntarily touched a hand to her belly, then quickly pulled it away.

Mr. Jamison didn't seem to notice. "You didn't enjoy Georgia State, I take it? They have so many great programs there."

Bea wrinkled her nose. "It was a nice school, but we decided to move to Santa Clara when we got married."

"And they don't have any schools in Santa Clara?"

Her face warmed. "They do."

He raised one eyebrow. "I see."

But he didn't. He didn't see at all.

"That broccoli looks rather leggy, don't you think?"

She turned a head over in her hands, noting the long, thin stems. "It's hard to get good produce here, you know."

He nodded sagely. Montana wasn't exactly known for its favorable growing conditions. Potatoes did well. Soybeans and wheat. But fruits and vegetables? Not so much.

Mr. Jamison selected a small bulb of garlic. "I suppose you heard about Earl."

She frowned. "No. What happened?"

"He's all right." Mr. Jamison patted her arm. "Only madder than a hornet. His grandkids got together and staged an intervention of sorts. Took away his keys."

"To the four-wheeler? Oh dear."

"I'm afraid so." Mr. Jamison threw up his hands. "They

didn't want him causing an accident, you know. Perfectly understandable. But the man is heartbroken."

Bea thought of Jeremy. He had been right. "I bet."

"Now they're threatening to get him signed up for one of those social workers for the elderly. They're supposed to keep tabs on you, I guess. Make sure you take your pills every day or something, I'm not really sure."

"I see."

"Anyway, I best be off." Mr. Jamison tipped his hat. "Have a good day, Ms. Michaels."

She set the last head of broccoli down as he walked away. It *was* pretty leggy. But did she want to care about that? Did she want to spend her time worrying about produce? This job was meant to be temporary, but that's what Kathy had intended when she first started here, too. And she ended up working the Food Farm morning shift for twenty-three years.

It wasn't that Bea hated the job. She liked stocking and organizing and keeping things tidy. She liked helping people and seeing familiar faces every day. But the meat cooler broke down once a week, and MacGregor spent the beginning of every shift grumbling about how Costco was killing him. This wasn't how she pictured her future. She'd always wanted to do something more . . . meaningful.

Her phone vibrated in her back pocket, and she pulled it out. MacGregor didn't mind his employees checking their messages during shifts, so long as they got their work done. It was a text from Jeremy.

> On break from potatoes. Have you called the doctor yet?

Her stomach sank. Since they weren't paying rent or utilities right now, her paychecks were going straight into savings. But every time she researched healthcare costs online, the number of expenses they should be prepared to pay grew larger.

No.

You promised.

I'll do it when I get off work.

She'd have to take the time to look up doctors in Ponderosa. No way was she going to call the clinic in Moose Creek. Ruth Anne, the LPN who worked there four days a week, had cared for hundreds of pregnant Moose Creek women over the years, even delivering many of their babies when the road to Ponderosa was impassable or there wasn't enough time to make the drive. But Bea didn't want to be seen going into the narrow yellow building on Mule Deer Road. No way.

How's it going on the belt?

I'm working alongside a 300-pound man with a handlebar mustache who likes to tell jokes.

Huh. She hadn't seen Big Ben in ages. How had the Duncans managed to wrangle him into working the belt?

Ask him about the time there was a moose in his bedroom.

?!?! Will do! Don't forget about the doctor.

She slipped her phone back into her pocket without responding. Don't forget? *Ha.* As if she could think of anything else but the child inside her every minute of every day.

The curious and charming face of Amber's baby popped into her mind for the hundredth time since last Friday, and she found her hand resting on her belly again. She dropped it. What would her baby look like? More like her or more like Jeremy? Her heart pounded just thinking about it. Was something wrong with her?

She opened another produce box and swallowed. A lump formed in her throat, and tears pricked her eyes.

Baby carrots.

She was crying over a vegetable.

Yep. Something was definitely wrong.

THIRTEEN

My whole body is shaking. The utter humiliation of it all. That my own husband and son would trick me into the truck. Drag me here. Talk with some quack as if I were a child. I could spit. I could just spit.

Wait until Caroline hears about this.

I dig my fingernails into my arm. The truck keys are in Mitch's coat pocket. I saw him put them there. He's so deep in conversation with Dr. What's-His-Name that I could grab them and be halfway to the parking lot before anyone noticed.

Mitch sees me move. "Mom, what are you doing?"

Anger seethes beneath every inch of my skin, but his face is so concerned. His tone of voice is so *concerned*.

"Nothing," I snap.

Mitch turns back to Dr. What's-His-Name, and I study Rand's face. Had this been his idea? Or Mitch's? As if I don't know who the president is. Or Mitch's phone number. Such stupid questions to ask. Even if I didn't know, who cares? We'll have a new president in a year or so, anyway. And if that man pokes me one more time, I will bite him.

I swear I will.

What I really don't understand is why Rand would tell this man such lies about me. Rand. The man I've loved since I was no more than a girl. The man who brings home handfuls of wild sunflowers to leave in a jar on the table. The man who saved me from . . . well, from myself.

No, not Caroline. Beatrice. Caroline is gone.

Oh, God, help me.

I focus on the doctor's face. Dr. Watson? Wilson? What was it? He doesn't look like a quack. Maybe I should listen to what he is saying. But his mouth is moving so fast. I hear phrases like *early onset* and *rapid decline*, but I'm not sure what they mean. Are they still talking about me? Then he says, "Hereditary."

My heart stops beating. Or maybe I stop breathing. Or maybe I'm dead. I reach to stick my hand in my pocket—to search for my penny so I'll know I'm alive and this is real—but it isn't there. Did I lose it? It was in the grass, but I went back for it.

I'm wearing a thin green gown. There is no pocket. A bitter chill washes over my body. I almost ran into the parking lot with no clothes on.

"Perhaps you'd like to go into the bathroom to change now," the doctor says, as if reading my mind.

I have a weak recollection that he mentioned this before he began talking to Mitch and Rand. I have a stronger recollection of vehemently refusing.

"Unless you have any questions?"

Ha. Do I have any questions? Everything is a question. I shake my head and stand unsteadily to my feet. Mitch hurries to my side to help me. I look at his face.

When did he get so old? He was just a baby. I had him in my arms, wrapped in a blanket, as Rand drove the truck over to Wilsall to visit his parents. He's a baby in my mind. Forever a baby.

My baby.

As I reach the bathroom and Mitch holds open the door, the doctor is telling Rand about some kind of test Rand must schedule, and I know I will have to come back here. I know as sure as the mountain stands that this isn't over.

The door clicks shut.

FOURTEEN

Is that a mullet?"

Bea jabbed Jeremy with her elbow and giggled. "Don't stare."

"Sorry." He lowered his voice. "I've just never seen one in person before."

They reached the top row of the gym bleachers, and he helped her take off her coat. She tucked her purse down by her feet and sat behind a kid wearing a gray T-shirt that read, *Education is important, but welding is importanter.*

She'd forgotten how uncomfortable the bleachers were. "The whole varsity football team is doing the mullet thing, I guess. For good luck."

"Where'd you hear about that?"

"At the store."

"Right. Of course." Jeremy sat down with a groan. "Oof. It hurts."

"What does?"

"Everything."

He'd spent the last two days working twelve-hour shifts on the belt down at the Duncan place. Last night in bed he'd told her he'd never had sore forearms before. She'd found it kind of funny and endearing but also troubling. His life had been so different from hers up until now. None of that had mattered when they first met. He'd made her smile again. Made her believe there was life after death. But now she was beginning to wonder how much they actually had in common.

A whistle blew, and the volleyball game started. She spotted Amber and her son near the bottom of the bleachers, and Amber's words ran through her mind: *"We should meet up for lunch sometime."* Maybe it would be nice to catch up with Amber. They'd never been close before or anything, but they were about to have a lot in common. She touched her belly.

Jeremy scanned the crowded gym. "Does anyone around here do anything for fun that doesn't involve school sports?"

"Yep." She ticked them off on her fingers. "Hunting. Skiing. Fishing."

"Okay."

"Rodeo. Snowmobiles. Hiking."

"Okay, okay." He held up his hands. "I get it. But all those things happen outdoors."

"So?"

"So the outdoors is pretty cold around here."

Bea patted his knee. "I hate to tell you this, but it's only the beginning of October. It's going to get much, much worse."

It had been a mild fall so far, but snow had dusted the tips of the Bridgers like powdered sugar ever since the freezing rain, and she could feel winter in the air.

"How much worse?" Jeremy asked.

"Ever felt forty below before?"

His eyes widened. "Forty below what? *Zero?*"

She nodded. "That's how much worse."

The storms she'd seen in Atlanta had been different from anything she'd experienced before, but it rarely froze there. Let alone fell below zero. And the weather in Santa Clara had been predictable. Mild.

Montana was a different story. In the spring and fall, the

temperature could swing fifty degrees in a twenty-four-hour period. In the winter, you could go days without seeing the thermometer top zero. And the summer? There was no telling what the weather might do during a Montana summer. A girl had to be ready for anything.

Atlanta and what happened there crossed her mind, and she shuddered. A girl had to be ready for anything living on her own in the big city, too.

That was a different kind of survival.

A tall blond girl hit a spike for the Moose Creek Spuds, and the crowd cheered. Bea spotted her dad entering the gym and waved as he headed in their direction. They had driven separately this time, at Jeremy's insistence, and he had embarrassed her to no end by activating the car locks on the Toyota in the parking lot. The loud beep-beep had caught everyone's attention as they turned to see who thought it was necessary to lock their vehicle outside the school.

Why had she given up her Blazer for a Matrix again?

They'd always locked their car in Santa Clara, of course. But in Moose Creek? Dad never even locked the house unless he went out of town, let alone the truck. Same with Grandpa and Grandma. "Got nothin' worth takin'," Grandpa Rand told her once.

Jeremy watched the volleyball fly back and forth over the net. "We'll be gone before the weather gets that bad."

Bea squirmed. Would they? How could he be sure? If they ended up stuck here longer than expected, would Jeremy be okay with that? No Starbucks or movie theater. No RadioShack. He was being a good sport now, but winter was coming. If Jeremy was questioning gym time already, how was he going to handle basketball doubleheaders?

As Dad climbed the bleachers toward them, she forced the conversation in a different direction. "Did you see that chocolate cake in the lobby? With Heath pieces on top?"

Jeremy nodded. "Are they having a bake sale or something?"

"A silent auction, I think." She scanned the game program and read aloud from the blurb on the front. "'For Breast Cancer Awareness Month this October, we are raising money for Susan Mullins, who is currently at the Cancer Center in Seattle receiving treatment for breast cancer. Please check out the items in the lobby and make your bids. The silent auction will close at eight.'"

Her voice stumbled over the words *breast cancer*, and she steeled herself against a slew of bad memories. She couldn't cry, not with Dad about to join them. She'd learned the hard way he didn't know what to do with her tears. And from what she'd heard at the store, Susan's cancer had been caught in the early stages. Before it could metastasize.

She was lucky.

Dad reached them and took a seat next to Bea. His expression looked as sick as she felt, and he awkwardly patted her knee. "Such a shame about Susan. I hadn't heard. I put a bid on that big chocolate cake."

Bea nodded. He would do all he could to support the Mullins family. The whole town would. "That's the one I want."

A strong chocolate craving had kicked in the moment she'd laid eyes on it. She'd never wanted a cake so badly in her life.

Jeremy leaned close so only she could hear. "There are five tables full of baked goods out there. How'd he know you'd want that one?"

She tried not to look at him like he was crazy. What else did she love more than chocolate cake? Did Jeremy know her at all?

"It's my favorite. Just . . ."

"What?"

Just like my mom. The words stuck in her throat. Mom had come to every single one of her volleyball games. Had sat up here in this same spot and cheered for Bea no matter how long she sat on the bench or how many mistakes she made. And if she were here right now, she'd stop at nothing to win that chocolate cake.

"Never mind."

The first set of the match ended with Moose Creek on top 25 to 18. As the teams switched sides, fans chatted and stretched and moved around the gym.

Jeremy pointed with his chin. "Look. There's another one."

A second mullet strolled by, and Bea laughed. "If it helps us make the play-offs, I'm all for it."

Jeremy stood. "I'll be right back."

"Okay. Check to make sure Dad still has the highest bid on that cake." She winced as he walked stiffly down the bleacher steps. Hopefully, harvest would go quickly this year. Everyone was scrambling to get their crops in before the first hard freeze, which could come any day.

She turned to her dad. "How did the appointment go?"

He'd mentioned this morning that he and Grandpa Rand were taking Grandma to an appointment in Ponderosa today. At the time, her mind had been preoccupied by her own appointment, which she had finally scheduled and was a mere four days away. Plus, she'd felt like she was going to die and had been trying to act normal so he wouldn't notice the cold sweat on her forehead or how nauseated she was. But now she wanted to know more.

Dad hesitated. "It was fine."

"Is Grandma okay? What was it for?"

Bea couldn't even picture Grandma June in a doctor's office. She'd given birth at home. Set her own broken finger with a switch from a lodgepole pine. Stitched Grandpa Rand's leg with sewing thread and whiskey after a run-in with some barbwire. She was the kind of woman who believed in taking care of herself. And yes, her finger was still crooked, as was Grandpa Rand's scar, but you didn't live your whole life in rural Montana if you weren't willing to remove an errant fishhook from your own neck.

She glanced over at Dad when he didn't answer right away. "*Is* she okay?"

"They need to do more tests."

Bea's stomach clenched. She'd heard those words before. "Is it . . . ?"

"No." Dad put a hand on her shoulder. "Sorry, B.B., I shouldn't have said that. It's not cancer."

Breathe. Okay, breathe. It wasn't cancer.

"What, then?"

Dad looked down at the court. "We were at the neurologist. Grandpa's worried about, uh . . ."

Bea frowned. About what? Why was it so hard for him to say it? All kinds of emotions began bubbling up inside her, roiling in her guts in an unfamiliar way. "A brain tumor?"

"No, no. Like I said, it's not cancer. She's just having trouble with her mind."

What was that supposed to mean? Bea thought back to her and Jeremy's visit to Grandpa and Grandma's house a few days ago. Grandma had been a little forgetful, but otherwise she'd seemed totally normal.

"There's nothing wrong with her mind."

"She was really agitated when we got to the office. She wasn't herself."

"Well, of course she was agitated. She hates doctors."

"It was more than that."

"You and Grandpa agreed about this?" Bea stuck her hands under her legs. How could they both believe Grandma was losing it? It didn't make sense.

"We just want to be sure." Dad kept his eyes on the game, refusing to look at her. "Don't you worry about it."

A spark of anger warmed her chest. How many times had he said that when Mom was sick? "*Don't you worry about it.*" How many times had he blown off her questions?

Jeremy reappeared and began his ascent to the top row. A

hollow spot opened up in Bea's stomach as she thought about her mother. Maybe that's what this whole thing with Grandma was really about. Dad always blamed himself for not insisting Mom go to the doctor sooner. Get help sooner. Now he was overcompensating with Grandma and seeing things that weren't there.

"Side out, Spuds," Dad shouted. "Come on."

He was well-versed in volleyball lingo. He'd been at all her games, too.

She took a deep breath and let it out. Grandma June was fine. Dad was worried for nothing. Once they ran more tests, everyone would see. He'd be able to put his mind at ease.

Jeremy reached their seats and gave her a bewildered look. "There's a peach cobbler out there going for almost two hundred dollars."

Bea set thoughts of Grandma aside and nodded. Moose Creek wasn't a wealthy community, but they took care of their own. And the most important thing in her life at this moment started with *choco* and ended with *late*. "Did you check on my cake? Is Dad winning?"

Jeremy sat down with a smug smile. "Not anymore."

❖   ❖   ❖

The second set was tied 22 to 22, yet Mitch tore his eyes from the volleyball action to stare at his son-in-law. "What do you mean 'not anymore'? Who's winning?"

Jeremy held his eyes without flinching. "It's *my* job to give Bea what she wants."

"Is that right." Mitch frowned. "And what do you know about jobs?"

"Guys." Bea looked back and forth between them. "Don't."

Okay, maybe that had been a low blow. But Jeremy was the one who'd decided to turn this into a competition.

Mitch stood. "I'll be right back."

"Dad." Bea gave him a meaningful look. "Stop."

No way. Not a chance. "It's for a good cause, B.B. Those cancer centers aren't cheap."

He scrambled down the steps before she could reply. Some nerve that kid had, trying to outbid him. As if he could without anything moderately resembling gainful employment.

The set ended with Moose Creek losing 26 to 24 as Mitch entered the lobby. A handful of people milled about the tables, perusing the goods. There were sugar cookies decorated like volleyballs, piles of Rice Krispies Treats, and plates of fudge. Brownies of every shape, size, and flavor imaginable—ooh, were those mint?

Mitch shook his head. Only the cake mattered now.

He laughed to himself as he read Jeremy's bid. Only five dollars more than his? He'd put an end to this right now.

He wrote a number one hundred dollars more. "That ought to do it."

A short woman appeared at his elbow. "What'd you say?"

"Oh." He felt his face flush as he glanced over at Marge. "Hi. Nothing."

She had a knack for showing up at the worst possible times. He uncharitably thought of her as Meddlesome Marge in his more juvenile moments.

"That looks delicious." She leaned over the bid sheet, her ample bosom brushing the paper. Not that he was looking at her—uh—chest, but it practically knocked the sheet off the table.

She caught a glimpse of his bid, and her eyes widened. "I had no idea you loved cake so much."

"It's for Bea."

"Ah." Marge smiled. "It must be nice having her back."

Guilt stabbed him. Marge's kids were spread out all over the country and hardly ever came to visit. He'd heard they blamed her for her and Bill's unamiable split. But after living next to them for years, Mitch knew if there was any blame to be shoveled out, it should land squarely as a pile of dung on Bill's boots.

"The house is so quiet when there's no one around," Marge continued. "Even when I take three shifts a week at the hospital, I still feel like I've got nothing to do. You know how it is."

Oh, he knew all right. The oppressive silence of an empty house. The imagined wisp of his wife's voice as he walked into a room. The dull and persistent ache of loss. Of missing her smell and her laugh and her everything.

His throat tightened. He'd never considered how similar Marge's loss was to his. He tried to swallow his grief and coughed.

Marge nodded knowingly and patted his hand. "You got any big plans for your birthday?"

His what? Oh yeah, he would be turning forty-three soon. How had she remembered that? He certainly had no idea when her birthday was.

He squeezed the back of his neck. "Hadn't thought about it."

She gave the bid sheet a meaningful glance. "Well, it looks like someone should bake you a chocolate cake."

He couldn't hold back a laugh. "Maybe so. And if they do, you'll have to come over and help us eat it."

At his words, her expression revealed a subtle shift, and Mitch mentally kicked himself. Why on earth had he said that?

She tucked her hair behind her ear. "That would be lovely."

It was suddenly difficult to breathe. He must walk away. Right this second before something bad happened. *Move your feet, Mitch. Move!*

He took a step toward the door. "I better get back in there."

With a grumble, he turned and fled before she could answer. Boy, oh boy, was he an idiot. He hurried into the gym and took a deep breath, consoling himself with the fact that he would most likely not have a birthday party anyway, so he would most likely not have to worry about Marge attending. Most likely. But the whole incident had his insides jumbled up worse than the tools in his toolbox.

Maybe he should talk to someone about this. Someone who could give him some perspective on why he would do such a dumb thing. Frank was no longer an option, so who? It definitely couldn't be big-mouth Ralph. Mitch needed someone with more discretion. And wisdom. Ralph was not overly blessed with either of those qualities.

The third set was ending as he collected his wits and returned to his seat. Moose Creek had lost another close one, 25 to 20. They'd better get their act together, or the match would soon be over.

He caught Jeremy scowling at him and indulged in an internal self-congratulation. Jeremy would never be able to outbid him. Mitch might've pulled an ill-advised move with Marge, but he was winning that cake, darn it all to heck.

He checked his watch. Aha. It was almost eight o'clock.

Bea furrowed her brow at him as if she knew what he was thinking. "Was that necessary, Dad?"

He held up his hands. "Did you know there's a layer of toffee frosting inside the cake?"

Her mouth opened. "You're kidding me."

"It says so on the sheet."

The fourth set began. Jeremy stood. "That's it."

Bea grabbed his arm. "Just leave it."

He pulled his arm away. "You were just telling me how bad you were craving the stupid cake. I want to do this for you."

Bea frowned. "If it's so stupid, then just forget about it."

Mitch looked between them, feeling a bite of remorse over the trouble he'd stirred up.

"That's not what I meant," Jeremy said.

Moose Creek served up an ace, and the crowd shouted encouragement.

"Let's do this, Spuds."

"Comeback time."

Bea frowned and nodded at the court. "Then let's just watch the game. What's the big deal?"

"The big deal"—Jeremy raised his voice to be heard over the crowd as they cheered for a miraculous dig—"is that *I* should be the one"—a collective gasp swept through the gym as Moose Creek's star player fell to the ground, hitting her head with a thunk—"taking care of my own pregnant wife."

Jeremy's words spewed forth just as the entire crowd grew quiet, anxious over the fallen player's fate. As his words reverberated throughout the abruptly silent gym, the entire home side of the bleachers turned to look up at them.

Mitch froze. Oh, great. Everyone was staring. Jeremy was making a fool of himself.

Hold on a minute.

Did he say *pregnant*?

FIFTEEN

B ea lay flat on her back in bed, her eyes clenched shut.
"I said I was sorry." Jeremy covered her hand with
his. "It was an accident."

"Now the whole school knows. Which might as well be the
whole town." It was melodramatic, but she couldn't help it.
Couldn't pull herself together. It was like she'd lost all control
of her heart and her mind and her mouth. Like a tiny alien
had invaded her body and taken over, which wasn't far from
the truth.

"I know. I'm sorry." Jeremy kept his voice low. "I don't know
how many times I can say it. But they were all going to find
out eventually."

"That's not the point." She hated how whiny she sounded.
Hated the tears springing from the corners of her eyes yet again.
"I wanted to tell him myself. When I was ready."

That was the worst part about the whole thing. She hadn't
had time to prepare herself for the look on Dad's face. The one
that held more than just hurt over learning such important news
at the same time as everyone else. It had also been chock-full
of disappointment.

"I'm sorry." The regret in Jeremy's voice matched the regret in her heart. But no amount of *sorrys* could take back what had happened. She sighed a heavy sigh and opened her eyes.

"Okay." She rolled toward him. "But it's not just that. The whole thing with the cake was—"

"I'm sorry."

"Stop saying that." Her sharp words struck Jeremy, and she could see the hurt take root on his face, yet her possessed mouth forged ahead. "Stop being sorry. And stop touching me."

She pulled her hand out from under his and rolled away. A strained silence filled the room like the lingering fumes from Earl's four-wheeler. Choking her. What a rotten night. She just wanted it to be over.

After Jeremy's unfortunate announcement, the injured player had been helped off the court, the Spuds had lost the game, and everyone had gone home. She hadn't spoken a word to Jeremy in the car and hadn't allowed either Jeremy or her dad to so much as look at her cake. They didn't deserve to partake in its goodness. She'd blown off Dad's attempts to talk and left Jeremy to explain the whole pregnancy thing while she'd hidden in the kitchen and eaten almost a third of it by herself.

She closed her eyes. Was all this really about what happened at the volleyball game? Her mother's face sprang to mind, and new tears began to form. Would she ever stop crying? Would she ever stop missing Mom? Would she ever be qualified to be a mom? How would she know what was best for her baby?

When would she start acting like she had a handle on her life?

With all her strength and will, she held back a sob, afraid if Jeremy noticed he would put a gentle hand on her shoulder, and she would give in to his comfort and weep in his arms until the morning light. And she didn't want to do that. She wanted to be angry.

Her thoughts moved to Grandma June and what Dad had done. Grandma must've been angry, too. Furious that he dragged her to the neurologist for no reason. What could've gotten into him?

Bea stiffened. Maybe he was keeping something from her just like when Mom was sick. If he would've been honest about how little time Mom had left . . .

She focused on making her breathing even so it would look like she was asleep. Her dad wasn't going to get away with that again. She would get to the bottom of this.

SIXTEEN

itch paced the kitchen Saturday morning, stewing. Why hadn't Bea told him she was having a baby? And what were they thinking, starting a family when they didn't even have their own home?

He didn't feel old enough to be a grandpa. He wasn't ready for this. And speaking of grandpas, he needed to call his dad. They hadn't been able to talk about yesterday's neurologist appointment with his mother in the truck.

Steve watched him stride back and forth with a wary eye. Mitch reluctantly acknowledged the cat with a slight nod. Who would've thought that out of everyone in his life, Steve would be the one causing him the least amount of trouble?

After eating chocolate cake for breakfast, Bea and Jeremy had gone for a walk, the temperature an unseasonably warm fifty degrees. He wanted to talk to her, wanted to find out more about the baby, but she was avoiding him. Something had changed between them since she got married.

He tapped his knuckles on the counter and frowned. Okay, maybe it had changed before that.

Caroline always used to tell him to give her time. When he would want to jump in and pester Bea with questions—solve her problems—Caroline would pat his shoulder with a knowing smile. *"Give her time."*

After Caroline died, he'd given Bea nothing but time. Time and space. More than any teenage girl who'd just lost her mother could ever need.

What a mistake.

He slapped his phone against the palm of his hand. Bea and Jeremy would be back soon, so he should head to his room before calling his dad. If Bea were to come home and hear him discussing her grandmother's condition, it would only upset her more, and she was plenty upset with him already. He opened his bedroom door and stepped in, glowering as water seeped through his sock. He eyed the carpet. Another puddle. What on earth was going on in here?

He'd inspected the attic and found no leaks. He'd felt around the carpet in other areas, even under his bed, and found no dampness there. Only by the door. He'd blame Steve, but he never left his door open. Ever. And cats couldn't turn doorknobs, last time he checked.

It was an infuriating mystery but one that would have to wait.

Since cell service at his parents' place was unreliable, he dialed their landline. His father answered right away, his voice low.

"Mitch?"

"Yeah, Dad. It's me. How's Mom this morning?"

"I don't know. Kind of in a daze."

"Is she mad?"

"Worried, I think."

Mitch mulled that over. Was she worried about what might happen to her? What further testing might reveal?

"I'm worried, too," Rand continued. "The doctor's talk about that hereditary stuff's got me thinking about you. And Bea."

Mitch furrowed his brow. "And Bea's baby."

"What?"

103

"Bea's expecting. I found out last night."

"Well, don't that beat all. What if—"

"Let's not get ahead of ourselves." Mitch rubbed the space between his eyes. "The doctor said the kind of Alzheimer's that can be passed down through genes is very rare. The familial early-onset kind."

"And isn't it early?" The fear in his father's voice was unmistakable and unsettling.

Mitch sat on the bed. Dr. Wilson had explained that anyone developing Alzheimer's-like symptoms while under the age of sixty-five could potentially be considered for the early-onset variety, but he had encouraged them not to jump to any conclusions. In fact, he'd only spoken about it after Mitch pressed him about his mother's relatively young age. The doctor had assured them there were many other steps to take before considering such a drastic diagnosis.

Yet that didn't make Mitch feel any better. He remembered well the feeling of helplessness—the temptation to assume the worst—when Caroline had first fallen ill. The doctors had said the same things: *"It's too soon to tell." "Don't jump to any conclusions."*

He'd tried. For his wife's sake, he'd worked hard to think positively and convince himself he was overreacting. He'd nearly succeeded, too . . . just in time to find out she had three months to live.

"We'll figure it out, Dad." The words tasted bitter in his mouth, the same words he'd spoken with confidence three years ago. "We'll talk again soon."

He hung up and marched to the front door where he'd left his boots. He shoved his feet into them, wet sock and all, and grabbed his truck keys. As much as it galled him, there was only one person he could talk to about this stuff. Sure, he'd burned that bridge, but he was a decent swimmer. He'd find a way across. He was already wet anyway.

✦ ✦ ✦

The Take Your Best Shot guns-and-ammo store was not located on the same strip as the rest of Moose Creek's small businesses. It sat a little apart from town on the road leading to the gun range, and it had the rugged look of a log cabin. Inside, it was well-stocked with all the latest in hunting gear and technology, as well as the old, classic favorites.

Mitch was not surprised by all the vehicles parked in front of the store. Open season was only two weeks away. He pulled into one of the last empty spots but left the truck running as he stared at the store. Maybe this wasn't such a good idea. Frank might not be too thrilled to see him after the way they'd left things the last time they spoke. But Mitch didn't know where else to turn, and he was starting to feel a mite desperate.

A loud quack sounded as he opened the door to the store. That had been his idea, to replace the chime on the door with a duck call, way back when Frank first started working here to supplement his meager pastor's salary two decades ago. Mitch had suggested it as a joke, but Frank had taken him seriously. That's kind of what Frank did. He took things seriously.

Several men greeted him with a nod as he worked his way around the store looking for Frank. He found him deep in conversation with Jeff Bates, one hand on Jeff's shoulder as he nodded empathetically along with whatever Jeff was saying. It was a familiar pose. Frank's pastor pose.

Mitch hung back until Frank's conversation with Jeff ended, then he approached, hands shoved deep into the pockets of the Carhartt vest Caroline had given him the Christmas before she died.

"Hey," Mitch said.

If Frank felt any shock at seeing him, it didn't show. "Hey, Mitch. Good to see you."

"I was hoping we could talk."

"You know, I was just about to take an early lunch break." Frank gestured over his shoulder. "I'll meet you out back in five minutes."

Mitch nodded once and turned away. As the door quacked on his way out, he chuckled to himself thinking about inviting Jeremy to go hunting with him. That would be something. If the kid could barely handle a two-hour football game at twenty-eight degrees, he'd never survive a ten-degree morning up Brackett Creek.

He took his time circling around the store to the metal picnic table where he and Frank had had many a talk. His friend was already waiting. Or should he say former friend? Frank was definitely his former pastor, but the friendship thing was still up in the air as far as Mitch was concerned.

"I'm glad you're here." Frank paused while Mitch sat down, then gave him that probing, concerned look Mitch had seen a hundred times. "How are you?"

This was not the kind of man who would accept *fine* as an answer to that question.

Mitch shrugged. "Got a lot going on."

Frank nodded. "I heard about Bea. I can't believe you're going to be a grandpa before me."

"You can't win every time, Frank."

"It's not a competition."

A small spark of anger lit in Mitch's chest. "Don't use your pastor voice on me."

Frank sighed. "I'm sorry. It's a habit."

The sincerity of his apology threw sand on Mitch's internal fire. He let his shoulders relax and leaned his arms on the table. "Here's something else you won't believe. Bea's baby is the least of my worries right now."

Frank's eyebrows rose. "Tell me more."

"You know Marge? She keeps showing up. At my house. Bringing food and checking in and asking about my birthday."

"That's nice of her."

Was that a twinkle in his eye? Mitch frowned. "And then there's my mom. She's not doing well."

Frank visibly deflated at that news. "That explains why I haven't seen your parents at church in a while."

"Yeah." Now that the floodgates had been opened, Mitch couldn't get the words out fast enough. "I thought Dad was crazy at first when he told me something was wrong. She seemed the same as always, except for the pies. But when we took her to the neurologist for a consultation, she turned into a completely different person. Confused. Belligerent. They're going to do more tests. I think Dad's really struggling."

Frank tilted his head to one side. "The pies?"

"If they end up diagnosing her with Alzheimer's or something, what will happen? I don't know if Dad can take care of her all by himself, and you know there's no one else up there. Not for a mile on every side. And I work every day. But can you even fathom trying to get Juniper Jensen to move out of her house? I wouldn't be surprised if she chained herself to the stove. Bea thinks I'm being mean, making Mom go to the doctor. She won't believe there's anything wrong with her. And they have a cat. Bea and Jeremy. There is an actual live cat living in my house."

When Mitch finally ran out of words, he lowered his gaze to the table and began picking at a spot where the black paint was chipping away. It had been easier than he'd expected, unloading on Frank like he used to do. It was almost like no time had passed since the last time they sat at this table.

Almost.

Frank took his time responding, as was his way. Even in high school, years before Frank got the call to ministry, as he put it, he'd been the kind of guy to carefully deliberate before rushing into anything. Even words. Maybe especially words.

"You have a lot on your plate," he finally said. "Including pie, apparently."

One corner of Mitch's mouth lifted. "I guess you could say that."

"I'm good, by the way." Frank tapped his fingers on the table. "Hannah's doing great at the university. Seth graduates this year." His fingers stilled. "Dorothy and I are very proud."

Mitch looked up from the table, his face burning. He hadn't even thought to ask after Frank or his family. Had only been thinking about his own problems. And he was the one who had promised Frank all those years ago when Moose Creek Community Church had chosen to hire a well-intentioned but naïve twenty-five-year-old as their new pastor that he wouldn't let the ministry—the church—change things between them. He swore Frank would always be his best friend first. Pastor second.

Mitch scowled. "You don't have to rub it in."

"Rub what in?"

"My callous self-centeredness."

"I just thought you'd want to know."

"I shouldn't have come here."

Mitch met Frank's eyes with a challenge but didn't rise from the table.

"Then why did you?" Frank asked.

Mitch threw up his hands. "I don't know. Who else am I going to talk to about all this stuff? Ralph?"

A mischievous smile formed on Frank's face. "How about Marge?"

Mitch huffed. "That's not funny."

Frank fought a grin.

Mitch felt a tickle in his gut. "It's not."

Despite his insistence, or maybe because of it, a chuckle escaped.

Frank's shoulders began to shake. "I bet she's a good listener."

Mitch fought for breath as laughter overtook him. "She's

got to be a better listener than a cook. Her sloppy-joe casserole is terrible."

"I know." Frank pulled up his glasses to wipe the tears from his eyes. "She brings it to every single potluck."

"But the enchilada casserole's not half-bad."

"*Muy bueno.*"

It took several minutes for their amusement to abate. A sharp pang of grief touched Mitch's heart when he realized he hadn't laughed that hard since Caroline had passed. She'd always been able to make him smile. Even lying on her deathbed, she would look out the window and say, "That fat magpie must've eaten a gopher," knowing the only thing Mitch hated more than magpies was gophers.

Darn it all to heck, he missed her.

Once a certain amount of soberness had returned to the table, Frank wiped at his chin with the back of his hand and gave Mitch an unflinching look. "Why haven't you returned my calls?"

Mitch should've seen that coming, of course.

His shoulders drooped. "I didn't want to hear about how I needed to come back to church. How I was setting a bad example for Bea."

"That wasn't—"

"Don't." Mitch held up a hand. "Don't try to tell me that wasn't what you wanted to talk to me about."

Frank sat back with a sigh. "That wasn't the *only* thing."

"I needed a friend, Frank. Not a pastor."

"You needed both."

Mitch made a fist with one hand and softly hammered the table one, two, three times. Just like he'd promised Frank he wouldn't let the ministry change things between them, wouldn't ever see Frank as only a pastor and not a man he'd known his whole life, Frank had promised he'd never preach at

Mitch. Never make Mitch's relationship with him dependent on Mitch's relationship with God. But after Caroline died . . .

"You weren't the only one hurting, you know," Frank said. "We loved her, too."

Mitch recoiled. "Don't compare your pain to mine."

"Like I said." Frank looked him square in the eye. "This isn't a competition."

Mitch held his gaze. "You have no idea what it's been like."

"Because you've never told me."

Weariness gripped Mitch suddenly and fiercely. He'd had his reasons for avoiding his best friend. Avoiding the church. Avoiding . . . well, everything. Life. But now all he could think about was Bea having a baby and his mother losing her mind and Marge giving him that look and saying she'd love to come to his birthday party.

"Would you talk to Marge for me?" Mitch asked. "Tell her to back off a little?"

Frank's laugh was long and hard, coming up from the soles of his feet and bursting into the unseasonably warm air. "Not a chance, buddy. Not a chance."

SEVENTEEN

As Jeremy pulled up to the stoplight, Bea looked out the window and cringed. The jacked-up Ford F-350 in the neighboring lane towered over them like Saddle Peak. She was still getting used to being dwarfed on all sides when on the road. In California, the Toyota Matrix fit right in. In Montana, it stood out like a Shetland pony in a herd of wild mustangs. Plus, Dad wouldn't stop nagging about how its tires weren't fit to face a Montana winter. "Why'd you trade the Blazer for *that* thing?" he'd asked three times now.

In Santa Clara, it was all about gas mileage. But she'd missed the sound of a Power Stroke diesel engine.

"I still can't believe it." Jeremy reached over and squeezed her knee. "We heard our baby's heartbeat."

"Yep." Bea kept her eyes on the window. "Pretty amazing."

Jeremy didn't comment on the lack of enthusiasm in her voice. Maybe he didn't notice. It wasn't that she had been unmoved by the sound of her baby's heartbeat coming through the monitor when the doctor pressed the wand against her stomach. She had been. Very much. It was just that the resolute thumping sound had made it all so real. So tangible. So inevitable.

What was her problem? Seriously, she acted as if she were dreading the arrival of her own child. Why wasn't she crying happy tears every time she thought of holding the little bundle in her arms? Why couldn't she beam and count down the days like a normal person?

"Which do you want to get first," Jeremy asked, "the vitamins or the Orange Julius?"

The doctor had insisted she start taking prenatal vitamins with folic acid immediately.

"Orange Julius."

He smiled over at her. "You got it."

As Jeremy drove toward the mall, Bea surreptitiously studied his face. They'd had a good first year of marriage in Santa Clara. Despite a few bumps, they'd made a lot of great memories, but he'd never looked like this. Happy and content.

Okay, and sexy. Ha. Maybe that was her hormones talking. Or the ruddiness in his face and slightly more defined muscles in his shoulders that she could only attribute to the hours he'd put in on the Duncan farm.

"I think Montana agrees with you," she said.

His dimples appeared. "I'll admit, it's way different here than I expected."

"How do you mean?"

He shrugged. "I feel like I can breathe here. The world just stretches out in front of you for miles and miles."

She nodded. That was one of the things she'd missed the most. The wide-open spaces. The way you could look out over the valley and see pretty much the same thing people had been seeing for hundreds of years. There were farmhouses and little towns here and there, but for the most part the land was as untamed and rugged as the day the mountains were born.

She hadn't been many places, but Montana had to be one of the best.

A Luke Bryan song came on, and Jeremy turned down the radio. "We've heard this one at least five times today."

"That's the country station for you."

"And you know what else?" Jeremy waved a hand in the air. "These songs are always about Southern girls. Why aren't there any songs about Northern girls?"

Bea raised one eyebrow. "You been listening to the station a lot?"

Jeremy made a face. "Like I've had a choice."

"The older songs are best."

"I'll take your word for it."

"You've got to give it a chance." She turned the radio back up. "It'll grow on you, just like the big sky."

He gave her a wink. "If you say so."

They picked up their drinks and the vitamins and started back for Moose Creek. There had been snow on the peaks of the Bridgers for a couple of weeks, yet the back way home through the canyon was clear and dry. They'd opted for the scenic route rather than the interstate since it was such a nice day. Though the weatherman on the radio was calling for snow by late this weekend, today she hadn't even worn a coat.

"What's up with your dad's belt?" Jeremy asked as they passed Moreland Road.

She wrinkled her nose. Her dad's belt? "What made you think about that?"

"I saw that shop across from the mall, Jack's Custom Leather." He shrugged. "Your grandpa's got one and your dad's got one—I just wondered if it was a Montana thing."

"More like a Jensen thing, I guess. The Jensen men receive a belt embossed with their name on it from their fathers when they get married. It's a tradition."

He nodded and drove on as the canyon widened and the valley came into view. When they left Bridger Canyon Drive for Highway 288, Bea checked the time. "Don't forget to drop me off at The Baked Potato."

Jeremy glanced over. "I'm glad you decided to meet up with her."

Amber had stopped at the Food Farm the other day and greeted Bea like they'd grown up together. Which of course they had. As she hung a green basket on her arm, she'd repeated her sentiment from the football game: "We should meet up for lunch sometime."

As Amber wandered the store picking up a few items, Bea had tried to focus on unboxing the iceberg lettuce but found herself unable to shake off Amber's words. Had she meant them? Did she really want to be Bea's friend, or was she just being polite? Amber had probably been nervous to reveal her pregnancy, as well. How had *her* family reacted?

In the end, Bea's desperation to talk to someone—anyone—about the surrealness of being pregnant and the weird things happening to her body won out. She'd rung up Amber's groceries, handed her the receipt, and forced out the words, "I'm off on Tuesday."

Amber had said, "I'm free, too," with a smile, and they had made their plans.

Bea was surprised at how easy the whole thing was.

After stopping to allow a small flock of ducks to cross the street, Jeremy pulled up in front of The Baked Potato. "Have fun. Text me when you want me to pick you up."

"No." Bea opened the door. "I'll walk home."

"Are you sure? You don't want to overdo it."

She rolled her eyes but not so he could see. "I think I can handle it."

As he drove away, she fiddled with her phone, then slid it in her pocket. Why was she so nervous? Inside the diner, Amber and Hunter were already seated at a table. Amber was smiling—she always looked happy—but there were dark circles under her eyes and leftover smears of some kind of food on the shoulder of her shirt.

As Bea walked over to join them, Amber gave her a once-over and laughed. "I remember the days I could leave the house with nothing except what fit in my pockets. Now I have to pack half the house before going anywhere."

Bea sat down across from her. "Half the house?"

Amber indicated her son sitting in a high chair and the paraphernalia strewn around him. "Diapers, wipes, diaper cream, change of clothes, snacks, water bottle. Binky. Blanket. Light jacket and warm jacket in case the weather changes. His favorite toy. I even pack an extra shirt for myself, just in case."

Bea's eyes grew wide. "In case what?"

Amber laughed again. "In case he throws up on me or has a blowout or something. You never know."

Bea wondered what her unencumbered life looked like to Amber. "I guess I never thought about that."

Amber nodded knowingly. "You'll learn all about it soon enough."

Bea grimaced. "You heard?"

"Oh, honey." Amber folded her arms on the table and made a sympathetic sound. "Everybody heard."

Bea sighed. Nothing got past the moosevine.

"When are you due?" Amber asked.

The doctor had given them a date just that morning at the appointment. "May fourteenth."

"A spring baby." Amber clasped her hands together. "That's the perfect time to have a baby around here. You won't have to sweat through the summer, you can eat whatever you want at Christmas, and by the time you're recovered enough to want to go outside, it will be nice enough to do it."

"When was Hunter born?"

"February. It wouldn't have been so bad if the entire winter hadn't waited until the week after he was born to show up. We had to take him to his first well-child exam in two feet of snow."

We, she said. Bea had noticed Amber's left hand was conspicuously bare. She didn't want to jump to any conclusions, but she wondered about Hunter's father. It was hard enough for Bea to imagine becoming a mother and dealing with all that at her and Amber's age. But if she had to do it without Jeremy by her side . . .

The lone waitress on duty appeared at the table with two glasses of water, wearing jeans and a Moose Creek Spuds sweatshirt. Unlike the servers at the restaurants in Ponderosa, this woman wore no makeup and gave no hint that she was trying to impress anyone or angle for extra tips. She just kept her gray-streaked hair out of her face with a ponytail and tapped the table with her little notepad.

"Are you ready to order?"

Neither Bea nor Amber had looked at the menu, but they were ready. The offerings hadn't changed for as long as Bea could remember. The prices had gone up, but the Tuesday special was still the same.

"I'll have the deluxe cheeseburger, please. With extra fries." Amber tousled Hunter's hair. "Hunter loves fries."

The waitress jotted it down and turned expectant eyes on Bea.

"I'll have the same. With a chocolate milk shake."

After barely choking down half a bowl of cereal for breakfast, she was starving.

"Ooh, good idea." Amber's excitement made Bea happy. "We'll have a chocolate shake, too."

The waitress nodded and walked away. Bea could appreciate the lack of airs at The Baked Potato. It was the kind of place that never tried to be something it wasn't. Two-thirds of the floor was laid with gray-speckled linoleum, and the other third had gray-checkered linoleum because when the owners had gone to replace the part of the floor that had been damaged by a small fire, they discovered the speckles had been discontinued and decided the checkers were close enough.

Amber patted her stomach. "I won't be able to keep eating like this forever, but I'm still nursing so I think I can get away with it."

Bea worked to hide her surprise. She was still nursing? As in, breastfeeding Hunter? But he was sitting up. He ate fries. He had teeth!

She had so much to learn.

Amber was happy to fill in Bea's stunned silence. "My goal is to make it to his first birthday. The lady at the WIC office says a full year of breast milk is super beneficial. Of course, she would say that since they don't want to add formula to my WIC checks. That stuff costs a fortune."

Hunter somehow got hold of a napkin and tried to put it in his mouth. Amber pulled it away and wiped his tongue.

"What's WIC?" Bea asked.

Amber shrugged like she thought everyone should know. "It stands for Women, Infants, and Children. It's the program where the state gives vouchers for certain types of food to pregnant women, nursing women, and kids up to the age of five. If they qualify."

"Oh." Bea's mind swirled with a hundred questions she was too embarrassed to ask.

Amber continued, her persistent smile faltering for a moment. "I qualified easy since I only work part-time and I'm a single mom." Her face brightened. "I bet you'd qualify, too, since Jeremy's unemployed."

So she *was* a single mom. What had happened?

Bea mulled Amber's words over in her head. Jeremy was self-employed, not unemployed. At least that's what he was working toward. But aside from his limited stint at the Duncans', the amount of income he was bringing in was zero, regardless of what you called it, and her twenty-five hours a week at the Food Farm left a lot to be desired.

She wondered what Jeremy would say about WIC. How he would feel about it. Shouldn't she know something like that about her husband? Her family leaned so far toward the too-proud-to-accept-handouts side of the fence they were liable to fall off and break their necks. But what about Jeremy?

Bea poked at an ice cube in her glass with a straw. "What happened to Hunter's dad?"

Amber sighed and gave her son a smile. Ran a finger along his cheek and booped his nose. "Well . . ."

The waitress appeared with two milk shakes, each topped with a generous dollop of whipped cream. "Here you go, girls."

Hunter slapped the table and made happy gibberish sounds. Bea understood how he felt. The sight of all that cold chocolate goodness made her whole body take notice. She'd heard about cravings before but had never dreamed they could be so powerful.

Amber dipped the tip of her spoon into the whipped cream and let Hunter lick it. "The WIC lady would probably have a fit if she saw me doing this."

Bea had to suck hard to get the milk shake through her straw because it was so thick. "Well, there aren't any hidden cameras in here. I think you're safe."

Amber chuckled. "I suppose so." She gave Hunter another tiny lick and turned on her mushy mommy voice. "We just won't tell that mean old WIC lady, will we, buddy?" He babbled in response. Amber looked over at Bea. "She's not really mean. Just intrusive and opinionated."

It was Bea's turn to chuckle. The waitress appeared again with a plate in each hand.

She plunked them down on the table. "Two deluxe cheeseburgers with extra fries. You girls need anything else?"

"No, thank you," Bea said. "We're good."

There weren't many other people in the diner, so the waitress shuffled behind the counter to restock napkin dispensers.

Amber squeezed a giant pile of ketchup onto her plate. "Anyway, I was telling you about Hunter's dad."

Bea cringed. Hot coffee, she shouldn't have brought that up. "You don't have to."

Amber exchanged the ketchup bottle for the mustard and squeezed another pile. "No, it's fine. I'm surprised you haven't heard about it around town."

Bea pulled the onions from her burger. "Everyone's too busy talking about me, I guess."

"You're right." Amber's eyes twinkled, and she leaned forward like they were sharing a secret. "Thanks for taking the heat off me."

"Glad I could help."

"Do you remember Axel Scott? He was a couple years ahead of us in school."

Bea nodded. "The guy with the mohawk?"

Amber blushed. "Yes. We got together after I graduated. I moved in with him and everything. He was working at the auto shop, but he always talked about getting out of here. Leaving Moose Creek in the dust and all that. I guess when he found out about Hunter, he couldn't stand the thought of being tied to this place. He was gone before I could say, 'Get me some pickles and ice cream.'"

"Just like that?"

Amber raised one shoulder. "Just like that. I live with my mom now. She still works at the school, so I watch Hunter during the day and pick up a few hours at the gas station in the evenings."

"You didn't want to go to college?"

"I did." Amber swirled a spoon through her milk shake and looked Bea over with an assessing gaze before answering. "But a baby changes everything."

EIGHTEEN

I lean my head out of the bathroom into the hall and call to Rand, "You forgot to flush last night."

The distinct sound of his walk—*thump, slide, thump, slide*—draws closer until he appears around the corner. "What're you talking about?"

"Someone peed in this toilet." I point over my shoulder. "And it certainly wasn't me."

He watches me for three blinks, a variety of thoughts moving across his face like the flickering light of a campfire. I don't recognize any of them, his thoughts. I can't read them.

"You were up three or four times during the night." He takes another step, and his eyes look sad. "You must've gone in there at some point."

"I did no such thing. I slept like a baby."

I had, hadn't I? I don't remember getting up. Certainly not three or four times. And I feel very distant and disconnected from the rank, dark yellow liquid in the toilet bowl. I would know if it was mine.

I put my hands on my hips. "Just admit it. You forgot to flush."

Rand shakes his head wearily but gives me what I want. "Sorry, dear."

I huff and shove a hand into my pocket, rubbing my penny

between two fingers. "All right. Now what should I take out for dinner? You want to grill brats?"

Fridays are good days for grilling. We still have a couple of venison cheese brats left over from last season. Those normally don't last more than a few months before we eat them all—those Milligan Meat folks sure know how to make them—but I saw a package in the bottom of the chest freezer this morning. It was just sitting there. I don't know how I missed it all year.

"That would be fine," Rand says.

He returns to the kitchen to read the ag reports, and I dig the brats out of the freezer in the laundry room and set them in the sink to thaw. From the window above the sink, I can see the mountain. I don't know how many times I've studied it as I washed dishes or rinsed vegetables or scrubbed stained clothing in the sink, but it is as familiar and mysterious to me as Rand's face. I know each crease, each bend. Every rise and fall. I've noted every season as it has come and gone. Yet I wonder if I know them at all, these faces.

I feel Rand's eyes on my back as I leave the kitchen and take the front door out to the porch. The mountain draws me as if it has a message I alone can decipher. My heart thumps as the notion there's something important I need to remember shortens my breath. What was it? What had we been talking about? Someone had peed in the toilet. Who had been here? Who would do such a thing?

No, it had been Rand. You'd think he'd appreciate a good flush, growing up in a cabin with no indoor plumbing like he did. But he is getting old. We both are. Could it be that we've been married for forty-four years? Have we lived that much life together already?

It has been a good life. But there are clouds forming across the valley and moving closer. Dark clouds.

I lean against a post and wrap my arms around my body. There is a distinct chill in the air. What did I need to remember?

Though it's hours yet until the light appears on the mountain, I look up and think of Miner McGee. Always searching, searching, searching.

Searching.

My hand flies to my throat as I gasp. My son. That's what it is. He could be in danger. That doctor said some diseases of the mind are hereditary. And it must be true there's a disease in my mind. I sense it lying in wait, crouching like a mountain lion stalking its prey.

Tears sting my eyes, and I cover my mouth. Is this my punishment, God? My memories of his face and his tiny little hands are all I have left of him. Are you going to take them away to punish me for what I did? No, Lord. Please.

No.

I have to fight against the disease. I can't lose my son again. The mountain towers before me, and I picture Miner McGee, searching, searching. That crazy old man. If I've said it once, I've said it a million times—he'll never give up.

And neither will I.

NINETEEN

Mitch checked his watch and knocked on the door. How exactly had Frank talked him into this again? Heck of a way to spend his lunch break.

Frank's voice called from the other side of the door. "Come on in."

Mitch entered the office and found his old friend sitting behind a desk strewn with papers, books, and coffee mugs. A plastic bag sat on one edge, filled with maybe half a dozen frozen venison chubs.

Frank caught him looking at it. "Someone was cleaning out their freezer to make room for hunting season."

"So they gave you last year's meat?"

"It's from two years ago, actually." Frank leaned back in his swivel chair and shrugged. "You know how it is."

Yes, Mitch knew. He and Frank had shared many laughs the last twenty years over the gifts Frank often received from the well-meaning folks in his congregation. Some of them were welcome surprises, like when Miss Ellen would leave sugar cookies on the seat of Frank's car with a handwritten note. Others were less appealing, such as the couch the Westerly family "donated" to the youth room that only had three feet and was covered in mouse turds.

Mitch muttered something about firstfruits, and Frank gave him a half smile. "Dorothy and I are thankful for it. Have you seen the price of beef lately?"

Mitch grunted.

"But you're not here to talk about beef, are you?"

Mitch stiffened, and Frank must have noticed.

"No preacher stuff." Frank held up his hands. "I promise. I asked you to come in as a friend. That's it."

Mitch grumbled to himself and plopped down in an old armchair. The arms were threadbare, worn down by the anxious hands of old men seeking advice about how to divide up their land without destroying their families, married couples seeking counseling, and teenage boys wondering if the Bible *really* said fornication was a sin. And a man rubbing at the fabric and asking what he was supposed to do now that he was alone. How he was supposed to help Bea. What he was supposed to say to all the people telling him God had a plan when all he wanted to do was punch them in the face.

"Your parents missed the service again," Frank said. "When did you say your mom's CT scan is?"

"Next Friday morning."

"Will they be doing any other tests?"

"I think they'll do the full blood and urine tests at the same time. Dr. Wilson suggested doing it when we were there last week, but Mom was so upset we decided not to. I was afraid she might hurt someone if they tried to stick a needle in her arm."

"Your mother is a strong, independent woman."

"You can say that again."

"And how's Bea?"

"She had her first doctor's appointment this week. Said she's due May fourteenth."

Frank smiled like he meant it. "That's wonderful."

Mitch wasn't so sure, but he kept his doubts to himself. "Still can't believe I'm going to be a grandpa."

Without Caroline. It would've been the highlight of her life to hold a grandchild in her arms. To babysit. To knit little pink or blue booties and take a million pictures.

Mitch remembered his last conversation with Frank and looked Frank in the eye. "And how are *you* this week?"

Frank hesitated.

"And don't give me any sort of 'everything's fine and I'm just blessed to be serving the Lord' crap."

"It's not crap if it's true."

Mitch raised his eyebrows. "Okay, is it true?"

Frank heaved a sigh the size of a seventy-person congregation and slumped in his chair. "No."

Prickles of guilt jabbed Mitch's chest. He and Frank used to talk about everything. Mitch had prided himself on being the one person besides Dorothy whom Frank could unload on about challenges he faced as Moose Creek Community Church's only pastor.

Mitch shifted in his seat. "What's going on?"

Not that he had the right to ask.

Frank pinched his forehead. "Bob's stirring up trouble again. You know how he gets on different kicks and goes all in without thinking it over."

Mitch nodded. Bob was a repeat offender in that department. "What'd he do this time?"

"He started a new Bible study in his house about speaking in tongues."

Mitch waited.

"And told everyone I approved it."

"Ah."

"Now there's a small faction calling for my head."

It wasn't hard for Mitch to believe. It was a nondenominational church, technically, but the majority of folks had Baptist leanings. Bob had always tended more toward Pentecostal.

"It's my own fault," Frank continued. "He did ask if he could lead a Bible study from his home, and I said I didn't see why not."

"Well, now you see."

"Yes. It was a rookie mistake. I've just been busy and distracted by other things and didn't think it through."

Mitch knew Frank had walked this road before. As the pastor of a small church, he got less than half the praise he deserved for everything that went right and more than twice the blame for everything that didn't.

"So you're going to ask him to stop the study?"

"I tried that. He says he has the right to do whatever he wants in his own home. And he's right, of course. He just needs to stop telling people I approve of it. But he's insisting that I *did* approve. He's also convinced that if I just read this book he found, I'll come over to his side on the speaking-in-tongues thing."

"Danny still on the church board?"

Frank nodded. Danny was Bob's wife's brother. He was also related by marriage to Bob's daughter-in-law.

"Whose side is he on?"

"Bob's. He wants me to read the book. Everyone's quite interested in it now."

"The people who want your head—they're strongly against speaking in tongues, I take it?"

Frank laughed. "You wouldn't know it by how unrestrained they are with their own, but yes."

Mitch chuckled, too, even as the pangs of guilt in his chest grew in intensity. He'd had a hard couple of years and hadn't wanted to talk to anyone about God's will or His "perfect plan"—he still didn't—but who had been there to check in on Frank? Give him a listening ear?

"I'm sorry." Mitch dropped his hands to his knees, then put them back on the arms of the chair. "And not just for the tongues situation."

Frank gave him a similar look to the one he'd given when Mitch first told him about Caroline's diagnosis. "I've been worried about you. It's a frightening thing to me, to watch someone I care about turn their back on God."

Mitch squirmed. How could he explain it? He hadn't turned his back on God. You couldn't live in Montana and not consider Him. Couldn't look out over the valley or drive to Glacier without seeing His handiwork. Couldn't come within fifteen feet of a regal six-point bull elk without being awestruck by the wonder of creation. His relationship with the Almighty was different from what it used to be, but they were still on speaking terms.

"It wasn't that."

"What then? Why did you stop coming to church?"

Mitch scrounged for the right words. "I hated the sympathy. People would be talking and laughing in a group, and then when I would walk up, they'd get all serious. And they would say such stupid things. One woman would come up to me out of nowhere and say I needed to wait at least one full year before getting remarried. Like it's in the Bible or something. Five minutes later, another woman would come along and tell me about her hairdresser or niece or whatever who was single and looking to settle down."

"Wow."

"Yeah, and I couldn't tell you how many times I had to listen to 'We can't question God's plan' or 'Just be thankful she isn't suffering anymore.' Once Bea left for school, I didn't have the strength to keep putting myself through all that. Couldn't sit there in the pew and listen to everyone singing without Caroline's voice."

"I understand." Frank folded his arms on the desk. "But we need other people in our lives, Mitch. To help us carry our burdens. That's how God made us."

Mitch checked the time and frowned. He could carry his own

127

burdens. And what about Frank? Everyone was always dumping their burdens on him, not helping to carry them.

"Look, I gotta go." He stood. "Time to get back to work."

"Please don't blow off what I said."

"I'll think about it." Mitch moved toward the door. "Good to see you, Frank."

He dashed out of the office and into the parking lot. Ralph would grumble at him if he was late. As he strode to his truck, he replayed Frank's words in his head. *We need other people in our lives.* Frank meant well, but he had no idea what it was like to feel like an outsider in your own hometown. To feel like you no longer belonged to the same world as everyone else. He longed for his wife like the fields longed for rain.

At least Bea was back. Maybe he wasn't much of a friend or church member anymore, but he could help her get her life back on track, couldn't he? She didn't want to work at the Food Farm forever. She didn't know what was best for herself or her baby. And it couldn't be true that she didn't care about finishing college. He didn't know why she'd quit, but he was going to find out. It was the least he could do.

He started his truck with a renewed sense of purpose. He and Caroline had had such dreams for their daughter. Dreams that reached beyond the confines of Moose Creek. Beyond the Food Farm and Friday night football games. Caroline had even named her after two female pioneers in engineering with those dreams in mind.

He wouldn't let her down.

◆ ◆ ◆

Bea took her time driving out to Grandma and Grandpa's house. She hadn't driven a stick shift in two years, but she was thankful Dad had let her borrow his truck. She'd decided to go check on her grandparents after Jeremy called to let her know he was still in Ponderosa. "I've met so many interesting people," he'd said. "I've got so many ideas."

She'd thought of the bill for her last doctor's visit and barely swallowed back her father's words: *You can't eat ideas.* Instead, she'd said, "That's great." He'd promised to bring her back a surprise, and she'd quickly made plans to get out of the house. Didn't feel like dealing with her dad by herself. Plus, the football team was away tonight, so what else was there to do?

The days were getting noticeably shorter as winter neared. Because of the dense clouds, it was almost dark as she pulled up. She parked and studied the small but sturdy old house and the lights shining from inside. Maybe she should apologize to Grandma for what her dad had done.

She tapped on the door and let herself in. "Anyone home? It's Bea."

"Beatrice?" Grandma June was at the kitchen sink. She fixed Bea with a perplexed look. "What are you doing here? Why aren't you at school?"

Grandpa came out of his office. "She's not in school anymore, June. She got married, remember?"

Grandma swiped a soapy hand across her forehead, leaving a streak of suds. She gave him a withering look. "Of course I remember."

Bea looked back and forth between her grandparents. She'd never heard Grandma snap at Grandpa like that before.

"We just finished supper," Grandma said. "Did you eat?"

"I'm good." She was holding out for whatever Jeremy was going to bring home. "Thanks, though."

"I'll get you something to drink, then." Grandma pulled open the fridge. "I've got . . . um . . ."

Bea joined her at the fridge and peered over her shoulder while she dug around inside. Bea frowned. Where was all the food? She'd better put together a few groceries to bring out the next time she had a shift at the Food Farm.

And what was going on with Grandma's hair? She usually kept it short and tidy, but today it was sticking out all over the place.

Grandma clucked her tongue and pulled a can of Budweiser from the depths of the fridge. "This will have to do. It's the last one. I haven't been to the store in a while."

"Oh, um . . ." Bea held up her hands. "No, thanks. Grandpa can have it."

"Don't be silly. He doesn't need it. Here." Grandma shoved it into Bea's hands. "It's nice and cold."

Bea stared at the can, then gave Grandpa a sidelong look. Why was Grandma acting so strange? He looked back, his cloudy blue, almost gray eyes boring into her as if trying to tell her something, but he didn't speak.

Grandpa had a beer now and then, while Bea had never acquired a taste for it. Even if she had, she'd never consider it while she was pregnant. Had Grandma forgotten about the baby? She'd always complained about Grandpa's occasional Budweiser, but now here she stood, watching Bea expectantly.

Bea set the can down on the counter. "I'm not thirsty right now."

"Okay, if you're sure." Grandma wiped her hands on a towel and motioned toward the living room. "Why don't we sit down for a visit."

Bea smiled. This was more like it. She'd spent many evenings sitting with her grandparents, visiting. Her favorite times were when they would sit out on the porch and watch the sunset reflect off the mountain while they talked, except it was too cold and cloudy for that tonight.

Grandpa Rand carefully lowered his wiry frame into his leather recliner, one of the few nice things he'd ever purchased for himself. Behind him, a wooden shelf sagged under the weight of his Louis L'Amour books, and a sweat-stained cowboy hat hung from a hook on the wall.

Bea nestled into her favorite spot on the couch and brought her knees up to her chest. In a few short months, she wouldn't be able to do that anymore. Her stomach would be in the way. Or should she say the baby would be in the way?

Grandma settled onto the couch close to Bea. "What are you up to these days? Did you work this morning?"

Bea nodded. "I stayed longer than usual. It was busy today, so they needed extra help."

"I'm not surprised they needed you, dear." Grandma patted her knee. "You'll be running that whole place in no time, I'm sure."

Bea gave a smile she hoped was at least semiconvincing. Before she'd left the Food Farm this afternoon, MacGregor had said something along the same lines. Not that she'd be running the whole place, but he'd grumbled about how hard it was to find good help these days and hinted he'd be happy to see her move into a full-time position with an eye toward becoming assistant manager.

It would be a good job. Decent pay. Modest benefits. Better than the zero benefits she and Jeremy had now. She'd told MacGregor she'd think about it, but it wasn't possible. They weren't going to be sticking around that long. Were they?

"We'll see," she said.

"It'd be so handy, wouldn't it?" Grandma fidgeted with something in her pocket. "So close to home, and you wouldn't have to worry about running out of milk."

Grandpa cleared his throat. "Bea might not want to spend the rest of her life at the Food Farm, June."

Grandma turned on him. "And what would you know about what Bea might want?"

Her voice was sharp and cold. Bea's eyes widened.

Grandpa looked stricken, but he didn't back down. "You're right, I don't know. But maybe you should ask her instead of assuming."

"I'm not assuming anything." Grandma's voice had the bite of a rattler. "I'm only giving my opinion. Since when is giving my opinion a crime, Rand?"

A lump formed in Bea's chest, a hard pressure like a fist stuck in between her lungs. What was going on? She'd never heard Grandma speak like that to anyone before and especially not to Grandpa. He held the place of highest honor in her life. In fact, the only time she'd ever disciplined Bea—*ever*—was the time Bea was about six or seven and Grandpa asked her to take her muddy feet off the coffee table, and Bea had talked back to him. Grandma had swooped in with a spanking Bea still remembered to this day.

Nobody but nobody disrespected Juniper Jensen's husband.

Grandpa didn't respond. Bea looked between him and Grandma, searching for normalcy. Any minute now, Grandma would smile at Grandpa and tell him she was sorry for being snippy. Tell him she must be tired or something and didn't know what had come over her.

Bea set her feet down on the floor and sat up a little straighter. "It's something to think about, Grandma. But I'm not sure what I'm going to want to do when the baby comes."

After the baby news had come out in the middle of the volleyball game, Dad had told Grandma and Grandpa about it over the phone, afraid they'd hear it through the moosevine. But she hadn't yet talked with them in person.

Grandma's eyes narrowed, and she jerked her hand out of her pocket. "Baby?"

"Yeah, remember?" Bea put a hand on her belly. Dad *had* told them about it, right? "I'm having a baby."

She looked to Grandpa for confirmation, and he gave an encouraging nod. Grandma blinked once. Twice. A cloud passed over her face, and she stood. For a frightening moment, Bea barely recognized her twisted face. She and Grandpa Rand watched in stunned silence as Grandma spun around and stomped away. A moment later, the door to her room thudded to a close.

Tears stung the backs of Bea's eyes, and she fought them. Was Grandma angry with her? About getting pregnant? What exactly had Dad said to her? If her mom was still around, Bea knew she would be beside herself with excitement. She would've already knitted booties for the baby's feet and sewn curtains for the nursery. Grandma wasn't as showy with her emotions as all that, but Bea never expected this.

She looked to Grandpa for answers, for hope, but his shoulders drooped. "I'm sorry, Bea. Your grandmother's not feeling well today. Maybe you should go."

Bea's lip quivered as she rose to her feet, the hurt sinking deep. "Okay."

She slowly put her jacket on, staring down the hall toward Grandma's bedroom. *"Your grandmother's not feeling well."* The words tumbled around like a stone in her stomach. Dad had been right. Grandma wasn't herself. In fact, this wasn't Grandma at all.

Grandpa didn't resist when she gave him a hug. He wrapped his arms around her tighter than he'd ever done before. When she pulled away and looked in his eyes, it was like watching a gathering storm reflect off the waters of Canyon Ferry Lake. Like a boat fighting the wind to get across. Like a man reaching out from the water, silently begging for someone to throw him a rope.

She opened the door and looked back, her voice cracking under the strain of holding in her emotions. "Tell Grandma I love her."

TWENTY

When Bea turned on to Second Street and saw the Matrix in front of her dad's house—parked the correct way—she burst into tears. Jeremy was home. All she wanted in the world was to have his arms around her.

It was all she could do to park the truck in the carport without ramming into a post, the way her body shook. She killed the engine and covered her face with her hands. She couldn't get the shadowy look on Grandma's face out of her mind. Or the sharp words she had spoken.

She opened the door and flinched at the cold night air. The chill and the dark, lonely alley took her back to the walk home on campus that night in Atlanta. A sense of panic bubbled up in her chest. She knew it was illogical to be afraid. No one was lying in wait for her on Second Street in Moose Creek. But the feeling was hard to shake.

Wiping her face, she took a couple of deep breaths. She was safe. She was fine. What would Dad do if he thought she couldn't handle her life? What would Jeremy do? She was tougher than this. She marched around to the front door, eager to get inside, then slowed her steps when she saw her dad standing in Marge's yard. Talking. To Marge.

His back was to her, so she slipped past without calling to him, questions swirling in her mind. How much more did she have to endure tonight? Why was Marge giving Dad goo-goo eyes? Dad and Marge didn't have a . . . a *thing* going, did they?

Bea shook her head. No, of course not. That would never happen.

She found Jeremy in the kitchen, his full attention on his phone. Country music played from the speaker, making her smile despite the emotion still constricting her throat.

"Is that Alan Jackson?"

He jumped and spun around. "Oh, you're back. Yeah, I remembered he was one of your dad's favorites. Figured I better check him out."

"You're getting sucked in." Her tease was halfhearted, but that didn't stop him from protesting.

"No, I'm not."

Her eyes burned, and she swiped at them. "Mm-hmm."

"Wait." He stood and reached for her. "Are you okay?"

Are you okay? Are you okay? How many times had he asked her that in the past month?

She buried her face in his shoulder. Everything was upside-down. What was happening to her grandma? What was going on with Dad? Would she ever be able to stand alone on a dark street without all the fear rushing back?

She wanted her mom.

When she'd regained some control over herself, she pulled away. Jeremy rubbed his hands up and down her arms, concern on his face.

"What's going on? Were you at your grandma's this whole time?"

She sniffled. "Yes. I just wanted to visit, but Grandma . . ."

Jeremy's voice was gentle. "What?"

Dad appeared in the kitchen entryway. "You're home."

She turned to look at him, and his eyebrows raised. "What's the matter, B.B.?"

Jeremy put a protective arm around her shoulder. "Could you give us a minute, please?"

"Did something happen with your grandmother?"

"Mr. Jensen, could you please—"

"It's okay, Jeremy." Bea ducked out from under his arm and took a seat at the kitchen table. "He should hear this, too."

Resigned irritation puckered Jeremy's face as he joined her at the table.

She put one elbow down, leaned her chin into her hand, and looked sideways at her dad. "Did you say something to Grandpa and Grandma about me? Something about the baby?"

His eyes narrowed. "I told them the news is all. Why?"

"Nothing else?"

"What else is there to say?" Dad crossed his arms. "What's this all about?"

Bea sank further into her chair. "I think you were right. About Grandma. Something's going on with her."

Dad remained standing but moved closer, his voice tight with concern. "What happened?"

Bea chewed the inside of her cheek. "Nothing, really. She was just being so weird. She forgot that I wasn't in school, and then she yelled at Grandpa. And when I reminded her about the baby, she . . . I don't know. Shut down or something and left the room. Like she couldn't handle talking about it. I thought she would be happy."

Dad scrubbed a hand over his face. "What did your grandfather say?"

"That she wasn't feeling well, and I should go."

Jeremy covered her hand with his. "That must've been upsetting."

Dad gave him a sour look. "Thanks, Dr. Phil."

Another sob worked its way up from Bea's chest and flew

from her mouth. Why did he have to be so childish? Jeremy scooted his chair closer.

"And there was . . . hardly any food . . . in the fridge." Bea's words came in spurts through her sobs. "All Grandma had to offer me . . . was a beer."

Jeremy's eyes widened. "You didn't take it, did you?"

Dad glared at him. "Of course she didn't."

"I'm worried about her." Bea slumped back in her chair. "I'm sorry I didn't believe you, Dad. What did the doctor say at the consultation?"

She had dismissed his concerns as soon as she heard what the appointment had been for and hadn't given Dad a chance to explain any of the details. Now she turned to him with eyebrows raised. Ready to hear. Jeremy moved his thumb across the top of her hand.

"He wants to do more tests," Dad said. "We're taking her for a CT scan and blood work next Friday."

She hated to ask but needed to know. "Does he think she has dementia?" Her shoulders tightened as she waited for the answer.

Dad waved an arm. "He said not to jump to any conclusions."

"But he must've given you some information about—"

"Yes." Her dad joined them at the table, his face grim. "When I brought up your grandmother's age, how she's not even sixty-five, he admitted he was going to want to look into the possibility of the early-onset familial kind of Alzheimer's disease. But he said it's way too soon to know anything for sure."

Bea tensed. Familial? She put a hand on her stomach. "Does that mean it could be hereditary?" She heard the panic in her voice and told herself to calm down.

Dad held up his hands. "The chances are so slim there's no sense in worrying about it. Dr. Wilson said it could end up not even being a neurological problem at all. Her confusion and mood swings might be the result of some sort of chemical imbalance or nutritional deficiency or something."

Bea took a deep breath. A nutritional deficiency. That sounded like a solvable problem. Maybe that's all it was. Poor Grandma. No one had been making sure she was taking care of herself.

"Okay." She wiped her nose with a napkin. "I guess now we wait for the tests."

Jeremy gave her a reassuring nod and pushed back from the table. "Since there's nothing we can do about it until then, I think it's time for your surprise."

Bea sat up a little straighter. "What is it?"

He made a goofy face and opened the fridge. As he reached inside and grabbed ahold of something Bea couldn't see, the freezer-side door spit a handful of ice cubes onto the floor.

Bea gave her dad a look. "I thought you fixed that."

"I tried."

"May I present to you, my lady"—Jeremy spun around, one hand holding a white box and the other hidden behind him—"chicken and veggie lo mein from Hong Kong City."

"Ooh!" She grinned. "My favorite."

"And . . ." He pulled another box from behind his back. "A pumpkin, chocolate-chip cheesecake from Bighorn Bakery."

It was the most beautiful cake she'd ever seen. If she'd been the swooning type, she would've fainted from joy right then and there. *Oh, Jeremy.*

She snuck a kiss on his cheek as he set the food in front of her on the table. "You're the best."

◆ ◆ ◆

"You're the best." Pfft. The words rankled in Mitch's brain as he lay awake in bed. He'd raised her, given her everything she ever needed or wanted, paid for her to move to Georgia and go

to school, and all Jeremy had to do was give her a cheesecake, and *he* was the best? The kid couldn't even drive a truck with manual transmission.

He growled. He wasn't being fair. Daughters were meant to grow up and move on. Meant to give their hearts to another man and live a life apart from their fathers. He knew that. But he didn't have to like it. The tune to Heartland's "I Loved Her First" played in his mind. Boy, oh boy, did he feel that. And how had Jeremy paid for that food, anyway? With the money *Bea* had earned at the Food Farm?

Okay, okay, maybe Jeremy had made a little cash down at the Duncan place. But harvest was over.

Mitch turned to one side, then the other. This twin bed was not nearly as comfortable as his old queen. And he still hadn't gotten used to sleeping alone. Two years might as well have been two days. He could still hear Caroline breathing in the night if he was quiet enough.

The words to "Sweet Caroline" replaced Heartland's song, and Mitch grumbled to himself. He was never going to get any sleep at this rate. Then Marge's face popped into his mind.

"Aargh." He startled as if a boogeyman had jumped at him from the darkness.

What was she doing in his head? It was probably because of their exchange earlier. She'd caught him outside and reeled him into a conversation like he was nothing more than a northern pike on a line. And she'd brought up his birthday again. He'd said, "I'll think about it," but all he could think about now was how she kept touching his arm. It should've bothered him, but it didn't. He'd gone without a woman's touch for two years, and it had felt . . . nice. Two years on his own with many more ahead of him. Would he be alone for the rest of his life?

No one else had mentioned a thing about his birthday so far—not his parents, not Bea—while Marge had asked about it twice. He wasn't sure what that meant, but he wasn't interested in lying awake all night trying to figure it out. Or in making a big deal out of his birthday.

His mind turned to his mother. He was sorry Bea had gotten upset, yet he was glad she was no longer in denial about his mom's condition. Maybe she could help keep his mom calm for the next appointment. Maybe June would listen to her.

He rolled onto his back and groaned. How long had he been lying here? Was it midnight yet? At least he didn't have to work tomorrow. A muffled sound came from above him, and he tensed up. What was . . . ? Was that . . . ?

Oh no. No, no, no, no, no. He flipped onto his stomach and buried his face in his pillow, pulling it up on the sides to cover his ears. The lovebirds probably figured he was sound asleep by now, and boy, oh boy, did he wish he was.

TWENTY-ONE

Bea lounged on the couch, her hands resting on her stomach. "I'm so full. I shouldn't have eaten that third piece of cheesecake."

For breakfast. She'd had three slices of cheesecake for breakfast.

Jeremy gave her an affectionate look. "The baby must've been hungry."

Bea laid her head back. Her stomach bulged from her huge meal, but otherwise there was no evidence of a baby growing inside her. She thought her waist had thickened a little but not enough that anyone would notice. Jeremy certainly hadn't noticed last night.

She did a quick mental calculation. About ten weeks along. A quarter of the way through her pregnancy. When would she need to start wearing maternity clothes? Was her morning sickness over for good, or had she just been lucky the past couple of days?

"Hey, guess what?" Jeremy broke into her thoughts. "You know that antler shop downtown?"

She nodded.

"It doesn't even have a website." His expression was incredulous.

She shrugged. "I don't think Mr. Van Dyken has any idea how to make a website."

"He should at least be on Facebook or something. He could post pictures of each piece as he finishes it."

Bea scrunched her lips to one side. It made sense, but she wasn't sure if Mr. Van Dyken even knew what Facebook *was*.

Jeremy checked his phone for the time. "Well, I better get going."

"What are you going out there for again?"

Harvest at the Duncan place had wrapped up a few days before, but Jeremy was still making trips down there to help out. When she'd said Montana agreed with him, she'd been right.

He shrugged. "I'm trying to get a feel for the people around here. What their needs are. How they run their businesses." He winked. "It's research."

She made a face. "Okay, but what am I supposed to do here with my dad all day?"

They were currently hanging out in the living room because Dad was messing with the fridge again. He'd announced at breakfast that he was determined to get to the bottom of the problem if it was the last thing he did today. Bea planned to avoid the kitchen at all costs.

"You'll be fine." Jeremy stood and kissed the top of her head. "I won't stay long."

He pulled on a jacket, gloves, and boots. The temperature was only supposed to reach about twenty degrees.

"Don't forget my dad's making dinner tonight."

"As if I could forget." Jeremy gave her a half smile. Dad had been going on all week about how he was going to make them dinner. "I'll be back in plenty of time."

He gave her another wink and headed out the door. She pulled her feet up on the couch and groaned, the pumpkin cheesecake sitting like a boulder in her gut. It had been worth it, though. And if her mom had been here, she would've been right there eating it with her.

With the sound of Dad making demands of the refrigerator in the background, Bea tapped a button on her phone to wake it up. On her home screen was an app that allowed her to monitor her baby's development and keep track of how many weeks left until her due date. Jeremy had downloaded it for her.

Her finger hovered over the icon. What did her baby look like at ten weeks old? Was it the size of a thumbprint? A fist? She looked down at her stomach. How could something so small feel so big?

She shook her head and brought up the internet instead. As she typed *early-onset familial Alzheimer's disease* into a search engine, the haunted look on Grandma June's face burned in her brain. She hoped and prayed Grandma's tests would reveal nothing more than the nutritional deficiency Dad had mentioned. But she couldn't resist the pull of *what if?*

She knew how easy it was to get sucked into an online vortex of speculative information and terrifying diagnosis stories. She'd been through all that before when her mom got sick. Websites about miracle cures. Lists of which foods to eat and not eat. Testimonials about how one family prayed away their loved one's cancer, while another watched them die a slow and painful death. It wasn't exactly helpful. But she needed more information. If there was even the slightest possibility of Grandma's condition being hereditary, she wanted to know.

Search results were at her fingertips in an instant. She chose the most scholarly-looking article from the list and began to read. Phrases such as *unusually early age*, *incurable*, and *progressive loss of brain function* jumped out at her like a deer leaping from the underbrush along Highway 288.

The article said symptoms often appeared in a person's thirties, forties, and fifties, and in rare cases, in a person's twenties. Children with a parent diagnosed had a fifty-fifty chance of inheriting the disease. She looked up from the phone. Her dad was turning forty-three in a couple of weeks. What if she, Grandma June, and her dad all had the disease and didn't know it yet? Was that possible?

Her heart beat a little faster, and she forced herself to lean into the couch and breathe. She was being paranoid. It wasn't possible. But wasn't paranoia one of the symptoms? Hot coffee. And wasn't another symptom loss of ability to do things a person used to do? She thought of her dad in the kitchen. He'd always been able to fix anything. That kind of work came naturally to him. So why couldn't he figure out the ice maker?

She rested her head on the back of the couch. This wasn't helping. When her mom was diagnosed with breast cancer, Bea had convinced herself she had it, too. Now she was doing the same thing. She closed her eyes. *Stop getting carried away. Stop getting carried away*.

Her phone buzzed, and she peeked at the screen. A text message from Amber.

What are you doing today?

A welcome distraction. Bea readily typed a response.

Nothing, why?

I need a favor.

Bea sat up a little.

What's up?

Axel's back in town, and I need to talk to him.
But my mom's not around to watch Hunter.

Bea's brow furrowed. Why would Amber want to talk to Axel after what he'd done? She rubbed her temples. It did make a little bit of sense. He was Hunter's dad, after all. But why couldn't she take Hunter with her?

> Doesn't he want to see his son?

Amber's reply was a long minute in coming.

> No. Can I bring him to your house? It's just for a couple hours.

Bea was sitting up with her feet on the floor now. She scanned the room. What would she do with an eight-month-old for two hours? What kind of toys did he like? She was pretty sure he couldn't walk yet, but was he crawling? She eyed the sharp edges of the coffee table. This house was definitely not babyproof.

Amber texted again.

> Please?

Bea shook her head. She couldn't refuse to help her only friend. Surely she could keep one baby safe for two hours.

> Sure. Bring him over.

Amber's response was immediate, as if she knew Bea couldn't say no.

> Be there in ten.

Bea was on her feet already. Ten minutes? She had ten minutes to prepare for a child? Her heart did a funny little swoop as she pictured Hunter's face. She needed to do a sweep of the house to look for hazards. She needed to check the kitchen for food suitable for a baby. She needed to pee.

Why did Jeremy have to pick this morning of all mornings to be gone?

She slid her phone into her back pocket and put her hands on her hips. She could do this. She was a grown-up. She had her own baby coming in just under seven months. She didn't need Jeremy's help.

"Dad?"

◆ ◆ ◆

Hunter pulled himself to a standing position using the coffee table for support and banged his hand on the wood surface. *Bang, bang, bang.* He stopped, widened his eyes in surprise, then did it again. *Bang, bang, bang.*

"Should I stop him?" Bea sat on the floor behind him, ready to intervene. "What is he doing?"

Her dad grinned at Hunter. "You like to make noise, don't you, buddy?"

Hunter bounced and banged, drool running from his mouth.

"He's fine." Dad set a blue plastic cup on the table in front of Hunter. "It's just what kids do."

After a number of attempts, Hunter grabbed the cup by the rim and brought it to his mouth.

"No, don't." Bea reached over to pull the cup away. "That's dirty."

Hunter's face scrunched up, and he took a deep breath.

"It's fine, B.B." Dad quickly gave the cup back. "It's not going to hurt him."

It was too late. With his mouth open wide, Hunter began screaming. And screaming. Bea's neck and shoulders tightened. Amber had assured her Hunter hardly ever fussed.

Dad scooped him up. "It's okay, buddy. Look, you can have the cup."

He tried to put the cup back in Hunter's hand, but the kid would have none of it.

"What do we do?" Bea asked.

Other girls her age had made money babysitting during their high-school years, but Bea had always worked at the Food Farm.

And since she didn't have any cousins or nieces or nephews or anything, her childcare experience was painfully limited.

Dad set Hunter down in a standing position on the other side of the coffee table and placed a *Montana Outdoors* magazine in front of him. "Distraction."

Hunter stopped crying and hit the magazine with his palm. *Slap, slap.* Then got ahold of the cover and started jerking it back and forth.

Bea inched closer. "He's going to rip it."

Dad waved her away. "He's fine."

Part of her was thankful she didn't have to face Hunter alone. Another part wished she hadn't gotten Dad involved. "You keep saying that."

Dad chuckled as Hunter succeeded in tearing off the magazine cover and crumpling it up. "That's because it's true."

But how did he know? Bea remained on edge as Hunter proceeded to rip more pages out, one by one. How was she supposed to know if he was fine? If he was doing what he was supposed to be doing? If she should let him do what he wanted or intervene?

Dad must've read the anxiety on her face. "Don't worry. You've got lots of time to figure it out."

"Seven months is not 'lots of time.'" Bea gasped as Hunter lost his balance and fell backward onto his bottom. He made a little burbling sound but otherwise seemed unfazed, his diaper having cushioned his fall. "What if I don't know what to do?"

Oops. She hadn't meant to ask that question out loud. Dad already thought having a baby was a bad idea. The last thing she needed was for him to find out how unprepared and ill-equipped she really was.

Dad helped Hunter to his feet, then pressed his own back into the couch and put his hands on his knees. "One time, when you were a little younger than this guy, we went to Ponderosa for something—I don't remember what—and totally forgot to bring your diaper bag. We had no spare diapers, no wipes, no nothing, and you had this huge blowout in the middle of a Wendy's restaurant. It was so bad, we ended up throwing away everything you were wearing and wrapping you in my favorite T-shirt. Which was soaked in pee by the time we got home."

Bea's eyes widened. "Why would you tell me that?"

An old, familiar light sparked in his eyes. "Because we lived through it. We learned. Your mother and I never forgot the diaper bag again, and it wasn't nearly as big a deal as we thought it was at the time."

Emotion flooded her as she pictured herself as a baby in her mother's arms. "What about your T-shirt?"

"I threw it in the wash and kept wearing it. And told your mother that next time she had to sacrifice her own shirt."

Bea smiled to herself. Her mom and dad had been new parents once, too. Everyone had to start somewhere. She began to relax, but then her previous anxiety resurfaced. What if Grandma June did have familial Alzheimer's disease? What if Bea carried the gene? What if she'd already passed it on to her child?

She needed to stop fixating on the possibilities. Fixation was another symptom of mental deterioration.

The next hour passed quickly. When Hunter had arrived, Amber said he'd just woken up from a nap. As lunchtime passed and his mother did not return, it became evident he needed another one of those. Bea texted Amber to ask when she would be back but got no response.

She held a yawning Hunter on her hip and looked around the house. "Where is he going to lie down?"

Dad was unperturbed. "We'll move a couch cushion to the floor."

"What if he rolls off?"

"Watch this." He slid the couch so it was perpendicular to the wall and tucked a cushion into the ninety-degree angle formed on the floor. He stood a second cushion upright against the side of the makeshift bed opposite the couch and nodded.

"Set him so his feet are this way." He pointed to the one open side. "And he'll be fine."

He'll be fine. How many times could Dad say the word *fine* in one day?

"Are you sure?"

"He's not going to roll feet first. Just make sure he's asleep before you put him down so he doesn't try to escape."

"Okay." Bea was skeptical and didn't care if she sounded like it. "But can you at least put a blanket over the cushion or something? It's covered in cat hair."

"Well." Dad raised an eyebrow. "That's not my fault."

Hunter's eyes were almost closed. Bea moved him to her shoulder, and his body grew limp. She gave her dad a look, and he raised his hands and went to the linen closet to find something to lay on the cushion. By the time the makeshift bed was ready, Hunter was completely sacked out.

Bea stood over the cushion and looked down at the floor. It was so far away.

"How am I supposed to set him down without waking him up?" she whispered.

Dad gave her an amused look. "He's sound asleep. He won't even notice."

She knelt in slow motion, eyeing the distance to the cushion and praying silently the baby would not wake up. She laid him next to the blanket she'd pulled from his diaper bag as carefully as she could, slowly moving her hands out from under him and inching away. He twitched and made a snorting sound, then pulled the blanket to his chest and started to snore.

She backed away a little farther, then stood. Whew. That was stressful. She turned and gave her dad a triumphant smile. "We did it."

He pretended to wipe sweat from his forehead, and she

chuckled. *Quietly*. Together they tiptoed to the other side of the couch to head for the kitchen.

The front door flew open.

Jeremy entered, his arms spread open as he called out in a singsong voice, "Honey, I'm hooome."

"Shh!"

Bea and her dad both put a finger to their lips and shushed him at the same time.

His eyes widened. "What?"

Hunter began to cry.

◆ ◆ ◆

Bea frowned at her friend and shifted on her feet. "You could've at least texted me."

Amber nodded. "I'm sorry. I didn't know . . ."

Her voice trailed off, and Bea rubbed her forehead. She'd expected Amber around noon, and it was almost five o'clock and long after Hunter had woken up from his second attempt at a nap, and she'd fed him everything she could find in his diaper bag plus yogurt and Ritz crackers from the kitchen. But it couldn't have been easy for Amber to see Axel again.

Bea peered over her shoulder to make sure Jeremy and her dad were out of earshot. "What did he say?"

Amber kissed her fingers, then touched them to Hunter's nose. "You look so much like your daddy—did you know that?"

Hunter held his arms up, wanting to be held. Amber obliged. "He said he was sorry he left."

Bea fought off a frown. "Really."

Amber shrugged. "He said a lot of other things. I don't know what's going to happen."

"Is he moving back?"

"I don't know. He said he's got a job in Ponderosa."

Questions dangled on the tip of Bea's tongue. What kind

of job? Did he plan to support his family? Did he have any idea how much it cost to raise a child? Because holy cow it was expensive. How could he just show back up?

She didn't ask any of them out loud, but a warning rang out in her brain. "Does he want to see Hunter?"

Amber nuzzled her son's neck. "He said he isn't ready."

He wasn't ready. How nice. Bea wanted to call him a not-so-nice name, but she saw the expression on Amber's face and changed her mind. "I'm sorry. This must be really hard."

Amber looked up, her eyes glistening. "Thank you, Bea. For everything."

Bea looked down. She hadn't done much. Watched Hunter for a few hours and tried not to be too judgmental. Was that all it took to be a good friend? She'd never really had one before except her mom.

"You're welcome."

"I mean it. Other people from school wanted nothing to do with me once they found out about Hunter. It's like they were afraid my situation was contagious."

"That sucks."

"I get it, in a way." Amber blew a piece of hair from her face. "They wanted to party at the river and go to concerts and date each other. You can't do stuff like that with a baby."

Bea bit the inside of her bottom lip. She didn't care about parties or concerts or dating. But what other things might she lose from her life once her baby was born?

"Well, I better get this guy home." Amber slung Hunter's diaper bag over her shoulder and smiled at him. "Did you have fun with Auntie Bea?"

Hunter gave a happy-sounding gurgle as he and Amber headed for the door, and Bea's heart squeezed. Auntie? She was an only child. She'd never be a real aunt, but she sure liked the sound of it.

"See you later." Bea waved and closed the door after her friend.

Friend. Who would've ever thought she and Amber Moss would be friends? Jeremy appeared, drawn by the sound of the door.

"She gone?"

Bea nodded. "I'm exhausted."

"I'm sorry I missed most of it. I need all the practice I can get."

"I had no idea what I was doing."

"I'm sure you were great." Jeremy kissed her on the forehead. "I had quite a day, too. Ed showed me how to change a tire on the ten-wheeler. Then I stopped at that antler shop on my way home."

"You talked to Mr. Van Dyken?"

Jeremy nodded. "He showed me all these amazing pictures on his phone of his work. He even has a video about how to build an antler chandelier that he made for his grandson."

"Whoa, I would totally watch that."

"It needs some editing, but yes, it was really cool." Jeremy was fired up now, and his voice rose. "But all that stuff's just sitting there on his phone. Being wasted! I showed him how to set up a Facebook account and post pictures on it."

"Did he do it?"

"No." Jeremy deflated. "He said he wasn't ready for that sort of thing."

Bea harrumphed. "Well, is he ready to go out of business?"

"I said something along the same lines." Jeremy chuckled. "Except with a little more subtlety."

He steered her toward the kitchen. "Shall we go see what your dad has planned for this big dinner he keeps talking about?"

Bea was happy to turn her attention to dinner. They entered the kitchen and found Dad elbow-deep in raw meat. He was kneading a giant ball of burger in a glass bowl and forming patties with his hands. Containers of chili powder, seasoned salt, garlic powder, pepper, and Worcestershire sauce were scattered around the counter.

Bea perked right up. "Are you grilling?"

Dad nodded. "Just the way you like them."

Even though she thought she'd never be hungry again after her cheesecake breakfast, her stomach rumbled.

"Do you mean grilling on a grill?" Jeremy looked back and forth between her and her dad. "Like a barbecue grill?"

Dad broke off a handful of meat and began rolling it between his palms. "Of course."

Jeremy gaped. "It's twenty degrees outside."

Once the meat had formed to his satisfaction, Dad began flattening it into a patty. "Technically, it's only seventeen."

Bea washed her hands in the sink. "Anything I can do to help?"

"You can cut up cheese and pickles and such if you want."

Though he looked skeptical, Jeremy helped her pull everything from the fridge that could possibly go on a hamburger. While Dad took the plate of newly formed patties outside to place on the grill, she and Jeremy sliced tomatoes, cheese, pickles, and onions.

When tomato juice dripped down her arm, Jeremy had a rag in his hand to wipe it up before she asked. As he opened the bag with the block of cheese in it, she set a cutting board underneath before he could even look for it.

Bea thought of her mom. She and Dad had made a good team, too.

"Get down, Steve." Bea shooed the cat off a chair as she began to set the table. "Dad won't like you sitting up there."

Jeremy opened a bag of hamburger buns. "Was it fun?"

"What?"

"Taking care of Hunter."

"I don't know." Bea filled three glasses with water. "I was too nervous to have fun."

153

"I bet it's scarier with other people's kids." Jeremy ran a hand through his hair. "With your own, it just . . ."

She raised her eyebrows and waited for him to finish his sentence.

He shrugged and grinned. "Just comes natural."

She tried to smile, but it felt more like a grimace. That couldn't possibly be true. "But what if—"

The back door opened, and a blast of cold air stalked through the kitchen like a wolf on the prowl, stealing Bea's words away. Jeremy gave her a questioning look, but she shook her head. Maybe she wasn't ready to say it out loud, anyway.

Dad proudly set the burgers on the table. "Dinner's ready."

"Smells good." Bea took her seat. "Thanks, Dad."

"Yeah, thank you." Jeremy sat down beside her. "I'm starving."

Dad prayed over their meal, and then they all eagerly prepared hamburger buns to their liking. For Bea, that meant mayo, lettuce, tomato, two very thin slices of pickle, and a tiny bit of mustard. No ketchup, no onions, and definitely no barbecue sauce. Barbecue sauce on a burger was a sacrilege she only overlooked for the sake of family peace.

Jeremy loaded everything available onto his bun and took a huge bite.

"Did you get the fridge fixed, Dad?" Bea asked.

His face darkened. "Not yet."

"Uh, guys." Jeremy set his burger on his plate. "I think there's something wrong with this beef."

Dad smirked. "It's not beef."

Jeremy gave his plate a confused look. "Um . . ."

"It's venison," Bea said. "Deer meat."

"Oh." He picked the burger up and peered at it. "Oh."

"Something wrong?" Dad asked.

"No. I've just never had . . . that before. Is it . . . uh, did you . . . ?"

"Kill it? Yes. Last fall."

Bea eyed Jeremy thoughtfully. She'd grown up eating venison, elk, and even bison on occasion. Black bear once, too, come to think of it. She'd never given it a second thought. But she had no idea what Jeremy's stance on hunting was. Or whether he even had a stance. It had never come up in Santa Clara.

Maybe she'd taken for granted that not everyone in the country had as close a connection to the food on their table as the people of Moose Creek. People who watched the potato fields mature over the summer. Smelled the wheat when it was harvested every September. Dragged the 175-pound carcass of a mule deer two miles to where their truck was waiting. Exchanged trout from the Madison River for honey from Miss Arlee's bees.

"What do you think?" She tried to sound nonchalant. "Do you like it?"

Jeremy took another tentative bite. Dad pretended to be indifferent and absorbed in his own burger, but Bea could tell he had one eye on Jeremy as well, interested in his response. As if Jeremy's feelings about wild game were awfully important to him.

"It's different." Jeremy winked at her. "Just like you."

Her cheeks grew warm. It seemed like something she should smack him on the arm for, but the way he said it made her feel like it was the nicest thing anyone had ever said to her.

"Don't just sit there gawking at each other," Dad barked. "Eat up."

TWENTY-TWO

Mitch strode into the kitchen Sunday morning, toolbox in hand, determined to win his battle with the ice machine once and for all. He stopped short at the sight of Bea sitting at the table, staring at a can of 7UP.

"What are you doing here?"

She'd said she was going to walk to church with Jeremy, hadn't she? She'd even tried to convince him to go along.

Her face was pale. "I'm not feeling well. Decided to stay home."

"Oh." He set the box on the table with a metallic thunk. "You're sick, and he just left you here alone?"

"I'm not sick." Bea kept her eyes on the can. There was an edge in her voice. "And I'm not alone."

"Okay, okay." He held up his hands. "Seems like he's always off gallivanting around without you, that's all."

"*He* has a name, Dad. And when he's gone, it's for work. He also doesn't like missing church. His faith is important to him."

Mitch tilted his head at the way she said the words. "It's not to you?"

She looked up. "I'm still figuring that out, not that you have a right to talk to me about it. But it makes me happy to be around other believers. I actually like them."

156

He bristled. "I like those folks, too."

Her hand closed around the 7UP can as she eyed him carefully. "Then why do you avoid them like the plague?"

He crossed his arms over his chest and looked at the fridge. How had this happened? There were things he wanted to talk with his daughter about, but church wasn't one of them.

"Ever since Mom died," she continued, "you've been acting like it's all those people's fault or something. Pastor Frank told me about the incident with the chowder."

He stifled a growl. What'd Frank have to go and do that for? He looked out the window. Barbara Currington's ham-and-corn chowder had been the last straw. He'd continued to attend church after Caroline died for Bea's sake, hoping the looks of pity, nosiness, and condescending platitudes would taper off. But once Bea left for school, his attendance had rapidly declined.

"I didn't mean to dump it all over the pew."

"But you did mean to tell her to—how did Pastor Frank put it?—keep her corn to herself?"

An old, familiar anger began to build up in his chest. He'd never asked for any food, yet someone tried to hand off a pan of pasta or bowl of soup every time he showed his face inside Moose Creek Community Church. He'd never asked for any of the pity or the inappropriate hints about single cousins or nieces or hair stylists people knew. He'd never asked to hear about the "words of comfort" God had allegedly placed in someone's heart to share with him.

"I just couldn't take it anymore."

Bea's eyes burned a hole through his skull. "Take what? The fact so many people cared about you?"

"No." He searched for the right words like an outstretched hand groping for the light switch in the middle of the night. "The pressure to be thankful. The expectation that I should be grateful for whatever sympathy someone wanted to show, however they wanted to show it. No one ever asked me what I actually needed. They just shoved plates of muffins in my hands and expected me to be happy about it."

Bea was silent. His neck muscles tightened. It sounded terrible when he said it out loud, but he was only being honest. It had felt so unfair at the time, like the whole church was asking him to carry the burden of pretending on top of the burden of grief.

"So you dumped out Barbara's chowder?"

He scoffed. "It was an accident. I stood up too fast, trying to get away."

A small smile appeared on Bea's face. "I wish I could've seen it."

"I'm told they found chowder over three pews away." He didn't stick around for the cleanup efforts, so he couldn't confirm that. But it was impressive if true.

Bea folded her arms on the table. "They were just trying to help, you know. They all loved Mom, too."

Her words scratched at a raw place in Mitch's heart. A place he'd thought had scarred over by now. The words to "Sweet Caroline" came to mind unbidden, and he yanked the lid of his toolbox open to drown out the melody in his head. Caroline was gone. He couldn't change that, and he couldn't take back what had happened with his church family afterward. But maybe there was one thing he could still change.

"Have you thought about your plans for the future, B.B.?"

She wrinkled her nose. "What do you mean?"

The wariness in her voice should've been a warning. Nevertheless, he forged ahead. "I mean going back to college. Getting a degree. Choosing a career. You can't work at the Food Farm forever."

Some rosiness began to appear in her pale cheeks. "I don't know if I'm ever going back to school, Dad. I'm not sure what the point would be. And you know the Food Farm is only temporary."

"'What the point would be'?" He pulled a screwdriver from the toolbox and waved it around. "The point is, you can't just give up on your dreams. Jeremy's ambitions are not more important than yours."

Her nostrils flared. "It has nothing to do with that. He would support me going back to school if that's what I wanted."

"And why isn't it? You always liked school."

She pressed her lips together and didn't respond. She looked so much like Caroline when her eyes sparked like that. Caroline had always wanted to give Bea the world. Before she died, she'd made him promise he wouldn't let her death hold Bea back. He hadn't done a great job of that. Hadn't wanted to accept she was leaving him. That everything was going to change. But it wasn't too late.

"I know it might not seem like it right now"—he dropped the screwdriver back in the box and leaned his hands on the table, facing her—"but there's so much life ahead of you. So many opportunities. We didn't name you after Beatrice Shilling *and* Beatrice Hicks so you could organize produce while your husband wanders around doing who-knows-what."

She pushed back from the table and stood. "You know very well what he's doing. He's working on starting his own company. It's going to take time—"

"I don't know what it's like in California, but around here, a man does whatever he has to do to support his family."

"So does a woman." Bea put her hands on her hips. "And if that means organizing produce at the Food Farm for a few months, then that's what I'm going to do. I can't just think about what I want anymore, Dad. I have to think about the baby."

A baby Caroline would never get to see. A fleeting image of Caroline holding a baby and smiling up at him flashed like lightning in his brain, and he took a step back from the table. It hurt. It hurt so much.

He had to make Bea see how much potential lay ahead of her. "You're only twenty-one. I don't want you to waste your life—"

"Waste my life?" She dropped her hands and clenched her fists. "That's what you think about my being pregnant? Mom was my age when she had me. Did she waste *her* life?"

His voice rose. "No, of course not."

She narrowed her eyes. He wasn't even sure what he was trying to say. What he wanted. He just knew this was nothing like how he pictured his life, or Bea's, three years ago.

"And what about you, Dad? You mope around here like an old man. Talk about wasting your life."

"We're not talking about me."

"No, of course not." Bea slapped the table with an open palm. "We're not ever allowed to talk about *you*. But *you* don't have a say in my decisions anymore. Don't have a right to tell me what I should or shouldn't do."

"I'm still your father, and I don't want to see you give up. College is still an option."

Her chin quivered. "You don't understand. You don't know how hard it was for me."

His brow furrowed. She'd never shied away from hard work, and her grades had been good that year at Georgia State. "And you thought getting married would be easier?"

"No." She flinched. "I don't know. I missed Mom."

"So you settled for the first guy who came along?"

Her cheeks were bright red now. He shook his head. That wasn't what he meant. "I—"

"Real nice, Dad." Her eyes flashed with fire. "You don't know anything about it."

"Because you never told me. I can't stand how you never tell me anything anymore." He took another step back and tripped over Steve, who yowled and ran off. "And I can't stand having that cat around."

"Well, that's an easy problem to fix." She spun around in a

huff and called over her shoulder. "We'll all be out of your hair as soon as possible."

He held up a hand. "No, that's not—"

She marched out of the kitchen and down the hall.

"Where are you going?" He hurried after her. "B.B., wait."

"It's Bea." She pulled her coat from the rack and snatched the keys to the Toyota off the hook on the wall. "And I need some fresh air. Tell Jeremy I'll be back in a little while."

Mitch opened his mouth in protest, but she slipped through the door and slammed it behind her, leaving a blast of cold air and her angry words lingering in the hall. He hadn't meant it about Jeremy. It wasn't Jeremy he blamed, it was himself. And he hadn't meant it about the cat, either. Steve hadn't given him any trouble. He'd keep them all here forever if he could, but wasn't he allowed to be concerned about his only child? About her future?

What about two years ago? Had he shown concern for her then or only himself?

He'd blown it big-time.

An elk bugle broke into his thoughts, and he realized he was still staring at the door. Shaking his head, he hurried to the kitchen to find his phone. Who would be calling him on a Sunday? It better not be the town office calling about another pothole emergency.

He saw his father's name on the phone screen, and his throat constricted.

"Hello? Dad?"

"Mitch, it's your mother."

His heart dropped a beat. "What happened?"

"I spent the morning riding Rattler. I needed some time. I took the truck keys with me, in case she got any ideas, but I never dreamed . . ."

"What is it? Tell me."

"Your mother." It was the voice of a man who blamed himself. "She's gone."

TWENTY-THREE

The car jolted over a pothole as Bea raced out of Moose Creek, knocking the Toyota off track. She yelped and jerked the steering wheel to correct her course. What was Dad's problem? How could he say those things? Ever since she and Jeremy had arrived, he'd been looking to pick a fight.

It wasn't his life. She should've known coming back here wouldn't work. Nothing had been the same since Mom died, especially her relationship with her father. He couldn't even look at her the same way anymore.

The miles flew past under her pathetic little tires as she ignored the speed-limit signs. The farther from Moose Creek she drove, the better she felt.

The morning sickness had hit her hard this morning. Every smell throughout the entire house had wrenched her stomach enough to make her want to gag. She cracked her window and turned up Pass Creek Road. Ah, the smell of the mountain. That was more like it. Her life was coming apart at the seams, but the mountain? The mountain made more sense than anything else.

Tiny flakes of snow blew into the car as she drove. Why couldn't Dad be supportive of what Jeremy was trying to do? And why did he have to keep pestering her about college? There was a baby growing inside her. An actual human child. She had a lot more important things to worry about than higher education. How dare he insinuate she married Jeremy because . . . what? She was sad about Mom and desperate for comfort? Is that what he thought?

That couldn't be true.

She swallowed.

Could it?

When she reached the turnoff that would take her to her grandparents' house, she hesitated. It should've been a no-brainer to head in their direction if she was seeking solace. In the past, Grandma June would know exactly how to make Bea feel better. A cup of hot cocoa. A sympathetic ear. An offer of a trail ride, maybe. But what would Bea find if she visited today? She didn't know if she could handle being called Caroline or being asked to leave.

She stayed on Pass Creek Road. What would she say to Grandma and Grandpa anyway? She could never explain why she was so upset. Her hormones were raging out of control. Sobs welled up in her throat, only to be followed by laughter.

She was going crazy.

The flakes flying into the car grew thicker. She rolled up her window and glanced around. She'd been driving with her eyes pinned straight ahead, caring only about the road in front of her and the memories behind. Now she fixed a wary eye on the sky. Those clouds were heavy with snow. What was already falling was only the beginning. Not another soul was on the road. She checked her phone. No service.

This was foolish. She was nuts. Jeremy would be worried sick when he got home from church in—she consulted the clock on the dash—twenty minutes to find her gone. But she wasn't ready to go back. She pulled up in front of the Pass Creek schoolhouse and put the Toyota into park. She needed to get ahold of herself.

She leaned her head back against the seat and took a deep breath. In through her nose, out through her mouth. And again.

What if Dad was right?

A figure passed by the passenger window, and she snapped upright. No one should be out walking right now. She leaned forward and peered out the windshield at the back of a wiry, elderly person marching resolutely forward as if late for work. It looked like . . . was that . . . ?

She flung open her door and scrambled from the car. "Grandma."

The woman did not stop.

Bea raised her voice. "Grandma June."

Grandma paused for a moment and cocked her head, then continued on. Bea dashed after her, cold snow stinging her face.

It was just her, Grandma, and the mountain.

TWENTY-FOUR

The snowflakes are gentle on my face. Reassuring me. Showing me the way. I won't stop. Not now. Not when I'm so close to finding my son. Rand will never understand, but I can't hide from the truth any longer. I can only hope he loves me enough.

The wind howls all sorts of mysterious messages to me. It screams my name, *Juniper. Juniper.*

"Grandma."

That's not the wind. I clutch my chest as a young woman appears beside me. Where did she come from? I don't want to talk to her. Don't want to talk to anyone. This is a mission I must complete on my own.

"Grandma, stop. What are you doing?"

She grasps my arm, but I pull away. How dare she.

"Where are you going?"

I hurry on, but she is faster than me. I will my legs to move, but I cannot escape. She grabs my arm again, and I turn on her. "Leave me alone."

Puffs of steamy air are spewing from her mouth. "Please, let me give you a ride home."

How does she know I'm not on my way home right now? I eye her with suspicion. Something about her is unsettling.

"I can't go home." I march on, and she keeps step with me. "I need to find someone."

The young woman remains at my side, matching my steps. "You'll never find them on foot. Let me give you a ride."

I stop and turn my gaze on Hardscrabble Peak, looming before me like a grizzly standing on its hind legs, daring me to come closer. She makes a good point. It's a long way up the mountain, and these old legs have seen better days. But what is she going to do? Carry me?

"It's freezing out here." She wraps her arms around herself to prove her point. "And the snow is only going to get worse. Let's go back to my car."

Her car? I spin around and see a yuppie-looking silver vehicle parked in front of the schoolhouse. I'm almost inclined to say I have more faith in my feet to get me up the mountain than that thing, but the wind pushes against me, crying, crying, that it will not make it easy for me. It will fight back.

I plant my feet in the middle of the road and cross my arms over my chest while staring at the car.

The woman gets my hint and takes a tentative step away from me. "I'll be right back. Don't move."

I give her my best glare but remain planted.

She hurries toward her car, looking back every five seconds to shout, "Don't move." Like I'm a child or an injured puppy. I wonder what my son is doing now. Is he cold on the mountain? *Oh, God, I hope he's not alone. You're with him, aren't you? Of course. You would never make him suffer for my sins.*

The silver car pulls up beside me with the passenger window down.

"Please get in," the woman says. "We'll get you all warmed up."

We? I check the back seat. There's no one else in there. This lady must be crazy. But she has a car, and I don't. I open the door.

"Come on, let's get you home."

I shut the door and step back. "No. I can't go home."

She puts the car in park, jumps out, and hurries over to me. "Grandma, please. Let me take you home."

Now I know she's crazy. I'm not anybody's grandma. Not yet. This woman shouldn't be out here by herself.

She opens the passenger door again, but I stand my ground. "I have to go up the mountain. I have to find him."

She shivers against the cold. Poor thing should put a coat on. I can see one right there on the front seat, yet she doesn't have enough sense to put it on.

"Find who?" she asks. "Grandpa?"

I don't want to tell her the truth, so I just nod.

She narrows her eyes. "Where is he?"

"There's a light up there." I point about halfway between the foothills and Hardscrabble Peak. "You can't see it right now, but that's where he is."

I'm sure of it. There, tucked away safely in the folds of the mountain, lies the greatest treasure in the world.

Her face contorts as she looks at me, then her shoulders slump. "Okay."

"Okay?"

"I'll take you wherever you want to go, as long as you'll get in the car."

I study her for a moment. Even though she's crazy, something tells me I can trust her. As if I knew her before, in a different life. She steps aside, and I sink low to slide into the passenger seat. I've never been in such a short car before. The woman scoots around the front and gets in behind the wheel, shutting the door with a thud and a gust of air. Her hands are red from the cold as she shifts the car into drive. I give the coat that now sits between us a meaningful look but don't say anything. If she wants to freeze to death, that's her business.

"To the mountain?" She looks at me for reassurance, fear in her eyes. Poor dear.

I nod. "To the mountain."

TWENTY-FIVE

One time, years ago, after he and Caroline first bought their house in Moose Creek, Mitch drove to his parents' house in record time after receiving a call from his mother that his father had been thrown from his horse and was dangling from a barbwire fence. By the time Mitch arrived, his father had cut himself free with the knife on his belt despite a dislocated right shoulder and had given his horse a dressing down that caused the mare to hang her head in remorse.

Dad had been angry that Mom had bothered Mitch over "such a silly thing." Mitch had insisted on taking him to the clinic, but Dad had rammed his shoulder into the side of the house on the way to the truck and popped it back into place. His mother had fussed over him at first but had eventually taken Dad's side. "Now he can finish his chores before dark," she'd said. "Everything's fine."

This time was different. As his truck charged down his parents' gravel drive, Mitch knew things were *not* fine. Would not be fine. His father was not physically injured. He was broken inside. And his mother was not waiting, hands on hips, to fuss over his father or him or anyone else. She was missing.

How had she gone from undercooking apple pies to wandering off in a snowstorm in a matter of weeks?

The sight of his parents' truck parked next to the house brought little comfort. About six months ago, his mom had had an incident with some loose gravel on their drive, ended up in the ditch, and stubbornly decided she wasn't going to drive ever again. At the time, he'd figured it was just a phase, but looking back, he could see it had been a warning sign. Now he was glad he didn't have to worry about her getting into an accident, but if she'd taken the truck, at least she'd have some protection from the elements. On foot she was entirely exposed.

He jumped out of his truck and jogged toward the house. His dad was waiting on the porch, wringing his hat in his hands. He took the steps as quickly as his bum leg would allow and met Mitch. "I'm sorry, son. I never should've left her alone."

"It's not your fault." Mitch gripped his father's shoulder. "I should've been helping more."

Rand wiped a hand over his face. "I tried tracking her, but the snow's falling too fast. It's already covered any prints."

The snow in Montana was often fine and dry, blowing and swirling like desert sand in the subzero temperatures of winter. But the snow today was thick and heavy, covering the ground with alarming speed.

"Which way do you think she went? Where would she want to go?"

Rand jammed his hat back on his head and shoved his hands into the pockets of his wool-lined coat. "Maybe toward town, but you would've seen her. I think she's headed for the mountain. She's always going on about that treasure."

"Then let's go." Mitch jogged back to his truck, and his father followed. "She can't have gotten far."

"Mebbe." Rand heaved himself into the passenger seat and pulled his right leg in with a grunt. "But I don't know how long she's been gone. And you know your mother."

Mitch turned the key in the ignition and scowled to himself. He didn't feel like he knew her at all anymore, actually. But his dad was referring to his mother's stubbornness and iron will, and Mitch did know about that. If she wanted to climb the mountain, she would find a way to climb the mountain.

He turned the truck around and headed back to the road. "We'll find her."

Neither of them spoke as he drove up Pass Creek Road. The snow fell faster and thicker. Mitch punched a button on his phone and called Bea for the third time since leaving the house, and for the third time, it went straight to voicemail. He threw the phone down on the seat with a growl.

"What?" Rand's gnarled fingers gripped the knees of his worn denim jeans. "Where's Bea?"

"I don't know. She went for a drive."

"In this weather?"

"She was mad."

Rand peered intently out the window. "I don't like this. Maybe we should call the sheriff."

Mitch nodded. "Keep your eyes out. If we don't see any sign of her before the schoolhouse, we'll call."

He said it with confidence, but Mitch knew how long it could take to get anyone out to help them. On a good day, the emergency response times were slow. During the first big storm of the season, when everyone realized they'd forgotten how to drive in the snow and ended up stuck in a ditch down on the interstate? Every police officer and ambulance for fifty miles would be busy for hours.

Though he was tempted to race down the road, Mitch took it slow so they could examine every suspicious-looking figure or heap or hiding place they passed. A half mile before the schoolhouse, he pulled the truck over and hopped out when he saw what looked like a jacket lying next to the road. It was a black garbage bag.

He kicked it and climbed back into the truck, giving his father a guarded look. "It's getting colder."

Rand worked the knees of his jeans, his callused palms rubbing the fabric like June's kneading dough. "You reckon it's time to call for help?"

Mitch checked his phone. "No signal here. And might not be any if we keep going. Maybe we should head back and come up with a better plan. What if we drove all over the mountain and she was at the house looking for you the whole time?"

It had been foolish to head out without leaving a note. His mother could've been hiding out in the barn for all they knew. He hadn't even asked Dad if he'd checked around the property or called any of the neighbors.

Rand nodded reluctantly. Visibility was so poor they both knew spotting June would be nearly impossible unless she was standing in the middle of the road. And what if she *was* waiting for them?

Mitch pictured his mother wandering the house, alone and confused. Pictured her in a ditch somewhere, the snow slowly covering her body. He drummed the steering wheel so hard it hurt and prayed.

He turned the truck around and drove faster, his mind working the problem while his hands and feet went into autopilot to get him back to the house. He would have his dad call all the neighbors as soon as his phone had service. Then he and Rand would split up and search every inch of the house and the property. If that failed to net any results, then there was only one thing left to do.

✦ ✦ ✦

Bea hadn't driven up Whitetail Pass Road in a long time and never in a vehicle with low-profile tires. But she knew that even if the car managed to navigate the worsening conditions, this road wasn't going to take them anywhere near Hardscrabble Peak like Grandma June wanted.

Grandma leaned forward in her seat, staring intently out the windshield. The wipers scraped at full speed, trying to keep the snow at bay. Bea tightened her hold on the wheel, struggling to accept that the person beside her was the same person she'd known her whole life.

"I don't think we should go any farther." Bea slowed the car and peered through the falling flakes, looking for a place to turn around. She'd humored her grandmother long enough.

"We're almost there." Grandma's gaze darted around like a hummingbird in August, alighting for a moment on one thing before darting to something else. "He's close. I can feel him."

Goose bumps rose on Bea's arms. Who was Grandma talking about? She couldn't possibly be searching for Grandpa Rand. Why would he be up here? An SUV drove by in the other lane at a reckless speed, spraying the Toyota with slush from the road. Bea's hands hurt from her death grip on the wheel. Maybe if she could distract Grandma enough, she wouldn't notice if Bea turned around.

"I bet he went back home." Bea slowed the car even more, hoping no one would come driving up and ram her from behind. As soon as she found a suitable turnout, she would take it and head back down the mountain. "He's probably wondering where you are right now."

A gasp blew from Grandma's mouth. "What if he's wondered all these years? What if he thinks I forgot about him?"

Bea didn't know what to say. None of this made any sense. Grandma started rocking back and forth, moaning words that sounded like they belonged to someone else.

"I will never forget. I will never forget. I will never forget."

A turnout appeared, and Bea breathed a sigh of relief. The snow was piling up, but the trees had kept the snow covering the dirt turnout from becoming too deep. She silently thanked the Lord and eased the car off the road, careful not to brake too hard. The last thing she wanted was to start sliding. Dad's warnings about someone losing sight of their house from ten feet away suddenly weren't so hard to believe.

Carefully, she drove the little half circle until she was back facing the road. Though it was unlikely she would see anyone, she stopped to look for cars before pulling out. She looked right. Looked left.

A blast of cold air struck her, and she spun around. "Grandma."

Grandma June was out of the car and looking around as if trying to decide which way to go. Her gray hair, which had grown even longer and wilder since Bea saw her last, turned white with snow in an instant.

Bea slammed the Toyota into park. "Hot coffee."

She pulled on her coat and climbed out into the snow, leaving the car running. "Grandma."

Grandma nodded as if making up her mind and started walking.

Bea held up a hand and shouted, "Wait. Stop."

The falling snow muffled her words. Her grandmother did not slow down. Bea's tennis shoes were soaked through by the time she caught up with her grandma, who wasn't wearing boots, either.

She grabbed one of Grandma's hands, which was ice-cold. Neither of them had gloves. She'd always kept a stash of hats, gloves, and blankets in the back of her Blazer at Dad's insistence, not to mention a jug of water and box of granola bars, but the Toyota had no such provisions.

Bea tugged on Grandma's hand. "Come back to the car where it's warm." Her voice was desperate. "Please."

Grandma ignored her. Panic rose up in Bea's chest. What was she supposed to do? She pulled her phone from the back pocket of her jeans with her other hand. No signal and a low battery. This was not good. Grandma dragged her along as she continued up the road, past two little white crosses marking the site of a fatal accident. Grandma didn't notice them.

Where was she getting her strength? She was a couple of inches taller than Bea, who took after her petite mother in size, but Bea never expected that Grandma could pull her along like a toddler.

The snow muted all sounds except their feet clomping along the road. They rounded a bend, and Bea looked back. She couldn't see the car anymore and had serious doubts about getting it back on the road without help. But she needed to get Grandma back inside it, and she needed to do it now. What would convince her?

She resisted as much as possible, slowing Grandma's progress, and checked her phone again. Just up ahead, at the top of a hill, was something of a clearing. If they reached it, perhaps she would be able to pick up one bar of service. That was all she needed. One measly bar.

She pulled up her messaging app with one hand and hesitated. At the top of the list were two names: Jeremy and Dad. She'd only have the chance to send one text, if any. She began to type, unable to look at the screen as she stumbled along. She hoped the words would make sense if they went through.

Grandma gave Bea's hand an extra hard tug, and Bea lost her balance. Pain shot up her leg as her right knee hit the pavement with a cold, wet splash. She winced, but Grandma wasn't about to slow down. She dragged Bea to her feet and continued walking. Bea prayed no cars would come around the bend.

"Let's go back, Grandma."

Grandma June reached the clearing and stopped, panting. Bea thanked God under her breath and quickly checked her phone. She'd been right. There was one bar. She held the phone above her head, said another prayer, and hit send.

Grandma looked at her with hollow eyes. "I will never forget."

"Of course not." Bea shoved her phone into her coat pocket, having no idea whether her message went through. "And I will never forget this trip up the mountain. Now let's go back to the car."

Her grandma let go of her hand and turned in circles, disoriented. Bea bit back her fear and racked her brain for something to convince Grandma June to listen. The snow showed no sign of letting up, and she thought of the blizzard that had nearly been the demise of old Miner McGee.

Wait.

That was it.

"Grandma." She gently put her hands on Grandma's shoulders. "Tell me the story about the light on the mountain."

Something flickered in Grandma June's eyes. "The light on the mountain?"

"Yes." Bea took her hand and pulled. In response, Grandma took a faltering step toward the car. "It's my favorite story. Please, won't you tell it?"

Grandma's hair was soaked, her fingers frozen. When Bea saw how badly Grandma was trembling, she quickened her pace.

Grandma allowed Bea to lead her. "But I need to find him. What if he needs me?"

Bea still had no clue who *he* was, but maybe she could use him to her advantage. "He would want you to tell the story, don't you think?"

The Toyota came into view, still idling.

Water streamed down Grandma's face. Bea didn't know if it was snow or tears. Maybe it was both.

Grandma's voice was small. "He would've liked that story."

"Who, Grandma?"

"My baby."

Bea's forehead wrinkled. "Let's pretend he's here. Once upon a time . . ."

They neared the car. Grandma didn't speak. Bea opened the passenger door and nudged Grandma inside. Her body was shaking too badly to put up a fight. For the first time, Bea wondered how long Grandma could last in these conditions. She'd been so caught up in the drama, she hadn't noticed how pale Grandma was. How blue her lips.

Bea ran around the car to get in, thankful she'd left it running. It was toasty inside. She jerked the car into drive and hit the gas. The car slid backward. The tires spun uselessly.

"Hot coffee."

She tried again, but it was pointless. The snow had deepened and was beginning to freeze into ruts the Toyota would never climb out of on its own. Not with its narrow tires and low clearance. It might as well be a toy car.

They needed help. She checked her phone, but it was dead. Nothing drained a phone battery faster than searching for service in the mountains. There was no way to know if her message had gone through.

As the inside of the windows fogged up from their wet clothes, she worried Grandma might make another break for it. But it only took a glance to realize that wasn't the biggest concern anymore.

"Let's get you out of that wet coat." Bea helped Grandma unzip it and pull it off. She needed to keep her awake. "Now, about that story. Once upon a time . . ."

This time a small light appeared in Grandma's eyes. "Once upon a time, many years ago, there was a man named Miner McGee. He had spent his whole life searching for treasure but never struck it rich."

Her words came slow and thick. The shifter between the two front seats poked into Bea's side, and her injured knee protested as she twisted and reached over to pull the socks and shoes from Grandma's feet. She tossed them on the back seat, then grasped Grandma's hands between her own, rubbing them briskly.

"What happened to him?" she asked.

"The people of Moose Creek told him of an enormous diamond hidden away on the mountain." Grandma sounded far away. "The Big Sky Diamond. He stocked up on supplies . . . and strapped on his headlamp . . ."

Her voice trailed off, and Bea's chest tightened. "And then what happened, Grandma? Tell me the story."

Grandma leaned her head back against the seat.

"Please, Grandma." Bea's voice was small and thin. "Tell me the story."

TWENTY-SIX

Mitch cupped his cold hands in front of his mouth and blew on them. The temperature had continued to drop. He hurried into the house to find his dad. There was nowhere else his mother could be. They'd checked every possible hiding place outside once and every inch of the house twice. What had possessed her to leave? What had she been thinking?

His father hung up the landline phone with a fearful look in his eye. "That was the last of 'em, and they ain't seen her neither. Said they'd call if she shows up."

Mitch nodded slowly. That was that, then. Only one thing left to do.

He checked his phone. No service, but he'd spent enough time in this house to know where the sweet spots were. He moved to the back of the kitchen and leaned close to the window. Aha. Two bars. He quickly punched some buttons and held the phone to his ear.

It rang once. Twice.

"I'm still at the church, locking up," Frank said. "Is Bea all right?"

Mitch's blood froze. "What do you mean?"

Had Frank heard something about Bea? If anything happened to her, he would have only himself to blame.

"She wasn't at the service this morning."

"Oh, right. No, it's my mother."

"What happened?"

Mitch moved away from his father and lowered his voice. "She ran off. We can't find her."

"Oh my. Lord, protect her. Did you contact the sheriff?"

"Not yet. The department's probably all tied up down at the interstate. I thought . . ."

His stomach clenched. Did he really want to do this? It was the stupid prayer chain that had first strained his relationship with Frank, back when Caroline got diagnosed. Frank had put the message out about Caroline's sickness before Mitch could agree. Before Mitch was ready for the onslaught of people saying, "We're praying for you," and, "We're so sorry to hear that."

Mitch's chest tightened. The blatant invasion of privacy. The argument he and Frank had had afterward. And what right did Mitch have now, calling on Frank and the people of Moose Creek Community Church for help in his time of need, after the way he'd treated them the past two years? And yet he was desperate.

"You want me to activate the chain?" Frank had his pastor voice on.

"I . . ." Mitch gripped the phone. If he said yes, help would be on the way in no time. The church's prayer chain would spread the news faster than a grass fire in July, and dozens of people would be here in less than an hour. All the same people who had intruded on his life when Caroline died, refusing him the courtesy of grieving on his own terms.

"Mitch?"

His phone beeped, and he pulled it from his ear to check the screen. A text had come through. "Hold on, Frank."

He swiped the screen, and the message appeared. His heart

caught. It was from Bea. He squinted at it, trying to decipher the words.

> Stick up wife tail password road. Ned help. Grsdnma j with me.

What on earth? He read the words again, and a swell of hope washed over him.

He pulled his truck keys from his pocket. "Never mind the prayer chain, Frank. I know where she is. We're leaving right now."

If Frank responded, Mitch didn't hear. He was already headed for the front door, jerking his chin at his dad to follow him.

"Mom is with Bea." He held the door open for his father. "They're stuck up on Whitetail Pass Road."

◆ ◆ ◆

Bea prodded Grandma June and called her name. She pinched her arm and even blew in her face. Nothing. A rattlesnake of dread coiled in her stomach, ready to strike. How had she let herself get into this mess?

A truck with a round bale in the back drove up, its headlights shining through the pelting snow. Bea waved an arm, but it sped right past. She turned back to Grandma June, failing to keep tears from falling.

"What happened to Miner McGee?" she shouted.

Grandma's eyes flew open. "He refused to wait until spring, so up the mountain he went. Just as the worst blizzard Moose Creek had ever seen fell upon the land."

Bea's throat tightened as she reached over and held her grandmother's hand.

"The snow fell for three whole days," Grandma continued, her voice soft as if remembering. "When it finally stopped, the people of Moose Creek gathered to decide whether to send a search party for Miner McGee's body right then or wait . . ."

Bea's whole body tensed, willing Grandma June to go on. To keep talking. The snow outside was still falling but not piling up as fast. The flakes were smaller now. Bea glanced at the Toyota's gas gauge. Less than a quarter of a tank. How long would she be able to keep the car running and warm?

"What did the people decide, Grandma?"

Grandma June shook her head. "What?"

"What did the people of Moose Creek decide to do about Miner McGee's body?"

"Oh." Grandma sat up a little straighter. "Yes. Well, as they were talking, the sun sank low in the sky, and someone shouted, 'Look!' And there on the mountain was Miner McGee's headlamp, shining bright for all to see as he searched for his treasure." She looked out the window, and her shoulders slumped.

Bea tugged on her hand. "Grandma?"

"Ever since that day, whenever the sun sinks low in the sky, you can see his lamp click on."

Bea swallowed hard. "What if he never finds the Big Sky Diamond?"

Grandma June pulled her hand away and touched the glass. "I will find him. I'll never give up."

A shiver ran down Bea's spine. She wished she knew what her grandma was talking about. Who she was talking about. And she wished she knew what else to say to keep her alert now that the story was finished.

"Who are you looking for, Grandma? Tell me about him."

Grandma June turned blank eyes on Bea. Her eyelids drooped.

Bea forced a smile. "Grandma?"

There was no answer except the whump-whump-whump of the windshield wipers sliding back and forth. Bea checked her phone again, as if somehow it would've recharged itself. The black screen caused an empty feeling to open up in her chest. She hated being helpless. Vulnerable. Like that night in Atlanta when she was walking back to her dorm after a late dinner . . .

A low growl broke through her thoughts. What was that? She sat up. A truck. And not just any truck. She knew that engine.

She used her sleeve to wipe at the foggy window and peered through. Dad's truck pulled off the road onto the turnout and stopped. Dad and Grandpa Rand hopped out.

Bea began to sob.

TWENTY-SEVEN

Jeremy squeezed her shoulder. "Are you sure you're okay?"

"Stop asking me that." Bea flinched at the sharpness of her words. She closed her eyes and softened her voice. "Please."

Her head hurt. She was exhausted. Dad and Grandpa Rand had helped Grandma June into Dad's truck so they could take her straight to the hospital. Then they'd helped Bea get the Toyota back on the road and insisted she drive straight home. She'd argued that she wanted to go along with them, but Dad wouldn't hear it. "Jeremy's expecting you," he'd said. "And I suspect Frank'll be there, too."

Dad had followed her in the truck until she turned onto Second Street, then continued driving down Highway 288 to the interstate. Bea had turned in her seat to watch as they drove on. Never had Ponderosa seemed so far away.

"Thank the Lord you found your grandma when you did." Pastor Frank shook his head. He'd been waiting with Jeremy when she arrived, just like Dad predicted. "God was watching out."

"Yeah." She stared at the table.

"That God would lead you to be driving way out there at

the same time she wandered off . . ." He smiled. "It's nothing short of a miracle."

She tried to smile back. It had been bittersweet to come home and find him sitting at their kitchen table. Sweet because he was such a dear old friend with whom she shared many fond memories. Bitter because the last time he'd been in their house was the day of Mom's funeral.

"I can't believe they let you drive yourself back." Jeremy set the hot tea he'd prepared for her on the table near her elbow. "You were in no condition to—"

"I'm fine." She wrapped her hands around the warm mug. "It was fine. Grandma was the main concern."

"Well, you're *my* main concern." Jeremy frowned. "Are you sure you're—"

She shot him a look.

He held up his hands. "Sorry, but I was really worried."

She took a sip of tea and leaned her arms on the table. When she'd gotten home, it had taken every bit of energy she could muster to change out of her wet clothes and take a hot shower. Jeremy had taken one look at her wet hair and ordered her back upstairs to blow-dry it, as if it would make any difference now. Still, she appreciated his concern.

Her phone rang from where it was charging on the counter. When she moved to stand and grab it, Jeremy held up a hand. "I'll get it."

He handed her the phone, and she glimpsed Dad's name on the screen. "Hi, Dad. Did you make it? How's Grandma?"

The voice on the other end was crisp and clear, as if an entire mountain didn't stand between them. "The roads were terrible. Wrecks everywhere, like I figured. But they took her back right away and are giving her fluids and checking everything. She'll be spending at least one night. Maybe more. That's all I know right now."

Jeremy and Pastor Frank leaned toward her, eager for news.

"Did she wake up? Does she feel okay?"

"She woke up all right." Dad snorted. "Halfway to Ponderosa, she panicked and started screaming about searching for treasure. Then when we tried to get her into a wheelchair to wheel her into the hospital, she sat down on the ground, right in the snow, and refused to move."

Bea nodded to herself. It was amazing how strong and stubborn Grandma could be when she set her mind on something. Bea had learned that the hard way. She rubbed her right knee. It was going to be sore for a while.

"Are you going to stay there?" she asked.

Dad hesitated. "I think your grandpa's going to insist on spending the night. I should probably stay with him."

She wanted to ask how Grandma could get so bad so fast. How the doctors were going to explain the seeming stranger she'd picked up at Pass Creek School. Instead, she finished with "Okay. Keep us posted."

"Will do."

She hung up the phone and filled Jeremy and Pastor Frank in on what she'd learned.

Pastor Frank tapped the table thoughtfully. "I think I'll head over to the hospital if they're going to stay awhile, now that I know you're okay. Is there anything you need?"

Bea shook her head. "Thanks for coming."

"Of course." Pastor Frank patted her hand. "Dorothy and I will be praying for all of you. And if there's anything else I can do . . ."

"Okay."

He gave Jeremy a meaningful look. "You got my number?"

Jeremy nodded.

"I'll see myself out."

She listened to Pastor Frank clomp down the hall and out the door. Having him around was so familiar and yet so strange. His family and hers used to come and go from each other's houses as if they were related. But everything was different now.

Jeremy pulled up a chair beside her as she took another sip of tea. "Can I get you anything? Are you hungry?"

Stop fussing over me, she wanted to scream. But she took one look at the concern on her husband's face and felt tears well up in her eyes. Hot coffee, not again.

She fought back the waterworks as best she could. "A little. Are you?"

He put a gentle hand on her back. "A little. I wish there was a pizza place I could call for delivery."

The only places open on a Sunday evening in Moose Creek were the gas station and the bars. Peggy's Place was actually a bar and grill and made pretty good chicken-strip baskets, but they definitely didn't deliver.

"What's in the fridge?"

Jeremy stood to find out. "There are a few things I miss about the big city."

"Pizza delivery's not that special."

"That's not what I meant." Rogue ice cubes spit from the freezer and onto the floor when he opened the fridge. "I was thinking of uninterrupted cell service."

"Oh. Yeah."

He pulled out leftover venison burgers and slid them onto a plate and into the microwave. "It scared me when I couldn't reach you, and no one was here."

"That's just the way it is out here."

"You must've known you were going to lose service. You could've called before that."

She held back a huff. "It's not like I planned this, Jeremy. Plus, my battery died. Cell service doesn't matter if your phone's dead."

He turned his back on her to glare at the microwave. "You managed to text your dad. You let *him* know where you were."

"Is that what this is about?" She cursed the pain and weariness in her forehead. "I was lucky to send any texts at all."

"But why him and not me?"

"It all happened so fast. I knew he'd be able to figure out what I meant."

"And I wouldn't?"

She threw up her hands. "I don't know—you tell me. Do you know where Whitetail Pass Road is?"

The microwave dinged, and he pushed the button to open it. He pulled the plate out and practically flung it on the counter, still not looking at her. "No. But I would've found it. I would've done whatever it took to get to you."

"And how would you have gotten there?" Her voice was strained and heated. "I had your stupid car, and you don't know how to drive Dad's truck."

He spun around, hurt darkening the blue of his eyes. "It's *our* stupid car. And I could've gotten your dad to drive."

"Which is why I texted him in the first place."

There. She'd said it. The words hung unappealing and ominous between them, but they were true. When the split-second moment of decision had come, she'd known her dad was the better person to contact. Even if he had been the reason she'd gone out in the first place. Even if he was going to say "I told you so" about the tires on the car. She'd known she could count on him.

Jeremy was her husband, and she loved him, but in the moment of crisis, he'd seemed so untested. What had they really been through together? How would she know if she could trust him to come through?

He set a plate in front of her with a clunk. "You should eat something."

She stared at her lap, avoiding his eyes. "What about you?"

"I'm not hungry anymore."

He turned to leave, and those pesky tears welled up again. They burned.

"Please." Her constricted throat barely allowed the word to slip through. "I'm sorry. Don't leave me alone."

Her body trembled as she fought against the sobs that wanted to burst from her mouth. What a horrible day. What a stinking, rotten pile-of-hot-coffee kind of day.

Jeremy's hand landed lightly on her shoulder.

She stiffened in surprise, then leaned her cheek against his tattooed forearm, feeling the cross on her skin. "I don't know what to say." Her voice was low and strained. "I don't know what you need from me."

No one had ever told her marriage would be this hard.

"I need you to choose me."

Tears fell from the corner of her eye onto his hand. She'd married him, hadn't she? Yet it seemed like that wasn't enough, and she wasn't sure why. If her mom were here, she would understand. She would tell Bea what she was supposed to do. But Bea was alone. Grandma June was in the hospital. Dad and Grandpa Rand had left Bea to take care of herself. Mom was dead. Bea had only Jeremy, and she didn't know how to tell him about the turmoil in her heart.

If he would ask her again if she was okay, just one more time, she would say no. Admit that she was afraid and unsure and ask for help.

But he didn't.

TWENTY-EIGHT

I'm calm now, apparently. That's what everyone says when they come in the room and see me lying here like an infant. "She's so calm." As if I can't hear them. As if it's some sort of miracle that I'm not flailing around in a tizzy. Well, maybe it is.

Rand's hound-dog face is enough to make me wonder if there's something they're not telling me. He just sits there looking sad, patting my hand and saying he's sorry. I don't know what he's sorry about. I'm pretty sure I'm the one who's got everybody worked up. I slide one hand under my covers and search for a pocket, but whatever I'm wearing's got none.

My body aches from this bed. They tell me I've been lying here since yesterday afternoon, so I guess that explains that. I don't remember being here yesterday afternoon. I just remember waking up this morning and my eyes bugging out when I saw Rand sleeping in an ugly gray chair next to me. He never has liked us being too far apart. Over the years, if he had to drive somewhere, he always insisted I go along. I never minded.

Then Mitch came waltzing into the room without even knocking, all astonished to see me looking at him. Not long after that, a doctor came in talking in some sort of cryptic language. It's been a couple hours now, and I've had about as much of this—whatever *this* is—as I can take.

"Where's Bea?" I ask.

Mitch is messing with his phone, but he looks up when he hears me speak. "She's at home. Resting."

Resting? "Is she okay?"

"Yeah." Mitch exchanges a look with Rand. "She's fine. Just a little tired after your ordeal yesterday."

My ordeal? That sounds awfully dramatic. "What happened?"

He gives Rand that same look again. Mylanta.

"We told you all about it when you woke up this morning." He speaks slowly and carefully like I'm three years old. "Do you remember that?"

I frown. I remember being cold. Really cold. I remember waking up. I remember the doctor and everyone talking, talking, talking. But what had they said about yesterday? My cheeks burn with shame. I want to remember. I shake my head.

Mitch stands and moves over to my bed. I can't read what that is in his eyes. He puts a hand on my arm. "You walked away from the house when Dad was out riding. Got caught out in the snow. Bea found you and drove you up the mountain."

My brows wrinkle. "Why would she do that?"

"She said you insisted. She said you were looking for someone. Do you remember?"

Icy hands press against my chest, making it hard to breathe. The snow is falling on my face. My son is out there somewhere, waiting for me. Wondering where I am.

"Mom?"

I take a deep breath. Mitch is my son. And he's right here. I look up at his face. "Bea's okay?"

He pats my arm. "She's fine. Everyone's fine."

"Then why am I here?"

Mitch looks back at Rand, who clears his throat. "You have an infection, June. A bad one."

"What do you mean? What infection?"

He looks embarrassed. "A urinary tract infection. They've got you on antibiotics."

I scowl. "I don't want antibiotics."

"The doctors are also running some tests." His look is more sheepish than embarrassed now. "On your blood."

I stare at him, an ember of anger warming my chest where moments ago it had been frozen. They took my blood, and I didn't even know it. I couldn't even remember. Who gave them permission?

"We're waiting for the results," Mitch says. "They don't want you to leave until you're stable."

I feel perfectly stable, but I say nothing. Whatever it is in Mitch's eyes is in Rand's eyes, too. Fear rises in my throat like words I wish I could say.

"How much longer?"

My son hesitates. "We don't know yet."

"I want to go home."

"I know." He rubs the back of his neck. "I know. But, Mom, you walked away into a snowstorm. You could've—"

He clears his throat. I blink. He straightens, standing tall. "You could've died. If Bea hadn't found you . . ."

I try to push through the fog surrounding his words to hear what he's really trying to say, but my mind can't seem to fight its way through. The fog is thick and heavy. Shadowy. Dangerous.

Sometimes when the clouds are low, the Bridger Mountains disappear. A person can drive past on the interstate and never even know they're there. The clouds are like a cloak. A shroud. But if you know where the mountains are, you can feel them. You can sense their towering presence and know that everything is where it should be, even if you can't see it.

I peer at Mitch's face and search for the mountain through the clouds. I know it's there. I squint and lean closer, straining to make out the shape of my memories. To distinguish between the figures and shapes, the lies and the truth. The real and imagined.

"I want to go home," I say again, and that's when I see it. The outline of what Mitch was trying to say.

He can't trust me anymore. I am not safe.

There is a tall, stark mountain peak cutting through the mist like a knife. And I can't drive by and pretend it isn't there.

TWENTY-NINE

Mitch shifted the truck into park in front of his parents' house and let out a slow breath. It had been a long couple of days. Kenny Chesney's hit "Don't Blink" faded from the radio speakers, and Mitch looked over at his mother in the passenger seat. The song was about how fast life goes by. How fast things change. It was fitting.

As he moved to open his door, his father reached up from the back seat and put a hand on his arm.

"No need to walk us in. We'll be all right."

Mitch turned and gaped at him. They would be all right? How did he figure that? His mother had just spent two nights in the hospital because she thought she could climb the mountain on foot searching for lost treasure. What about that was "all right"? Then he noted the hard set of his father's jaw, the determination in his eyes. Mitch didn't want to pick a fight.

He took his hand off the door handle. "Are you sure?"

June opened her door and stepped outside. The October sky was clear, the sun reflecting off the new snow blinding. She stood there with her face turned up, and Mitch could see the woman who used to race him to the barn and churn homemade ice cream and swat his backside. The woman who used to remember everything.

She stuck one hand in her pocket, held the other out to the side as if welcoming whatever was to come, and started walking unhurriedly toward the house.

Rand moved to open his door and follow her.

"Dad, wait."

He paused.

Mitch cleared his throat. "I don't feel right about this."

"It's not up to you."

"But—"

"I won't leave her again." His father's voice was resolute with a hint of defensiveness.

Mitch studied his mother through the windshield as she climbed the porch steps. "You can't watch her every second. You have to sleep."

"You heard what the doctor said about her blood work. Her system's all out of whack." Rand held up a plastic bag. "I got all her supplements right here. I'll see that she takes them. And now that her infection's under control . . ."

"Is the list in there?"

Rand nodded. The doctor had printed off a list of do's and don'ts for what kinds of things his mom should be eating and drinking. He'd told them there was no cure for dementia but managing her health would help with her symptoms and slow the rate of deterioration. Especially if they could keep her UTI from returning.

The doctor had been optimistic about the improvements they might see if they got his mother's levels under control, but Mitch was less certain. Any positive changes, if they ever came, weren't going to happen overnight.

"You'll call me if you need anything?"

"Yeah."

"And you'll lock the doors at night?"

Rand hesitated. "She knows how to unlock doors, son."

"She might forget. It might slow her down."

Rand slid out of the truck and looked at Mitch through the open door, clutching the bag. "You'll come get us Friday for the CT scan?"

That was another thing Mitch worried about. Though his father's cataracts were fairly mild, they were enough to make driving in the dark dangerous. And the long nights of winter were only just beginning. "Of course."

Rand jerked his chin once, shut the door, then limped toward the house. Mitch growled like a cornered raccoon. If something happened while he wasn't here, he'd never forgive himself. But it wasn't his house. Wasn't his decision. He and his father needed to have a talk about his mom's future, but that would have to wait for another day. Maybe the doctor was right and a steady diet of omega-3 and cranberry juice would make all the difference in the world.

Mitch turned the truck around and drove slowly down the snow-packed gravel drive. He didn't know if he was doing the right thing. He didn't know if Caroline would believe his mother was going to be fine, or if she would insist on moving his mother out of that house right this instant. He didn't know how to do this by himself.

Why'd you have to take her, God? It would've been better if God had taken him instead. He wasn't himself without Caroline.

Taylor Swift's "Back to December" came on the radio, and Mitch stiffened. *Oh, Lord, not Taylor Swift. Not now.* He wasn't sure his heart could take it.

He reached to change the station, but as the words filled the cab—poignant words about loss and regret—his hand hesitated. He imagined Caroline riding beside him, singing along, and pain roared through the gully in his heart like snowmelt rushing down the mountain, washing out everything in its path.

The song might be called "Back to December," but there was no going back.

❖ ❖ ❖

"Sorry to leave you hanging for a couple days, Ralph." Mitch filled his thermos with coffee from the pot and glanced around the town office. "And with all that snow to clear."

Ralph shrugged. "Jimmy pitched in. And Janice didn't mind my working late. She said that Frank said your mom's doing better?"

Mitch took a swig of coffee. Same as him, Ralph never called Frank "Pastor Frank" like most everyone else. He'd rather go a couple of rounds with a grizzly than darken the door of Moose Creek Community Church. But Janice was a faithful attender.

"I don't know about better, but she's home."

"Lucky Bea found her when she did."

The story had already spread through town. Mitch nodded, his mind struggling to focus, to shake off the image of his wife sitting beside him in the truck, singing along to the radio. He clenched his jaw. He had a lot of work to do, and it was time to get to it. He was lucky he'd been able to take Monday and Tuesday off, no questions asked.

He and Ralph pulled on their coats and left the office to step into the sunshine. Mitch squinted in the sudden brightness.

"You want to start north, and I'll start south?" Ralph asked. "Meet in the middle?"

It was twelve degrees this morning, although temperatures were expected to rise to the upper forties by Friday. They needed to inspect all the town drains before the snow started melting. Clear any obstructions to avoid flooding.

"Sure."

Ralph gave him a two-finger salute and headed toward one town truck as Mitch headed for the other. Before either of them reached their vehicles, a voice rang out through the crisp air.

"Yoo-hoo."

Mitch froze. Funny how sound carried farther and more clearly when it was cold.

"Mitch, I was hoping I'd run into you."

He spun to face the woman approaching him. Marge. He glanced over at Ralph, hoping he had gotten in his truck and would soon drive away, but no such luck. Ralph had stopped midstride and turned around to watch. Boy, oh boy.

Marge came closer and smiled. "I stopped by your house, and Jeremy said you were back at work today."

Of course he had. And what else had Jeremy told her?

"I haven't had a shift yet this week, but if I'd been at the hospital, I would've stopped by June's room to check on everybody." Marge fussed with her hair, which frizzed around her face and reminded him of dandelions. Always popping up everywhere no matter what you did to get them under control.

"Uh, yeah." He didn't need her checking in or stopping by. "Which department do you work in again?"

"Pediatrics. But I could've snuck over to see you."

He fiddled with the zipper on his jacket. "It's probably good you didn't have to make the drive to Ponderosa in the snow."

"I wouldn't have minded." She gave him a steady look.

He looked away. "Well, I gotta—"

"I dropped off a pot of chili, but I wanted to see if there's anything else you need." Her smile grew bigger, if that was possible. "Such a scary incident with your mom. I bet you're glad to be home." She looked around, and her smile faltered. "Not that you're home, I just mean, um . . ."

"Thanks." He tried to return her smile and put her at ease. "That's nice of you, but we're fine."

"Okay." She crossed her arms, then uncrossed them. Then clasped her hands behind her back. "I was just thinking that with everything going on, you probably haven't given any more thought to your birthday party."

"My birth—?" He could feel Ralph's eyes on his back. "Oh, right. Well, it's still weeks away."

"Less than two weeks."

He opened his mouth but darned if he wasn't flat-out speechless.

"Anyway," Marge continued, "I wanted to offer to make your cake."

"My cake?"

"One less thing for you to worry about. German chocolate's your favorite, right?"

A birthday cake was not on the list of things he was or had ever been worried about. But she just stood there, shifting from foot to foot, waiting for a response. It was almost endearing. Wait, how did she know his favorite . . . ?

"You don't have to decide now. We'll talk again later." She turned to go. "I'll let you get back to work."

As she scurried off, Mitch clamped his lips together and pulled his keys from his pocket. What had just happened? Against his better judgment, he allowed his gaze to slip over to where Ralph stood. Ralph raised his eyebrows, made a show of looking in the direction Marge had gone, then climbed into his truck.

Oh, heck. It was a done deal now. Some kind of story about him and Marge would be all over town by the time he got home from work. And he had Jeremy to thank for it.

THIRTY

Mitch inched down Second Street at the end of the day, his mind on his mother and his daughter instead of the road. As he sang the melancholy words of "Desperado" along with Clint Black, he couldn't help but think of Marge, as well. He was convinced he was fine on his own. Didn't need anyone else in his life after losing the only person who was everything.

But that was what the desperado thought, too, and old Clint didn't seem to think that was going to turn out so well.

A flash of movement caught Mitch's eye, and he slammed on the brakes. A deer darted in front of his truck, pausing on the side of the road to stare at him a moment before bounding out of sight. His heart pounded. Deer wandered through town a lot this time of year, snitching apples that had fallen to the ground and leaving scat in everyone's backyards. He needed to pay more attention. That was too close.

On full alert now, he noticed a Suburban parked in front of his house. He eyed it as he pulled the truck into the alley. Frank. What was he doing here?

Dusk softened the edges of the mountain as Mitch walked around the outside of the house. After Caroline died, the distance from the carport to the front door had grown with the distance between him and the last time she'd been here waiting for him. But as he reached the door this time, it struck him that the distance had shortened the past few weeks, not lengthened. Was it because his eyes had moved somewhat toward the future instead of just the past?

Frank was in the living room, sitting on the couch with his fingers laced behind his head.

"Who let you in?" Mitch tried to put a growl in his voice, but Frank was unfazed.

"Bea and Jeremy went for a walk. None of us knew how late you'd be working."

"You could've texted."

"I could've."

Mitch hung up his jacket and keys and kicked off his boots. "You eat yet?"

"No." Frank let his arms down and moved his hands to his knees. "But Dorothy would kill me if I had dinner with you. She's waiting for me."

"Then you better say whatever you came here to say so you can get home to her." Mitch wanted to add something about how Frank didn't know how lucky he was to have someone to go home to, but he couldn't bring himself to do it. And he had a feeling Frank did know.

Frank indicated the empty space next to him on the couch, and Mitch huffed. He chose the recliner across from the couch instead.

"Dorothy said that Barbara said that Ralph and MacGregor were talking about you and Marge at the store this afternoon."

Mitch groaned. "I knew it. It's all Jeremy's fault."

Frank's forehead wrinkled. "Don't see how that's possible."

"That's why you're here? Because of Marge?"

"No, I just wanted to mention it so I could see the look on your face."

Mitch scowled. "How's this for a look?"

Frank laughed. "Marge is a wonderful lady, you know. There's a lot more to her than you probably think."

"What'd you really come here for?"

"To check on you. To see how you're doing since bringing your parents home yesterday."

With his left hand, Mitch massaged his right shoulder where it was tight from shoveling all day. He had appreciated it when Frank showed up at the hospital Sunday. He knew Frank cared. But he wasn't too sure about all the checking up going on. First Marge, now Frank. And he wasn't too sure how he felt about Frank acting like they hadn't spent the last two years estranged.

"We're hopeful Mom will be less disoriented now that her infection is under control. The doctor's got her on supplements and antibiotics and a strict diet."

"That's good news. I'll keep praying for her. But I asked how *you* are doing. And don't say *fine*."

"Oh, please." Mitch leaned his head back on the chair. "Not this again."

Frank leaned toward him. "Not what?"

Mitch stifled another groan. It was like déjà vu, Frank looking all concerned and trying to pull the truth out of him with his pastor voice about how not fine Mitch really was. When they'd gotten the news about Caroline . . .

Mitch scrubbed a hand over his face. It'd be a lot easier to get mad at Frank if he wasn't so darn sincere about it all.

Frank softened his voice. "Am I not allowed to care about my best friend?"

"Well, how are *you* doing?"

Frank sat back.

Mitch shrugged. "I'll tell you how I'm doing if you go first."

"Okay." Frank nodded. "That's fair."

"And don't say *fine*."

Frank chuckled.

Mitch waited.

Frank studied the floor.

Mitch raised his eyebrows. "It's not so easy, is it?"

Frank clutched his knees with his fingers. "People usually jump at the chance to tell me about their problems, but no one ever wonders about mine."

"I'm wondering now. How's everything? How's your family?"

"Hannah's away at school, as you know. She wants to be a music teacher."

"That's great."

"Yeah." Frank rubbed his hands together. "We're very proud. You know how Dorothy loves music. Still getting used to all the college expenses, though. And Seth graduates in May, so the church . . ."

Mitch's stomach grumbled. Lunch was a long time ago, but food could wait. Something in Frank's voice made him tense up. "The church what?"

"Oh, it's nothing." Frank waved a hand as if clearing smoke. "Just some changes they want to make."

If it was nothing, Frank wouldn't have mentioned it. "What changes?"

For a minute, Frank didn't answer, and Mitch studied him, remembering what it had been like between them back before adulthood and families and church had gotten in the way. The hunting trips, the late-night talks about girls, the rescue missions to pick up friends too drunk to get themselves home. That would've been Mitch if not for Frank.

"There's a handful of people calling for a pay cut," Frank finally said. "When Seth leaves home. They figure Dorothy and I won't need as much income once we're empty nesters."

Mitch grimaced. "You're kidding."

"It's okay." Frank suddenly looked very weary. "The church has always struggled to make ends meet. That's just how it is. Decreasing my salary will help."

"But they can't do that." Mitch could feel his blood warming. "It's not fair. You aren't getting paid that much as it is. How are you supposed to put two kids through college on *less*?"

"It's not the church's responsibility to put my kids through college. Why should they pay for that when most of them can't send their own kids?"

"You're not being reasonable."

"I'm being realistic." Frank looked at the floor. "I shouldn't have said anything."

Mitch struggled to keep his mouth shut. Frank had faithfully served the folks of Moose Creek Community Church for twenty years—twenty years!—without complaint. He'd married them, baptized them, taught them, prayed for them, and buried them. He'd helped them during harvest and made countless trips to Ponderosa, visiting them in the hospital. Or in jail. And this was how they would thank him?

"I can always pick up more hours at Take Your Best Shot." Frank shook his head. "We all do what we have to do."

Mitch crossed his arms over his chest. "Well, I don't like it."

"I appreciate that." Some of the spark returned to Frank's eyes. "Now it's your turn. How are you handling this thing with your mom? And having Bea back?"

"Just taking it one day at a time, I guess. Mom seemed much better yesterday."

"And if she gets worse?"

Mitch hesitated. There'd been no official diagnosis yet, but from everything the doctors had said so far, there was no *if*. Only *when*. "We'll cross that bridge when we come to it."

"Do you think your dad can manage her okay by himself?"

He didn't answer, but Frank had always been exceptionally good at reading his face.

"You're worried," he said.

Mitch nodded. "We got lucky this time. With Bea finding her like that. But what if . . . ?"

"That wasn't luck, and you know it."

"The weather's only going to get worse from here. It's only going to get colder and darker. How long can a person survive out in the elements when it's twenty below?"

He hadn't meant to say all that. He preferred to keep his fears to himself. But Frank had a way of drawing people out.

"Have you talked with your dad about moving her somewhere?"

Mitch's shoulders slumped. "Not yet. But it needs to happen soon."

"And what about Bea? She doing okay?"

"I don't know. She's not speaking to me much right now."

Frank nodded knowingly. When his daughter, Hannah, was sixteen, she'd gone through a brief but intense rebellious phase. Ran away and everything. Mitch had never seen Frank so torn up.

Frank stood. "Well, I better go. I'll be praying for you."

Mitch walked him to the door. From anyone else, those words would feel trite. Condescending even. When Frank said them, though, he felt a small sense of relief, maybe because he knew Frank meant it. He spent hours in prayer. Mitch had caught him on his knees in his office more times than he could count.

"Thanks for coming by."

Frank squeezed his shoulder. "Talk to you soon."

Mitch closed the door after him and stood in the hallway for a moment, listening to the silence and remembering the time he'd shown Frank to the door and told him not to bother ever coming back. It had been his anger and grief talking—he knew that now. He only hoped Frank knew it then.

◆　◆　◆

The tip of Bea's nose was frozen, while the rest of her was surprisingly warm. Her coat, hat, and gloves, along with the brisk pace of their walk, were doing the trick. Beside her, Jeremy hummed a Mark Chesnutt tune.

"That's an old one," she said.

"I like the classic country station better than the other."

She smiled, pleased. "Me too."

They walked in silence for several minutes.

"Let me know when you want to head back," Jeremy said.

Bea chuckled to herself. That was his nonconfrontational way of saying he was about done with this whole walking around town in the dark and cold thing.

"In a minute."

She loved the peaceful feeling of Moose Creek tucking itself in for the night. All the Ponderosa commuters had made it home by now. Football and volleyball practices were over at the school. Families were finishing dinner and getting kids ready for bed. And that was it. There was nothing else going on.

"You think your grandma will be okay out on the ranch?" Jeremy's words formed puffs of steam in the cold air.

She shrugged. "I don't know. I'm scared she's going to end up in a nursing home somewhere."

"She's too young for a nursing home."

"But it seems like there's something really wrong. The things she said that day . . ."

"What do you mean?"

Things had been strained between her and Jeremy since Sunday, but she needed to talk to someone about Grandma June's unsettling words.

"She kept talking about how she needed to find someone. How he must be wondering where she was. I asked if she meant Grandpa Rand, and she said yes, but I don't think that was it."

"Why not?"

"I'm not sure."

Bea paused as they reached the end of Mule Deer Road and

looked up. The stars were starting to come out, flickering into view one at a time as the sky darkened.

"I've never seen so many stars," Jeremy said.

She'd missed them. The glare of the city lights had hidden all but the brightest stars and turned the blackness of night into a yellowish haze. Here, she could see every level of intensity, from the piercing light of a neighboring planet to the soft glow of the most distant star. The degrees of light gave the sky both dimension and depth. It reminded a person of how small they were in the grand scheme of things. And how big God was.

Bea stared at the great swirls of distant galaxies and thought of the snow swirling around her and grandma on the mountain. "She kept saying she would never forget."

Jeremy stood close, his arm touching hers. "Forget what?"

"Her baby? I don't know, it doesn't make sense. I tried to get her to tell me about Miner McGee, and she said her baby would've liked that story."

"Do you think she was confused about what year it was? Like her mind had taken her back to when your dad was born? And since there was no baby in her house, she could've thought something happened to him."

"Maybe."

"That could explain why she took off like that. She was just being a good mom."

Bea shivered, the cold catching up to her now that they had stopped walking. "What about saying she would never forget him? She sounded so sad."

"It's strange all right." Jeremy lowered his chin so the high collar of his jacket covered his mouth. "Your dad never had any siblings?"

Bea shook her head. "Unless . . ."

"What?"

"I don't know, maybe she lost a baby once. Like a miscarriage or something." Her gloved hands found their way to her belly, and she swallowed hard. "A lot of women delivered their babies at home back then. Anything could've happened."

"That would make sense." His jacket muffled his words. "And it wouldn't be surprising for her to fixate on a memory that traumatic. Maybe your dad knows something about it."

"Maybe."

"We could ask him. Or I could do a little digging online. It's amazing what you can find out on the internet."

"I've always wondered why my dad is an only child. Most people from my grandma's generation had like a dozen kids, especially farming families."

"You're an only child."

"I know, but that's more common now. Back then . . ."

"I'll do some research. See if I can find anything out."

"Okay." Bea drew in a slow, deep breath, then turned. Night had fallen in earnest. "We should head back."

As they walked side by side, she felt there was more Jeremy wanted to say, but he remained quiet. Snow and gravel crunched under their boots, unusually loud in the stillness. The snow-covered mountain glowed in the moonlight. As they approached a rugged old shiplap house, Bea slowed her pace.

"Look at that." She jerked her chin at the house.

"Isn't that your old teacher?"

"Yep."

"And the old guy from the four-wheeler? Ernest?"

"Earl."

"He looks happy."

Through the window, they could see Earl sitting at a table across from Mr. Jamison. A chessboard sat between them with various pieces placed all around as if the game was in full swing. Earl made a move, and Mr. Jamison threw his hands up in mock protest. Earl laughed. Maybe he didn't need a social worker for the elderly. He just needed someone like Mr. Jamison.

Bea couldn't help but smile. "His family all moved away, you know. On to bigger and better things. They come visit once in a while, mainly to tell him what to do, but for the most part he's on his own."

Jeremy stomped his feet, a sure sign he was losing feeling in his toes. "Looks like he found a friend."

Bea started walking again but looked back once before the house was out of sight. It was a powerful thing to have a friend. She'd never thought much about it before, but couldn't just one friend make a world of difference in someone's life? She thought of Amber. And her dad. He used to have Pastor Frank, but now he kind of had no one.

She had Jeremy. For better or worse. She reached out and took his hand, and he gripped hers back tightly. All those trillions of stars floating around the limitless sky, and she was a speck of dust in the vastness of forever. But she had Jeremy.

THIRTY-ONE

Her dad paused at the door, keys in hand. "Are you sure you don't want to come?"

Bea looked down at Steve as he rubbed his head against her ankle. Part of her wanted to tag along to Grandma June's appointment, while another part—the part that could barely drag itself out of bed this morning—screamed that this was a rare Friday morning off, and she needed to rest. Plus, she wasn't sure she wanted to be stuck in the truck with her dad.

"I think I'll just hang out and wait for my shift to start. You can tell me about it later."

"I don't like leaving you here without a vehicle."

She only barely resisted the urge to roll her eyes. "I'll be fine."

Dad flipped up the collar of his coat and opened the door. "Okay."

He left the house, and Bea looked back down at Steve, now sitting at her feet. "It's just you and me today, I guess."

Jeremy had gotten up early to go to Billings for "research." She'd asked him how much longer it might be before he had a solid business plan, and his eyes had dimmed. "I'm not sure," he'd said. "I'm still looking for my place in all this."

It had seemed so simple at first, when she and Jeremy got engaged. They loved each other and would figure it out as they

209

went along. What else did they need to know? Now here they were. A college dropout working part-time at a grocery store and an unemployed city kid trying to figure out rural life. With a baby on the way.

She wished she could go back to the day they moved into their crummy apartment in Santa Clara. They'd said, *"This will be an adventure. As long as we have each other, we'll be fine."* She had a few things to tell those two naïve kids. Like how humiliating it was going to be to move back in with her dad, for starters.

Bea plodded to the couch and flopped onto it. Wasn't she still just a naïve kid? Maybe Dad was right. Maybe she'd rushed into marrying Jeremy because of everything that happened with Mom. And maybe she didn't know him as well as she thought.

Steve jumped onto the back of the couch and curled up near her head, purring. She huffed. A cat's life was so uncomplicated. Her eyes began to drift closed, then flew back open at a knock on the door.

"Oh, man." She groaned as she pushed herself to her feet. If it was Marge coming by with another casserole, Bea was going to . . . well, she didn't know what she was going to do, but she wouldn't be too thrilled about it.

She flung open the door, ready to politely but firmly decline any and all food items, but it wasn't Marge. It was Amber and Hunter.

"Hey, guys." Bea smiled at Hunter as he nestled a sleepy face into his mom's shoulder. "Someone got a haircut."

Amber adjusted him on her hip and tousled his hair. "I did it myself. I always cut my mom's hair, so I figured I could do his. Saves money, you know."

"You did a good job. He looks very handsome." Bea stepped aside. "Come on in."

"Thanks." Amber kept a tight hold on Hunter as she

dropped his diaper bag on the floor. They both looked as tired as Bea felt.

Bea shut the door. "What are you guys up to?"

Amber looked a little nervous. "I was hoping you'd be able to watch Hunter again."

Bea raised her eyebrows. She'd been counting on getting some rest. And she was all alone. "Um . . ."

"I know I should've texted first. I'm sorry." Amber moved Hunter to the other side of her body. "Man, he's getting heavy."

"Is it Axel again?"

Amber nodded. "He says he's got some money for me."

Bea squirmed. That should be good news, right? Then why did it make her cringe inside? "Are you sure about this, Amber?"

"I need the money."

"No, I know." Bea spit out the words before she lost her nerve. "But I don't want you to get hurt again. I just wonder if he's really changed."

Amber glanced at Hunter, and a flash of uncertainty pinched her face before she gave Bea a big smile. "It's going to be fine. He wants to take me to breakfast. Just the two of us."

Bea eyed the baby warily. Despite her reservations about Axel, she did want to help her friend. Amber was the only person she'd connected with since coming back home. But after last time . . .

"When would you be back? I have to work at one."

Amber shifted on her feet. "Two hours, tops. I promise. It wasn't right for me to leave you hanging like that before."

Bea hesitated a moment more. Then her eyes landed on Hunter's newly trimmed head and an idea formed. "Okay." She forced some enthusiasm into her voice and reached for the baby. "But you owe me a favor in return."

Hunter whimpered as Amber released him. "Of course. Anything."

"Do you think you could cut my grandma's hair?"

Amber's face lit up. "Sure. I'd love to do that."

Hunter started to cry, and Bea frowned.

"I better go. He'll be fine." Amber opened the door. "He'll forget all about me in five minutes."

Bea did not feel as confident about that as Amber sounded. She nodded. "See you in two hours."

She took Hunter into the living room, where they watched out the window as Amber drove away.

"Mama," Hunter cried. He reached out and touched the glass. "Mama."

"It's okay, buddy." Bea massaged his back. "She'll be back soon."

Soon. Yep. Only one hour and fifty-nine minutes to go.

❖　❖　❖

Bea had tried everything. She had rocked him. Offered him snacks. Checked his diaper. She'd even sung a dozen songs. But Hunter was having none of it.

"What do you need, buddy?" She tousled his hair like she'd seen Amber do. "Do you miss your mom?"

He jerked around in her arms and wailed, "Mama! Mamaaaaaa . . ."

Oops. Shouldn't have brought up the M-word.

Steve stood nearby, ears perked. He meowed, clearly concerned.

"I know." She gave him an exasperated look. "I'm trying."

A quick check of the time told Bea they still had about fifty minutes to go. Her throat constricted, but she swallowed hard and steeled herself. She would not cry. She. Would. Not. Cry. The last thing anyone needed right now was more tears.

Hunter's wail raised itself an octave, and she winced. "Hot coffee."

Her back and shoulders ached from holding him. She eyed

the couch. If he was going to cry whether she was holding him or not, she might as well put him down for a minute. Just to stretch.

She laid him on the couch and raised her arms over her head. Ooh, that felt good. She twisted her torso back and forth. How did Amber do it? She pulled her phone out to check the time. Thirty-eight more minutes. She saw a flash of movement out of the corner of her eye, followed by a soft thud. Her heart stopped beating.

Hunter.

A piercing scream rent the air. Bea dove for the baby. He was on the floor. What had she been thinking setting him on the couch? She'd only been two steps away from him, but he had rolled onto the carpet.

"Are you okay, buddy?" Every muscle tensed as she scooped him up and examined him. "Are you hurt?"

She should've never agreed to watch him. Should've never turned her back. What kind of babysitter was she?

Oh, God, let him be okay. Let him be okay. Oh, Lord. Oh, God.

His face was red. Giant tears rolled down his cheeks. The screaming continued. She couldn't see any visible injuries, but how would she know if he was okay or not? Tears formed in her eyes, as well. This time she didn't fight them. Let them come. She was going to be a horrible mother just as she'd long suspected.

"Yoo-hoo. Bea?"

She knelt on the floor, rocking Hunter as he cried. Should she take him to the doctor? How was she going to explain this to Amber?

"Bea. My goodness."

Bea looked up. Marge stood in the hallway, hand on her chest. Where had she come from?

"I knocked, but no one answered." Marge took a step closer. "Then when I heard screaming . . ."

"He f-fell off the c-couch." Bea's chest heaved. Never in her life had she been so happy to see her neighbor. "I only looked away for t-two seconds."

"Oh, honey." Marge scurried over and joined her on the floor. She gently pulled Hunter from Bea's arms and kissed him on the forehead. "Who do we have here?"

Bea sniffled. "H-Hunter."

"Okay, Hunter, let's have a look at you." Marge talked softly to him as she carefully examined his arms and legs, his back and head, with the practiced movements of someone who worked with kids for a living. Hunter quieted and began to hiccup. "Where does it hurt?"

Snot ran from his nose, and he rubbed his eyes. Bea realized her fingernails were digging into her palms, and she shook out her hands.

"I think he's fine." Marge looked over at her. "I bet it scared him more than anything. Good thing you have this nice thick carpet in here."

Bea's brow furrowed. "He's fine?"

Marge nodded. "Completely fine."

"But he's been crying for over an hour. He wouldn't stop. I put him down to take a quick break, and—"

A small sob cut off her words. How could she have been so self-absorbed? Her thoughtlessness had endangered her friend's baby.

Marge stood Hunter up at the coffee table and stuck one hand in front of him to play with. While he pulled at her fingers, she placed her other hand on Bea's shoulder.

"I couldn't get him to stop," Bea said.

"Sometimes babies just cry. He probably misses his mother. Maybe he's extra tired. Maybe he has a tummy ache from gas."

"You got him to stop."

Marge shrugged. "He needed a distraction. And I have a lot more experience than you. You'll get the hang of it."

Bea watched Hunter poke Marge's hand. "I should wash his face."

"You go get a washcloth. I'll stay with him."

Bea scrambled to her feet and ran a washcloth under warm water in the bathroom. As she wrung it out, she took a deep breath. Then another. Hunter was fine. Amber would be back soon. Her life was not over.

Holy hormones.

She returned to the living room and held the washcloth out to Marge.

Marge didn't reach for it. "You go ahead."

Bea knelt beside Hunter but hesitated, sure he would start crying again if she touched him. But something needed to be done about the snot that had smeared all over his face and was starting to crust over. It had carpet fuzz stuck in it.

She carefully wiped his face. He pulled back, tossing his head back and forth, yet he didn't cry out. It took a couple of tries, but she got it all off.

"There." Marge smiled at the baby. "Good as new."

Bea resisted the urge to check the time. Probably only ten minutes or so until Amber's return. An awkward moment stretched between her and Marge as they watched Hunter play at the table.

"Thanks," Bea finally said. "For your help."

Marge waved a hand. "Sorry for barging in like that. I just got worried when I heard all the commotion."

"No, I'm glad you did."

"It wasn't locked."

"It never is."

Marge pushed a mass of wild curls from her face, revealing long earrings made from turquoise stones. They caught Hunter's eye, and he grabbed at them.

"No, no." Marge gently moved his hand away. "No touch."

"What did you need?" Bea asked. "I mean, what did you come over for? My dad's not home."

Marge blushed. "I know. I came to ask you about your plans for his birthday. I thought . . ."

She let the words hang there, pregnant with meaning. Bea stiffened. She thought *what*?

Bea forced her neck muscles to relax. Marge wasn't her enemy. She was her neighbor. A neighbor who had just helped her through a crisis. That the crisis turned out to be largely imaginary didn't negate the fact Bea was thankful Marge had shown up when she did.

"I hadn't thought much about it." Bea watched Hunter play. "I guess you could say I've had other things on my mind."

"I'd like to help."

Bea coughed. Her mom used to make a big deal out of Dad's birthday. She would prepare his favorite dinner and invite Grandma and Grandpa and Pastor Frank and his family. The crowning detail, though, had always been the homemade German chocolate cake. Every bit of it from scratch. A little hole opened up in her stomach. Had anyone made Dad a cake the past two years? Grandma June must have, right? Bea had been too preoccupied with herself to think about it.

"I don't know if he's made any plans."

Marge tickled Hunter's tummy, and he laughed. "He hasn't. He"—she seemed to be trying hard not to look at Bea—"told me."

Had he now. What else had he told her? It wasn't surprising that he hadn't made any plans. It *was* surprising that he'd mentioned that to Marge.

A small prick of panic poked at her chest. She didn't know how she felt about her dad and Marge talking. And there was no way Grandma June would be making Dad a cake this year. It was up to Bea. She wasn't much of a baker, but she knew where the recipe was, even though Mom had known it from memory and hadn't taken it out of the box in years. Bea could figure it out. Jeremy would help.

What if she ruined it?

"He hasn't mentioned anything to you?" Marge asked.

Bea wasn't about to tell her that she and her dad weren't talking much lately.

"It's on a Sunday, right?" Bea calculated the days in her head. "We'll probably do something after church."

Marge's voice turned airy, as if she was trying hard to sound nonchalant. "And is there anything I can do?"

Bea's mind raced. Had Dad invited Marge? She acted like she was coming, but why would she be? Why would he want her there?

Her heart rate sped up a little. *Did* he want her there? Were they . . . close? No. Dad wouldn't have anything to do with another woman. He'd loved Mom too much. Bea couldn't imagine him with anyone else. But then . . .

She remembered the time she'd come home to find Dad talking with Marge over in her yard. The time she'd found them chatting in the kitchen. All the times Marge had stopped by with food . . .

Marge was looking at her, waiting for an answer. If Mom were here, she would thank Marge for her offer and assign her a task. She would be completely sincere about it and impeccably kind and polite. Then again, if Mom were here, Marge would not be.

Bea cleared her throat, trying to dislodge the lump forming there. "Would you want to bring a salad?"

Maybe not exactly how Mom would've done it, but it was something.

Marge's eyes flickered with some kind of question, though Bea wasn't sure what it could be. "Sure. Is there anything else I can help with?"

She put an awful lot of emphasis on the word *else*. Bea fought a grimace. She was trying to be nice here, yet Marge wasn't making it easy. Did she think Bea incapable of putting a meal together?

"A salad would be helpful," she said flatly.

Marge put on a big smile. "Of course. I would be happy to. What time?"

"Noon?"

"Perfect."

Bea couldn't believe what had just happened. It should be her mom sitting here with her, not Marge. She turned her attention back to Hunter. "Looks like he's over his shock."

Marge pushed herself up off the floor. "Yes. What a doll. Well, I better be going."

Bea stayed put, not wanting to leave Hunter for even a second.

Marge reached the hall and turned back to wave. "Bye now."

Bea raised a hand and whispered, "Thank you," as Marge disappeared around the corner. Yes, it should've been Mom here with her, helping her through this, coming to her aid in a crisis. But Mom wasn't here. Wasn't going to be here ever again. Instead, it had been Marge.

Bea checked the time. The two hours had come and gone.

Hot coffee.

THIRTY-TWO

F irst down . . ."

Jeremy shouted in unison with the crowd, "Spud Town!"

Bea grinned and nudged him with her shoulder. "You're really getting into this."

He smiled back. "It's senior night."

Every year, the school gave a special introduction to each senior student from the team during the last home game of the regular season. The crowd always cheered extra loud, and the mothers always tried extra hard to hide their tears as it hit them that this was the last season of high school football their babies were ever going to play. But miracle of miracles, this wasn't the Spuds' last game. Moose Creek was going to the play-offs.

Dad sat on her other side, as usual. He'd already told her all there was to know about Grandma's appointment earlier in the day, which hadn't been much. It had taken some convincing to get Grandma to lie down for the CT scan, but they'd gotten it done. The office said they would call to set up an appointment to discuss the results early next week. Dad had said it seemed like Grandma was doing better. She hadn't had any incidents since getting home from the hospital.

Jeremy glanced at his phone and nudged her shoulder with his. "Look at this."

He held it out, and she leaned over to see a small rustic table with an antler base. "Is that . . . ?"

"Yep." He grinned. "Mr. Van Dyken decided to take my advice. He sent me a friend request this morning and posted two pictures. This one and another of an antler wall clock. They've been shared almost twenty times."

"Wow."

"Each."

Bea rarely went on Facebook, but it seemed like an impressive start. When Jeremy began tapping intently on his screen, she scooted closer, caught up in his excitement. "What are you doing now?"

"I'm asking him to send me that video I told you about. The one he made for his grandson. If I have some spare time, maybe I could edit it for him."

She gave him a half smile. "He's lucky you moved to town."

He smiled back. "How was work, by the way?"

She'd come straight from the store. "The usual. MacGregor brought up the assistant-manager job again."

Jeremy's expression gave nothing away. "He's known from the beginning you wouldn't be sticking around."

She picked at the hem of her coat. That had been the plan. But things were different now, weren't they? She couldn't leave Moose Creek with Grandma struggling the way she was. Couldn't leave Dad to deal with it all by himself. And if they were going to stay, she might as well have a good job. "He's offering benefits. Paid time off. Health insurance."

"Bea." Jeremy's eyes crinkled. "We're only going to be here for two more months."

What could she say? They'd had an agreement. But Jeremy still had no job, and Grandma . . .

An unfamiliar weight settled on her chest. This was how

small towns did it. How they sucked you in. By getting ahold of your heart one way or another and not letting go. It was what she'd feared from the beginning.

How had she gone from not knowing how to return to not knowing how to leave?

"Maybe we need to talk about our plan again."

Jeremy kept his eyes on the game. "We did talk about it. For hours."

She saw no way they would be going anywhere anytime soon. Even if Jeremy got his as-yet-unspecified company up and running, their most reliable income was in Moose Creek, along with their best prospect for health insurance. Yet she was afraid to say so. Afraid he would accuse her of taking her dad's side. Afraid of seeing that look on his face again—the one she'd seen after texting her dad in the snowstorm instead of him.

"I heard Joe Miller talking about the housing market at the store today." She looked at Jeremy from the corner of her eye. "He's a real estate agent. He said housing prices have gone up eight percent in Moose Creek over the past couple years and fifteen percent in Ponderosa. Can you believe that?"

Joe had also said wages had not increased to keep up with the change. Jeremy didn't respond. Instead, he joined in as the cheerleaders led the crowd in a cheer.

On her right, Dad started getting restless as the opposing team moved into the red zone.

"That was a hold," he shouted. Then he glanced over at her. "I see Jeremy finally learned how to dress."

She cringed at his tone. Why did he care, anyway? It was true that Jeremy was getting the hang of how to stay warm in Montana, but it didn't matter tonight. It was a balmy forty-two degrees.

"You won't have to worry about the cold tomorrow." She steered the conversation in a different direction.

He nodded. "If the forecast is right, it's going to be the

warmest opening day I can remember, which is too bad. We need cold weather to drive the animals down the mountain, you know."

"But you're going anyway?"

"Of course. I just wish your grandpa could go with me."

A twinge of sorrow squeezed her heart. While growing old was a part of life, it still made her sad to see her grandparents losing their strength and abilities. When she was a kid, she'd thought they could do anything.

Dad leaned forward to catch Jeremy's eye. "You ever shoot a gun?"

"No, sir."

"Huh."

Bea shot Dad a look. "Don't start."

He jumped to his feet. "That was a facemask. Come on, refs. Call it both ways."

"Sit down."

He acquiesced and looked over at Jeremy again. "You ever play football?"

Jeremy sighed. "No."

This time Bea jumped to her feet. "I'm going to go stretch my legs."

"Okay, B.B. Sorry." Dad raised his hands in surrender. "I'll stop. I was just trying to make conversation."

"I'll come with you," Jeremy said.

"No, thanks." Bea scooched around her father's knees. "I've got to go to the bathroom. I'll be right back. And it's just Bea now, remember?"

"Right. Sorry." Dad let her pass. "Way to go, Jeremy."

"What did *I* do?"

Bea made it to the aisle and stomped down the bleacher steps, not waiting around to find out how Jeremy and her dad would resolve their little spat, or whatever it was. Why couldn't they just get along? Why did her dad always have to take digs at Jeremy like that?

Behind the bleachers stood a small concession stand and a large shed where they stored equipment. As she passed the shed on her way to the school, she noticed a couple standing in the shadows behind it, talking.

Was that Amber and Axel? Bea didn't see Hunter. Amber had been almost thirty minutes late picking him up earlier today, but Bea hadn't been able to bring herself to be upset about it after the whole couch incident.

She paused for a second, wanting to call out and say hi to her friend but not wanting to intrude. Their voices grew louder, and Bea took a step back. No way did she want to get in the middle of an argument. But then Axel grabbed Amber's arm, and Amber yelped in pain.

"Let go!" Amber cried.

For a second, Bea froze. The dark shadows cast by the shed turned into the treelined sidewalk Bea always took back to her dorm room in Atlanta. She'd been with her roommate all evening. Only for the last couple of blocks was she alone.

A man had appeared out of nowhere and grabbed her arm. *"Let go!"* she had cried. He'd clapped a hand over her mouth and tried to pull her deeper into the trees, but her one panicked protest had been enough to draw the attention of a small group of people a block ahead of her. A guy in a Georgia Tech sweatshirt had started running in her direction with no hesitation, his arm raised, and he shouted—

"Hey!" Bea's hands formed into fists as adrenaline coursed through her veins. "Leave her alone."

Just what Jeremy had said that night. *Oh, God, if he hadn't been there . . .*

"Bea." Amber pulled free of Axel's grip and crossed her arms. "We're just talking."

"Beatrice Jensen? Is that you?" Axel turned to Amber. "This is the friend you've been hanging out with?"

Bea moved a couple of steps closer and glared at him. "What are you doing?"

"Having a private conversation."

"Get out of here, Bea." Amber's face was impossible to read in the shadows. "I don't need your help."

Bea wasn't so sure. She wanted to march right over to her friend and grab her hand. Tell her she didn't need to take any crap from this guy. Ask her where her son was. But she held her tongue and unclenched her fists. Had her own memories caused her to overreact? Axel didn't look threatening anymore, only annoyed.

"Fine." Bea took a few steps back. "But I'll talk to you later, okay?"

Amber nodded. As Bea turned away and hurried into the school, Amber's yelp of pain continued to ring in her mind. She wanted to let Amber know she was concerned. Wanted to ask her what exactly Axel's intentions were. Wanted to make sure her friend was okay.

But she still really needed to pee.

❖ ❖ ❖

Bea's eyelids drooped as she lay beside Jeremy in bed, watching Netflix on her phone while he worked on his laptop. She tried to focus on her show, but the click-click-click of the keys as Jeremy typed seemed to pound out the words she hadn't been able to get out of her mind. *"I need you to choose me. I need you to choose me."* The same words that had been hanging over her head every day since the snowstorm.

She rubbed her eyes and swiped the screen to shut off her show. Did Jeremy think about that conversation all the time, too?

Her body sagged. She couldn't wait for her first trimester to be over. The app Jeremy had downloaded said the extreme fatigue should fade soon. She pulled her earbuds out and set everything on her bedside table.

"You throwing in the towel?" Jeremy asked.

She nestled deeper under the covers and closed her eyes. "Mm-hmm."

"Mind if I work a little longer?"

"It won't bother me any."

She rolled on her side and wriggled so her back pressed against Jeremy's side. She wanted to be close to him. Feel his warmth. Tucked up against him like that, she felt safe. The tickety-tick as he continued to type lulled her toward sleep. *"I need you to choose me. I need you to choose me."*

"Bea? You still awake?"

She startled and opened her eyes. "Yep."

"I've been thinking."

"Okay."

"Remember when I said I would do some digging about your grandma losing a baby? I thought there might be a record of it."

"Uh-huh."

"I never found anything."

Her eyelids drooped again. "Maybe we were wrong."

"Exactly. Do you think there's any chance your grandma's aunt Gladys is still alive?"

"What?"

"I know she'd be pretty old, but there's a chance, right?"

Bea's sleepy brain worked to keep up with Jeremy. "She'd be in her late eighties at least."

"I'm going to search for her online. Do you think she still lives in Chicago?"

"I don't know." She yawned. Why was Jeremy so interested in Great-Aunt Gladys? "Grandma's never really talked about her. And when Grandpa Rand said they got married after

Grandma's visit to Chicago, that was the first I'd ever heard of any trip out east."

His fingers continued tapping on the keyboard. "Doesn't that make you wonder?"

Bea peered at Jeremy's face. He had that look he got whenever he started talking about family. A look of longing mixed with pain and questions about what could have been. She understood him well enough to know it was a look that meant this was important to him.

She sat up and waited.

"Found her. Gladys Fennel. Twenty-four East Meridian Drive in Chicago."

Bea's heart began to beat a little faster. "How did you—could it really be . . . ?"

"Only one way to find out. There's a phone number."

Her eyes bulged. "You're going to call her?"

"Not right *now*. But I have an important question, and I don't know who else to ask." Jeremy copied the number onto a scrap piece of paper from his nightstand. "Maybe Great-Aunt Gladys will have the answer."

Her brow furrowed. He was taking this really seriously. "What question?"

"Why did Grandma June go to Chicago that summer?"

Bea tilted her head. "Why not? Maybe she went every summer."

"I didn't get that impression, did you?"

"No." He was right. It hadn't seemed like an annual event. And Grandma hadn't been eager to talk about it. "Maybe she needed to get out of Moose Creek for a while. I can certainly relate to that."

"Okay, but why?"

A shiver of possibility tingled down her spine. "Do you think this has something to do with what Grandma was talking about on the mountain?"

"Maybe."

"A baby?"

"A secret baby."

Bea rested against Jeremy's shoulder and rubbed her forehead. She thought about the look on her grandma's face that time at her house when Bea reminded her she was pregnant. About Grandma's desperation to find a mysterious baby during the snowstorm. About her great-aunt Gladys.

Why *had* Grandma June gone to Chicago?

THIRTY-THREE

Mitch nursed a cup of coffee and listened to the men yarn. He enjoyed Wednesday mornings at The Baked Potato—they were so normal and familiar—but today he struggled to pay attention to the conversation. Too much else on his mind.

"How about you, Mitch?" Willy jerked his chin at him from across the table. "You have any luck over the weekend?"

"What?" Mitch shook his head. "Oh. No, I never saw a thing. If there were any elk up there, they had better camo on than me."

Willy chuckled. "Is that what's got your mug full of tears over there?"

One corner of Mitch's mouth lifted. "Got a lot going on is all."

Willy sobered. "Your mom still having a time?"

Mitch nodded. Dr. Wilson's office had called yesterday afternoon about bringing his mother in to discuss the results of her CT scan. When they'd said they could squeeze her in this Friday in Ponderosa, he had been relieved. He didn't want to wait any longer than necessary. But now that he'd had time to think about it, he wouldn't mind a little more distance between himself and the appointment. It felt like a moment of truth just waiting to smack him upside the head.

"You hear about George's boy?" Travis asked.

Heads shook all around the table.

"One of the only guys to get a shot off on Sunday, then he fell in some kind of hole tracking the dang thing and broke his leg in three places."

Willy's eyes widened. "You're kidding."

"Nope." Travis slid his chair back and pointed at his own leg. "Here, here, and here. Some cracked ribs, too. Gonna be laid up for months."

Willy tossed his fork down. "Well, shoot."

Mitch hated to hear that. George's "boy" was a twenty-six-year-old named CJ with a wife and two kids. The wife stayed home with the little ones, and Mitch would guess CJ's job barely paid their bills. They would've been counting on that meat to get them through the winter.

"What are they going to do?"

"Don't know." Travis shrugged. "It'd be a lot easier if their little rental wasn't out to heck and gone. The missus took cinnamon rolls over there yesterday, but her old car'll never make it up that hill once the roads get bad."

Mitch thought of his parents. Their house was more accessible than CJ's, but it was still difficult to check in on them as much as he would like. It wasn't on the way to anyplace, and by the time he got off work at six or seven, it was already getting dark. Most of the time, he was plumb wore out. But he needed to make more of an effort. His dad said they were doing better, but it didn't matter. He needed to be there for them.

He dropped a couple dollars on the table as he stood. "I better get to work."

The other men mumbled their farewells, and Mitch stopped at the register to pay for his usual: two eggs, hash browns, bacon, and toast.

As Debbie rang him up, he pulled an extra twenty from his wallet. "CJ Tucker's got a tab here, don't he?"

Debbie nodded.

He handed her the cash. "Put this on it."

◆ ◆ ◆

Mitch brought the truck to a stop with a grunt, his wrists resting on the steering wheel. Of all the houses to be sent to for water-meter maintenance, why'd it have to be Marge's? He'd tried to pass it off on Ralph, but Ralph had found great enjoyment in refusing. "I think she'd rather see your ugly mug at her door than mine," he'd said.

Mitch dragged himself from the truck and carried a bucket, toolbox, and replacement parts to the door.

Marge flung it open before he could knock. "Hi, there."

It'd been a while since he'd seen her without a big old smile on. She didn't seem as happy to have him standing at her door as she always was to be standing at his.

He nodded. "Howdy. Sorry to have to bother you like this, but it should only take me a few minutes to get your meter back on track."

"It's no bother." She stepped aside and ushered him in. "I'm just glad I didn't get called in to work today."

He caught a whiff of citrus as he passed her. Caroline never wore perfume, but she'd always smelled of vanilla from her shampoo. Vanilla made him think of home. Marge's scent made him think of sunshine.

She fidgeted as he glanced around the house, trying not to gawk. He hadn't been in here in a long time. It looked like nothing had changed since Bill and the kids left, almost as though the whole place were frozen in time, waiting for them to come back.

Like he could talk. Caroline's Bible, glasses, and favorite lotion were still perched on the nightstand next to her side of the bed. Her lotion was vanilla, too. His eyes fell on a grimy pack of Newport cigarettes, and he grunted. He could practically see Bill's fingerprints on it.

Marge's long shiny earrings jangled as she shifted on her feet. "I keep meaning to throw those away, you know? I just . . ."

"Yeah." He knew. They locked eyes for a second—a moment spanning the distance between them, a moment where he could see pieces of Marge in her eyes that he'd never seen before—then he cleared his throat. "Why don't you show me where the line comes in."

The moment passed.

She led Mitch down to the basement and pointed. "It's right over here."

He nodded and got straight to work, hoping to make his visit as short as possible. Being here alone with Marge gave him a peculiar feeling. Not bad necessarily, but different.

Most people left him to take care of business after showing him to the meter. Not Marge. She pulled a chair over, sat down, and crossed her short little legs. "Only four days until your birthday, can you believe it?"

He tugged at the collar of his shirt. That wasn't the *last* thing he wanted to talk about, but it was pretty close. "I suppose not."

"I know the party's at noon, but if you need me to come over earlier, just let me know."

The party was at noon? That was news to him. He didn't even know there *was* a party.

She must've read the confusion on his face. "I talked with Bea."

A light sheen of sweat formed on his forehead as he knelt beside the meter. Boy, oh boy. Bea and Marge talking?

"She's going to be a wonderful mom," Marge continued. "I just know it."

He tried to keep his face from giving anything away but must have failed.

"What?" Marge leaned closer. "You don't think so?"

His hands stilled. His voice lowered. "They're just so young. They don't even have a place to live."

Why was he talking to her about this?

"Of course they do. They live with you."

He let out a long breath. "Hardly the ideal situation to start a family."

Marge's eyes widened, then she laughed. She slapped her hand on her knee and let out a high-pitched hoot that made Mitch jump.

He frowned. "What's so funny?"

"Listen to yourself." She wiped at her eyes. "The 'ideal situation.' If everyone waited for the ideal situation, no families would *ever* start."

He slowly turned back to the meter, his brow furrowed. She had a point. But he didn't have to like it. He resumed his work while racking his brain for a different topic.

"You hear about CJ Tucker?" He shifted his body and jerked his wrist, making quick work of the meter's attachment. "George's boy?"

"No." She put a hand to her chest. "Everything okay?"

"Had an accident." Mitch leaned into the wrench and grunted. "Busted his leg real bad. I guess he'll be laid up for quite a while."

"That's awful. What with his wife expecting and everything."

He pulled a rag from his back pocket to mop up some water that had dripped onto the floor. "Expecting?"

"I heard she's pregnant again. Poor thing." Marge's cheeks flushed. "Because of CJ's accident, not because of the baby."

The family had been on his mind all day. And they were having another baby? Looked like Bea and Jeremy weren't the only expectant parents in a less-than-ideal situation. He wished there was something he could do to help.

"Puts them in a tight spot, that's for sure." He double-checked his work, then stood. "That should do it."

"Thank you." Marge rose from her chair, and they walked toward the stairway. "Can I get you anything before you go? I made banana bread."

"No, thanks. I better get moving."

"A cup of coffee?"

He reached the top of the stairs and paused. He couldn't take any longer than necessary, or Ralph would never let him hear the end of it. And he had a lot more work to do today, anyway. But he was surprised to find the thought of sitting down with Marge and having a cup of coffee didn't seem like the worst way in the world to spend the morning. There was a chance they had more in common than he thought.

He glanced at the box of cigarettes from the corner of his eye. "Maybe some other time."

Her big smile returned. "I'm going to hold you to that."

He gave her a small smile back. It wouldn't be so bad, would it? At least he wouldn't have to do much talking. "All right."

As she opened the door for him, she put a finger to her chin. "You know, I'm on the women's committee at church, and I'm wondering if we couldn't pull together a fundraiser for the Tuckers. A chili feed maybe. Who doesn't love chili and corn bread?"

He stopped on her front step and turned to her. It was the kind of thing Caroline would have said. Her corn bread had been the envy of every woman in Moose Creek.

His smile was bigger this time, and it tingled a little as it stretched his face. He hadn't smiled much in the past two years. "That's a darn good idea."

THIRTY-FOUR

Bea sank onto the couch with a sigh. It felt good being in the living room with Jeremy, just the two of them. She rarely got home before her dad, but he was working late tonight.

Jeremy put his arm around her and pulled her close. "This is nice. I like snuggling when your dad's not around."

She leaned into him. "Have you called Great-Aunt Gladys yet?"

He brushed a finger over her cheek. "Your skin is so soft."

"Okaaay."

"Maybe we should make out."

"Jeremy." She squealed and smacked his knee. "Did you talk to Aunt Gladys or not?"

He laughed. "All right, we'll save the making out for later. No, I have not. I thought we could do it right now."

Bea gulped. "Now?"

He pulled out his phone. "Sure, why not?"

Her chest tightened. Why did the thought of talking to Great-Aunt Gladys make her so nervous?

Jeremy punched in the phone number and held out his phone. "Just hit talk when you're ready."

She shrank back. "Me?"

"Well, of course." He gave her a puzzled look. "She won't know who *I* am."

Bea wasn't so sure her great-aunt would know who she was either, but she took the phone from Jeremy's hand. That look on his face was back. She couldn't refuse him.

She pushed talk and listened to three rings. Four. Five. It was an hour later in Chicago. Maybe Aunt Gladys had already gone to bed. She could feel Jeremy tensing up.

"Hello?"

"Oh, uh, hello." Bea cleared her throat. "Is this Gladys Fennel?"

"Yes, yes." The voice was warbly and soft. "This is Gladys. Who is this?"

"Um, well . . ." Bea glanced at Jeremy, and he nodded his encouragement. "This is Beatrice Jensen. Juniper Jensen's granddaughter."

There was a long pause, and Bea could almost hear Aunt Gladys blinking.

"Put it on speaker," Jeremy whispered.

Bea hit the button.

"I haven't talked to Junie in ages," Aunt Gladys finally said. "How is she? Is she still living in that old house?"

"Yes, she is. She's . . . okay. She's having a few health problems right now."

"Oh, I'm sorry to hear that." Aunt Gladys clucked her tongue. "Does she know you're calling me, Beatrice?"

"Um." Bea hesitated. "No. But she mentioned her stay with you in Chicago, and I was wondering—"

"She told you about that?"

Bea held the phone tight. "Yes." It wasn't exactly a lie.

"Poor Junie. She never was the same after everything with the baby. Wouldn't speak to me after that."

Bea glanced at Jeremy, her heart jumping. "Baby?"

"I thought it was awful the way her parents pressured her

235

to give him up." Aunt Gladys sniffed. "I never agreed with it. That's why I told her she could live here with me. We could raise him together. But she was so young . . ."

Bea swallowed. What a hard position to be in. "What happened?"

"Oh, I'm sure you've heard it all already. She got pregnant out of wedlock, and her parents were ashamed. They said she couldn't come home unless she put him up for adoption. She was scared, you know. Hated the big city."

"Him?"

"Yes, indeed. A mighty fine baby boy, born right over at Mercy Hospital."

"When?" Jeremy asked.

"Oh! Who is that?" Aunt Gladys asked.

"That's my husband, Jeremy."

"You're married? How wonderful."

Bea smiled but didn't want Aunt Gladys to get sidetracked. "So when was he born?"

"I can't believe Junie has a granddaughter old enough to be married. Makes me feel ancient."

"Aunt Gladys—"

"I am, of course. Ancient. Only two more months and I'll be eighty-nine."

"Yes, that's amazing. But when was the baby born?"

"I'll never forget." Aunt Gladys paused. "I've never seen a woman so broken. It was August 17, 1976. Junie was barely eighteen. She thought the adoption would be better for everyone, but . . ."

Bea chewed her top lip. She wasn't that far from eighteen herself. "That's a big decision to make at that age."

The same words Dad had used to protest her marriage to Jeremy.

Aunt Gladys sighed. "I wish I knew what happened to him."

She wasn't the only one. Bea fumbled for something to say. Had Grandma really kept a secret this big all these years?

Before she could speak, Aunt Gladys began questioning her about other family members, trying to catch up on all the family news. Bea did her best to answer for several minutes, then said good-bye. Her eyes were wide when she turned to Jeremy.

His eyes were bright and sharp. "I think I got all the information I need."

"All the information—?" Bea's face twisted in confusion. "For what?"

He raised his eyebrows. "To find him."

She sat back. *Him*. Grandma kept saying she was looking for "him." But why had she never said anything before? Where was her firstborn son now? Did he know about any of this?

Bea pulled her knees up to her chest and wrapped her arms around them. It was unbelievable. Somewhere out there, she had an uncle. He could have kids. She could have cousins! And Dad . . .

Dad had a brother.

The moosevine was going to have a heyday with this one.

"What are we going to do?"

Jeremy twisted a lock of her hair around his finger. "There are a lot of ways to search. I'll start with the hospital records and birth certificate."

"Are you sure that's the right thing to do?"

He grew still. Solemn. "You know I lost track of my dad when my parents split up. And you know he died before I could find him." His eyes flashed, begging her to understand. "I have to do this."

Her mind raced. There was no talking him out of it—she could see that. "Should we tell Dad?"

Jeremy rubbed his chin. "We should wait until we have more information. We might not be able to find him. Or something might've happened to him, and he could be dead. There's no telling."

Bea nodded. The longer they could keep it a secret, the better. Dad had enough on his plate already. She leaned into Jeremy again and considered the possibilities. There were so many questions. What would Dad think of all this? What would Grandma do if she had the chance to meet her firstborn son? Who was the father?

Bea's heart sank a little. Did Grandpa Rand know about the baby? And the most unsettling question of all was . . . what if her uncle didn't want to be found?

THIRTY-FIVE

I don't like Ponderosa. I don't like driving to Ponderosa. I don't even like talking about Ponderosa.

Rand and I used to load Mitch up and make the drive once a month to stock up on supplies, but now that our ranching days are over and Mitch has his own place, we try to stay away. It's too crowded. Too city. But here we are again.

We were just here for a test or a scan or whatever. Why did we have to drive all the way back to *talk* about the test? Or scan. Or whatever. Our telephone is perfectly functional.

I peek over at Rand from the corner of my eye as we wait in a quiet, sterile room for someone to call us back. He looks tired. He looks like an old man. I reach over and tuck my hand in his. He turns his head to me in surprise. Like he doesn't know who I am. But I'm the one losing my mind, not him.

I find the penny in my pocket with my other hand and rub a finger over it. Will I stick my hand in my pocket one day—and will it be soon?—and wonder why there's a penny in there? Will I pull it out and toss it in the cupholder of Rand's truck with all the other change? I can't imagine that. Can't fathom not knowing what this penny means to me. But Rand's face when he looks at me makes me afraid.

A young woman in green scrubs appears. "Juniper Jensen?"

Mitch raises his hand. "That's us."

Rand helps me to my feet, and we follow the woman to a small room that looks more like an office than an exam room. The woman tells us to sit, and we shuffle around each other like chickens settling in to roost.

I used to have chickens. I raised them so they would recognize my voice and come eat out of my palm. I used to have a lot of things.

The woman in green stands in the doorway. "Dr. Wilson will be with you shortly."

"Thank you," Mitch says.

She closes the door behind her, and I turn to my son. "Why are we here?"

He puts on his patient face. "I told you, Mom. The doctor wants to talk to us about the results of your CT scan."

I know this already. "But why are we *here*?"

It seems like a reasonable question to me, but Mitch's face twists like he bit into a sour apple. Doesn't it bother him to have to drive all the way back here just to talk? Doesn't he wonder about Dr. Wilson's aversion to using the telephone?

He works his mouth as though he's searching for the right words. Rand says nothing, but when I start shifting in my seat and wringing my hands, he pats my shoulder.

A crisp knock and the door opens.

Dr. Wilson comes straight to me. "Good morning, June. It's good to see you again."

I shake the hand he offers me. "I suppose that's probably true."

After all, it's like walking into a room and finding stacks of money sitting in chairs waiting for you, isn't it? If I were him, I'd be happy about it, too.

We've never had much money, Rand and I. Like many people in the valley, we were land rich and cash poor. Now we have some money from selling the fields, although not enough to pay specialists as fancy as Dr. Wilson. Rand worked too hard all those years for us to throw money away on a man who doesn't even know how to use a phone.

I realize Mitch and Rand are answering Dr. Wilson's questions for me. What had he been saying? The green woman returns with a large folder and hands it to him, and he flips a light on some sort of screen contraption on the wall. He pulls something from the folder and props it up on the screen.

My stomach wobbles. I think that's my brain. He sets a couple more pictures up, like a kid displaying his crayon art on the fridge. Except his face is grave.

He uses a pen to point at the lit-up pictures and begins to string together words I am not able to follow. It's like he's talking too fast and yet his mouth is moving in slow motion. Mitch nods while Rand furrows his brow and clears his throat.

Dr. Wilson points at this bright spot here and that dark spot there. I stare at my brain and wonder if God took a piece of it away every time I sinned, and this is how I will pay for my mistakes. Here's a chunk of my brain, God. Here's another memory. And another. Until there is nothing left.

Mitch asks a lot of questions, and I stop trying to keep up. He will explain everything to me on the drive home in a way I can understand. That's what I'm hoping for. Eventually, Dr. Wilson and Mitch stand and shake hands.

"Thank you, Doctor," Mitch says.

It takes Rand a little longer before he stands, too. I wait until Dr. Wilson is gone before rising to my feet.

"It's okay, Mom. Don't worry." Mitch cups my elbow as he holds the door open for me. "We'll figure all this out."

I love my son. He means well. But I've already figured it out.

THIRTY-SIX

Mitch leaned against the kitchen counter, coffee in hand, and watched Bea flit around the kitchen like the queen of England was coming for Sunday brunch.

"Are you sure about this?" he asked.

She wiped her forehead with her arm. "Yep."

Her face looked a little green, and he was pretty sure she'd been throwing up in the bathroom earlier this morning.

"I don't need a big to-do."

Bea added more ingredients to the Crock-Pot. "I already invited everyone."

A rather large hole opened up inside him, somewhere between his lungs and ribs. "Everyone" included his parents. The ride home from Ponderosa on Friday had been quiet and pensive. No one had wanted to address the elephant in the room, or rather, elephant in the truck. No one had wanted to repeat the words Dr. Wilson had spoken: *"Clear evidence of dementia."* Mitch hadn't been able to think of much else since. But right now, he needed to focus on his daughter.

He used his coffee mug to gesture at Jeremy. "You could let us help you."

The oven timer beeped, and Bea rushed over to look inside. "I got it."

"We could skip church," Jeremy said.

"No." Bea pulled two round pans of chocolate cake from the oven. "I've got everything planned. Our lunch will be cooked in the Crock-Pot by the time we get back, and the cake will be cooled. All we'll have to do is set the table and add the frosting."

Jeremy gave her a worried look.

She pointed at him with a toothpick. "Which I already made." She poked each cake with the toothpick, then set them on the stovetop. "Perfect."

Mitch sipped his coffee with a snort. She had a plan, all right. One would think a man should have some say in the goings-on for his own birthday, but what did he know?

Jeremy checked the time on his phone. "Did you want to walk to church or drive?"

Bea wiped her hands on a towel. "Drive, so we can get home right away and set up."

"Okay. Will you be ready to leave in ten minutes?"

Bea gave Jeremy a withering look. "I *am* ready."

Mitch chuckled into his mug. The poor guy hadn't yet learned that was not the kind of question you asked your wife. At the stricken look on Jeremy's face, Mitch felt a touch of pity for him and cleared his throat.

"Is there anything I can do while you're gone, B.B.?"

She turned on him. "You're not coming?"

"Haven't been in two years. Don't see why I'd start now."

"Because it's your birthday. Everyone will want to see you. And I thought you and Pastor Frank were friends again. He's coming to the party."

Mitch set his mug down and pushed off the counter. "No one will notice if I'm there or not. And we were never *not* friends."

"Then why are you still staying home?"

"It's complicated."

She gave him a look. How could he explain it to her? He wasn't too sure himself.

"Fine." She tucked her hair behind her ears and grabbed her purse from the back of a chair. "But don't ruin anything while I'm gone."

She stormed out of the kitchen, Jeremy close behind. A minute later, the front door shut, and a small handful of ice cubes rattled from the fridge door. One skidded to a stop in front of Steve, who turned his nose up at it with practiced disdain.

Mitch eyed the fridge with the same look. Now that he was alone in the house, maybe he could do what he wanted. It was *his* birthday, after all.

"All right, fridge." Mitch clapped his hands together once. "It's just you and me. Let's wrassle."

◆ ◆ ◆

The moment the church service was over, Bea made a beeline for the door. She had no idea what Pastor Frank's sermon had been about. Her mind had been preoccupied with her dad's birthday party the whole time he was talking. Hopefully, the subject wouldn't come up at lunch.

Jeremy caught up with her and opened the passenger door of the Toyota. "What's the big rush? Aren't people coming at noon?"

She slid in and buckled. "Yep."

"It's 11:32."

"Which means we better hurry."

Jeremy walked around the front of the car and got in. Why hadn't she told everyone to come at twelve-thirty? What had she been thinking? Pastor Frank never got out of the building by noon on a Sunday.

Jeremy started the car and drove out of the parking lot,

singing along to Alabama on the radio. Bea was too distracted to even tease him about it.

He turned onto Town Road. "Why are you so stressed about a birthday party?"

"I'm not stressed."

"You are."

She clasped her hands together and looked out the window. It was hard to explain. She wasn't sure she even wanted to. He always got so sad when she brought up her mom. But maybe this was part of what he meant when he said he needed her to choose him.

"My mom always made a big deal about birthdays." She tucked her hands under her legs. "And was obsessive about Dad's German chocolate cake. It was always perfect. I helped her in the kitchen a lot growing up, but that was one thing she insisted on doing herself. Something she wanted to do for him. I've never made one myself."

"I'm sure it will be great." Jeremy turned onto Second Street. In front of them, a mass of stratus clouds cut the Bridgers in half, covering the peaks so the mountains looked like buttes. "How hard can it be?"

Bea felt tears forming and fought them back. No. She would not cry again. He didn't mean anything by it. The voice telling her he was dismissing her concerns was only her hormones trying to destroy her life. But what a thoughtless thing to say.

"Pretty hard, actually." The words erupted from her mouth. "Have *you* ever made a German chocolate cake?"

He looked at her from the corner of his eye. "Uh, no."

"Then you don't know." Her words were fast and sharp.

His were slow and careful. "You're right. I don't know."

He pulled a U-turn and parked in front of the house.

Bea covered her face with her hands. "I'm sorry. I just . . ."

He turned off the car and gently tugged her hands down. "Hey."

She stared at her knees, unwilling to be undone.

"Bea."

She chanced a look up at his face.

He smiled. "We're in this together, okay? We're going to figure it out. All of it."

"But what if everyth—" She pressed her lips together. "What if the cake falls apart?"

He squeezed her hands. "Then we'll eat it anyway, and no one will give it a second thought."

It wasn't that simple. She wanted to prove herself. Make her dad see she wasn't wasting her life. Prove that she could be a good wife and mother and daughter and take care of everyone, just like Mom used to do. If she could bake the perfect cake . . .

She took a deep breath, opened her door, and climbed out. Company would be here soon. She needed to make this happen. Jeremy would help. They held hands as they walked to the house. Though the low-lying clouds hovered over the mountains to the east, the sun shone on them from overhead. Jeremy held the door open for her.

"Hey, Dad," she called. "We're home."

"In the kitchen." His reply was muffled as if he were bent over something.

She quickly hung up her coat and headed that way, eager to get to work on her final preparations. She turned the corner and froze, eyes wide.

There were bags of frozen vegetables on the counter. Ice cream cartons and a Stouffer's lasagna in the sink. The freezer-side door of the fridge was detached and lying across the table. Dad stood next to it, one arm crossed over his chest and the other propped on it, fingers drumming his chin.

"What are you doing?" Her voice was shrill, but she didn't care. "People will be here in—" she checked the time—"eighteen minutes."

"I think I finally figured it out." Dad lifted the door off the table.

She stuck her fingers in her hair. "This is not okay."

Dad stood the door on the floor and gave her a sheepish look. "I might've gotten carried away. But Jeremy will help me, and we'll have everything back in place in no time. Right, Jeremy?"

His mouth was hanging open a little, but Jeremy nodded. "Sure."

Bea pressed her lips together. Jeremy was supposed to help *her*.

"You do whatever you need to do." Dad's sheepish look turned serious. "And don't worry about us."

Bea pinched the bridge of her nose. What had he been thinking? This was not how her preparations were supposed to go. Not how she plotted it in her head during Pastor Frank's sermon. But crying wouldn't change anything. Crying wouldn't get her cake ready in time.

She mentally blocked Dad and Jeremy out of her mind and picked up one of the cake pans. If she focused, she could still make this work. She had to. The plate she planned to turn the cake out on was already on the counter, so she quickly slid a butter knife around the edge and flipped the pan.

Nothing.

She shook the pan. "Come on, come on."

There. Out it came. Her heart lurched. Huge chunks were missing, still stuck to the pan. This was not good. But that was one of the best things about frosting, right? It covered up mistakes. Plus, her mother's recipe called for both chocolate and coconut-pecan frosting, so there was twice as much frosting available for cover-up.

She grabbed the two metal bowls from the fridge, along with a small rubber spatula, and dipped into the chocolate frosting. She gulped. It was as hard as a rock. Okay, maybe not a rock, but it was definitely not scoopable, spreadable, or any other

247

-*able*. Was it too cold? There wasn't near enough time to let it warm up to room temperature.

Her chest tightened, but she choked down her panic. The chocolate frosting wasn't required. It was just an extra bonus. She could skip straight to the coconut-pecan frosting, and Dad would probably never notice.

Before she could get to the other bowl, her phone beeped. A text from Dorothy, Pastor Frank's wife.

> Frank is meeting with a church member in crisis, so we're going to be late. Start without us!

Bea turned the screen off without replying and massaged her temples. Could nothing go according to plan? *Don't panic.* They would be here eventually. She'd save them some cake.

She wiped the spatula on a paper towel and dipped into the other bowl. The frosting was gooey and decadent, just like it was supposed to be. She plopped a glob of it on top of the first layer of cake to spread and growled to herself. Something was wrong with it. It was supposed to have more texture.

Her heart clattered to the floor. The coconut. How could she have forgotten the coconut in the coconut-pecan frosting?

A thin layer of perspiration formed on her forehead and the back of her neck. And under her arms. She stared at the cake with trepidation, and her mother's face stared back at her. *There's my girl.*

Bea's eyes stung. *Mom, I'm sorry. I didn't know you'd be gone so fast. I didn't know this would be so hard. I tried, Mom. The cake . . .*

A knock sounded at the door as a lump formed in her throat. She shook her head to clear it. The clock on the stove said *11:50*.

The knock came again. Hot coffee. She should still have ten more minutes. She wasn't ready. A quick glance told her Jeremy and her dad had their hands full, so she set the spatula down with a groan. Fine. Maybe Grandma could help her salvage the cake.

She hurried down the hall and pulled open the door.

Marge.

Grinning.

Holding a beautiful, magazine-worthy German chocolate cake in her arms.

Bea burst into tears.

THIRTY-SEVEN

itch wasn't sure what the big deal was. Why had Bea gotten so bent out of shape over a birthday party he never even asked for? He shook his head while she stabbed at her lunch, and Marge batted her eyes at him.

"I had no idea you were making the cake, Bea," Marge said. "I'm so sorry."

His mother perked up. "Cake?"

She and Rand had arrived two minutes after Marge and three minutes before Bea had gotten ahold of herself.

Bea didn't look up. "It's fine."

"Is it your famous German chocolate cake, Caroline?" June asked. Then she looked up with a frown. "I mean, Beatrice."

A jolt of pain Mitch could feel from the other side of the table flashed across Bea's face. Mitch glanced at his father, wondering what he was thinking. He seemed so unfazed by all the little lapses his mother made, as if he were already used to it. But how did you get used to such a thing? They needed to discuss his mother's future, and they needed to do it soon.

Marge reached over and patted June's hand. "Of course it is, June. And it's perfect. Isn't that wonderful?"

June smiled at Bea. "I knew you wouldn't forget."

His mother resumed eating with a happy humming sound,

and Bea pushed meat around her plate with a sickly expression. Jeremy set a gentle hand on her shoulder.

Marge leaned closer to Bea and spoke quietly. "I should've known you would want to do it. You just never said anything about a cake, and I didn't want Mitch's birthday to go by without—"

"You could've just asked."

Marge nodded. "I thought—"

"You *should've* asked."

Mitch's eyes widened. "Bea."

"No, no. It's fine." Marge waved away his objection. "You're absolutely right, Bea. I'm sorry."

Bea gave her a sidelong look. "Did you use my mom's recipe?"

Marge's face tightened. Mitch held his breath, suddenly realizing why the cake was such a big deal. How could he have been so clueless? How many times had he made it worse for Bea since Caroline died by sticking his head up his butt and leaving it there?

Marge set her fork down. "Yes. I did. She copied it for me years ago."

He braced himself for Bea to start crying again. Instead, Bea's pinched face relaxed. "Good."

Phew. He let out his breath and eyed the cake on the counter. He'd rather die than tell Bea, but he, for one, was glad Marge had made it.

As everyone finished eating, Bea stood to collect the dirty plates. Jeremy jumped up to help. Mitch had to give the kid one thing at least. He was helpful.

Even though Marge had some sort of clip holding back her hair today, it still spiraled and jutted out in all directions like octopus tentacles. She patted it down to no avail and turned to his mom and dad. "I bet it's beautiful out at your place this time of year."

June nodded. "It's always beautiful."

"Of course." Marge smiled. She was ever smiling. "You've lived there your whole life, right, June? It was your parents' ranch?"

"Yes." June's wrinkled hands rested on the table. "I was born in that house. So was Mitch. 'Course, it looked a lot different then. Rand put a lot of work into fixing it up when we got married."

"I can't imagine what it would be like living in the same place for that long," Jeremy said. "My family moved every couple of years when I was growing up."

"That's the trouble with people these days," June said. "Never staying put. I've never lived anywhere but the valley, and I never will."

"Except when you went to your aunt's in Chicago," Jeremy said.

June's head jerked up. "What?"

Mitch gave Jeremy a sidelong look. Boy, oh boy. His mother didn't like talking about her past. She always said, "Today's more important than yesterday." How did Jeremy even know about that trip?

Jeremy continued, all wide-eyed and earnest. "Grandpa Rand said you lived with your aunt in Chicago before you got married."

June moved her hands onto her lap. "Oh yes. Well. That was temporary."

"How long were you there?" Jeremy asked.

The kid was skating on thin ice. Mitch watched his mother to see what she would do.

June fidgeted. "I . . ."

His father came to the rescue. "About four months or so. Right, dear?"

She sank lower in her chair as if the exchange had stolen all her strength. "Yes. That's right."

Marge rose from the table. "How about some cake?"

Mitch was glad for the distraction. He worried whether a conversation about the past might confuse his mother. Could her recollection of the past even be trusted anymore?

There was a loud knock, then the door opened, and Frank called out, "We made it."

"Just in time," Mitch called back. "We're about to have cake."

Frank and Dorothy bustled into the kitchen and greeted everyone, not batting so much as an eyelash at the sight of Marge standing in Mitch's kitchen. They'd seen it all, those two.

"Sorry we're late," Frank said. "You know how it is."

Frank was always the first person to arrive at the church building and the last person to leave. And he always dropped everything when someone needed to talk.

"Don't worry about it." Mitch gestured for them to find a seat. "We're glad you're here."

Bea fished around in the junk drawer and came up with a handful of candles and a lighter while Marge took out little plates from the cupboard. She knew right where they were. Mitch watched her warily, hoping Frank wouldn't notice. She seemed so at home here.

He tried to examine his heart to see if that bothered him, but it was too full of memories of Caroline. All the birthday cakes she'd made. All the birthday kisses. Year after year of little surprises hidden around the house, just for him.

He didn't need those things. He could get by just fine without gifts, or a cake for that matter. But without Caroline?

Bea stuck the candles in the cake and lit them. "Ready?"

As she carried the cake over and set it in front of him, everyone sang the birthday song. Frank belted it out as if leading the congregation. Marge's eyes twinkled like the amethyst stones hanging from the bottom of her metal hoop earrings.

She caught him looking and sang a little louder. "Happy birthday, dear Miiitch . . ."

All of a sudden, he couldn't remember Caroline's voice singing the familiar song. Couldn't hear it.

"Happy birthday to you."

THIRTY-EIGHT

Mitch snuck one more bite of cake from the plate before covering it with plastic wrap. "You look beat, B.B. Why don't you go sit on the couch. Jeremy and I can finish up."

She scrubbed at one of the cake pans and shook her head. "I'm fine."

Their company had gone home about an hour ago after sticking around to visit for quite a while. He'd practically had to push Marge out the door. Then he and Jeremy and Bea had eaten some meat sticks and leftover cake for dinner and started cleaning up the kitchen. He'd thrown Bea's unused baking attempt in the garbage when she wasn't looking.

Jeremy took the pan from her hands and gently nudged her aside. "He's right. You should go rest."

She looked back and forth between their faces as if trying to gauge how serious they were, then held up her hands. "All right. I surrender."

She trudged from the kitchen and disappeared. Mitch grabbed a dishrag from the sink to wipe the table.

Jeremy rinsed the cake pan and set it on a towel. "She doesn't like that name, you know."

Mitch frowned. "What name?"

"B.B. She doesn't want people calling her that anymore."

Mitch's neck tensed. "It's just an old habit. She doesn't mind."

"Yes, she does."

"Then why hasn't she said anything?"

His words were accusatory, but his tone fell flat. She had. Several times.

"She's not a kid anymore."

Mitch tossed the rag back into the sink, and it hit the dishwater with a splash. "I'm well aware of that."

Jeremy set to work on the second pan and didn't respond.

The ceramic bowl from the Crock-Pot was still soaking, but Mitch picked up the base and put it away in the cupboard. "You've been gone a lot lately."

"Yeah. Meeting a lot of people. Getting a lot of good ideas."

Ideas again. Mitch huffed.

Jeremy stopped scrubbing and set his hands on the edge of the counter. "You can't eat ideas. I know. But I'm going to make this work. For Bea and our baby."

"But they need you *now*." Mitch lowered his voice to be sure she couldn't overhear from the living room. "Bea's on her feet all day. I worry about her stress level, and how are you going to pay the medical bills for the baby?"

"With all due respect, it's not your job to worry about any of that."

Mitch could feel his face heating up. "Well, if you're not going to . . ."

Jeremy turned to face him, his eyes alight with a fire Mitch had never seen in them before. "I take my responsibility very seriously. I *will* provide for my family. I *will* do whatever it takes. But I won't stand by and watch you disregard Bea's wishes or dismiss my contributions to our family."

He wiped his hands on his jeans and marched out of the kitchen. Mitch realized his mouth was hanging open and snapped it shut.

"Huh." He shared a look with Steve, who had been lurking underfoot ever since scoring a bite of meat stick from Bea. "What do you know."

He'd never seen this side of Jeremy before. Never would've guessed he had it in him.

Maybe Jeremy had what it took to be what Bea needed after all.

THIRTY-NINE

Thanks for coming with me, B.B." Mitch drummed the steering wheel with his fingers. "I mean Bea. Sorry."

Her eyes remained fixed on something far in the distance. "What are you going to say to him?"

Mitch let out a long breath through his nose. Good question. He knew he needed to have the hard conversation with his dad about what to do about his mother's condition, and after spending a couple of days trying to figure out how to talk to Dad without his mom listening in, Mitch had come up with the solution of bringing Bea along to distract her. He'd even finished his typical Tuesday work ahead of schedule so he could get off early.

But he still hadn't figured out what to say.

"We need to talk about the future." He raised two fingers in the standard country-road salute as another truck drove by in the other lane. "I'm just not sure what he's thinking."

"Grandma can't stay out here." Bea turned to him. "She needs to come live at the house."

"I can't watch her all the time."

"I'll watch her."

Mitch huffed. He couldn't agree to that. Couldn't expect Bea to take on his mother's care.

"You're not going to be around much longer, so then what?"

She narrowed her eyes. "You're trying to get rid of us again?"

His heart squeezed. That was the last thing he wanted. It had been miserable having her gone the past two years. But . . .

"Do you really want to live with your dad forever?"

Bea moved a hand to her stomach. "We'll find a place in town."

It'd be a dream come true for him, wouldn't it? Keeping her close. Watching over her. A bubble of hope began to rise in his chest.

Bea gave a confident nod. "Then I'd be available anytime."

The bubble popped. Mitch turned onto the gravel drive. Anytime? Sure, except when she had to work or take care of her baby. She had no idea what kind of commitment that was going to be. "You can't just give up your own life."

Her eyes flashed. "You can't just shut me out of this like you did with Mom."

Oh yes, he could. If that's what was best for her. "We don't even know what your grandfather's going to say."

"You need to tell him I want to help."

Mitch grunted but didn't respond. He couldn't tie Bea down like that. He wouldn't. It was his job to protect her, just like when Caroline was diagnosed. Whether she liked it or not.

"Even If It Breaks Your Heart" by Eli Young Band came on the radio, and Mitch glanced over at his daughter. The song was about never giving up on your dreams, but all he could think about was whether he was willing to break his own heart for Bea's sake and tell her he didn't want her staying in Moose Creek. Could he really push her away like that?

There was already a distance between them he didn't know how to breach—a distance he had caused—but if he told her she shouldn't stick around, told her she could have no part in her grandmother's care, she might leave and never come back.

That wasn't what he wanted. But what *he* wanted hadn't mattered when Caroline was sick, and it didn't matter now.

◆ ◆ ◆

Bea hung back as Dad hopped out of the truck and headed for Grandma and Grandpa's house. He was doing it again. Acting like he didn't want her around anymore, just like after Mom died. Should she move across the country a fourth time? Would that make him happy?

Not that she could afford to do that.

She neared the house and checked her phone before climbing the porch steps. Cell service was better outside. She raised her eyebrows at a text from Amber.

Are you home?

She wasn't sure what to make of that. Wasn't exactly in the mood to do Amber any more favors after the way she'd told Bea to "get out of here" the other night. But what if Hunter needed her?

No. I'm at my grandma's. What's up?

Dad paused at the front door and called back to her, "You coming?"

"Be right there."

Just hoping we could talk. I could meet you there for that haircut we talked about.

Haircut? Bea pursed her lips to one side. She'd forgotten all about that. It would be the perfect distraction to keep Grandma occupied while Dad talked with Grandpa.

Hunter too?

Of course.

Okay, see you in a few.

She stuck her phone in her pocket and walked to the house with a hint of hesitation in her step. It would be thirty minutes before Amber and Hunter arrived, but a small pit of dread was already forming in her stomach. What did Amber want to talk about?

Inside, her dad was sitting in the living room with Grandma and Grandpa, talking about food. A flood of relief washed over Bea when Grandma June smiled at her in greeting. Nothing like the look she'd given her the last time Bea visited.

"Come in, come in." Grandma gestured to the couch. "Have a seat. You look wonderful, Bea."

Bea sat down. "Thanks."

"Your father was just pestering me about my diet."

"I wasn't pestering." Dad leaned forward and rested his elbows on his knees. "I was merely asking if you'd been taking your supplements."

Grandma sat up straight and regal and looked down her nose at him. "And how about you, Mitch? What did *you* have for breakfast today?"

"Okay, okay." Dad conceded defeat and pushed himself to his feet. "Never mind. I think Dad and I are going to go for a walk now, Mom."

Grandma tilted her head. "Bea and I will come, too."

Grandpa Rand wobbled a bit as he rose from his chair. "Now, June, I don't think—"

"It's a beautiful day. Some sunshine will do me good." Grandma hopped to her feet, her spryness in stark contrast to Grandpa's slow, unsteady steps.

Dad caught Bea's eye, and she gave a slight nod. She knew what her job was, yet she also knew she had to do it in such a way that Grandma wouldn't be suspicious.

"How about Grandma and I go for a walk and you guys

261

stay here?" A walk would kill time until Amber arrived for Grandma's haircut. "You guys could never keep up with us anyway, right, Grandma?"

Grandma snorted. "Of course not."

Grandpa sank back into his chair and waved his hand. "Sure, all right. We wouldn't want to slow you down."

Grandma had already pulled on her walking shoes and a light jacket. She put her hands on her hips and jerked her chin at Bea. "Don't just stand there. Let's go."

Bea chuckled and followed her grandma to the door and out into the sunshine. Grandma was right. It was a beautiful day.

They started down the gravel drive in silence. Some days the mountains were sharp and jagged as if carved from stone, but today they were soft. They looked as if they'd been shaped from blue-and-green sand and could collapse at any moment under the weight of the sky.

Bea took a deep breath of fresh air, enjoying how it felt to move and stretch her changing body. To work the ligaments in her hips that seemed to be loosening more each day as her body prepared itself for what was to come. She looked south and southwest at the Spanish Peaks and the Tobacco Root Mountains. They were both far grander in scale than the Bridgers, but their distance tamed them. The mountain in her backyard always appeared to be the most fearsome mountain of all.

Grandma June stopped, and Bea pulled up beside her.

"Look." Grandma pointed.

Bea followed her finger to a small harem of elk in a field about a hundred yards beyond the jackleg fence. There was one strikingly handsome bull and about half a dozen cows with their yearlings. They'd almost walked right by without noticing.

"Wonder what they're doing down here?"

Grandma studied them carefully. "Enjoying the day, I would say."

After watching them for a few minutes, she started walking

again, and Bea followed suit. It felt so normal. So easy. Hope surged in her heart. Maybe Grandma was going to be okay. Maybe her condition wasn't as big a deal as everyone thought.

Bea glanced at the mountain and remembered the snow-storm. The helplessness. The fear. The woman she'd tried to help that day was not the same woman who walked beside her now. What if that other Grandma reappeared and this Grandma never came back?

Bea thought about what she and Jeremy had learned from Great-Aunt Gladys. The son out there somewhere who'd never met his biological mother. If they didn't find him soon, he might never get the chance. This Grandma—his mother—could be gone.

They reached the end of the drive and turned around.

Bea stuck her hands in her pockets. "Did you ever want more kids, Grandma?"

Grandma didn't slow down or look at Bea. "You have no idea what a handful your father was as a child, dear. He was all I could manage."

Bea didn't know how hard to push, but a sense of urgency compelled her to ask another question. "Didn't he wish for a sibling?"

A cloud passed over Grandma's face. "We wish for a lot of things in life, Beatrice. But wishing doesn't change what we have. It only makes what we do have harder to love."

Bea's throat constricted as she realized her hands were touch-ing her stomach. She'd spent a lot of time the past few weeks wishing for a different life. What if all those wishes for what could've been were keeping her from loving what was? What if Grandma and her firstborn son were better off not wondering what might've been?

As they neared the house, gravel crunched behind them. Bea spun around. From the driver's seat of her Ford Explorer, Amber waved and brought the vehicle to a stop.

"Be right back, Grandma." Bea jogged over to the window as Amber rolled it down. "Hey."

"Hey." Amber's smile was tentative. "Thanks for letting me come over. I'm sorry I acted like such a jerk the other night."

"I've been worried about you."

Amber nodded. "I think you were right about Axel. I told him he can't just be around for the fun times. He needs to prove he can be around for the hard times, too."

"What did he say?"

"Not much. He took off again."

Bea's shoulders drooped. "I'm so sorry."

Amber opened the door and climbed out. "I was tired of doing this parenting thing on my own. I wanted to believe . . ."

"I wanted that for you, too. I really did. I just—"

"I know. I wish you'd been wrong." Amber lifted one shoulder and gave a small smile. "You're lucky, you know."

Bea thought about Jeremy. He wasn't perfect. They were still learning what it meant to be married, and now they had to figure out what it meant to be parents on top of that. But she loved Jeremy. More than she'd ever thought possible. And as scary as it was to think of becoming a parent, at least she didn't have to face it alone.

"I know."

Amber opened the back passenger door to unhook Hunter from his car seat.

"Who's that?" Grandma called.

Bea turned and smiled. "I have a surprise for you."

FORTY

The little boy won't stop looking at me. It's like he can see things in my face no one else can see. He jabbers and bats at my feet as his mother trims my hair, and I want to scoop him up and hold him close. Smell his hair and kiss his hands. Press my face into his neck and cry.

"No hitting, Hunter," Amber says. "Leave Miss June alone."

"No, no." I smile at the boy. "He's fine."

It feels good as Amber pulls a comb through my damp hair. We're sitting in the front yard, letting the hair disappear into the grass. I didn't realize how long it had gotten, but as it falls away, I feel a lightness I haven't felt in a long time.

Bea sits at my feet to keep an eye on Hunter. She is radiant in the late-afternoon light. Her cheeks are rosy with life, and the sun shines on her hair like an anointing. I can't believe she's going to have a baby, but her soft glow declares the truth as plain as day.

She's so young. Still has so much to learn. But she's older than I was when I became a mother.

The little boy—what is his name? It starts with an *H*. He sits on his bottom and runs his hands over the grass, then grabs a clump and shoves it in his mouth.

"Hunter, no," Bea says.

That's right. His name is Hunter.

She sticks a finger in his mouth to clear out the grass. "Icky."

Tears fill his eyes, and his chin quivers. Oh, Mylanta, it hurts me to look at him. Hurts to see anguish on a little boy's face after spending forty-five years imagining what pain would look like on the face of my firstborn son. Imagining it and knowing there was nothing I could do to make it go away. I wonder if the pain was ever because of me.

I pat my lap. "Come here, Hunter. Don't cry."

Please. Please don't cry.

He cocks his head and sniffles. Studies me again. Then holds up his chubby arms. My heart catches. *Oh, God, thank you. You have given me this moment. I don't deserve it, but I am grateful.*

Bea helps him onto my lap, and his bright red sneakers leave wet marks on my knees. The warmth and weight of him is like an anchor, holding me fast to this life. These people. These fleeting memories. After my first son was born, I didn't think I'd ever hold another child. *But you brought Mitch along for Rand's sake, didn't you, Lord? It certainly wasn't for mine.* Holding Mitch sealed up the festering wound in my heart enough for me to go on living. Scarred and disfigured, but living.

Hunter nestles into me, forming to my body. He smells of grass and Cheerios and sunshine. I put my hands on his sides to steady him, and he pokes at them. His fingers are wet with drool.

"Almost done, Miss June," Amber says.

I say, "Okay," though I wish this could go on forever. Wish I could always remember everything about this day, down to the tiniest detail. But it's like I told Bea. Wishing doesn't change what you have. And what I have is limited time.

I don't remember when Bea's baby is due, but I know I won't be around to see it. Not around like this, anyway. I'll be someone else by then. This is as close as I will ever get to being a great-grandmother. I don't know how I know exactly, but it's as sure and inevitable as an early season snowfall in September.

I gently pinch Hunter's thighs, and he giggles. It's the sound of happiness and regret.

"There." Amber pulls the towel from my shoulders and steps back. "You look beautiful."

"Thank you." I pull the baby a little closer with a smile. "Feels good."

FORTY-ONE

Mitch stared straight ahead down the gravel road as he drove away from his parents' house, but he could still see the look on his daughter's face from the corner of his eye.

She raised her eyebrows expectantly. "So? How did it go?"

He cringed. It had been torture trying to get his father to admit he couldn't be responsible for his mom by himself. Even harder for Mitch to admit that he couldn't take her in, either. He had to work. In the end, he'd been forced to remind his father how horrible it had felt when his mom went missing and how they couldn't afford to allow that to happen again. It was too dangerous.

"We agreed to look into assisted-living homes in Ponderosa."

"You've got to be kidding."

"There are a lot of nice places, B.B. Bea. I've looked at some on the internet and—"

"No." Bea's voice rose with her indignation. "There's no way you're sticking her in some nursing home somewhere."

"Calm down. It's assisted living, not a nursing home. And it's Ponderosa, not somewhere."

"Same thing." Her voice was thick with emotion.

He grimaced. It wasn't like he wanted to move his mother out of the house she'd lived in her entire life. It felt like giving up—like failure—but he was backed into a corner. He still had twenty-some years before he could retire, and Caroline was gone.

"No, it's not the same."

Bea smacked a palm against her leg. "I'm not going to let you do this."

Mitch wiped a hand over his face. "It's not up to you."

He'd said the same thing when Bea had protested his and Caroline's decision to forgo cancer treatment. She'd been angry then, as well.

"She's *my* grandma. And I live here now, too."

He kept his eyes on the road, afraid to look at her. Here they were again. He couldn't sacrifice Bea's future for his mother's sake. June wouldn't want that.

The song returned to his mind. *"Even if it breaks your heart . . ."*

"You can't stay here forever."

She sniffled. "I'll take the assistant-manager position at the Food Farm."

"I can't let you do that."

"You have no say in it."

"Jeremy does." It rankled down deep, but it had to be done. "And I'm betting he would agree with me on this one."

She turned toward the window with a huff and didn't answer. For two miles, Hank Williams sang "A Country Boy Can Survive," and Mitch gripped the wheel. When Bea drove her black Blazer out of Moose Creek, leaving him alone in an empty house with stinging memories lurking in every corner, it had felt like losing Caroline all over again. Now here he was, driving Bea away on purpose.

When she finally spoke, it was in a whisper. "How would they pay for it?"

Mitch's shoulders drooped. That was the worst part of the whole thing. "They'll have to sell their house as soon as possible."

They drove the rest of the way to town in strained silence. He pulled up in front of the house with a sigh and put the truck in park. Jeremy's car was gone.

The frustration that had been building since they left this morning reached a boiling point. He'd had about enough of his son-in-law's disappearing act. "Where's he off to this time?"

Bea glared. "His name is Jeremy."

"Well, has Jeremy made any progress on those ideas of his?"

"Really, Dad? You want to do this again? Now?"

"What? You can tell me what to do, but I can't even ask if there's hope of employment in your husband's future?"

"He's going to figure it out."

"So you trust him to figure that out, but you don't trust me to know what's best for my own mother?"

Bea flinched, and Mitch mentally kicked himself. He was pretty sure it was his helplessness talking. Caroline would be shaking her head at him right about now.

He checked the time. He had five minutes to be at the church. "Look, I've got to get to a meeting."

Bea turned red, watery eyes at him. "With who?"

Refusing to answer would be worse than telling the truth, but he didn't have to tell the *whole* truth. "Frank."

She hopped out of the truck and slammed the door behind her.

He rolled the passenger window down. "Don't hold dinner for me."

"Fine."

She rounded the front of the truck and started up the walk. He was shifting the truck into drive to pull away when a movement caught his eye.

Marge came bustling across the yard, waving an arm at him. "Yoo-hoo."

Bea stopped. Mitch gulped. When Marge waved her arm again, he rolled his window down.

"You headed to the church?" Marge stopped a couple of feet from the truck and put a hand to her chest. "Whew. I'm out of shape. Anyway, I was on my way, too. I'll just hop in with you."

Mitch resisted the urge to look to Bea for her reaction, but he knew she was watching and judging and jumping to conclusions. He could feel it.

"Uh . . . sure." He put the truck back in park. "Might as well."

This was what he'd tried to hide from Bea. That Marge was part of the meeting. Actually, it was Marge's meeting to begin with. She wanted to talk with Frank about using the church building for a fundraiser for CJ's family. According to Frank, she had big plans. And somehow Mitch had gotten roped into them.

Mitch hadn't realized it was possible to bounce into a truck, but that was what Marge did. Everything about her was bouncy. She buckled her seat belt with more energy than he'd had in months.

Before he could roll his window back up, Bea called to him with a smirk, "You kids have fun."

He was sure the tips of his ears were flaming red.

Turning the truck around, he headed toward the church, praying with greater fervency in his soul than he'd had in a while that Frank would not see him and Marge drive up together. Nothing like a woman to send Mitch pleading at the foot of the Almighty's throne.

Marge leaned toward him as much as the seat belt would allow. "What were you and Bea up to today?"

"We were just up at the ranch is all."

"Your mom seemed to be doing well on Sunday at the party. Did I hear you mention you were back at the neurologist's last week?"

He hadn't told her about that, had he? Taking his mother to the neurologist wasn't something he would mention.

"Dorothy said that Frank said that you took Friday morning off work again."

Aha.

"Yes." Mitch turned down Main Street and cringed as several people peered into his truck as they drove past. Why hadn't he gone the back way? "We had a follow-up appointment."

"How did it go?"

Still reeling from his painful conversations with his dad and Bea, he shook his head. He didn't want to talk about it. Not again.

"I'm sure this whole thing has been very difficult for you." She made a sympathetic humming kind of sound. "Has the doctor given you a diagnosis?"

Mitch pulled into the church parking lot. *Diagnosis.* What an ugly word. "They're pretty sure it's Alzheimer's."

"Oh, Mitch." Marge put a hand to her mouth. "I'm so sorry. Is there anything I can do?"

It wasn't her problem. Wasn't her mother. Wasn't even her business, though whether something was or was not her business didn't seem to impact her knowledge or interest in the something. Mitch killed the engine and grunted. She meant well. At least she cared. But . . .

"We'll be fine," he said.

She followed him out of the truck and into the building. He walked at a fast pace, hoping to deter any further questions. They paused in front of Frank's office, and Mitch knocked.

"Come on in."

Mitch held the door open for Marge and ushered her inside.

Frank sat behind his desk with a grin on his face. "It's good to see you two."

He didn't tack the word *together* on the end, but Mitch could read it all over his face. Oh, brother. How had he gotten himself into this again?

✦ ✦ ✦

Mitch had been raised to tackle his problems head-on. So when Dorothy arrived and took Marge to the community room to start planning decorations for the fundraiser, Mitch didn't waste any time.

"Go ahead and say it."

Frank leaned back in his chair with an amused expression. "It's nice to see you getting out more. Getting involved."

"And?"

"And nothing."

"You don't want to say anything about"—he glanced over his shoulder at the still-open door and lowered his voice—"Marge?"

"What's there to say? You're both concerned about the Tuckers and want to help. That's all there is to it, right?"

"Right." Mitch let out a breath. "Exactly. That's all there is to it."

"And even if there *was* more to it, you wouldn't want me pointing it out or talking about it."

Mitch narrowed his eyes. "Right."

"And you definitely wouldn't want me asking all kinds of probing and embarrassing questions about your feelings or intentions."

"My *what*?"

Frank raised his hands in surrender. "You brought it up, not me."

Mitch shook his head. "You're the worst."

"She's very enthusiastic."

"I thought you said I don't want to talk about it."

"We don't always get what we want." Frank laced his fingers together behind his head. "Besides, what you want and what you need are not always the same thing."

"There's nothing going on."

"Does she know that?"

"She won't leave me alone."

"Is that such a bad thing?"

Mitch squeezed the back of his neck. "Has the church board changed their minds yet about your salary?"

"You're changing the subject."

"I still think you're getting screwed over."

Frank set his hands back on his knees and scooted his chair closer to his desk, his playful demeanor gone. "It's not worth worrying about. It's just money. God will provide."

"That doesn't make it right, what they're doing."

"Maybe not. But—"

"You're not going to at least tell them how you feel?" Mitch waved a hand. "Ask them to reconsider?"

"I might. I haven't decided. But at the end of the day, my relationships are more important to me than my finances."

"That sounds like a standard pastor cop-out."

"Well, I *am* a pastor. But it's not a cop-out; it's the way things are."

Mitch huffed. Even though they'd been estranged for two years, Frank was still his best friend. He wanted him to be treated fairly. And it wasn't just the pay cut. How many times in the past twenty years had Frank gotten the short end of the stick from these people? How many times had he been taken advantage of and taken for granted?

"I just don't know how you put up with them."

Frank sighed, sliding over a to-go box from The Baked Potato so he could rest his elbows on the desk. "How did you put up with Caroline?"

The hairs on the back of Mitch's neck rose. "What the heck—"

"No, listen." Frank cut him off, serious now. "Caroline was an amazing woman, but she wasn't perfect, was she?"

"Yes." Mitch stumbled over the words. "She was."

"No. She wasn't. But you loved her anyway. More than anything or anyone else. Right?"

Mitch's blood raced through his veins. How dare Frank bring Caroline into this? "Of course."

"Even if she made a mistake or acted irrationally or was selfish sometimes, you loved her. You still do."

Emotions clawed at the back of Mitch's throat. Grief. Anger. Confusion. Sorrow. He would never stop loving her. Ever.

"It's the same with the church." Frank's voice softened. The wrinkles on his forehead smoothed out. "She isn't perfect, and she never will be. But I love her anyway. Warts and all."

Mitch stared at the box of takeout food on Frank's desk. Studied the potato lying on a towel sunbathing, which was The Baked Potato's logo. He understood what Frank was saying. Sort of. But it was hard to keep loving someone who hurt you over and over. Hadn't Caroline done it, though? How many times had Mitch hurt her over the years with his stupidity and pride? Yet her love for him had never changed.

"Well," he grumbled. "None of that means I have to like what they're doing."

Frank raised an index finger. "*Like* is a feeling. *Love* is a choice."

"Yeah, yeah." Mitch rolled his eyes. "But for the record, Caroline didn't have any warts."

Frank chuckled. "I'll take your word for it."

A thump and a whoosh made Mitch jump. Marge appeared beside his chair, breathless.

"Dorothy had so many creative ideas." Her eyes were bright. "We set the date for Saturday, November twenty-seventh."

"That's great," Frank said.

"It doesn't give us much time, but everyone's going to pitch in."

Frank nodded. "Just let me know what you need from me."

His eyes turned on Mitch, and Marge's followed. They looked at him expectantly.

"Uh, yeah, me too," he said, swallowing hard. "Whatever you need."

FORTY-TWO

Bea peered at the screen. "This looks amazing."

The website was simple but attractive. She scrolled through it on Jeremy's laptop, clicking buttons and skimming the information. He had created an impressive internet home for Mr. Van Dyken's store.

Jeremy nodded. "I'm pretty happy with it. Mr. Van Dyken still has his doubts, but he said he's sold five pieces since he started posting on Facebook."

"That's probably more than he sold all last month."

"Actually, more than he sold in three months."

She raised her eyebrows. "Wow."

"And you want to know the best part?" Jeremy leaned his elbows on the kitchen table.

"What?"

"He paid me twenty bucks."

Bea laughed. "Twenty whole dollars?"

Jeremy shrugged. "I just wanted to help. I knew he had to have customers out there if he could just reach them."

She pointed at the screen. "I like this graphic."

"A guy named Spencer helped me with that. He's interested in partnering with me. He's really talented."

She tilted her head. "Partnering?"

276

Jeremy moved the laptop away and took Bea's hands. "I want to help people like Mr. Van Dyken. At least half of the businesses I visited over the past few weeks are struggling to find customers. Spencer and I were talking, and we think—we *know*—we can help them build or revamp their websites, come up with new marketing ideas, and reach new customers."

"And they would pay you to do that?"

"Well." Jeremy gave her a self-conscious look. "Maybe not much at first. Some of the people I've talked to have been kind of skeptical. But when the changes we make start bringing in business, people will realize that what we have to offer is valuable. In fact, I'm waiting to hear back from three potential clients as we speak."

Bea loved the spark in Jeremy's eyes as he talked about it. Loved the look of the website and even the idea of partnering with another person who could help share the load and responsibility. But how long would it take before there was a profit?

The assistant-manager position at Food Farm was looking harder and harder to resist.

"That's really great, Jeremy. Really. But what about—"

A knock on the door cut her off. She glanced at the time. Dad should be returning from his day out hunting anytime now, but he wouldn't knock. She frowned. *Please, not Marge again.*

She pushed away from the table with a groan. "I'll get it."

Jeremy and Steve followed her down the hall. She braced herself for a burst of Marge's gusto as she pulled open the door.

A man about her dad's age stood on the step in a very expensive jacket. "Hello."

Her eyes widened slightly. "Hi."

"Is this the Jensen residence?"

He didn't look like a salesman, and Mormons typically traveled in pairs. Who was this guy? He looked familiar, but she couldn't place him. "Yes."

He shifted on his feet. "I'm Ken. Ken Thurgood."

"I'm Bea. Can I help you with something? Are you lost?"

You couldn't exactly pass through Moose Creek by accident. How did he get here?

"Bea?" Ken's eyebrows rose in an almost hopeful way. "You're Bea?"

She nodded slowly, ready for this strange exchange to make sense. Jeremy cleared his throat behind her.

"Uh, honey?"

She glanced over her shoulder at him. "What?"

"I think Ken might be your uncle."

✦   ✦   ✦

"What were you thinking?" If a whisper could be described as shrill, that's what Bea's was. "Why didn't you tell me?"

Jeremy peeked around the corner into the living room, where Ken sat on the couch thumbing through a Jensen-family photo album. He hung his head. "I was afraid it might be a dead end, and I know what it feels like to get your hopes up for nothing. I was waiting for a response."

She made a broad gesture in Ken's direction. "There's your response."

"I was trying to protect you. We don't even know if it's really him."

Bea glanced out the window, hoping to see Dad's truck. She'd sent him a text as soon as Jeremy had told her who Ken might possibly be, asking when he would be home. He hadn't answered, which meant he was either far afield and had no reception or was already driving back. He never checked his messages while driving.

"He does look a lot like Dad. And he seems to be the right age."

"When I found him on the website, I thought it had to be the wrong guy. It seemed too easy. He never even wrote me back. He just . . . showed up."

Jeremy had explained about the website he'd found, designed for people searching for their birth families. Explained how there was a way to send confidential messages in hopes of matching families up with their long-lost relatives.

She paced the floor. "When exactly were you planning to fill me in on all this?"

"I'm sorry." He tried to grab her hand as she passed, but she pulled it out of reach. "I didn't want to stress you out until I knew for sure there was something to it."

"You don't think this is stressful?" Her neck muscles strained with the pressure of shouting indignantly in a whisper.

"There was no way I could know he would show up like this."

She realized her fists were clenched and forced them to release. She shook out her hands. Part of her understood the reasonableness of what Jeremy was saying and the decisions he'd made. Another part wanted to wring his neck. Weren't they supposed to tell each other everything?

Well. Maybe there were a few things she hadn't been one hundred percent forthright about with him, either.

Her shoulders relaxed the slightest bit. "What do we do now?"

"I can't believe I'm going to say this, but . . . I wish your dad was here."

The corners of her mouth twitched. Jeremy caught her eye and smiled a sheepish half smile.

"See?" She chuckled. "He comes in handy once in a while."

Jeremy gave an exaggerated sigh of exasperation. "Okay, fine. He might be good for something."

"He'll be thrilled to hear that."

"You wouldn't dare."

She raised an eyebrow. "Wouldn't I?"

He grabbed her around the waist and pulled her to him,

tickling her side. "I'm not letting go until you promise not to tell him."

She squealed and gasped for breath. "Okay, okay. I promise."

"Should we ask Ken some more questions?" Jeremy reluctantly let her go and peeked around the corner again. "Offer him a glass of water or something?"

Bea gave him a sly grin. "So we can pull his fingerprints off the glass?" A low rumble caught her ear. "That's Dad's truck."

She hoped he was in a good mood. Hoped he wouldn't freak out. Hoped it wasn't all a terrible mistake. She held her breath as an awfully long moment passed. Then they heard the front door swing open. She and Jeremy stumbled over each other to meet her dad at the door.

He clomped into the house, indicating the road with a jerk of his head. "Whose car is parked the wrong way out there?"

Her mind went blank of everything except the peaceful look on Grandma June's face the last time Bea was at her house. She'd been happy. Content. Bea didn't want to ruin that. Should they have left the whole thing alone?

"Uh . . ."

Jeremy stepped up. "Well, you see . . ."

Ken appeared.

Dad's eyes registered a quick flash of surprise before his manners kicked in. "Hello, I'm Mitch."

Ken took her dad's outstretched hand and clasped it, hope and hurt and hesitation in his eyes. "Ken. Ken Thurgood." His voice cracked. "I'm your big brother."

❖　❖　❖

Mitch looked around the table, his eyes stopping briefly on each of the other people before returning to the mug of coffee Bea had set before him. "You're telling me that my mother, Juniper Marie Jensen, had a baby, gave him up, and then lived the rest of her life as if nothing happened? And she never told a soul?"

"Dad." Bea's voice was sympathetic but firm. "We've been over the whole thing three times now."

He wrinkled his forehead. "It's just so hard to believe. I can't wrap my mind around it."

Even after Ken had shown him a copy of a birth certificate that listed J. Reynolds as the mother of a baby born on a date that was most definitely not *his* birthdate . . . even after Bea repeated her entire conversation with Aunt Gladys, which Mitch at first dismissed as the ramblings of a senile old woman before feeling bad and recanting . . . even after looking into his own eyes, the ones he and he alone had always shared with his mother, which stared back at him from across the table, he was still struggling to come to grips with the truth.

He narrowed his eyes at Jeremy. "And you just posted our address on the internet?"

Jeremy raised his hands. "No, I—"

"That's my fault," Ken interrupted. "Once I had some names to go on, it wasn't hard to find your house."

"But why come here?" Mitch asked.

Ken hesitated. "I thought it would be easier . . ."

Everyone waited.

"If I was going to find out my biological family wanted nothing to do with me"—Ken struggled to meet Mitch's eyes—"I thought it would be easier coming from you."

Mitch tried to put himself in Ken's shoes. Though it had taken a lot of courage on Ken's part to come all this way, the man had no definitive proof to back up his claims. Yes, Mitch's mother was in Chicago the summer Ken was born. Yes, her maiden name was Reynolds, and Great-Aunt Gladys had corroborated the story. But still. Mitch just couldn't believe—

"I know what you're thinking." Ken drummed the table with his fingers, something Mitch often found himself doing, as well.

"Maybe this whole thing is a long shot. But I'd really like to visit her and see if she can explain."

Right. That. Mitch shifted uncomfortably in his seat. As far as he knew, Ken was completely unaware of his—their?—mother's tenuous condition. Unaware of how unpredictable her grip on reality was and how catastrophic a meeting like Ken was suggesting could be for her mental clarity.

"Should we call Grandpa?" Bea asked.

"Your grandpa." Ken cleared his throat. "Is he my . . . ?"

Mitch shook his head. "No. He would've never allowed my mother to be sent away. There's no way."

Ken hung his head. "I don't suppose you have any idea . . . ?"

"I think there's only one person who can give you any answers about that. If, and I do mean *if*, there's any truth to this whole thing." Mitch sighed. "I'll call my dad."

He pushed away from the table and left the kitchen. The whole thing was inconceivable. Could it be real? Could his mother have kept this a secret his entire life? He'd always wanted a brother. Used to beg for one like it was a puppy you could pick up at the store. But he never dreamed it would happen like this.

If it was even true. For all he knew, Ken could be some kind of scammer. A con artist with fake papers. What if he *did* know about Mitch's mother's condition and was planning to use her confusion against her? Against all of them?

Mitch slipped down the hall to his room and stepped inside. Oh, great. Another carpet puddle. As if he needed another mystery in his life.

The water seeped through his sock as he dialed up his parents' landline with shaking hands.

One ring. Two rings. Three. Maybe this was a bad idea. He should hang up.

"Hello?"

The gruff voice his father always used to answer the phone

brought the situation into sharp focus. If Ken was who he said he was, it would change everything. It could destroy his parents and the forty-four years of marital trust they had established. It could compromise the progress his mother had recently made with her health. It could mean this Ken person had some sort of claim on the house Mitch grew up in. His mother's house.

His father spoke again. "Hello?"

Mitch plunked down on his bed and pulled off his wet sock. He could try to avoid bringing it up, but Ken could easily find his parents' house and confront them anytime he wanted now that he'd come this far. Better to get it over with on his own terms and not leave it up to Ken. Better to get to the bottom of it.

"Yeah, Dad, it's Mitch."

"Any luck out there today?"

"No." His usual go-to spots for hunting had failed him so far this season, but that was the least of his worries. "Listen, are you and Mom up for a visit?"

His father chuckled. "You can come by anytime; you know that. You don't have to call first."

"I know. It's just, we all want to come. Me and Bea and Jeremy. And . . ."

His dad waited. Settled into the silence.

Mitch looked up at the ceiling. "And there's someone else who wants to see you. Er, Mom. See you both, I guess. Is that okay?"

"Who is it?"

"It's a little hard to explain."

More silence.

"How's Mom doing today?"

"Oh, about the same. Kind of quiet."

Mitch didn't want to upset her. Maybe he could ask Ken to let them all sleep on it for a couple days before doing anything. What harm could a few more days do after so many years?

He stared at his one bare foot and thought about how quickly his mother's mental faculties could change. How quickly she could deteriorate. If he wanted the truth, maybe a couple of days did matter.

"We'll head over soon, then."

His father grunted. "Well, all right. See you in a few."

"Sure. See you."

He hung up and stared at his phone. He'd never missed Caroline more.

FORTY-THREE

I don't know how long I've been sitting here. Goose bumps prickle on my arms, but the thought of going inside to find a coat is overwhelming. I just want to sit here watching the clouds cast moving shadows on the mountain.

"You're cold."

Rand's voice startles me. I forgot he was here.

I turn my head slowly to look at him in the rocking chair next to mine. "I'm okay."

He pushes out of the chair with a groan and takes a shuffling step toward the house.

"No, don't." My hand feels as if it weighs a hundred pounds as I raise it in protest. "I'm okay."

"I'll just grab a blanket."

I do not answer. A lump forms in my throat. I don't deserve that man. I never did.

I turn my face back to the mountain and blink, clearing my vision. Won't the light be appearing soon? I've lost all sense of time. I sit up a little straighter, suddenly feeling it's very important that I see the light.

Rand returns and tucks a blanket over my lap. It feels nice.

He peers into my face. "What's wrong?"

"The light." I shift to look past him, around him. "I can't see it."

He tugs his rocking chair a little closer and sinks into it. "It's early yet."

"But I can't see it anymore, Rand." I shove my hand in my pocket and grab the penny tightly in my palm. "I need to see it."

"You just gotta wait is all." He rubs my knee. "Just a little longer."

Okay. Wait. My grip on the penny loosens, and I examine his hand. It's so wrinkled and worn. So familiar and comforting. Of all the memories I stand to lose, the feel of his hand will be one of the most precious.

Gravel crunches and I stiffen. "Someone's here."

"I told you Mitch was coming out, remember?" Rand stands again. "With the kids?"

Oh. Right. His truck appears over the little hill along the drive. "And they're bringing someone?"

Rand nods and descends the steps. *Thud, drag. Thud, drag.* He waits at the bottom of the stairs, knowing they will come. I would jump up to meet them, too, but I am so tired today. Just so tired.

Another car I've never seen pulls up behind the truck. That must be the someone. Last time it was Amber who came out. I liked that. I don't know who they're bringing today.

Mitch, Beatrice, and Jeremy climb out of the truck. Bea waves at me, and I lift a hand. I think I smile. She looks so much like Caroline. Another man joins them, and he watches me as the four of them walk over to the house.

"Howdy," Rand says.

Mitch nods. Jeremy reaches out to hold Bea's hand. That makes me happy, even though I still think they're practically children.

"Hi, Mom," Mitch says. "How are you?"

"Good."

I narrow my eyes at the stranger, and Mitch understands. "Uh, this is Ken. He . . . well, maybe we should all go inside and talk?"

I'm quite happy on the porch. I'm waiting for the light. But Mitch looks so serious, and the stranger's eyes fixed on me are so unnerving that I push myself to my feet. Rand stands ready at my elbow as if I might topple over, but the rush of activity has given me a jolt of energy. I go inside, and everyone follows me to the kitchen.

"What can I get out?" I ask. "Let me cut up some cheese and salami."

"No, Mom." Mitch waves a hand. "We're all fine. We don't need anything."

I open the cupboard. "Let me pour some drinks."

"June." Rand pulls out a chair and gestures toward it with his chin. "They said they're fine. Why don't you come and sit."

It's like he knows something I don't. A small match of anger bursts to flame in my chest. No one needs to tell me what to do in my own house. But I catch a glimpse of Bea's face and realize perhaps someone has died. That is why they're here. But then who is this man? Why is he looking at me like that? His eyes . . .

"Mom, we need to ask you about something important," Mitch says. Everyone is sitting now.

I feel my hands tremble slightly in my lap. Something important? What if I don't know the answer? "Okay."

"Do you remember your aunt from Chicago? Gladys Fennel?"

I tilt my head. Aunt Gladys? Is it Aunt Gladys who has died? I sigh. We haven't been in touch in years. She was a good woman, but I lost her long ago.

"Mom? Do you remember?"

"Yes."

Will they expect me to be sad?

287

"And do you remember going to stay with her the summer after you graduated high school?"

My stomach twists. I wish he would just tell me she's dead. "Yes."

"I was hoping you would be willing to talk to us about why you went to Chicago that summer."

My heart pounds loud enough that I wonder if everyone can hear it. None of this will bring Aunt Gladys back. There's no point . . .

"I'm not sure why that's important now."

The stranger flinches, and Mitch clears his throat. "Well, Mom, I think it *is* important. Because this man here"—he points with his thumb—"this is Ken, remember? And Ken was born at Mercy Hospital in Chicago on August 17, 1976."

I hear a newborn cry, and I gasp. It's such a beautiful, horrible, vulnerable sound. I long to see his face. To touch his hand. But they are carrying him away.

"No," I shout. I cry. My baby. My sweet, precious, perfect baby. "No!"

Bring him back. Bring him back.

Oh, God, what have I done?

FORTY-FOUR

Fear and confusion twisted his mother's face as she shouted, and Mitch wished he could take it back. The whole thing. But they were here, and Ken sat beside him, intense and intent, not going anywhere.

Rand reached toward June as if to comfort her or hold her down, but then pulled his hand away. Unsteady. He addressed Mitch while turning a suspicious eye on Ken. "What's this about, son?"

Mitch let out a deep breath through his nose. Bea and Jeremy seemed to know more about it than he did, but they'd agreed on the drive over that he should take the lead in this conversation.

He grasped at straws. "Will you tell us about your visit to Chicago, Mom?"

She made an unintelligible sound and stared at the table as if seeing something else entirely. Mitch was glad he'd warned Ken about her condition before they drove over. Her appearance was improved from the last time he'd seen her—that haircut had done wonders—yet her behavior remained unpredictable.

His father's voice grew impatient. "Mitch?"

Mitch drummed the table with his fingers. Boy, oh boy. There was nothing for it but to dive in.

"Ken has a birth certificate that says he was born in 1976 in Chicago to J. Reynolds."

Rand's eyebrows shot up. He looked at June. Looked at Ken.

"Did you ever wonder what she went there for, Dad?" Mitch tried to keep his voice calm and level. "Did you ever ask?"

"You know what she always says." His voice sounded far away, an echo in the bottom of a well. "'Today's more important than yesterday.' I never gave it much thought. June?"

Mitch held his breath as five pairs of eyes fixed on his mother.

Rand persisted, his voice harder now. "Juniper?"

She made a sound like a whimper.

Ken leaned forward and spoke for the first time. "Mom?"

Her eyes snapped up to meet his. All the air was sucked from the room. Mitch felt it leave his lungs and disappear. The moment hung there, weightless yet immovable.

"Marshall." June's voice was small and strained, but her eyes were clear. "My boy."

"Mom." Ken sprang from his chair and hurried around the table to crouch beside her. "I knew it was you the moment I saw you."

"I'm so sorry, Marshall. So sorry." She reached a tentative, shaking hand toward his face but stopped short.

"Go ahead," Ken said.

She touched his cheek. Touched his hair. "I've missed you every day of your life. I've thought of you every minute. I'm so sorry."

Mitch's neck tensed. Maybe there'd been a mistake. This man's name wasn't Marshall; it was Ken. He snuck a glance at his father. His expression was cloudy, his jaw tight. If Mitch had harbored any suspicions that his father knew about Ken before today, they were gone now. What was he thinking? Mitch felt a stab of grief on his behalf. How would he feel if he learned his wife had kept a secret from him for over forty years?

"What happened, Mom?" Mitch glanced at Bea and Jeremy, reading the same desire to know more on their faces.

Rand shook his head. "June, is this true?"

"Please tell us." Ken stood and pulled his chair over next to June. "Who is my father? Why did you give . . . Why didn't you keep me?"

Mitch glared. "Don't push her."

"It's all right." June folded trembling hands in her lap. "There was a boy in my class. A nice boy. I'd never been involved with anyone before, but he promised we would get married. I let it all go to my head. I should've known better."

"He left you?" Ken asked.

She stared past Mitch's head, as if watching her past play out on the wall. "He enlisted the day after graduation, and I never heard from him again. My parents sent me away to Chicago."

A pit grew in Mitch's stomach as she told them about her desperation and humiliation. The young girl she described was nothing like the strong, capable, almost defiant woman he'd always known. The one who never let anyone tell her what to do or where to go or what was best.

"The moment they took you away and wouldn't let me see you, I knew I'd made a mistake." His mother's voice broke. "But it was too late. I did nothing but scream and cry for days, and Aunt Gladys . . . well, she did what she could with me. Eventually, I took a bus home. Everything about Chicago was a reminder."

She looked at Rand. "That's when you started paying attention to me. And you were so good and honest and strong."

His father looked back, his eyes trying to tell her something, but Mitch didn't know what it was.

"I should've told you." She hung her head. "I was afraid you'd change your mind about me. I—I'm sorry."

Ken shifted in his seat. "What was my father's name?"

"Ethan." June sniffled. "Ethan Swenson."

"His name's not on the certificate."

"No." She raised her head. "I refused to tell them. He didn't deserve any part in it."

Ken was opening his mouth to ask more questions when Mitch caught his eye and shook his head. There'd been enough questions already.

June looked around the table at each person. "Forgive me. All of you."

Rand rose from the table and paused, the lines on his face deep as trenches. Then he left the kitchen.

"Dad," Mitch called.

"Leave him alone." June motioned for Mitch to stay where he was. "He's right to be upset."

Mitch remained in his chair, but his heart hung heavy in his chest. The front door creaked open and slammed shut. He couldn't remember ever seeing his father angry at his mother. They'd always had such a strong bond. Always presented such a united front. It felt wrong to witness this distance between them.

"Now." June nodded at Ken, her eyes bright with unshed tears. "Tell me everything."

❖ ❖ ❖

Bea listened to Ken's life story with rapt attention. She was delighted to learn she had five cousins, ranging in age from four years old to seventeen. Ken had not gotten married and started a family at such a young age as Dad.

Grandma June hung on every word, laughing or crying at every detail Ken shared. He insisted several times that he'd had a good life, that his parents loved him. He flipped through pictures on his phone and told Grandma the names of her other grandchildren over and over, which she struggled to keep straight.

As his story wrapped up, Jeremy asked one of the questions that had been on Bea's mind, as well. "How long have you been looking for us?"

"I didn't even know I was adopted until about five years ago when my dad had a heart attack." Ken slid his phone back in his pants pocket. "He told me everything before going in for double bypass surgery. In case he didn't make it out."

Bea's eyes widened. "Did he?"

Ken smiled. "Yes. Thankfully. But his surgery made me face the fact my parents wouldn't be around forever. Got me wondering how long I had before I missed my chance to meet my biological parents. It wasn't long after that I decided to start searching. I registered on that adoption website about two years ago."

Grandma June stared at his face as if memorizing it. Or as if she'd known it all along.

Bea's father shifted to peer out the window. "Where do you think Dad went? It'll be dark soon."

"What?" Grandma's brow furrowed as she looked around the table. "Oh. Yes. I'm sure he's fine."

A feeling of impending loss tightened Bea's chest. She'd been reading up on Alzheimer's disease and had learned about *sundowning*, when people struggling with dementia grew more confused and disoriented at the end of the day. She made note of the worried look on Grandma's face and feared they were losing her.

She nudged her father and leaned close to his ear. "Maybe we should go. Before . . ."

He pressed his lips together. "You might be right. But we can't leave until your grandpa's back."

Ken overheard them and said, "I have so many questions I want to ask still. I told her my whole story, but she hasn't told me hers."

"You can stay with us tonight." Mitch looked out the window

again. "Maybe we can come back in the morning. Oh, there he is."

The front door opened, and they all listened to the sound of boots scraping against the entryway rug. Bea stood, and Jeremy followed her lead. It was time to go home. But Ken wasn't ready.

"Why did you call me Marshall?" Ken took Grandma's hand in his. "Just tell me that one thing. Did you name me before they took me away?"

Grandma was quiet for a long moment, and Bea held her breath, afraid Grandma might say she didn't remember. Or worse, might ask Ken who he was and what he was doing in her house. Grandpa Rand appeared in the kitchen entrance and stopped, leaning against the wall. Grandma didn't see him.

"Rand's middle name is Marshall." Grandma's voice was higher and shakier than before, like the wind whistling through a hole in the barn. "I told Aunt Gladys that if you were a boy, I wanted to name you after a good man. Someone with a good heart. I'd known Rand my whole life and couldn't think of anyone better than him. I wanted you to grow up to be like that."

"It says *Ken* on my birth certificate."

Grandma stuck her hand in her pocket and nodded. "They didn't let me choose. Your . . . uh, parents, they had already told the nurse what your name should be. But to me, you were always Marshall."

She looked over at Mitch and smiled. "My two boys. Marshall and Mitch. Mylanta."

"Thank you for telling me." Ken rose to his feet. "Can I come back tomorrow? I'll have a little time before I have to catch my flight home."

Grandma didn't answer. She stared at her lap.

Ken noticed Grandpa Rand standing by the wall. "Would that be all right with you, sir?"

Grandpa nodded.

Bea nudged her dad toward the door. "We'll let you get some rest now, Grandma."

Still no answer. Bea, Jeremy, and Dad moved to leave the kitchen. After a moment of hesitation, Ken reluctantly turned to follow.

"Wait." Grandma's head shot up. "Marshall."

Ken jerked to a stop. "Yes?"

She pulled her hand from her pocket and opened it. On her palm rested an old worn penny. "I want you to have this."

He gingerly took the offered gift and examined it closely. "Does that say 1976?"

She nodded. "I picked it up from the floor of Mercy Hospital as I was leaving. 'Course, it was brand-new then."

Ken's voice was thick with emotion. "You've kept it all this time?"

"I've never been without it. I've held it ten thousand times, praying that someday God would let me know that you were okay. But I don't need it anymore."

His fingers closed around the penny.

She smiled. "Now you're here."

FORTY-FIVE

When Bea opened her eyes Sunday morning, she was back in high school for a split second. In her old bedroom, under the comforter she'd had since she was thirteen. She had no responsibilities. Dad was cooking sausage links for breakfast. Mom was alive and well.

She sat up with a groan. This wasn't her comforter. It was Mom and Dad's quilt.

Reality made its presence felt. As she scrambled down the hall to the bathroom, clutching her stomach, she thought about Grandma June. What was it like for her to wake up some days in a different life? A different time? Thinking it was the past. Thinking things were one way when they weren't.

Her own brief fantasy had been right about one thing. The sausage. She dry-heaved as the smell of it wafted into the bathroom.

Jeremy tapped lightly on the door. "You need anything?"

She sank to the floor and leaned back against the tub, crossing her arms over her tender breasts. "Just give me a minute."

"I'm going to get dressed."

"Okay."

Perspiration covered her forehead and the back of her neck.

Gross. Wasn't the whole morning sickness thing supposed to be over by now?

Her hands found their way to her stomach as they seemed to do often and rested lightly on her lower abdomen, which was tight and ever so slightly swollen. She'd need to go shopping for maternity clothes soon. Mom would've loved that.

She let her head rest against the tub and took a couple deep breaths, concentrating to block out the smell of sausage. Mom would've been ecstatic to find out about Ken. *Uncle* Ken. She'd loved everything to do with family. She probably would've asked Ken to send her some of his photos and already printed them out and hung them on the fridge.

It was weird, knowing he was here. Staying in their house. Dad's half brother. It might take a while to get used to that. Would she get to meet her cousins? Were his adoptive parents nice?

With another groan, she slowly rose to her feet and splashed water on her face. She didn't want everyone waiting on her. Back in the bedroom, she found Jeremy sitting on the bed, dressed and ready.

He watched her search for an outfit in the closet. "Pretty crazy weekend, huh?"

"Very crazy."

They hadn't talked much about it last night. By the time they'd gotten home and gotten Uncle Ken settled, Bea had been ready to fall straight to sleep. She hadn't known what to say, anyway. It was a lot to process.

"Ken seems nice."

"I like him." Bea settled on her loosest pair of Wranglers and a sunset-orange sweater. "But I still can't believe it."

"That must've been hard for your grandma. Giving him up like that. What a burden to carry."

Bea touched her stomach again as she buttoned her pants. *A burden to carry.* Was that how she'd been viewing the child inside her? She thought about how devastating it had been for Grandma to lose her baby. How much he had been a part of her, even after he was gone, and how alone she'd been. Carrying such a tragic secret for so long was a burden. A heavy burden. But carrying a child . . .

She pulled the sweater over her head and ran her fingers through her tangled hair. Sure, maybe she'd have to cut it when her baby was born. Yes, maybe everything would change like Amber had said. But she was going to be a mother, and she was not alone.

Jeremy gave her a lazy smile and nodded toward the door. "Ready?"

She smiled back, believing for the first time that maybe she was.

◆ ◆ ◆

They rode out to his parents' house all together this time. Bea and Jeremy kept to themselves in the back of the truck, but Mitch kept glancing over at the passenger seat, reminding himself that man over there was his brother. Only half, technically, but more brother than he'd ever had.

Ken watched the world go by through the window. "It's beautiful out here."

"I'm partial to it myself."

"I saw pictures in your house of you with a dark-haired woman."

Mitch's forehead wrinkled. "Caroline."

"What happened?"

"Cancer. Two years ago."

Ken tore his gaze from the scenery and looked at him. "I'm sorry."

Mitch nodded. He'd heard all about Ken's wife, Marianne, yesterday, as well as plenty of other details about Ken's life that would normally take a number of visits to discover. Ken, though, knew next to nothing about Mitch or his life. Had no idea what he faced now with his mother's health, well, *their* mother's health, going downhill like it was.

"Look, about yesterday—"

"How long has she been this way?" Ken cut in. "Confused, I mean."

"It happened fast." Mitch searched his memory for a definite sign—something unmistakable to point to and say *this is where it all began*—but couldn't find one. There was only before he realized his mom had changed and after. "We're still getting used to it."

Ken turned his face back to the window. "And she never said anything about me at all? Not even when you were a kid?"

The longing in his voice was a seedling reaching its green arms to the sky. Hopeful but prepared to be crushed underfoot. Mitch slowly shook his head.

"How could she just let me go?"

Ken's words seemed to be directed at himself, but Mitch answered anyway. "We may never know the whole story."

"If only I'd found her sooner. I thought if I could just get here, everything would make sense. I wish . . ."

The road and the silence stretched out before them. Mitch didn't need Ken to finish telling him what he wished. Mitch knew. It was the same thing he wished. That things could've turned out differently.

"Me too," he said.

Ken glanced over. Mitch had one eye on the road, but with the other he caught a subtle change in his brother's expression.

Ken sighed. "You're losing her, too."

Though the words held a note of painful finality, somehow Mitch found comfort in them. For just a moment, he was not alone.

"I'd like you to meet my family sometime." Ken drummed his leg with his fingers. "If you want."

Mitch nodded. "I'd like that."

As they neared the house, he checked the time: 9:42 a.m. He'd hoped to get out the door sooner, but Bea had been moving slowly. He had to get Ken back to his rental car by noon if he was going to make it to Ponderosa in time to catch his flight. That didn't give them much time.

The sky was clear overhead, but clouds charged over the ridge of the mountains like an army surging into battle. The temperature had dropped steadily the past three days, and snow threatened. It would drive more animals into the foothills. Had Ken ever been hunting? Did he know anything about running a ranch?

Mitch parked close to the house, and they all climbed out. Rand's limp seemed more pronounced today as he walked over to meet them. The hard look he'd had in his eyes yesterday was gone.

"Hey, Dad. You doing okay?"

Rand took several breaths, hooked his thumbs in the belt loops of his jeans, and studied the mountain before answering. "I was mad."

The others took their cue from Mitch and waited.

"Just don't see how anyone could ever treat June like that," Rand said. "Made me want to wring Ethan's neck. If I would've known at the time . . ."

Mitch peered at his father's face, remembering what Frank had said about loving the church no matter what she did. His dad hadn't been angry about his wife having a child without him. About her keeping it a secret. He'd been angry at how she'd been hurt.

"How's Mom today? After all that?"

Rand looked down. "I'm afraid she's not doing so good."

Ken frowned. "What's the matter? Is she sick?"

"Mebbe."

Mitch's heart sank. He and Bea had both worried last night that his mom had overdone it. "Where is she?"

"Inside. On the couch. You can go on in, but don't expect much."

A feeling of irony stung Mitch as he watched Ken hurry into the house. It wasn't fair. To be reunited with your mother, to learn she'd never forgotten you all this time, only to watch her memories fade away.

They all crowded into the house and shuffled to find seats. Ken and Bea joined his mom on the couch, one on each side.

She smiled at them politely, as if they were strangers on the train. "Hello."

"Hi." Ken fidgeted like he didn't know what to do with his hands. "Do you remember me?"

"Hmm." She tilted her head, eyeing him intently. "Aren't you that nice boy from the Food Farm? The one they hired for the meat counter?"

"No, Mom. It's Ken. Uh, Marshall."

"Ken Marshall? Oh, well, it's nice to meet you. I'm Juniper." She patted his knee. "I'm sorry, I thought you were Todd. From the meat counter."

Mitch gave his dad a quizzical look and whispered, "Todd?"

Rand shrugged. "I think there was a man there named Todd when we were kids."

Mitch felt like he'd been punched. He wasn't prepared for this. Wasn't ready. His mother's deterioration was supposed to be more gradual. He was supposed to have more time to figure out a way to come to grips with it.

Ken was right. He was losing her.

For half an hour, Ken and Bea asked his mother questions and tried to explain who they were. She smiled graciously, nodded her head, and said, "Aren't you a character?" while the dread in Mitch's heart grew far and wide. His shoulders tightened. *"Far and wide as the open arms of Jesus,"* as his mother would say.

When she began to wring her hands and laugh nervously, Rand cleared his throat. "Maybe I can show you around the ranch a bit, Ken. Then I think you all better go."

Ken's face fell, and Mitch frowned. He hated that Ken might never get to see his mother how she'd been, with all the spunk and spark Mitch had always taken for granted. Might never be the recipient of the withering glare she gave when someone used the Lord's name in vain, or take a big bite of her apple pie the way it was meant to be.

"Okay." Ken stood and gave June a little bow. "It was nice to meet you, Mom . . . uh, Ms. Juniper."

Her eyes darted around the room. "Yes, yes. Nice to meet you, too, dear."

Jeremy stood as well and joined Ken. "I haven't gotten the grand tour, either. Mind if I tag along?"

Mitch glanced over at Bea.

She waved a hand. "You guys go ahead. I'll stay with Grandma."

Mitch followed his father, brother, and son-in-law out the door, thankful the weather today lent itself to showcasing the ranch in its best light. He had so many things he wanted Ken to see. The places that had been special to him as a child. The places where he and Ken would've built forts or snuck cigarettes if Ken had been here. He'd missed so much.

As Mitch stepped off the porch, he watched Ken slow his pace to match Rand's and pressed his lips together. Maybe it was better not to dwell on all the things Ken had missed. Maybe he should just let his brother enjoy what was.

Today was more important than yesterday, after all.

FORTY-SIX

Ken stood in the front hall, his small duffel at his feet. Mitch stood close by, clearing his throat, trying to figure out how to say good-bye.

"I wish there was something I could do to help." Ken nudged his bag with his toe. "I'm expected at work tomorrow."

"Of course." Mitch rubbed his eyes. He hadn't gotten much sleep last night. "I understand. I wish you could've had more time with her."

Ken nodded. "I'm sorry I turned up unannounced, but if I'd waited any longer . . ."

"I'm glad you came when you did."

Ken picked up his bag. "Christmas is in six weeks. Do you think it'd be all right if we came back for a few days? Me and Marianne?"

Mitch hesitated, surprised. Even after his mom's behavior this morning, he wanted to visit again so soon?

"We don't have to." Ken shifted on his feet. "I don't want to impose."

"No, no, that would be great." Mitch held out a hand. "We'd love to have you. You'll stay here with us."

"Are you sure?"

"Of course."

Ken shook his hand, then pulled him in for a hug. Mitch wasn't much of a hugger, but you only meet your long-lost brother for the first time once. They squeezed each other tightly, then Mitch pulled away.

"Well, you don't want to miss your flight," he said.

Ken cleared his throat, grabbed his bag, and opened the door. "We'll talk soon."

"Okay." Mitch gave his brother a nod. "Soon."

Ken waved down the hall at Bea and walked out, closing the door behind him.

Mitch moved to the living room and watched through the window as Ken hopped into his rental car and drove away. Mitch hated how he was losing his mother. Hated the helplessness. Hated how dementia could turn a vibrant and flourishing brain into a gray, murky wasteland. And yet God was bringing something good from it all. For all his losing, it looked like he was gaining, too.

"Dad? You okay?"

He turned around. There before him was another significant gain: a grandchild. He'd almost lost Bea once, pushing her away like he did when Caroline died. Then he'd looked at her having to move back home as proof he'd been right about her marrying Jeremy. But what if it was just God's way of giving him another chance?

A chance he'd almost blown. But she wasn't gone yet.

"I need to tell you something."

Bea waited.

"I never should've said what I said about you and Jeremy."

"Dad—"

"I was wrong. And I'm sorry I wasn't there for you after your mother died. I got . . . lost." Mitch pictured Caroline's face. Her hands. The shape of her legs and the curve of her neck when he brushed her chestnut hair out of the way to kiss it. He hadn't been ready to say good-bye. "It's been hard to figure out what to do without her. How to be. But your marrying Jeremy wasn't a mistake."

Unshed tears shone in Bea's eyes. "It was hard for me, too."

"I know."

"I thought getting away from here would help—I thought I could move on—but at college I was so alone. I didn't fit in. Something was always missing. Until I met Jeremy."

"Is that why you quit school? Because you didn't fit in?" He wanted to understand. She'd always insisted it wasn't because of her marriage, but what else could it have been?

"That was part of it."

He moved closer, wanting to hold her but unsure if he'd ever be able to let go. "What was the other part?"

"I was scared, okay? I didn't know what I wanted to do. I didn't want to disappoint you. And there were bad memories there. I was attacked—" She cut herself off and looked away as if she hadn't meant to say the words. Blood pounded in his temples.

"You were *what*?"

She held up her hands. "Nothing happened. Jeremy saved me. I know I told you we met through a mutual friend, but that wasn't really true. He rescued me from an assault."

Mitch's mouth went dry. His baby girl *attacked*? "Why didn't you tell me?"

She hesitated. "I shouldn't have been walking alone. I wanted to pretend it never happened."

Anger and regret rolled around in his mouth like a pinch of chew from a Skoal can. "You should be able to walk wherever you want." His fists clenched. "Did he hurt you?"

"No. It just . . ."

"Just what?"

"Scared me."

He shook out his hands. Took a deep breath. He hadn't been there to protect her. "Jeremy saved you?"

She nodded.

"And you're okay?"

She nodded again. "I promise."

He couldn't hold back any longer. He wrapped his arms around her, knowing it was like trying to grasp a snowflake in his hand. "I'm so sorry."

She submitted to the hug for a moment, then pulled away. "It was Jeremy's idea to take a break from school for a little while. He knew how much I was struggling."

Jeremy knew. Mitch hung his head. He hadn't known. He'd been too buried under his own grief. Too unbending in his expectations. Too quick to judge. "I'm glad you did."

She gave him a skeptical look. "You are?"

"You guys were right to make that decision together. That's how it should be."

It had been easy for him to question Jeremy's place in Bea's life—to want to always be the one she turned to in times of trouble—but he knew what Caroline would do if she were here. She'd hum Bob Carlisle's "Butterfly Kisses," pat his cheek, and tell him to get over it.

His voice was thick. "Your mother would be proud of you."

"I miss her so much."

"Me too."

"I wish we could talk about her."

"We will." He'd thought holding the pain and memories inside, keeping them to himself, would prevent Caroline from slowly fading away. But all it had done was put up a wall. "From now on, we can talk about her anytime you want."

Bea nodded. "Okay."

He put a hand on her shoulder, and for a moment they stood together, remembering. Then a low rumble caught his attention.

Bea put a hand on her stomach. "Can we eat lunch now? The baby's hungry."

Mitch studied his daughter. Marge had been right. This baby was coming whether the ideal situation ever did or not. "I can't wait to meet this baby."

Bea's eyes widened. "Really?"

"He's going to take after his grandpa, I bet." Mitch grinned and held out his arm. "Right this way to the kitchen."

They found Jeremy there, pulling items from the fridge to make sandwiches. Mitch caught his eye and nodded.

Jeremy nodded back. "Ken get on the road okay?"

Bea grabbed an apple from the bowl and began slicing it. "Yep. I feel bad Grandma didn't recognize him today."

"That was rough." Jeremy snuck a potato chip from an open bag. "Did the doctor say she could get so bad so fast?"

Mitch shook his head. "He never said she couldn't. He said dementia is very unpredictable."

Bea pulled three plates from the cupboard. "I don't like seeing her that way."

"Me neither." Mitch watched Bea take bread from a bag. Maybe there would be another good thing to come out of all this. Maybe now Bea would understand why they had to move his mother to an assisted-living home in Ponderosa. "Which reminds me—I've narrowed it down to two places for Mom in Ponderosa. I've got meetings with both of them on Saturday."

Bea dropped the butter knife she was holding into a jar of mayonnaise. "You're still on that? No."

"It's up to me to figure this out. Not you."

Bea threw up her hands. "You can't fix this one by yourself, Dad."

His nostrils flared. Yes, he could. He had to. Who else was there? He was on his own. Caroline was gone. Bea wasn't his anymore. Even Ken was gone.

The whole thing stunk like cow pies in the sun. He eyed the chair nearest him and shoved it in, slamming it against the table.

The freezer spit out three small chunks of ice in response. They clattered off the tray and onto the floor.

One piece landed in front of Steve, who jumped to his feet and batted it across the floor. It shot out of the kitchen. Steve chased it, sending it skidding down the hall. Mitch followed the sliding of the ice and the scritch-scratch of the cat's claws on the laminate floor with his ears until there was silence. A few moments later, Steve reappeared, looking downcast, no ice cube in sight.

"Where'd it go, Steve?" Jeremy asked.

Mitch narrowed his eyes. Wait a minute. Wait just a minute. He hurried down the hall to his bedroom, and Steve eagerly followed. Mitch opened the door.

Aha.

There, sitting on the carpet just inside his room, was the piece of ice, already beginning to melt. Steve pounced on it, sending it back into the hall.

A tickle of laughter started in Mitch's stomach and worked its way up to his throat. "You really had me stumped, you little rascal."

He headed back to the kitchen, a new lightness in his step. Maybe Bea was right. He couldn't fix the problem with his parents on his own. Or maybe at all. And apparently, he couldn't fix the fridge to save his life. But that didn't mean things weren't going to be okay.

A light tap at the front door stopped him on his way to the kitchen. He changed course and pulled it open.

"Hi, there." Marge smoothed her hair with one hand and held a plate covered in foil with the other. "Who was that you had over here last night?"

He stepped aside and gestured for her to enter, which she seemed more than happy to do.

"You'll never believe it," he said.

And he found he couldn't wait to tell her all about it.

✦ ✦ ✦

Bea chewed her sandwich and watched warily as her dad and Marge chatted on the other side of the table. He was telling her the whole story about Ken and Grandma June, and she was eating it up.

"I didn't want to say anything earlier." Jeremy leaned close so that only she could hear. "But I think it's time to quit the Food Farm."

"The assistant-manager job would get us through until your business takes off. It wouldn't be that bad."

"But I have good news."

She finished her bite and gave him her full attention. "Really? What?"

"I found us a place."

"You found . . . ? Like, to live?"

He smiled. "Thanks to working the belt for the Duncans, we've got enough in savings for the deposit and first two months' rent. It's small, but it's better than our apartment in Santa Clara."

Apartment? Bea chewed the inside of her cheek. There were only a few apartments in Moose Creek. None of them could be considered better than where they lived in Santa Clara.

"Is it over someone's garage or something? I didn't know there were any apartments available around here."

"No. Bea." Jeremy set his sandwich down and glanced over at her dad. "It's in Ponderosa."

She looked down. What? Their only source of income was here. Dad needed her here. He'd never agree to move Grandma and Grandpa into the house if she moved away. And she'd just mentioned it to Amber the other day, and she said she'd be happy to stop in once a week to keep an eye on Grandma. Between her and Amber . . .

"I can't run my company from here." Jeremy's eyes pleaded

with her to understand. "Those three clients I told you about? They're ready to sign. All of them. But I need to be more available. I need to be around other businesses."

She opened her mouth. Closed it.

He raised his eyebrows. "I need better internet. I need . . ."

She felt the familiar stirring of uncontrollable emotions in her chest and struggled to conquer them. Of course, she knew they couldn't live with Dad forever. They'd put a three-month limit on that. And she'd never imagined herself settling down in Moose Creek. But Dad was all alone. He needed her. Grandma and Grandpa needed her. And her only friend lived here. The pull of inertia was strong.

Jeremy's words from before echoed in her mind. *"I need you to choose me."* She looked over at Dad, talking animatedly with Marge. He'd come a long way from the broken man Bea left behind two years ago. Back then he'd been angry and hurt at her leaving. But now?

She dropped her hands to her lap, and her fingertips brushed her upper left thigh where her commitment to Jeremy was etched forever into her skin with black ink. Then her fingers moved to her belly. This was her family now. Jeremy and this little one she could almost feel in her arms.

"It's a great place." Jeremy reached for her hand. "Money will be tight for a while, but if I do a good job with these three clients, more will come. I know it."

His voice, his expression, asked her to trust him. To choose. She swallowed the lump in her throat and put on a smile. It wasn't the brightest and most convincing smile she'd ever given, but it was a start.

"When do we move in?"

FORTY-SEVEN

M itch stood in front of his house, waiting. It was awkward. There was no reason for him to attend another meeting at the church about the Tucker fundraiser, but Marge had quite firmly requested his presence and asked him to give her a ride there. For some reason, he'd agreed.

Almost a week had passed since he'd told her all about his unexpected brother. He'd been surprised how easy it was to confide in her. How nice it was to have someone to talk to. But since that day, he'd felt uneasy whenever he saw her. Which was quite often. She never seemed to run out of reasons to stop by.

"Yoo-hoo." She closed the front door of her house and jogged across her yard. "Sorry to keep you waiting."

He shrugged and gestured toward his truck. They got in, and he started it up, letting out a long breath. What a day. He'd scheduled both care facility interviews for today so he wouldn't miss any more work. Ralph had covered for him enough lately. He didn't want to make the trip to Ponderosa twice anyway, and there was that stop at Jack's Custom Leather he'd needed to take care of. But now he was tired. The care facilities had put him on edge, and he'd been disappointed to learn their protocol as one spouse deteriorated was to separate them from the other spouse. It made him ill to think of his parents being separated.

"Did you just get home?" Marge asked.

"Yeah."

"And what have you been up to all day?"

He hesitated but couldn't think of one good reason not to tell her. "Touring assisted-living homes in Ponderosa. For my mom."

"Oh." Marge struggled to adjust her seat belt. "I didn't realize . . ."

"Didn't realize what?"

"Oh, nothing." She flicked a hand. "It's not my place or anything."

He grunted. "Okay."

She messed with the strap some more. "It's just I didn't think you'd send her away. I mean, she's lived in Moose Creek her whole life."

A flash of annoyance scrunched his face. First Bea and now Marge? Maybe there was one good reason not to tell her.

She had no idea how he'd agonized over this decision. How he felt backed into a corner. He wasn't sending her away. He was getting her the help she—and his father—needed. It wasn't like he wanted to do this. It wasn't like he was happy to be losing his mother only two short years after losing his wife.

He kept his mouth shut and remembered to drive the back way to the church this time.

"I suppose you don't feel you have much choice," Marge continued, "since you're working full-time, and they live so far out of town. Obviously, it would be hard to keep an eye on them yourself."

He suppressed a sigh. If it was so obvious, why was she surprised?

"And with Bea and Jeremy already living with you, it's not like you can take in more family members."

His heart squeezed. Bea had dropped the bomb on Wednesday. They were moving out next weekend.

"Not for long," he muttered.

"What's that?" She leaned closer and fluttered her eyelashes at him. "What'd you say?"

He waved a hand. "Nothing. Just . . . Bea and Jeremy got a new place. In Ponderosa."

Her eyes widened. "Hmm."

Hmm? What was that supposed to mean? The church parking lot was empty except for Frank's Suburban. He parked next to it and turned off the engine.

She unbuckled with a thoughtful look on her face. "Now that's something to think about."

He slid from his seat and furrowed his brow. Whatever it was, he had the feeling he didn't really want her thinking about it.

❖ ❖ ❖

The meeting had been short. Frank had made faces at him whenever Marge wasn't looking and remarked several times about how nice it was they could just ride over together. Mitch wanted to punch him. They used to do that kind of thing a lot when they were younger. Box and wrestle until they were laughing too hard to continue. Frank had been the brother Mitch always wished he had. He'd have to sit down with him soon and tell him all about the biological brother he now had, as well.

Mitch parked the truck in the carport. Marge had barely spoken on the ride home, which made him nervous. He didn't mind the quiet or anything—in fact, he rather enjoyed it—but when had he ever known Marge to be quiet?

They walked around to the front of the house.

Marge fiddled with a giant star-shaped wire earring. "Thanks for the ride."

"I've got your plate from the other day." Mitch scratched the top of his head. "You want to come in and grab it? Those muffins were good."

313

A huge smile split her face. "I just wanted to share. Couldn't eat them all myself, you know." She patted the curve of her hip. "I've got nowhere left to put it."

He cleared his throat and tried not to stare at her abundant behind as she led the way into the house. She'd put just the right amount there, as far as he was concerned. He shook his head—he shouldn't be thinking like that.

They headed for the kitchen. He hoped Bea and Jeremy were on a walk or a drive or in their room or something . . .

Nope. They sat at the kitchen table, drinking an orange smoothie in a large glass with two straws.

"Hey, guys." Bea smiled at him. "How was your meeting?"

"Uh . . ." Mitch pointed at the counter. "Marge is just picking up her plate."

The plate had been washed and sitting on the counter for a couple of days. He handed it to Marge, the tips of his ears burning. He already felt weird around Marge, but when Bea was around, it was a hundred times worse.

Marge took the plate and sat down at the table. "Your father tells me you're moving to Ponderosa."

Bea nodded, a look of amusement in her eyes.

Marge turned around to face him, putting one arm on the back of the chair. "I've been thinking."

That's exactly what Mitch had been afraid of. "Oh?"

She stared at him for several seconds, her neck twisting awkwardly, before he realized he was being rude. He moved to the table and sat down.

"Much better." She sat up straight. "Now, I know you've had a tough few years and that you've had a lot on your mind lately."

He pinched the inside of his elbow. Where the heck was she going with this?

"I also know you don't want to move your parents to Ponderosa," she continued. "So here's what I'm thinking. The hospital just bumped me down to two shifts a week, and at first I was disappointed, but now I see it was all for a reason."

She paused for a breath, and Mitch sat perfectly still, afraid to look at Bea because he suspected she found this whole situation far too entertaining.

"You work Monday to Friday." Marge gave him a serious look, and he noticed the wrinkles around her eyes were more pronounced when she did that. He liked it. "I work Wednesday and Friday. We're both home on the weekends. That means there are only two days a week you would need to have someone available for your parents."

His nose scrunched. What was she talking about?

Bea pushed the smoothie glass over to Jeremy, her voice full of excitement. "And Amber already said she would love to visit with Grandma once a week. Grandma loves Hunter."

"Wonderful." Marge tucked her hair behind her ears. "That only leaves one day a week. I don't think I'll have any trouble getting volunteers for that."

Mitch looked from Marge to Bea and back. "For what?"

"It's settled then." Bea squealed. "Grandma and Grandpa can live here. They don't have to go to Ponderosa."

Mitch gaped. This conversation had gotten away from him fast. As his brain caught up with what Marge and Bea meant, an uncomfortable feeling grew in his gut. The care facilities he'd visited today had both been nice. Clean and comfortable. The staff had been courteous and competent. But neither place had felt quite right. Neither place had a large outdoor area, and neither could offer the one thing his mother found more comforting than anything else in the world: a view of the Bridger Mountains.

But that didn't mean he could move his parents into his house and allow all these random people to help care for them. Okay, maybe they weren't random people, but still. They were *his* parents. *His* responsibility.

Marge touched his elbow, and he startled. "I know what you're thinking."

It seemed an impossibility, but he searched her face and believed her.

Bea folded her hands in front of her. "Dad, I get it, too. But people want to help. They love you, and they love Grandma and Grandpa. I think you should let Marge do this."

He was still a little fuzzy on the details. "Do what exactly?"

"Help you." Marge smiled. "Organize a schedule to have someone available for your parents every day of the week. Give you the opportunity to say no to those icky places you looked at in Ponderosa."

"They weren't icky."

Bea turned solemn eyes on him. "But they weren't home, either. Those people aren't family."

He huffed. Marge wasn't either. Amber wasn't. Whoever else Marge had in mind wasn't. And he wanted to say so. He almost did. But then he thought of Frank. As real a brother as a guy could hope for all this time, despite no shared blood.

"What do you say, Mitch?" Marge asked.

Caroline would be a puddle of tears right about now if she were here. His mother would be silent and stubborn, insisting on her independence. His father would not speak, but his eyes would be steely and determined. None of that mattered, though. It was up to him now.

"I'll think about it."

FORTY-EIGHT

Bea felt a little guilty about moving ahead with Marge's plan before Dad had made his decision, but not much.

"Which day would work better for you?" She pinned her phone between her ear and shoulder to lift her suitcase onto her bed. "Wednesday or Friday?"

Amber didn't hesitate. "Wednesday. It would be the perfect way to break up our week. Me and Hunter are always looking for reasons to get out of the house."

"Great." Bea opened her closet and eyed her clothes. "I'll let Marge know. Thanks, Amber."

"We're excited about it." Her voice changed to baby talk. "Aren't we, little mister?"

Bea smiled. "Cool. Well, I better get back to packing."

"I'm not excited about that part," Amber said.

"I know." Bea looked around her little bedroom. It was familiar and comfortable, but it was time to move on. "We'll come back to visit as often as we can."

"It won't be the same."

"Hunter will be walking soon."

"So?"

"So you'll be way too busy to think about me."

Amber laughed. "That's true."

They said good-bye, and Bea tossed her phone on the bed. How had she gotten so settled into this place in less than three months? She was going to need another bag if she was going to take her winter gear. And where had her vitamins gone? She couldn't keep track of anything these days.

She thought again about Grandma June, and her heart twisted. What exactly had Dad told her? From the beginning, the doctor had mentioned the possibility of the disease being classified as early onset due to Grandma's age and had warned them about the rare familial variety. But had anything ever been determined for sure? She hadn't been to any of the appointments and had relied on Dad for the information.

He'd been more irritable than usual and unable to fix the fridge. She'd been forgetful and had lost everything from her hair dryer to her favorite pair of socks. A chill swept over her. As unlikely as it seemed, she couldn't help but wonder. Familial Alzheimer's? She'd tried to put it out of her mind from the beginning, not wanting to overreact. It wasn't a serious consideration. But what if . . .

"Yoo-hoo. Anyone home?"

Bea shook the unpleasant thoughts from her mind and stuck her head out the door into the hall. "I'm up here."

It no longer surprised, shocked, or dismayed her when Marge showed up at the house. It was still awkward, but at this point, Bea was just happy her dad had another friend. Frank was great and all, but he had seventy-some congregants constantly vying for his attention.

"Oh my." Marge bounced up the stairs and stood in Bea's doorway. "You're busy."

"Just packing." She opened and closed the little drawer in her bedside table. Where had she put her vitamins?

"We're going to miss you."

Her use of the word *we* kind of made Bea cringe but also made her smile. "You'll have your hands full with my grandma."

"I suppose so. What's the matter?"

Bea stuck her fingers in her hair. This kept happening. She swore she just had her vitamins. Fear nipped at her. "I keep losing things. My brain just won't work right. It's almost like . . ."

Marge plopped onto the bed. "Like what?"

"Nothing." Bea dropped her hands to her sides. "I've just never been so forgetful."

"Ah, baby brain." Marge picked up some clothes and started folding them. "I remember it well."

Bea's brow furrowed. "Baby brain?"

"Of course. Everyone gets it. Between the hormones and tiredness and extra stress, your brain goes haywire when you're pregnant. It's like it starts redirecting half of its resources to preparing for the baby."

"But it feels like it's not working at all sometimes."

Marge nodded. "When I was pregnant with Jonathan, I forgot my own birthday."

Hope burst and spread in Bea's chest like an egg cracking open. Her forgetfulness was normal?

"One time—I think this was when I was pregnant with Sarah—I ordered takeout from The Baked Potato and then never picked it up and made spaghetti instead."

Bea laughed. "They didn't call you about the order?"

"Well, they *did*." Marge grinned. "But I couldn't find the phone."

They both giggled. Bea never would've imagined herself giggling with Marge, but it wasn't so terrible. Marge was kind of pushy. And nosy. But nice.

"I was afraid I was losing it," Bea confessed.

"You're not losing your mind, sweetie." Marge's smile remained, but her expression grew more serious. "You're becoming a mom."

❖　❖　❖

As Mitch drove home from his parents' house, clouds hovered over the mountains, blocking out the highest peaks. He wondered if that was where the answers were. Up at the very top. Hidden.

He'd gone out to see his mom and dad after work for the past four days, but he was still conflicted about what to do moving forward. His mom had alternated between knowing what day it was and thinking it was 1998. Neither he nor his father had been able to figure out what made the difference. Why some days were worse than others. Even so, Mitch felt sure about one thing. Whatever was going on in her mind, she was more at peace now than maybe ever before.

Mitch had talked to the doctor by phone, who told him it was unusual but not unheard of for an Alzheimer's patient to suffer so inconsistently and deteriorate so quickly. Dr. Wilson had also asked about her diet and recommended more tests to check for any new infections or issues. Mitch had scheduled the tests for Friday just to cover all the bases. Something told him, though, that they weren't going to find any underlying causes for her decline.

The only thing he knew for sure was that his parents couldn't stay on the ranch. Every time he drove away, he sent up a fervent prayer that nothing serious would happen before he could return again. Then he spent most of the night startling awake, checking his phone in case his dad had tried to reach him. He couldn't live like this much longer.

When he reached Second Street, Jeremy was arriving at the house just before him. He'd been driving to Ponderosa every day, even during the whiteout on Monday, and getting home late. Jeremy couldn't live like this much longer, either.

Mitch pressed his lips together. They would celebrate Thanksgiving tomorrow, and then Bea and Jeremy were leaving on Saturday. Just when he was starting to get used to having them around. Just when he was starting to appreciate Jeremy.

But it was for the best. He could see now how he had been holding Bea back from giving Jeremy the commitment he deserved. It would sting to let her go again—sting like the dickens—yet he was determined to make Caroline proud of him, in case she was watching. He wouldn't give Bea a guilt trip. Wouldn't give Jeremy a lecture. He would smile and send them off, even if it broke his heart.

Oh, Caroline. Sweet Caroline.

He entered the house to the sound of laughter in the kitchen. Two laughs that were subdued, and one more boisterous than puppies on their first day out of the pen. Marge was here.

Bea smiled at him when he walked in. "Hey, Dad. I was just fixing Jeremy a plate. I'll make one for you, too."

"That's all right." He pulled a plate from the cupboard. "I'll do it."

Bea pulled foil off the top of a pan of enchiladas. "We tried to wait for you guys, but we were starving."

It took Mitch a second to realize the *we* Bea referred to was her and Marge. One eyebrow twitched, but he said nothing. Looked like Marge had wormed her way into Bea's heart.

His neck muscles tensed. What about his?

"We were just telling Marge about Steve and the ice cubes," Jeremy said.

Mitch chuckled. "Is that right."

Marge wiped at her eyes. "I haven't laughed that hard in ages."

Bea slid Jeremy's plate from the microwave, and Mitch slid his in. He turned it on high for one minute. "It figures the ice is just the right size to slip under the door."

Once everyone was seated at the table, the room grew quiet. Not quiet like everyone was too busy eating to talk, but quiet like something was up.

Mitch glanced around at everyone's faces. "What's going on?"

321

Bea and Jeremy exchanged a look but didn't answer.

Marge pulled a piece of paper from her back pocket and set it on the table. "I have something to show you."

He narrowed his eyes at the paper. She pushed it closer.

"What is it?" he asked.

She pointed to the left side of the paper. "This is the list of all the people who want to volunteer to help with your mom." She pointed to the right side. "And this is the calendar of who would help when, Monday through Friday, for the first three months, starting next week."

"And we'll visit most weekends." Bea nodded at Jeremy, and he nodded back. "For extra support."

He stared at the list of names. So many people. Almost everyone he knew from church was on there, including Corn Chowder Barbara. Something shifted in his heart, like when the sun hit just right and the light on the mountain sparked to life.

He shook his head. "I can't believe—"

"I'm sorry." Marge wrung her hands. "I know you haven't made any decisions yet, but—"

"No." He held up a hand. "It's okay. I mean I can't believe all these people would be willing to help me."

After how he'd treated them. After avoiding them for two years. After shunning the only kind of love and support they'd known how to give during the hardest time of his life. He should never have expected them to be perfect. To handle a terrible, tragic situation they'd never faced before perfectly. He sure hadn't.

"What do you say, Dad?" Bea's eyes were wide. Hopeful. "Can we give this a try?"

It went against everything in him. He'd been raised to solve his own problems. Clean up his own messes. Independence and grit were the way of the West. The way of the pioneers and trailblazers who had settled the wilds of Montana and North Dakota and Wyoming. But country living was also about community. Sharing with neighbors.

He thought about Susan Mullins, who had recently returned from her treatment in Seattle to find everyone on her block had pitched in to build her a new deck. He thought about the chili feed coming up on Saturday, where he was sure the town would raise thousands of dollars for the Tucker family. *This* was the Montana way.

"Okay." He looked at the paper again and nodded. "Let's do it."

FORTY-NINE

Bea dropped her bag on the floor and looked around. Jeremy had been right. This was way nicer than their apartment in California. Brand-new carpet. Sliding glass door that opened to a small balcony. A second bedroom—tiny but big enough for a crib.

"And not a speck of mold in the whole place." Jeremy put his arm around her shoulder. "I checked."

She smiled, and it was a full ear-to-ear smile this time. It wasn't her big dream or anything, to live in an apartment in Ponderosa, but this was a great place for another new start.

"Best of all," Jeremy continued, "we can make out anytime we want."

"Shh." She smacked his shoulder and pointed to her stomach. "She'll hear you."

His eyebrows rose. "He."

She laughed, but half her mind was stuck on how hard it was going to be on Dad when Grandma and Grandpa moved in, and the laugh rang a little hollow.

"I know it doesn't have a very good view of the mountains, and there's no yard"—Jeremy spoke quickly, earnestly—"but the rent is doable and—"

"It's perfect." She kissed him on the cheek. "I love it. And I'm sorry we couldn't bring Steve."

No pets allowed. Jeremy had been crushed, though his eagerness to get their own place had outweighed his sentimentality about the cat. She'd almost died of shock when Dad offered to keep the frisky feline. "Just for now," he'd said.

Jeremy spun her around and put his hands on her shoulders. "Thank you."

"For what?"

"For choosing me. For bringing home the bacon while I figured out how to do all this. For being the mother of my child."

She leaned closer. "MacGregor was pretty upset when I gave him my two-weeks' notice."

Jeremy moved his hands down her arms. "I bet."

"I'm going to have to find another job, you know. At least until your client list grows a little more."

"We'll see." Jeremy took a step back and studied her. "But if you do, it should be something you can get excited about this time."

"Like what?" Her eyebrows shot up. Hot coffee. The question had come out of nowhere.

"Whatever you want." He cocked his head. "You could do anything you set your mind to."

Bea's smile drooped a little. Was that true?

"And what do you want, Bea?" There was no furniture in the apartment yet, so Jeremy sat on the floor and indicated his suitcase for her to use as a chair. "You used to say you were going to go back to school after getting settled in Santa Clara, but then . . ."

Bea plopped onto the suitcase with a sigh. Then? Then everything changed. She got pregnant, and they had to move, and her return to Moose Creek had given her a lot to think about.

"I wish I could do more for Grandma. There's this thing called social workers for the elderly."

"You think your grandma needs one of those?"

"Yes." Bea shook her head. "Well, no. I mean, I think I want to *be* one. But you have to get a bachelor's degree."

"So?"

"It would take a long time, especially now that we're having a baby." She rubbed her stomach. "It would be years before I could actually help anyone, and we could never afford it."

"Is it what you want?"

She sat up a little straighter as the truth struck her. "Yes."

"Then that's what we'll do."

"But—"

"I'll visit every single business in Ponderosa looking for clients. I'll work extra hours."

A low, tremulous buzz of excitement started in her chest and worked its way up to her brain. She thought of her grandparents and Earl and all the other people in Moose Creek and even more remote places who had to find someone to drive them an hour or more just to see a doctor. Who needed help buying groceries or figuring out their health-insurance paperwork but had no idea what kind of resources were available. She could help them.

"But—"

Jeremy laughed. "No more buts. You can apply for scholarships, and I'm sure you'll qualify for grant money. We'll figure it out."

A sharp sliver of dread jabbed at her growing excitement. She looked down at her belly. "*But* I'm going to be very busy soon. What if it's harder than I thought? I'd have to research programs and fill out a bunch of applications, and you know how slow I type. It'll take forever."

"I didn't say it was going to be easy." He gave her a playful grin. "*But* it will be worth it. And I know a guy who's willing to help out."

"You do, huh?" Bea's shoulders relaxed under the gentle

weight of possibility. She smiled back. "Does this guy happen to take kisses as payment for all his help?"

Jeremy pulled her over until she was sitting on his lap. "He sure does."

◆ ◆ ◆

Maybe he should've taken one day to himself before trading Bea and Jeremy for his mom and dad like Marge had suggested, but Mitch couldn't bear the thought of one more sleepless night, worrying that his father wouldn't hear it if his mom woke up and wandered off. Or fell down the porch steps. Or who knew what else?

It didn't hurt that it gave Mitch an excuse to miss the chili feed, either. He was ready to start facing the world again, but he wasn't ready for *that*. Marge was never going to let him hear the end of it.

He pulled up in front of his house and drummed the steering wheel. "Here we are."

Rand made no move to open the passenger door. "Are you sure about this, son?"

Mitch knew his dad wasn't a fan of the whole moving-in-with-him thing. Knew it was a blow to his pride. He had protested the possibility at first. But Dad's love and concern for his wife had eventually overshadowed his doubts.

"Of course." Mitch glanced at his mother, who was sitting quietly in the back seat, hands folded in her lap, looking out the window as if they were on a scenic Sunday-afternoon drive. "I wouldn't have it any other way."

It was true. He'd had his doubts at first, too. But the idea had grown on him more with every day that passed. He'd be able to check on them during his lunch break whenever he wanted. He wouldn't have to drive all the way out to the ranch to pick them up for appointments.

And he wouldn't be alone.

Rand gripped the door handle. "Let's go then."

There were a few bags and boxes in the back of the truck, but they'd left most of his parents' things behind. They'd have to figure that out later. For now, the Tucker family was renting the house for next to nothing in exchange for keeping up the place. That had been Marge's idea, too.

He helped his mother out of the truck and walked arm in arm with her to the house. Mitch wasn't sure how much she understood about what was happening, but she'd known him today when he picked them up and had been happy to see him. As long as she could see the mountains from her bedroom window when she woke up in the morning, he had a feeling she was going to be okay.

When they entered the house, he helped his mom to the couch and went back for her trunk. It was the big, clunky kind new brides used to put their wedding dresses and homemade quilts in. The trunk had originally been his great-grandmother's. He carried it into the bedroom, pleased to see there were no puddles on the carpet now that he kept the door open. He was giving up his room on the main floor and moving to the guest room upstairs so his parents wouldn't have to navigate the steps. He'd leave Bea's room open so she and Jeremy could come stay whenever they wanted.

It had been bittersweet, cleaning his and Caroline's stuff out of here. She was everywhere in this room, and it made his heart ache to think of sleeping somewhere else. But life kept moving forward, and he knew she would tell him it was time to let go. Not of her or the memories or the years of life they'd shared, but of his claim on the pain her leaving had caused. He'd held on to it like a prized possession for two years, afraid if he let it go he might not feel anything at all, but there was a lot of life to live outside of his pain. A lot of other people to love.

Rand appeared in the doorway holding a cardboard box. "Where should I put this?"

"Wherever you want." Mitch stepped aside and smiled. "It's your room now."

FIFTY

When did Rand get to be so old? I don't understand. Sometimes he puts his hand on my hand and I don't believe it belongs to him, with its spots and wrinkles. I wonder where my husband went. But then I see his eyes and remember. He's always here.

Mitch is here, too. In and out of this place all the time like he has many important things to do. I'm sure he does. I wonder what Caroline would say if she could see him buzzing around like a worker bee.

Caroline is gone.

Rand tells me sometimes.

This is Mitch's house, I suppose. I don't know how I ended up here, but there are two chairs on the back deck where Rand and I can sit and watch the mountains. A short, round lady with wild hair was here earlier, and she brought banana bread. She was nice.

Sometimes when I'm watching the mountains in the evening, a light appears, just for a minute, and I find myself reaching into my pocket for something, but nothing's there. Shadows dance across my mind like clouds across the sky, and I can't always figure out what the sun is revealing before it's cast in shadow again. Cast in shadow and gone. I never know if the sun will reveal it again or if it will remain in darkness forever.

I walk through the house and see a cat. It meows at me and tangles itself in my legs, almost knocking me over. I steady myself against the wall.

Rand is beside me, his hand on my elbow. "Are you okay?"

"When did we get a cat?"

"It's Bea and Jeremy's cat, remember?"

"Beatrice."

"Yes."

"But she's not here."

Rand's eyes are deep and wild as Alder Gulch. "She and Jeremy moved to Ponderosa, remember? They've got their own place now. They're going to have a baby."

Baby. My hand slides into my pocket. I had a baby. The shadows shift and darkness covers him. Where is he?

I look down at the cat.

Where is who?

Rand leads me to a kitchen table.

This must be Mitch's house.

Caroline is gone.

"Is Mitch home?"

Rand pulls out a chair for me. "Not yet."

After I sit, Rand sits, too. He's never in a hurry. Never has more important places to be. No matter how many shadows form, I know that if a storm comes, he'll be right here next to me. Holding my hand. Peering through the shadows to find me, wherever I might go.

FIFTY-ONE

When Mitch got home from work, Frank's Suburban was there. It was the end of the first week of the schedule Marge had put together. Of course, Frank had signed up for the first Friday available.

Mitch tromped into the house and found Frank playing checkers with his father in the living room. His mother sat nearby, watching closely.

"Howdy." Dad greeted him without looking up from the board.

"You're giving Frank a run for his money, I hope."

"Mebbe."

Mitch caught Frank's eye. "You don't have to spend all afternoon here, you know."

The deal had been that people scheduled to help on any given day would stop in twice to check on his parents, but otherwise would just be on call in case something came up.

Frank threw up his hands with a groan as Rand finished off the last of his pieces. "You got me again." He solemnly shook Rand's hand, then stood to face Mitch. "I was waiting for you."

As if by unspoken agreement, they walked together to the kitchen.

Mitch draped his CINCH jacket over the back of a chair. "Everything go okay here?"

He'd felt like a nervous first-time parent all week, every time he left for work. But Marge had been wonderful, texting him several times a day that she'd been over and things were fine. And on Wednesday, when he got home, Rand had reported that Amber and Hunter had been by, and June had sat entranced, watching the baby play the entire time.

"It was great." Frank leaned a hip against the table and folded his arms across his chest. "I talked with your dad about coming to the service this Sunday."

"You think that's a good idea?"

It would be easy enough on one hand, but on the other hand, the one consistent thing that seemed to make his mother confused and irritable was a lot of people. And Mitch knew from experience the well-meaning folks at Moose Creek Community Church—God bless them—would be unlikely to give his mother privacy and space.

Frank shrugged. "Only one way to find out. But people could also take turns staying home with your mom so Rand could go. He's going to need a break now and then. And so will you."

Mitch's face twisted into a scowl for a second and then smoothed back out.

"I know, I know." Frank held up his hands. "That's something a pastor would say."

Well, yes, it was. But also something a friend would say.

"You're right." Mitch's neck muscles relaxed a little. "I'll talk to him about it."

"And talk to Marge about you getting out of here to do something fun once in a while."

"I can't ask her to watch my parents any more than she already is."

Frank laughed. So hard he bent over at the waist and put his hands on his knees. "I meant take her with you, you idiot. Go out to dinner or something."

Mitch felt his face flush.

"And I don't mean at The Baked Potato."

"I don't know about that. I'm not . . ."

"What?" Frank stared him down, a twinkle in his eye. "Good-looking? Sane? Smart?"

Mitch looked at the floor. "Ready."

"Look, man." Frank put a hand on his shoulder. "No one's ever ready."

Mitch hung his head. That was definitely true. He hadn't been ready when Caroline got sick. Hadn't been ready to say good-bye. Hadn't been ready for Bea to get married. Still wasn't ready to become a grandpa.

"I'll think about it."

"You do that." Frank clapped him on the back. "I better get going."

He was about to leave the kitchen when Mitch raised a hand. "Frank."

Frank stopped and spun around.

"I'm sorry." Mitch rubbed the back of his neck. "For everything. I never should've shut you out. I didn't know what to do."

Frank gave him a little smile. "I'm just glad to have you back. I missed you."

"Thanks."

"But I'm not the only one." Frank gestured with one arm in the general direction of the church building. "A lot of other people have been missing you, too."

Mitch wanted to say something sharp about how they wouldn't even notice if he drove off a cliff. Instead, he glanced at the schedule Marge had made, hanging on the fridge door, and couldn't do it. "I'll—"

"Yeah, yeah," Frank interrupted. "You'll think about it."

He saluted and showed himself out of the house, saying

a loud good-bye to Mitch's parents on his way. Mitch never could've imagined so many people coming and going from his house. Caroline would've loved it.

He wiped his hands on his jeans and looked around the kitchen as his stomach grumbled. What he wouldn't give right about now for one of Marge's—

"Yoo-hoo." The front door slammed shut, and Marge's voice carried down the hall. "I brought dinner."

One side of Mitch's mouth lifted. Now *that* he was ready for.

FIFTY-TWO

As they took the Highway 288 exit and headed north, Bea leaned forward to watch the mountains fill the windshield. Even though she was becoming more familiar with the back side of the Bridgers, the dips and peaks and jagged edges here were like an old friend. Today her old friend was wrapped tightly in a sweater of snow and ice, winter's merciless fingers pressing, pressing, pressing in, with the mountain refusing to yield.

"We're lucky the roads weren't too bad," she said.

When Jeremy didn't answer, she glanced over. The final lines of Tim McGraw's "Don't Take the Girl" played, and Jeremy wiped at his face.

Her eyebrows rose. "Are you crying?"

He sniffed. "No."

A grin spread across her face. "Yes, you are."

"It's a powerful song, okay?" He dabbed at one eye. "Does the girl die?"

"The song doesn't say." Bea put a hand on his shoulder. "I like to think she makes it."

"Me too."

Red-and-silver tinsel hung from the light poles on Main Street in Moose Creek. The roads were covered in hard-packed

336

ice, but they gave the new tires on the Toyota no trouble. Even when Jeremy flipped around to park the right way in front of the house.

As they walked to the door, Bea nudged Jeremy's new leather belt with her elbow. "Looks good on you."

His chest puffed out a little. "I'm surprised he didn't misspell my name on purpose."

She smiled and smacked his shoulder. "Oh, stop it."

They reached the door, and Bea knocked as she opened it. "Anybody home?"

Jeremy followed her inside, and they looked around. No one appeared to greet them.

"Hello?"

Dad poked his head into the hall from the kitchen. "Oh, you're here."

"Everything okay? Where's Grandma?"

"Yes, yes, of course." Dad waved her over. "Sorry, your grandpa and I were just talking at the table. Grandma's been in her room all morning. We're trying to figure out what might convince her to come out."

"She's not doing well? Hi, Grandpa."

Grandpa gave her a wink and lopsided grin.

Dad shook Jeremy's hand. "She's just been quiet today is all."

"Oh." Bea wasn't sure what to make of her dad's tone. Was he worried? He seemed distracted. "You still planning to run some errands while we're here?"

When she'd told him over the phone they would be coming today, he'd mentioned he might take the opportunity to run out and take care of a few things.

A funny look passed over Dad's face. "Yes. If that's all right with you."

"Of course."

Grandpa frowned. "I don't need a babysitter."

"I know." Dad appeared flustered. "But I don't like leaving you alone for too long."

Dad's explanation did nothing to alleviate Grandpa's frown. "How long are your errands gonna take?"

"Uh . . ."

Bea tried to keep her voice upbeat. "It's fine, Grandpa. This just means we'll be able to talk about him while he's gone." She turned to her dad. "Where will you be going?"

Dad scratched the top of his head. "Well . . ."

The door opened and shut.

"Yoo-hoo! Ready to go?"

Dad's face reddened.

Bea smirked. "I see. Well, I'm sure we'll all be just fine while you're on your date."

"Keep your voice down." Dad's face was horror-stricken. "It's not a date."

"You know what your mother would say." Grandpa's frown threatened to flip upside down. "If it looks like a duck, and walks like a duck . . ."

"Cut it out." Dad pleaded with his eyes as Marge joined them in the kitchen. "Bea, why don't you go down and see your grandma. See if you can talk her into coming out for lunch."

Ha. She could take a hint.

"Hi, Marge." She smiled at their neighbor and glanced at Jeremy, who indicated he would stay in the kitchen. "All right. See you later, Dad."

She gave Marge a small wave and excused herself. Dad would have some explaining to do when he got back, but right now she would focus on her grandma. That's why she was here.

Bea walked slowly down the hall, admiring the family photos that hung all along the wall. Suddenly, a tiny twinge from somewhere beneath her belly button stopped her. Her eyes widened. She put her hands on her stomach. "Is that you, little one?"

She stilled and breathed gently, hoping to feel it again. The app on her phone had told her she might start to feel her baby move soon, but nothing else happened as she waited. Her mind must be playing tricks on her.

When she reached the bedroom door, she paused. Even though it had been weeks since she moved out and her grandparents moved in, it was still strange that the room that had been her parents' her whole life was someone else's now. Nothing could stay the same forever. She was learning that was okay. Sometimes it was even good, because it forced people to consider things they never would've otherwise. Like going back to school to become a social worker.

The bedroom door stood open about an inch, and she tapped on it. "Grandma?" She strained to listen but heard no response. "It's Bea." She tapped again. "Beatrice."

The bed creaked. Bea waited. A wizened face appeared in the crack. Bea expected her grandma to say, "Don't just stand there, come in, come in," but instead, she just pulled the door open and stepped back.

Bea forced a smile and entered, struck anew by how different the room looked now. Mom and Dad's wedding photos were gone. Bright yellow curtains were tied back on the picture window, and Grandma's rocking chair from the porch at the ranch was positioned there so she could look outside.

"It's good to see you, Grandma."

Grandma tilted her head, then let her eyes drop to Bea's midsection. Bea placed a hand there and flushed. Though she was almost to the twenty-week mark, her baby bump was still barely noticeable. Could Grandma see it? Something flashed in her eyes, then was gone.

While Bea watched, unsure what to do, Grandma carefully lowered herself into the rocking chair and stared out the window. Bea let out a long breath. She thought she'd been prepared for this. Dad had warned her that Grandma's good days were getting fewer and farther between. Yet seeing it for herself was like having an elbow injury you could almost forget about if you didn't keep bumping it into things.

She sat on the plaid love seat along the wall near Grandma's rocker. It was the color of wild roses and amber sunsets. She watched Grandma rock back and forth, white spots appearing on the knuckles of her hands as she gripped the arms of her chair.

"Do you want to go to the kitchen for some lunch?" Bea asked.

Grandma rocked. Bea stuck her hands under her legs to keep from fidgeting.

"It's almost Christmas," Bea tried again. "Uncle Ken's coming to visit, remember?"

Nothing. Bea studied her closely. It wasn't that she seemed sad necessarily. People with dementia often suffered from depression, but Grandma was just . . . somewhere else.

"I know you're in there," Bea whispered.

Her heart felt the sting of loss—there'd been a lot of that the last few years—but she didn't sink into it. Wishing couldn't change what she had or didn't have. Grandma had taught her that. So she didn't wish her mother were here. Didn't wish Grandma would speak to her. Recognize her. She just sat and tried to be thankful Grandma seemed content.

After a few quiet minutes, Bea leaned over to look outside, too. To see what Grandma was seeing. The Bridger Mountains crowded the window, somehow still startling in their immensity and closeness even after twenty-one years of looking at them. Did Grandma miss her old house? Did she wonder what had happened to her? Did she recognize the mountains even when her brain held no memory of Bea's face?

Another twinge, the tiniest of movements deep in her core, caused Bea to sit up straighter. There was no mistaking it this time. Warmth flooded her chest and spread.

She was going to be a mom.

"Once upon a time, there was a man named Miner McGee," Bea said.

Grandma stopped rocking. Bea licked her lips. She hadn't meant to do it, but the story came tumbling out.

"He'd spent his life traveling the country, searching for treasure, but never struck it rich. And that's what he wanted more than anything. To strike it rich. Eventually, his travels brought him to Moose Creek on the first day of winter. The same day the town was buzzing with a *fantastical* rumor."

Bea would never be able to tell the story like Grandma, but she couldn't help giving extra emphasis to Grandma's favorite word. Grandma still wouldn't look at her, but Bea swore she leaned a little closer.

"The rumor told of the enormous Big Sky Diamond hidden away on the mountain," Bea continued. "Miner McGee couldn't believe his ears. He'd waited his whole life to find a treasure like that. So he stocked up on supplies, strapped on his headlamp, and headed up the mountain."

The hair on Bea's arms stood up. Grandma was looking now. Peering intently into Bea's face.

"Miner McGee went up the mountain just as the worst blizzard Moose Creek had ever seen swept over the land. The wind blew, the snow fell, and the roads became impassable. When the sky finally cleared after three days, the people of Moose Creek gathered to decide whether to send a search party up the mountain for Miner McGee's body right then and there or wait until the thaw."

Grandma covered her mouth with her hand and waited.

Bea's heart swelled. Her voice rose. "As the townspeople talked, the sun sank low in the sky, and someone shouted, 'Look!' Everyone looked, and there on the mountain was Miner McGee's headlamp, shining bright for all to see as he searched for the diamond."

A small gasp from Grandma caught Bea's attention, and

she lowered her voice. "Ever since that day, if you look over at the mountain when the sun sinks low in the sky, you will see his lamp click on."

Grandma's eyes widened. Bea held her breath. Memories swirled around them like the blizzard in the story.

"What if he never finds it?" Grandma asked, her voice a lone tumbleweed scraping along a dirt road.

"He will." Bea rested a hand on her stomach and smiled. "He'll never give up."

Acknowledgments

Thank you to everyone at Bethany House—and I do mean everyone—for all your hard work behind the scenes. From the people managing the mail and the book orders to the people in charge of design (shout out to Susan Zucker for the beautiful cover!) and marketing and schedules, I appreciate you all very much. I'm particularly grateful for my editors Dave Long and Luke Hinrichs, who diligently strive to keep me from embarrassing myself, and Kate Deppe, whose attention to detail helps me sleep better at night.

Many thanks to Sarah Carson, Janice Parker, Kerry Johnson, Emily Conrad, and Mary Freeman, who were gracious enough to offer feedback on early versions of the story. Your input and enthusiasm were invaluable to me during the awkward early drafts. I don't know where I'd be without you.

Thank you to Grandma Julie for pointing out the light on the mountain when I was a kid and telling me the story of the old miner and his lamp. I've carried that story around with me for many years, and I'm glad I finally had the chance to tell it myself. I wish you were here to see this.

To everyone watching a loved one suffer from dementia, I

hope you have a Light in your life that gives you hope. It is such a hard road.

To everyone kind enough to give my first book, *The Sowing Season*, a chance, I can't thank you enough. Your support has been amazing.

A special thanks to Baby B for bringing so much joy to my life, and a special *no thanks* to the dumpster fire that was 2020 for doing everything you could to keep this book from ever being completed.

A big, mushy *I love you* to my family—especially my husband, Andy; my kids; and my mom—for all your support and help and all-around awesomeness. You guys are the best.

About the Author

Katie Powner, author of *The Sowing Season*, grew up on a dairy farm in the Pacific Northwest but has called Montana home for almost twenty years. She is a biological, adoptive, and foster mom who loves Jesus, red shoes, and candy. In addition to writing contemporary fiction, Katie blogs about family in all its many forms and advocates for more families to open their homes to children in need. To learn more, visit her website at www.katiepowner.com.

About the Author

Sign Up for Katie's Newsletter

Keep up to date with Katie's latest news on book releases and events by signing up for her email list at katiepowner.com.

More from Katie Powner

Forced to sell his family farm after sacrificing everything, 63-year-old Gerrit Laninga no longer knows what to do with himself. 15-year-old Rae Walters has growing doubts about The Plan her parents set to help her follow in her father's footsteps. When their paths cross just as they need a friend the most, Gerrit's and Rae's lives change in unexpected ways.

The Sowing Season

 BETHANYHOUSE

 Stay up to date on your favorite books and authors with our free e-newsletters. Sign up today at bethanyhouse.com.

f facebook.com/bethanyhousepublishers   @bethanyhousefiction

OB Free exclusive resources for your book group at bethanyhouseopenbook.com

You May Also Like . . .

When a renowned profiler is found dead in his hotel room and it becomes clear the killer is targeting agents in Alex Donovan's unit, she is called to work on the strangest case she's ever faced. Things get personal when the brilliant killer strikes close to home, and Alex will do anything to find the killer—even at the risk of her own life.

Dead Fall by Nancy Mehl
THE QUANITCO FILES #2
nancymehl.com

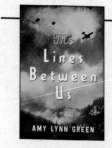

After Pearl Harbor, sweethearts Gordon Hooper and Dorie Armitage were broken up by their convictions. As a conscientious objector, he went west to fight fires as a smokejumper, while she joined the Army Corps. When a tragic accident raises suspicions, they're forced to work together, but the truth they uncover may lead to an impossible—and dangerous—choice.

The Lines Between Us by Amy Lynn Green
amygreenbooks.com

After an abusive relationship derails her plans, Adri Rivera struggles to regain her independence and achieve her dream of becoming an MMA fighter. She gets a second chance, but the man who offers it to her is Max Lyons—her former training partner, whom she left heartbroken years before. As she fights for her future, will Adri be able to confront her past?

After She Falls by Carmen Schober
carmenschober.com

BETHANYHOUSE

More from Bethany House

When lawyer Patrick O'Neill agrees to resurrect an old mystery and challenge the Blackstones' legacy of greed and corruption, he doesn't expect to be derailed by the kindhearted family heiress, Gwen Kellerman. She is tasked with getting him to drop the case, but when the mystery takes a shocking twist, he is the only ally she has.

Carved in Stone by Elizabeth Camden
THE BLACKSTONE LEGACY #1
elizabethcamden.com

After a deadly explosion at the Chilwell factory, munitions worker Rosalind Graham leaves the painful life she's dreamt of escaping by assuming the identity of her deceased friend. When RAF Captain Alex Baird is ordered to surveil her for suspected sabotage, the danger of her deception intensifies. Will Rose's daring bid for freedom be her greatest undoing?

As Dawn Breaks by Kate Breslin
katebreslin.com

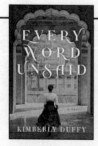

As the nation's most fearless travel columnist, Augusta Travers explores the country, spinning stories for women unable to leave hearth and home. Suddenly caught in a scandal, she escapes to India to visit old friends, promising great tales of boldness. But instead she encounters a plague, new affections, and the realization that she can't outrun her past.

Every Word Unsaid by Kimberly Duffy
kimberlyduffy.com

◆ BETHANYHOUSE